PLEASE READ

FROM

OTHER END

THE DESTINY SECRET:

A plot to change the world.

By Guy Clinton

AUTHOR'S BIOGRAPHY

Guy Clinton is British. He grew up in a middle class, middle of the road family who moved to the Middle East in his mid-teens, where he encountered his first dead person, lying in a gutter in Bahrain. The man had died from starvation and it left a lasting impression on him.

Since then he has lived in many different parts of the world including: California, Spain, Holland and Australia. He is a passionate advocate of freedom, fishing and fine food - a superb cook.

I met him when he was editing film scripts in California, where he developed a reputation for writing powerful humor.

He started writing this book a few years back and I have been involved in it from the start. I know he will not enjoy me saying this, but it must be said – he is a remarkable author. Remarkable not because he is a superb thriller writer but because he has an uncanny, quite unnerving ability, to perceive the future. There are many things that are not in this book. We made him remove them because they occurred after he wrote them but before publication: the fall of the Euro, fixed term parliaments, Obama campaigning under the banner 'Change'. It's quite a list. I first read them in the book outline some years ago. At the time I thought them far fetched, but now know they have actually occurred. Everyone involved must be as shocked as I am over that aspect - it is truly remarkable. I trust that many of the ideas he left in, will follow the same path. That is the good news Guy - change is accelerating. You were right about that too, but wrong about the rate of change - it is breathtaking. It must be a wonderful feeling to be wrong about that aspect. It has even made a cynic like me realise that all is possible.

Guy has now moved back to Britain to be near his ageing parents and lives quietly and discreetly in rural Sussex. He is single, straight and fortyish. If you meet him, he is unlikely to divulge his occupation or any detail of his career. He is shy of any form of publicity because he thinks people treat those who are known, differently. He is kind, loyal past the point of foolishness, guards his privacy, and enjoys a normal existence.

We all miss him. Take good care of him, Britain. Then send him back to us - safely and soon.

John Simons, Shark Bay California, May 15 2010

HARDBACK ISBN 978-0-9566032-1-0

SOFTBACK ISBN 978-0-9566032-0-3

Published by Coolclear Publishing
February 2010 publisher prefix 97809566032

Web sites
The DestinySecret.com   Guyclinton.com

Printed and bound in the UK by
CPI Mackays, Chatham ME5 8TD

ACKNOWLEDGEMENTS

I would like to thank all of my friends and family who assisted with the writing of this book. You are wonderful people. A joy to know. Truly glorious. The dinners and conversation we shared are forever enshrined in a sanctuary of my mind. Thank you. Without your assistance and openness I doubt I would have ever finished writing this book: one all.

To all my friends in California: Thank you for your warmth, generosity and, the kind. You taught me more than I ever dreamed.

An inspired Thank You to my father, Morland, for his comment after hearing the book outline. 'If I were you, I'd pick up the typewriter tomorrow.' Without that comment, Dad, this book would not have been birthed.

My thanks to Lydia Wanstall, for providing her editing skills early on, and to Dee Kyne and John Parsons for donating their intellectual balance which, I am still considering.

To Josie – the graphic designer who sprinkled beauty on the page – for her patience and precision.

My delighted Thankyous to P, Adam, Hilary, Eddie, Wolfgang, Ashley, Helena, Ingrid, Gav, Christy, Mark, Kaz, and the many others who have helped, for your comments and positive encouragement along the way. Thank you for travelling with the production of this book. You each made the journey extraordinary.

My especial thanks, my highest accolade and my deepest gratitude, go to two people who stepped boldly over the line of good, common sense. Throwing their pragmatism and time overboard, they kept our ship afloat. Through tempest and becalm, they brought this book safely to harbour; setting her high and proud in the water; shipshape; shining like a mirror; Bristol fashion. You both fought hard. You each fought well. On occasion you had to grapple demonically, but you always did so with care, kindness and consideration. I am blessed with an eternal regard for your skill and determination. You never stopped bailing - you never once bailed:

Vicky Tinker and Chrissy Catchpole, you are so exceptional, your abilities so exemplary, that you have resurrected a sensation I have rarely felt: I am truly lost for the words to describe how I cherish what you each gave me.

Having hunted through the Thesaurus until the early hours: I am certain they do not exist.

Always

gx

This book is dedicated to the memory Dr David Kelly, who lost his life in the service of his country.

A very brave man, highly aware of the risk he was taking on behalf of his fellow countrymen, he singlehandedly went into battle against the British and American Governments, riding under the flag of truth. Those who wish to join me in my campaign to have him awarded the George Cross posthumously for his bravery, can do so by registering on my web site at GuyClinton.com .

He is an example to us all.

BOOK 1

The moment each and every descendant of the killer ape understands and accepts that one man's terrorist will always be another man's freedom fighter, we instantly unshackle ourselves from the forged manacles of war.

THE COURAGEOUS OR COMPASSIONATE APE

Julie spun the helm hard-a-port, nudging the throttles down to put the engines into reverse. The propellers churned the seawater to milk as the stern of the cutter swung obediently towards the wharf. Three heartbeats after the fishing boat started to move she eased the twin diesels back into neutral, stopping the boat 6 inches from the side. Hopping nimbly out of the cabin she grabbed the spring line and looped it over a cleat before running to the bow and roping that to the dock. Satisfied the boat was secure she went back into the cabin and turned off the engines; shouting down to William in the ensuing silence, 'Let's get the fish loaded, honey, then we'll wash her down.'

'Oh lordy, I hate this part.' Will said, trudging over to lift the hatch of the holding tank. He gazed down at the 'fish' which eyed him back with evil intent. The problem with these 'fish' was they had a particularly bad attitude and were extremely well armed.

'Okay, then you net them and I'll put the rubbers on,' Julie offered.

Exaggerating a sigh of relief, Will picked up the long-handled net and dipped it into the tank. Swirling it around like a giant spoon he scooped up four, lifting them out and onto one of the grey plastic trays stacked on the dock.

With an ease that only comes from years of practice, Julie shot her hand past a snapping claw to pick up one of the kicking lobsters. Twisting it upside down to make it still, she snapped a wide elastic band around each of its claws and plopped it into the tank of seawater bubbling away behind her.

'One down – *only 56 to go*,' she teased, with an elfish grin on her face.

'Okay, okay, when they're all on the dock I'll band with you,' Will offered, refusing to rise to her bait.

'I'll never understand how a man who can face down boardrooms full of crocodiles is scared of little old Louie Lobsters.'

'And I'll never understand why a girl who doesn't like getting wet runs a lobster boat,' Will smiled, swinging another netful onto the dock.

'Shh, she can hear every word you say. And she's not a boat – she's a cutter. She's my baby and she's a good girl, aren't you?' Julie crooned, patting the rail consolingly to mitigate his faux pas. 'You've always got mummy home through good weather and foul, haven't you baby,' and she blew it a kiss.

'I sometimes think you love this...cutter more than me.'

'I don't love her more, but I've loved her longer....muuuuch longer,' she giggled. 'We've been together for nine years fishing these fine American shores so you're the new boy on the block. Anyway, you must know I love you because if I didn't, I wouldn't let you steer her,' Julie smiled her perfect feminine logic at him fondly.

'The pain of getting my thumb snipped off by one of these monsters is nothing compared to your tender love, my sweet,' he replied, grinning the joke back at her.

'Come now, babe. As long as you do everything I say, all of the time, you've nothing to worry about. Let's get these lobsters unloaded. You wash her down while I finish banding then I'll peel those cold wet clothes off you and throw you into a nice hot bed. Any resistance and I'll clunk a couple of these round your wrists,' she said, flicking a band at him which thunked on his chest.

'Now that's an offer I can't refuse. Oh Gentlest of the Gentle.'

Glancing past his shoulder Julie did a quick double take, her smile melting into a frown. She stood up straight, saluting her hand to shield her eyes from the slanting sunlight. 'That's a storm coming, Will... A bad one.'

Turning half around, he followed her gaze to see a black line sitting on the horizon with herring bone clouds streaming off it. 'Huh, that's odd. I didn't hear that on the forecast this morning. It said medium seas, wind 15 knots tonight.'

'You're right, and they were dead wrong. That's a real mother building out there. Come on, let's speed things up or we'll get wet.'

Hours after the sun had gone down and with their passion spent, they lay back in the easy silence of lovers. Will stared up at the bedroom ceiling of the old net man's cottage while she rested her head on his shoulder and played with the hair on his chest.

'I had a curious conversation with Alex Spyder yesterday,' Will said quietly.

'Alex Spyder? He's the head of CrystalCorp, isn't he?'

'That's his day job, but he also acts as a silent go-between for both Democrats and Republicans, which makes him pretty unique and highly revered. They accord him enormous respect, mainly because his ideas tend to be right on the pulse of public opinion and he's never been known to take sides for purely political reasons.'

'Really? I had no idea. What did he want?'

'Oh, nothing really… He just asked me a few questions about what I might do if I were the next President.'

'What? Well, you're the fairest man I've ever met. You would make a fantastic President, darling. What did you say?'

'I told him my wife used me as a deck hand on Fridays and the office needed me the rest of the week – so I was far too busy.'

'Don't keep me in suspense,' Julie sat up and shook him gently.

'I said the biggest problem any president faced was how easily a few powerful men had got a grip on this great nation of ours and the power needed to be put back in the hands of the populace.'

'Foolish dreamer,' Julie smiled, prodding him with her fingernail.

'He grilled me about it. How things could be changed without getting myself assassinated in the process. I said there was a large group of likeminded people who would jump at the chance to hand more Federal authority to each State – providing they were satisfied that corruption would be reduced and each stage was given time to bed in and mature.'

'Assassinated?'

'Look what happened to JFK: killed four days after he started saying there were people his Office had to answer to – that he was going to expose them and put a stop to it. Ever since then it's been quietly understood that if you go up against the power behind the throne, assassination becomes part of the job description.'

'Anything that's right is worth fighting for, but I don't think it's worth dying for, Will.'

'Fighting always involves risk. Don't worry, the solution is simple. We make sure we have enough people onboard before we attempt anything. Enough to guarantee that cutting off one head won't kill their demon. Assassination then becomes counter productive. It would reveal their hand and they can only operate in the dark. They are terrified of public awareness and rightly so. Shine that light anywhere near them and they scurry away.'

'I'll kill you if you get yourself killed.'

Will's thoughts wound their way back to his meeting with Spyder. In his mind's eye he could see Alex looking at him cautiously, 'Give the People the right to decide things for themselves? I recall some Greeks tried that once – worked pretty well...Of course it would mean a change to the Constitution,' Alex had added, his sharp mind hitting on the practical issue first time.

'When the Founding Fathers wrote the Constitution they gave the People the right to bear arms to safeguard freedom. They realised our open society was vulnerable to extreme forms of government. If they knew what you and I know today, Alex, they would be calling on the population to rise up and tear down this sorry state of affairs,' Will heard himself replying.

'Yes, there's no doubt they've got their hooks enmeshed in the political process,' Alex said cautiously. 'They've swapped military might for financial power and strength. That's a hard thing to go up against, Will.'

'Maybe not, times have changed,' he had countered. 'There are now a lot of people who suspect what's really going on and many more who feel our social orientation is too lopsided, too self-serving, too inhumane. Even the ordinary man in the street knows the care has gone out of our government. They want it back.'

Julie leaned over Will. 'What are you going to do?'

'If I'm going to carry a stick as big as that, I think I must tread very carefully indeed... and with the utmost diplomacy.'

'How did you leave it with Alex?'

'He asked me if I would bring you over for dinner next week.'

'Oh darling, I'd love to go. I've heard his wife is a scream. You're in Washington on Wednesday, I'll fly down if you like. How nice of him to invite us over.'

'It wasn't really an invitation.'

'Then what was it?'

'It sounded like a summons. A summons to the court of Alex Spyder – the King Maker.'

The crash and boom of thunder shook him awake in the small hours of the night. The front edge of the storm had moved directly overhead; Will turned over and felt the bed cold and empty beside him. Sounds of a muted electronic crackle were coming up the stairs from the kitchen below. With a gnawing concern, he jumped out of bed and hurried down to the kitchen still naked, to find Julie hunched over the pine breakfast table with her face squeezed anxiously between her palms, her head tilted towards the ship-to-shore radio. She flicked her eyes up at him anxiously as he stood opposite her.

The transmissions were fading in and out with the storm: 'We've got seas of 15-to-18 feet and building… We're 5 miles southwest of the lighthouse, over.'

'Roger that Argonaut. Do you need assistance? Over,' replied the voice Will knew was the controller of the Coast Guard station, 80 miles up the coast.

'No, that's-a-negative. We are taking on a little water but we should make it back, over.'

'I'm glad to hear that, Argonaut. We're pretty stretched here as you can imagine, over.' There was a pause then the same voice asked, 'What's your position and status Sea Wolf?'

'We are 23 miles due south the harbour. Same seas, wind 40 knots gusting 55. I've made the decision to pump out the hold, over.'

Julie suddenly looked up at Will, worry rioting across her face. 'That's Linton, the Captain of the Sea Wolf. We fished together a few years ago. He wouldn't be emptying his hold unless he thought there was a real chance of it dragging them under.'

She snatched up the microphone. 'Linton Linton, this is Julie of the SeaBelle. What's your exact status, over.'

'Julie? You're not out in this are you? Over.'

'No, the boat's on the dock.'

'Thank the Lord. It's wild out here. We're taking on more sea that we can pump out. They said it would be winds 20 knots but it's double that. We've got foam on the top of the waves now and if it builds any more it will get murderous. We're close to our limit Julie, over.'

'Okay, I'm staying up to monitor your status and position. Let's say every 5 minutes, over. Argonaut Argonaut, this is Julie of the SeaBelle. Do you copy, over?'

'Copy you Julie. We're 5 miles southwest of the Jenny lighthouse, over.'

'Okay, report your position every 5 minutes. Time now 2:41 over.'

'Roger that – and Julie. Thank you, over.'

She put down the handset and looked up at Will. 'I need you to go down to the SeaBelle and warm up the engines for me – just in case.'

Will stood stock still at her request, staring at her silently for nearly half a minute; their eyes exchanging countless arguments for and against her decision. They normally used this form of communication to signal their thoughts and feelings in company, but with the pendulum of danger swinging towards them it took on a much deeper significance. A storm squall hammered hard rain against the windows as Julie broke the silence between them.

'I have no choice, Will. They would do the same for me and the nearest lifeboat is 70 miles from their position. We are only 20 or so at most...I love you darling but you must do as I say, I might need every second.'

'Only if I come with.'

'Thanks, I'm sure that together we can handle anything...Oh and Will,' she called after him as he raced upstairs to throw some clothes on, 'take everything off the boat except the charts and life jackets...and drop the anchor and chain into the harbour.'

'I'll turn on the ship's radio. If you're coming – I'll know.'

'One more thing, Will.'

'Whatever you need, honey.'

'I'm the Captain on this one, okay?'

'Aye aye, Skipper,' he replied, deadly serious.

As Will leapt out of the car in the harbour car park, the weight of the wind hit him hard on his side trying for a quick knockdown, but he leaned against it and ran doubled over to the bucking gangway which led on down to the docks.

The harbour boats were raging at their bonds. Some were throwing themselves repeatedly at the front of their docks in a suicidal bid for freedom. He looked over anxiously to where the SeaBelle was moored. The contrast was startling. The 28ft East Coast Lobster Cutter was at the end of the T dock and he saw how well she was riding the waves being driven in by the storm. Her bow was rising and falling sedately with the four foot rollers and he smiled as she curtseyed evenly over a giant six foot swell. 'Looks like I'm the only one of us three who doesn't want to go out tonight,' Will said in greeting, as he stepped aboard.

Climbing into the relative peace of the cabin, he flicked the light switch and turned on the diesels, patiently watching the dials to make sure the engines were running correctly. Then he reached up to the ceiling of the cabin and clicked the radio into life, tuning it to channel 9. Instantly, Julie's voice filled the cabin, 'Copy that Linton, we're on our way, over...Did you read that, Will, over?'

'Roger that...Captain, over,' he answered, and started grabbing gear to throw it out onto the dock. Five minutes later he watched the anchor chain slither eagerly towards the place it had been trying to get to, ever since it had been put on the boat. Hearing a faint but rhythmic thumping on the wooden dock, he glanced between his legs to see Julie leaping aboard and going straight for the helm.

He stood upright, narrowing his eyes against the ferocious blasts of wind. 'I can't believe were going out in this hell. This storm's a bitch on wheels,' William Mann said through tightly clenched teeth, as he felt the buffetting rain turning to sleet on the back of his hands.

THE CLEVER APE

Leah felt nervous as she stood outside the study door. It didn't help that she was twenty minutes late – the Professor had a well known intolerance of tardiness. 'I wonder what he'll be like. Bearded and smelly, I bet,' she thought.

Picking up the weighty door knocker, she let it freefall on its metal stud. The noise boomed loudly and a voice called back in annoyance, 'Come in, come in, and for God's sake stop that dreadful banging – it's enough to awaken Neptune from his slumber.'

Opening the door, Leah stepped in and smiled with a confidence she wasn't feeling. For the past two weeks she had Googled him extensively, surprised to discover there wasn't a single photograph of him, anywhere. She had unearthed reams of articles and references to him in the press, detailing his advice and guidance to many different governments over the years – but no picture. It was noticeably odd in a person so intrinsically involved with the world. Looking over somewhat cautiously, she saw him for the first time. He was the complete opposite of the image she had formed in her mind.

The Professor stood tall and straight, but poised. Emanating a *présence royale*, as if he were on the brink of orchestrating some momentous event. His white hair was swept back behind his ears and grown long, rolling down his neck like a mane. He was clean shaven and looked barely fifty, but she knew from her research that he was really sixty-four. What stopped her abruptly were his eyes: the left was bright emerald green, while his right was the deep blue of a Mediterranean current.

'Ah, you are no doubt a Miss Leah Samantha Karen Mandrille,' he said as though announcing her name in court; his eyes holding hers, steadily.

'Yes, I am,' she replied, trying to make her voice sound confident

8

and mature.

Breaking his stare, he gestured her over to the far corner of the room. 'Let's go and sit in the window seat, which currently serves as my dining room.'

She walked over and sat down sideways, swivelling her legs under the ancient oak dining table, sweeping her gaze around to take in her surroundings more fully. The room was large and there were books everywhere. The ceiling was double-height and his library covered every square inch the walls could offer up.

It wasn't nearly enough. Zigzag columns of books and tomes were balancing precariously on the floor and chairs, some left open defying gravity. Sheaves of documents sat in loose piles all the way around the edge of the room, shouldering each other out of the way for any available space. Rising up through these were random outcrops of antique furniture and a dark Edwardian drinks cabinet. A blackened fireplace at the far end of the room was courted by a velvet Louis XV chaise-longue and two stunningly beautiful armchairs. Though they looked quite lovely, their canary yellow silk warred with the sombre browns, greens and blacks of the bookshelves. Hidden amongst the confused sea of volumes was an island formed by a round table, on which sat a huge chess set with the pieces laid out: the white king's pawn already advanced two squares, as if trying to tempt an invisible black opponent into making the next move.

Leah looked up at the Professor who had chosen not to sit, but stand. He was looking down at her with a slight quiver of amusement tugging at the corners of his mouth. 'Given that you are twenty minutes late, I thought we should celebrate. May I offer you a dry sherry?'

'I'm so sorry I'm late but someone...' and instantly the Professor held his left hand up, stopping her in mid-sentence as he poured the wine into two Renaissance glasses.

'Please don't apologise. I prefer to celebrate your victory over the Jaws of Death, or some other terrible cataclysm which no doubt effected your delay,' he said, handing her a glass which spun diamonds around the room. Holding up his own in salute, he offered a toast.

'To the Jaws of Death. Without them, the hallowed halls of life would be valueless.'

She raised hers with him, trying to maintain a level and open demeanour. Young, but extremely astute, Leah had been able to read hearts and minds from an early age and she now turned her full instincts onto him; but as she tried to gauge his emotions, her sight kept being drawn to his green eye. It was flecked with gold and she felt herself being pulled towards its source, but the deeper she went, the further she seemed to get from any insight to the man. Becoming aware of her stare, she switched over to his blue eye and went hunting there for clues to his persona. Nothing at first, then slowly she saw it. Nestling deep in the sapphire blue ring glistened a small flicker of humour; as in a joke unsaid or the glint of an imaginary irony perhaps; the same look her younger brothers shared, moments before they did something truly horrid.

Forcing herself to relax, Leah sipped at her sherry. After a brief silence the Professor reached down to pluck a worn clipboard off the dining table. He glanced down at the A4 sheets, waving his free hand airily, 'It says here you wish to study Political Theory, Human Psychology, Political History, blah, Political Science, more blah, with an emphasis on...blah, which just happens to include all nine of the subjects I teach. Now please help me my girl, because I am unable to ascertain whether this constitutes flattery or gluttony. What is your opinion?'

'Definitely flattery...It's one of the few things I never underestimate,' Leah added, trying to soften the compliment with a little humour.

'Hmmm, I wouldn't underestimate the lure of gluttony when it comes to the *body politic*,' the Professor smiled back. It was a lovely smile heartfelt and open, with only a hint of guile.

'The thing is, Leah, most of the students who come here are eighteen to twenty years old and our system of teaching supports them well. There is a certain understanding of the world that only comes with age and, with all due respect to what you have achieved in the exam room, I strongly recommend you take a year or two off before enrolling. At seventeen, you will gain far less from Oxford than you will in a year or two. Take some time off. Travel – get tattooed. Then you could come back here to Oxford, relaxed in the sure and certain knowledge that for once, you were perfectly on time.'

So there it was. Deftly thrown onto the table between them in under a minute.

He didn't feel she should take up her place at the University because she was one year early and twenty minutes late. She wondered whether to play it back with subservient acquiescence or a more surefooted confidence. Definitely neither, she realised. To quench her thirst for the knowledge and achievement she could sense was out there, hiding just beyond the horizon of this interview, she must show genuine substance to convince this man she was mature enough to enrol in twelve weeks time. Her reply needed to be considered and intelligent to win back his approval. After weighing her options carefully, she decided on a full frontal attack.

'Let's see...my mother died of cancer when I was seven, so I had to grow up quickly. She left me with four brothers. Two of them younger and my father, who went on from Oxford to become a career diplomat. By twelve, I was fluent in various dialects of Arabic, Farsi, French and Italian and was fighting my elder two siblings while nurturing the other two. At fourteen, my oldest brother Simon and I, sneaked out to climb a section of Mt Blanc where I had my first near-death experience. Sadly, Simon was less fortunate. My father took it badly and I had to nurse him through our awful loss. In seven short years he had lost his wife and first child, while I had lost my mother and my best friend.'

'I am sorry to hear that, but misfortune and tragedy often worship at the same altar – pray continue.'

'My father and I became interdependent for a while. He asked me to hostess the dinner parties and luncheons which he frequently held at home as part of his diplomatic position. I learned a great deal from this exposure and taught myself composure. By fifteen, he extended my role to being his official escort at diplomatic functions. At first they terrified me. Now I wonder what could. Most of my schooling was done on my own or online and with the exception of chemistry my grades were always As – as you can see. Taken together, these experiences have given me a greater maturity and worldliness than most twenty-five-year-olds. Plus of course, I have one thing they have lost.'

'What might that be?' prompted the Professor gently.

And she pulled the trigger.

'I'm a blank coin on which you can make your stamp. I trust this means that by the time I am twenty-one, I will have my Masters in both Political Science and Human Psychology. These, along with my languages and the experience I gained from my father, will make me the youngest Ambassador Britain has ever fielded. I am aware that you are one of the world's foremost political thinkers. I also know you have hand-steered the democratic growth of many countries during your lifetime. A few I spoke with, confided you are a sought-after advisor to several Governments' think-tanks which compete for your patronage and advice. I thought if I prove worthy, you might advise me how to launch my own career in the diplomatic corps. That is why I applied for all of your courses first, fitting in the others around them. I'm here because I believe you can help me achieve my ambition.' Then deciding to give the knife of her logic a playful twist, she added, 'quicker than I could on my own.'

Leah lifted her glass and sipped, watching him closely, hoping her tectonic determination and minimal use of language would reveal an understanding beyond her years.

'What an extraordinary woman,' the professor thought, finding that he had to remind himself she had only just turned seventeen. Her aura of maturity couldn't be the result of her life experiences, he felt, so it had to be in conjunction with insight. Which he knew was very hard to teach – if not impossible. Nevertheless, what about her resolve for the task ahead? He decided to venture over to this tree of doubt and see if he could shake a small bruised fruit off one of its low-lying branches.

'My dear girl,' he blustered slightly. 'Let me give you some very good advice. I have been here for nearly twenty-six years and have never seen anyone to date, prove me wrong in this. I implore you to reconsider. You will be trading the cream of your youth for late-night essay writing and lectures – a mistake which often ends in tears. 'Wisely and slow, they stumble that run fast,' he threw Shakespeare at her, 'is very good advice indeed.'

Leah placed her glass back on the table. 'I hope you don't mind if I pass on that advice, because I like to pass on good advice, it's the only thing to do with it,' she fired back Oscar Wilde in riposte.

'And what in your opinion differentiates good advice from bad?' the Professor asked quickly.

'Apart from the end result there isn't much to distinguish them. But in my limited experience, the motive of the advisor often makes the crucial difference,' this time quoting one of her father's oft-repeated mantras, thinking it unwise to volunteer the source. With a small sliver of satisfaction she watched the Professor languorously pull out a chair and sit down opposite. The act seemed to have an air of resignation to it.

'Whoever it was that said: "Youth is wasted on the young", was a genius who deserves to be better known.' He cocked a mischievous blue eye at her as he reached for the decanter to refill their glasses, hers first, before continuing. 'I see now, how you managed to pass the entrance exams with such ease. No mean feat at your age, or any age for that matter. I did however notice, that on your English paper the 8, the last digit of your birth date, looked very much like a 5; which, if simply glanced at would add three years to your age. Something I doubt most tired examiners would ever expect or check up on. This happened either by accident or through *design*,' he said, drawing out the word and looking at her intently, 'because I found this to be the case on all of your exam papers.'

Leah's heart banged to a stop. She froze in her chair. The unexpected shock of his words had turned her blood to ice and she dare not speak in case her voice added betrayal. Barely able to contain her neutral expression, she picked up her glass again and sipped, forcing as much serenity into the act as possible.

Gazing up vacantly at the ceiling over her head while tapping at his chin with a long tapering finger, he mused aloud: 'They must have thought they were reading the paper of a twenty-year-old. Not adding the intellectual snobbery and scorn they would have undoubtedly poured onto a seventeen-year-old's exam answers.'

The fact that he was right was not easing Leah's comfort level. His last comment had widened her eyes and bleached her face. Not only had he identified her little ruse, but correctly guessed her motive.

'Busted…I'm absolutely busted,' she thought fearfully.

Leah had intentionally styled her answers to reflect the views of an older student to imply she was twenty. Believing this approach stood a better chance for success than shouting that she was young, she had deliberately switched it around the other way: imprinting a 5 darkly on her exam papers, then tracing a thin line to make the diagonal forming the 8; expecting any closer examination to exonerate her from the accusation of cheating. Once her Oxbridge entrance results had come through, she thought that particular door had closed behind her.

Looking up at him nervously, she was surprised to see her acute concern reflecting back in his expression. He was looking at her in a way that was – kind.

'Please don't trouble yourself, my girl. There is nothing to be afraid of because your secret is quite safe with me. Actually, I applaud your ingenuity. In my experience, cheating in exams sometimes occurs when a person pretends to be younger – not older. And personally, I have never had much regard for the intelligence of examiners *per se*. In fact if your exam marks had been lower I might have phoned them up, insisting your papers were reassessed to produce a higher grade. From my point of view it is most unfortunate that wasn't required…I rather enjoy an intellectual spat after breakfast.'

Reaching across the table, he gently took her left hand in his, turning it palm up before covering it with his other. With his green eye sparkling gold-dust in the late evening sunlight, he spoke in the hushed tone of a co-conspirator, 'Funnily enough, it made me put my foot down and insist I should be the one to interview you for your place here at the University. You have my word that the only people who will ever know of your sleight of hand are sitting in this room right now. You can be certain, because although I read your exam papers with the utmost care, by the time I re-filed them I happened to notice that, annoyingly, they were all missing the top right hand corner of the first page. The corner which happens to hold the DOBs,' and he pressed his top hand down on hers in the same way he might secretly tip the maitre d' of a restaurant.

She could feel the small pieces of paper being given to her and smiled at him with relief; in time to see, just for a moment, a flickering twinkle appear genie-like, in his right blue eye.

'It is my great honour to welcome you to Oxford University, Miss Leah Mandrille. You will be the youngest girl I have ever taught.'

'Thank you so much. You won't regret your decision, Professor.'

'My name is Victor. Feel free to use it and never address me in private as "Professor Simmius", or I will call you "Student Mandrille".'

'Thank you…Victor,' she smiled, feeling her composure flooding back warmly; as a stronger feeling pricked at her perception, demanding to be heard. The bell of intuition was tolling loudly in her middle mind revealing something Leah had rarely felt before. For she somehow knew, and with absolute certainty, that all secrets would be safe with this man.

And as is so often the way with instinct, she was very nearly one hundred percent correct.

'Had you worried there for a moment, didn't I? My apologies, but I needed to be sure of both you, *and* your commitment.'

'Victor, I can never thank you enough… but I would love to know who said "Youth is wasted on the young". I've never heard that expression before.

'Some say George Bernard Shaw plagiarised Oscar Wilde, but

most people accuse me of the crime.'

On hearing this, Leah broke into sincere and uncontrolled fits of laughter. It was contagious, and as her second bout came around, Victor joined in.

THE PSYCHOTIC OR GUILTFREE APE

Children in a playground can be cruel, but children in an orphanage can be vicious past the point of savagery. The constant ache of their loss is sharpened on the stone of a loveless survival to the twin points of anger and revenge – at far too young an age for it not to impact the remainder of their lives. Their chimp-like behaviour operates at its most powerful in troupes or gangs. They generally pick on anything weaker, smaller, or different from themselves and unfortunately for Abdul, he fitted all three categories perfectly. He was only four feet tall at twelve years old and thin, from years of semi-starvation, but it was his eyes which turned him into a constant target for their spleen. Instead of being brown, one was green, the other bright blue.

He looked around fearfully, in panic, but there was nowhere left to run. Cornered; with too many of them to fight his way out, he was going to take a serious beating. The gang advanced on him haltingly; wary of his raised fists and desperate expression. For a boy so small and slight, his punches were painfully accurate and lightning fast. They had bitter memories of his ability to defend himself and none of them wanted to take a hit from those weaving hands. A standoff ensued, until the leader of the gang shouted, '3-2-1. Grab him!'

Seven boys lunged at him as one, but they hadn't seen the handful of coarse sand in his right fist. He flung it into their eyes, blinding three who recoiled, before a surge from the rear of the pack pushed them back onto him and he was quickly overwhelmed. A deluge of punches rained down and he grunted with the blows, making each hit sound as painful as possible. The battering intensified, forcing him to stagger sideways. Seeing the rest of the pack diving over the other boys to attack him, Abdul fell over backwards, pretending to be stricken.

The gang circled him, staring down on their prey which writhed on the baked earth in agony. Bashaar took control again. 'Pick him up,' he commanded.

They hoisted him by his arms and legs, and feeling their tight grip Abdul went deadweight – taking all the sport out their torment. His nonchalance quickly infected the gang, who began to lose interest in carrying their burden.

Bashaar saw what Abdul was doing. He leaned across his captive's limp form, putting his face only an inch away. 'I know, let's throw him down the well,' then he jumped back, pointing and squealing with sadistic glee as Abdul began struggling violently.

'Not the well, Bashaar, I can't swim. You'll kill me.'

'We've had enough of your lies,' Bashaar grinned, striding towards the well. Taking hold of the handle he wound the wooden bucket up from the dark water below. 'Put him in the bucket!' he ordered.

Four boys manhandled Abdul's feet into it and forced his hands around the rope, then instantly let go to watch him swing across the void. 'Oh dear,' Bashaar said quietly, making Abdul grip the rope for all he was worth – he had never learnt to swim. 'All those dates you've eaten are making you terribly heavy...I can't hold your weight any longer,' and he let go of the handle; laughing hysterically as Abdul dropped straight into the black, like a convict on the gallows.

The buoyancy of the bucket combined with its speed to crumple him to his knees as it smacked down on the hard surface, but he managed to stay inside. Jeers and laughter rang down, then Bashaar's dark profile broke across his round patch of sky. 'If you piss or shit in it we won't pull you out.' This was vitally important as they all drank from the well. His gang nodded sagely at the wise words – none of them had considered that side to it.

'If you admit to eating Hamid's dates we will come and get you at sunset, unless you really can't swim,' he said derisively. 'Then we will have to pull you out with a hook before you stink up the water.'

Abdul hadn't taken the dates. He felt certain that it was Bashaar, and foolishly, told the bigger boy to check inside his own pockets first, right in front of Bashaar's second-in-command. The gang leader had flown into a rage, rounding up his gang to punish the upstart for insubordination. Abdul had fled. Shouting his innocence. But someone had to pay for this theft and it wasn't going to be the godfather of the biggest gang in the orphanage.

'If I admit to stealing them will you pull me out now?' Abdul called up his gambit.

'Course,' came Bashaar's too quick reply.

'Okay, pull me up and I will tell you how I did it.'

'Aha you admit to it! I thought so. Tie off the handle,' he told the boy on his right. 'Hold onto the rope until we come back at sunset…and don't swim off anywhere,' he quipped, to even greater hilarity from his troupe.

Abdul waited until he was certain they had left him alone to his fate then began climbing the rope; getting half-way up before the ache in his arms and legs told him he would never make it to the top. He slithered back down, the coarse rope burning the skin off his palms until his feet touched the bucket and he collapsed back into it. He plunged one of his hands into the cool water, trying to remove the fiery pain, before swapping it with the one holding the rope. The water provided an instant balm but when he changed hands it seemed to make the pain much worse. He gave up; then started whimpering out loud in fear and self pity; wondering if he would make it through the three long hours till sundown.

After what seemed like an eternity, he heard a soft voice calling his name from above. Looking up expectantly, Abdul could see a small dark head silhouetted against the blue. 'Shhh, say nothing,' the young voice echoed down. 'We must be very quiet. They are nearby. I will try to wind you up but you must not tell them I got you out. You must say you climbed out on your own. Swear it on the soul of the Prophet.'

'I swear on the soul of the Prophet I will never say you helped me. Now pull me up, I beg you,' Abdul croaked back.

It was hard going, but the little boy managed to inch Abdul up to the surface. As his hands touched the round wooden bar which coiled the rope, he saw the features of his ally for the first time. It was Ali.

'Thank you for your mercy, Ali Bin Mohammed,' he gasped, clambering out of the bucket onto solid ground. 'Let us get away from here.'

One month later, Victor arrived at the orphanage and took Abdul back to England. He had spent four desolate years looking for his lost son, after the bombing of the Beirut Hilton which had wrought havoc on so many lives. It was doubly tragic in their case because it also claimed Victor's wife, costing Abdul his mother. Shell-shocked and dazed, Abdul had wandered away from the explosion into the slum quarter; where a kindly man found him begging for food and took him in.

The kindness stopped the moment he got him alone. One night and three terrible years of slavery later, Abdul noticed a knife gleaming at him from under the alabaster table opposite his bed. His molester used it for cutting up cakes of Lebanese hashish which he sold to tourists in the expensive hotels by the beach at a hugely inflated price. In a stupor, the beast had dropped the large knife to the floor before collapsing onto his bed. Abdul waited until his snoring reached floor-quivering height, then crept over to the table: feeding out his ankle chain with one hand; holding it clear of the floor with his other, to avoid waking the monster. The chain was just long enough to reach and stretching out, he managed to get hold of the sharp point and spin the knife towards him.

Abdul tested the edge of the blade in the moonlight reflecting off the ghost-white table and to his delight, saw a thin black line appear like magic on his thumb. Wiping the blade clean, he stole back under his blanket. He had to wait patiently now, because his tether wasn't long enough to reach the man's wooden cot. Wisely, his tormentor had measured the chain and cut it to length, ensuring he would rest in peace.

At daybreak, as the abuser went about his ritual assault before attending the morning prayer, Abdul punched the knife into his side in a cold rage then pushed him off – stabbing in a frenzy of fear. Only when certain the man was dead, did he begin sawing his way through the wire that bound his foot to the chain. It took him over an hour. Halfway through his labours the man groaned out his death rattle and Abdul, fearing he was still alive, stabbed the corpse repeatedly – churning the man's chest and stomach to a bloody pulp.

When he finally got free of the shackle, Abdul went over to the bucket of water by his bed, washed the blood off his hands, then pulled the knife out the body and cleaned it. He quickly ransacked the room but couldn't find any money, so he took the hashish. As he put the last chunk into a small wicker basket, his eye fell on a pair of oil lamps by the table. He unscrewed the bottom of one, shook the oil over the body, then searched through the man's pockets for some matches. Stepping back, he took one last lingering look at his torturer, spat on him, then struck a match and tossed it into the mess.

The flames attacked the corpse eagerly. They seemed to purge all trace and memory of the man with their hot, clean breath. All the self-doubt, he had harboured during his years of mental and physical torture, melted away as the heat withered the body, reducing it to nothing more dangerous than roasting meat.

The fire roared as it devoured the bed. Abdul stood watching: Silent; smiling for the first time in three miserable years. Statue-still; mesmerised by the display; he waited until the last possible moment when the room filled with thick black smoke, before turning away to walk calmly out of the house into the relative sanctuary of the streets. After his long years of suffering he was free. Never again would he feel sorrow for anyone or anything in his life – no more self-doubt, no pity, no regret and never any remorse.

Abdul sold the hashish that evening, but didn't realise the value of the money he was given in return. Because he had been brought up in Britain, he wrongly assumed that 10,000 pounds was an enormous sum, but after the dealer had scurried off, he discovered to his horror that ten thousand Lebanese pounds would barely buy him breakfast. The man had noted his pallor, and the rest was easy.

Two days later Abdul ran out of money and began begging on a street corner but he didn't even make it till nightfall. One of the local gangs spotted him on their patch and when he couldn't pay their tax, they beat him up in the park next to the Al-Omari mosque warning that if they caught him again, it would be the very last time.

An imam from the mosque saw Abdul nursing his injuries. Finding the boy was severely bruised and bleeding, he took pity on him and drove Abdul to a nearby hospital. As he handed over the money for Abdul's care, he told the doctors it was as much of his generosity as he could afford; that he would prefer them not to reveal his name.

It took a full week for Abdul's bruising to fade to a light blemishing. The ward nurse tried every trick in the book to find out what had happened, but when he steadfastly refused to say anything about himself, she grew suspicious and called the police. The years of trauma had made him highly suspicious of everyone and with the knowledge of his recent crime burning a hole in his mind, he told the police nothing; except some vague detail about the bombing and how he was sure it had claimed his mother. Hearing this, the police relented and passed him on to the callous care of the orphanage. They felt it kinder than leaving him to beg on the streets and, believing he had not committed a crime, never recorded the incident. This compounded the tragedy of his life because if they had charged him with anything at all, Victor would have found him sooner.

Ten months later the policeman who had taken Abdul to the orphanage, noticed the reward Victor had posted in Anmag, the Beirut newspaper. When he read the description of Abdul's eyes he telephoned Victor in England and told him where his son was staying. Unable to get a flight for two days, Victor begged a favour from one of his political friends and they flew over in the man's private jet, landing at Beirut Airport the next morning. Though it had been four years since he last set eyes on his son, Victor recognised him immediately and brought him straight back to London.

At first things went well for them both as Victor took on the role of teacher, to bring his education up to speed in preparation for western schooling. He was amazed by how quickly his son picked up the lessons and after only twenty months, entered him into a leading Public School as a boarder, one year below his peer group. This however, proved to be a dreadful mistake. He wasn't liked by the other boys and they bullied him. Not with the same sadistic cruelty he had experienced in the orphanage, but they called him 'raghead' and forced him into servitude, deeply wounding his pride.

One break time, a doughnut hit him on the back of the neck splattering its thick red jam all over him. Abdul exploded in fury. Attacking the older boy with a speed and ferocity that knocked him straight down. As his antagoniser rolled on the floor in a daze, groaning, Abdul picked up a heavy wooden chair and started smashing it into him. Fortunately, he was so wild that he didn't aim the blows or he would have caused more serious injury – possibly worse. Five boys rushed in to help their friend, wrestling Abdul to the ground, shouting: 'Enough, Abdul, that's enough.'

They lifted their injured friend gently onto a bench and carried him to the school sanatorium; with a 3-inch long cut on his arm, extensively bruised ribs and a severe concussion.

'He sort of fell down the stairs,' they mumbled at the matron, which didn't fool her for a minute and she reported it to the Headmaster the moment the boy was stable.

The Headmaster called them all into his study and quickly got to the truth of the matter. As the truth unfolded, he was genuinely shocked and more than a little frightened. He telephoned Victor, telling him to come and collect his son, adding that he might have to expel Abdul – permanently. Victor arrived at the school the next morning and listened to the gruesome details soberly, waiting for the right moment to pitch his pre-planned plea.

'Look Headmaster, I took him out of a very rough orphanage only two years ago. Let me take him home for a week to cool off and I will discipline him. As a trained teacher myself, I fully appreciate you will have to expel him if he behaves like this again. But we have a duty to educate all children, which should include the more traumatised ones. Isn't that the real challenge of our profession? Why not interview him yourself next week and see if you can take him back? I implore you.'

'Traumatised is an understatement,' the Headmaster replied gravely. 'Twenty-eight years of teaching and I thought I'd seen it all. But the savagery of his attack, and his violent use of a chair as a weapon is aberrant, and extremely dangerous. Good God, he could have killed the boy!'

'I know, I know, but he was provoked. And I understand from him that he has been bullied daily since I placed him in your care,' Victor countered, carefully playing the only ace in his hand.

'Yesss, I too was surprised to learn that,' replied the Headmaster a little unconvincingly. 'Perhaps this is an exceptional circumstance. Two years is little time to adjust to our culture and more civilised way of doing things. I'll tell you what: bring him back after half-term and we'll start again. But if he repeats this behaviour, in any way whatsoever, then he must leave immediately.'

'Thank you for your understanding,' Victor said gratefully, before collecting Abdul from the ante-chamber outside the Headmaster's office.

Four days before the end of that same term, Abdul almost drowned a boy who had ducked him from behind in the swimming pool. Only the quick intervention of the coach, diving in fully clothed, prevented real tragedy. He had to perform mouth-to-mouth on the boy, pushing the water out of his lungs to revive him. In utter outrage and trembling with fear and anger, he marched Abdul straight into the Headmaster's office, demanding serious punishment and saying he refused to have him in any of his classes. Six hours later Abdul was back home with Victor; who had cried all the way down and shouted at his son all the way back.

After a turbulent nine months of applications and rejection, no school would take him and reluctantly, Victor asked for a sabbatical to resume his son's tuition. In this however, Victor was not disappointed – he was surprised. Very. The speed at which Abdul could memorise a page then repeat it back word for word, was astonishing.

Victor surreptitiously invited an eminent child psychologist over for dinner. After eating together and gaining the boy's confidence, they all sat on the floor in front of a blazing winter fire and played 'games' before he went up to bed.

When the two men were seated alone, the doctor looked at Victor thoughtfully. 'There's no doubting that his memory is extraordinary. In layman's terms – photographic. He only got two cards from the entire deck wrong. That doesn't mean he understands what he memorises, but it does mean he can recall virtually everything he has read or seen. Parrot-fashion at the very least.'

'That's very handy for passing exams,' Victor observed.

'It's handy for passing science and maths exams,' corrected the psychologist.

But everything else proved worrisome. Victor was forced to keep Abdul at a distance from the local boys to prevent the fighting which invariably broke out. To make up for his son's isolation, Victor came home one day with a games computer, promising a different game each month. He was slightly disturbed by the subject matter of the games Abdul invariably picked out, all of which seemed to have a violent theme, but when he tried to suggest alternatives he had replied defensively, 'Get real Dad. Even Tom and Jerry is violent.'

'As long as you keep up your studies you can have whatever you wish,' Victor encouraged, desperate to avoid any further confrontation, and in the belief that his son was headed for a full scholarship at any university he chose.

The offer letters from three universities arrived in mid August and they sat down to discuss them. To Victor's annoyance, Abdul announced that he was enrolling at Cairo University to study Computer Science and Economics. They rowed, with Abdul storming up to his room shouting that in one month's time when he was eighteen, there would be nothing Victor could do to stop him going. In the weeks that followed there were many heated discussions. They would lock horns, until Abdul began screaming that his father's actions had ransacked *his* country and caused the death of *his* mother. The barb tore into Victor's heart, and he suspected his son was all too aware of it.

Victor came downstairs one morning, to find a hastily written letter propped against an empty coffee mug on the breakfast table. In it, Abdul explained that he had left for Cairo University and by the time Victor read the note, he would already be on the 7:30 am flight. It went on to vilify everything his father stood for and believed in – how ashamed he was to call him 'Dad'. It had a cruel post script: 'Don't contact me – I'll call you.'

He never did.

Arriving in Cairo, Abdul enrolled and managed to get a part-time job in a restaurant to help pay his way through the three year course. He worked as a waiter and with his spare money he signed up for two correspondence courses: one in America and one in Tel Aviv. Unusually, he chose exactly the same degrees, Computer Science and Economics but with an emphasis on security software and the associated protocols which operate them.

After getting his Bachelor of Science degree three times over, Abdul got a job as a junior analyst at a Swiss investment bank. It didn't take him long to pick up the nuances of the business and he was quickly promoted. They asked him to project manage the building of a medium sized computer system to automate the complexities of the bank's Foreign Exchange Trading division. It became obvious to him at an early stage that the budget was insufficient, but instead of alerting his boss, Abdul reduced the scope of the system and took to working late – copying the best parts of the developing programming then splicing in additional functionality with his own code. As a result he dramatically enhanced the system that he built, but only passed on the software the bank was expecting him to deliver. When the beta test ended successfully, Abdul handed in his notice, stole his employment contract with its non-disclosure agreement, and left.

He went on safari, hunting four of the Big Five for six months, then took his superior software to the competitor banks. They paid top dollar to have his enhanced trading system right away, as they were all competing on the same foreign exchange markets, mainly against each other. A system with far greater functionality, delivering more information a hundred times faster than their in-house software, was an advantage they did not want their competitors to have the sole rights to.

'It's simply more profitable to compete on a level playing field,' became Abdul's sales close, and his company mushroomed rapidly. Until one evening on an overnight flight to New York, the person seated next to him in the first class cabin leaned over and said, 'We have need of you,' in perfect Cairene, the ancient Egyptian dialect of the street.

'How did you know I was Egyptian?' Abdul lied smoothly.

'We know many things about you. We have watched you closely for over a year. We even know who it was that killed your mother all those years ago,' the man whispered. 'Would you like to know who he is, and where? Because I am authorised to tell you.'

Abdul fixed a still blue eye on him, to hide his flash of anger. 'Of course I would,' he said evenly.

'He's sitting right next to you,' came the shocking reply.

When the flight took off from Geneva, Abdul had been a millionaire who owned a small but profitable software house. By the time he landed in New York he had accepted the position of CEO and had negotiated a 51 per cent shareholding in a new foreign exchange trading fund with initial cash reserves of just over 2 billion dollars. The first tranche of money he processed through his new company.

'We must rewrite the software platforms to steal a march on the other banks' trading desks,' Abdul said, shaking the same hand which had triggered the bomb that killed his mother and sent his life spinning away on its tragic trajectory. 'One day you will be brought before me to watch your family being tortured. Then after your own suffering, you will beg me to end your filthy life,' he comforted himself with the thought; while smiling warmly at the man and saying, 'It will take eight months to complete and might be advantageous not to announce that I was the CEO. I wonder…could you arrange another identity for me?'

'That is an excellent precaution. How many would you like?' the stranger asked.

By the time Abdul returned to Geneva, he was Abdul-Aliyy Saqr Khalifa: the man who became known for marrying the modern banking system of the West with the ancient financial network of the East. Hawala had opened its vaults to the West for the first time in six centuries, opening them almost exclusively through him.

Abdul had chosen his new identity in the full knowledge that only those supplying his investment funding would ever know what the name signified. The Western banks, from which he carved their joint fortunes, were unaware at the time that Arabic names all have ancient meaning – so they had no idea to look into it. While Abdul's delighted Arab backers knew it would be foolish to point it out to them – so they never did. In fact, it amused them greatly to know that Abdul-Aliyy Saqr means 'The Falcon Servant of the Most High'. Extremely fast and rarely seen – yet pinpoint accurate and deadly. In private conversations amongst themselves they referred to him in code, as 'The Hawk'.

He became fabulously wealthy over the ensuing five years; counting the heads of several governments as friends. He was known to support many charities – especially orphanages – and liked to meet the children in person. An unusual act for a man in his position and more than a little dangerous, as the care homes he set up were always situated in war-ravaged, more shattered parts of the world. Abdul set one precondition before granting any funding: he stipulated that English was properly and actively taught as a language. As he was happy to underwrite this additional cost his offer was readily accepted; with those benefiting from his philanthropy thinking him exceptionally generous: in both the size of his donations and his extraordinary personal effort.

Then one crisp morning, just as the leaves were beginning to fall in Central Park, Abdul sold every one of his shares on the New York Stock Exchange for seven billion dollars, then vanished. Leaving no trace of where he, or his fabulous fortune, had gone.

GREAT APES

Julie's voice echoed out of the loudspeaker, cutting through shrieks of the gale force wind, 'Throw the lines or cut 'em Will. We're outta here.'

A moment later the bow swung away from the dock and Julie pushed the throttles up, feeling the weight of the sea fall away as the cutter came alive under her feet. The sharp prow began slicing through the top of the ocean rollers; the low growl from her twin diesels warning defiance at the elemental storm raging against her hull. Slowly and majestically the Seabelle rose up in the water as she began to gather speed.

'That's my girl,' Julie encouraged, inching the throttles forward. The SeaBelle responded eagerly: lifting her shoulders over the swells; the chaos of the ocean becoming more even, as her keel began knifing through the waves with a hiss of contempt at the sea beneath.

'Life jackets on and make sure your safety line is always tied off,' Julie said to Will, as he bumped his way into the cabin. 'We're with the sea on the way out and against it all the way back. So you take the helm, Will, and I'll navigate us in to a mile of their last position. Then I'll take over. I'm going to need all of my reserves to get us back safely.'

'With pleasure,' Will replied, matching her calmness. 'What's our heading?'

'One eighty – due south.'

'Julie, would you tell the Captain of this boat that I love her madly,' he smiled at her.

'There's no need. The Captain of this boat already knows you're mad,' and they burst out laughing together, revelling in the thrill of their perilous adventure; which they knew most experienced crews would never wish to attempt.

Julie leaned against Will's back, circling her arms around his waist, 'I love you too my wonderful husband. Don't worry, as long as we pay attention we'll get through this.'

'I don't doubt it Captain.'

'The Sea Wolf lost an engine. If they lose the other the sea will swamp their boat, so we're going to get them. And as you found out the hard way, my love, I always get my man.'

The monotone hum of the VHF burst into life with the most heart rending message that can ever cross the sea: 'Mayday Mayday. This is the Sea Wolf. Julie? Anyone? Over.'

Julie snatched the mike down from the roof of the cabin. 'Roger that Sea Wolf. We're underway. State your position, over.'

'Same position, Julie. We're only just holding our own against this, but we're taking on more water than we can handle. I don't think we'll stay afloat longer than 10 minutes. What's your ETA, over?'

'We're about 11 miles away, closing at 15 knots. 45 minutes to you, over.'

'I might have to abandon ship way before that, over.'

'How many of you aboard Linton, over?'

'Four. I repeat: four in total. We've got an orange life raft aboard but it won't last long in this – may God have mercy.'

'Linton, you're going to have to stay afloat or we might not find you. Our visibility is 50 yards best, over.'

'Roger that. We've got flares but with this low cloud base they won't be much use. Then it's strobe light beacons – maybe 200 yards, over.'

Will looked back over his shoulder. 'His boat is fibreglass hulled isn't it?'

'Yes. Why?'

'Fibreglass floats. Will the boat float if it's swamped?'

'No, the weight of the engines will drag her down.'

'I see…if the water is coming in from waves breaking over them, he might do better if the boat was upside down. Providing they shut all the stop cocks first, the hull will trap the air. It should provide enough buoyancy to stay afloat. Then they can tie their raft to it. An upturned boat won't move far in this sea and that's the key to solving this. Even if they fire flares we might not see them and we have a much better chance of spotting an upturned boat than a small life raft,' he reasoned.

'Jeepers Will – you really are mad. Roll the boat deliberately? Only a land-crab would suggest that.'

'Think about it. If they get into an inflatable raft it will shoot off to God knows where in this wind, *and then* how are we going to find them? If anything goes wrong like we lose radio contact or their GPS gets wet, they'll be two miles from their position in fifteen minutes. We can only see fifty yards at best. To find them, we will have to drive over them.'

'You're asking Linton to roll his own boat deliberately, then use it as a sea anchor to hold them in position? You're crazy!'

'Yeah, like a fox. But if the boat goes down they lose their sea anchor and with it – their position. That raft will be driven across the sea and swamped in a few hours. At current wind speed that's four square miles we've got to search, 15 minutes after their boat sinks. We'll never find them.'

'I've never heard of anything like this, Will. What if Sea Wolf goes straight down?'

'You know it might, but it sounds like it's going to sink anyway. At least they get half a chance and if the boat does have enough air to stay afloat, it will hold a position. *And we know their position.* We get a really good chance of finding them, instead of virtually none.'

'Is that why you were a director of NASA for so long?'

'Look, it's not working as a boat, so turn it over and it becomes a sealed float. Better still, one that won't move far in this sea and we know where they are. If their boat sinks and they get into that raft – they're gone.'

'He won't do it...but I'll tell him anyway,' and she relayed his suggestion to Linton.

'Jesus, Mary and Joseph, Julie. Let me think about that.'

In the background they could hear him shouting for someone to check the hold and see how much water was in the boat already. A slow minute passed then his voice came back on. 'It's touch and go Julie. We're being swamped every third wave and it looks like you won't make it in time, over.'

'Roger that. We're about 40 minutes away, over.'

'I can't believe I'm saying this, but we have no choice...I'm gonna try it, over.'

'Roger Linton. Fire a flare in thirty minutes – three zero minutes. Then every five. When you see our flare fire another. When you hear our engines or see our lights – fire two, over.'

'Copy that Julie; and whatever happens – thank you. If you don't find us within 60 minutes of getting to our position, you must go back to the harbour, okay?'

'You're not giving the orders on my boat, skipper. Take all the weight you can off her before you roll and don't worry, we're coming. I'm putting the coffee on now and there's a bottle of rum aboard with your name on it.'

'You're probably our only hope, Julie. Come and get us.'

'On our way Linton, over.'

'There's a light to port,' Will nodded.

'That's the Argonaut,' she replied. 'SeaBelle to Argonaut. Do you read, over?'

'Roger Julie. I monitored your transmissions. You're going after them then?' he said, using the sailor's code of being intentionally ambiguous, to avert the calamitous hex of speaking a certainty at the sea.

'Roger that. How are you doing? Over.'

'We're battened down and running for port. If I had enough fuel I would have gone myself, over.'

'Okay, report in every 5 minutes. How much fuel do you have left? Over.'

'Less than quarter of a tank. We're down to five knots at 2000 rpm. It's hard slogging but we should make it – if there's a God in heaven, over.'

'Roger that.'

'For what it's worth Julie, I've never met a better helmsman than you. If anyone can get them in this – you can. Watch for rogues off your starboard, we had a small one hit us two minutes ago, over.'

'Copy that.' Julie looked anxiously at Will. He was already scanning the ocean on the right side of the boat.

They now stood in the stony silence of concentration. Rogue waves are one of the terrors of the sea. Contrary to what most imagine, it is not their size which makes them deadly, but their direction. Boats ride waves by going over them bow first, and waves travel in the same direction as the wind. Rogue waves don't follow this principle. Rather, they come from the side. They can run at 90 degrees to the other waves; flipping a boat over before the helm has a chance to reply. When coupled with size they become deadly, instantly. They both knew that where there's one there are probably several more. The icy fingers of apprehension gripped them both and they fell into a concentrated stare – oblivious to the slash of the rain on the windows and the wind howling through the stays.

Julie looked at her watch, then the GPS. '35 minutes to ETA. I think there's some lukewarm coffee in the thermos. Want some?...Are you okay, Will?'

'Aye skipper,' he smiled, but raw anxiety was etched into his face. Before, he had known the calculated risk they were taking; but the odds had swung against them with that last transmission.

'Hey, you know what?' Julie offered encouragingly. 'Why don't you get the coffee and I'll take the helm.'

'That's a superb idea,' Will replied. He was only too aware that if they were to have a chance against a rogue, it was with Julie at the helm.

'And Will, if I shout "Rogue" brace yourself. The ceiling is best, okay?'

'No problem,' he said slowly, grabbing hand holds to pull himself over to the galley. Joining her in trying to ward off the opaque fear stagnating the air of the cabin, he asked offhandedly, 'How do we get them aboard?'

'Your good looks and my stubbornness.' They both laughed loudly, their bravado adding a ring of hysteria to the sound. 'Seriously though, Will. I'll hold the boat on station, upwind of them. You tie yourself off outside then lower the life ring and pull them aboard one by one. How does that sound?'

'Sounds good to me.'

'Make sure you do it from amidships. Don't go near stern. The props will suck in anything that comes their way, including your lifeline. If you get the chance, pull their life raft aboard and tie it to the deck. It's always good to have a little insurance and our raft only takes three.'

Will brought her back a mug of sweetened black coffee. They

sipped slowly, in silence, then as he offered to refill her mug the faint glow of a flare tinted the blackness in front them, slightly off to the portside.

'They're alive Will. They're alive!' Julie shouted, glancing at the compass in front of her to fix the flare's position. She swung the helm over, adding 5 degrees to the compass bearing to allow for the wind and current pushing them off true. 'There's a flare gun in the seat behind the table, Will. Fire it out the door.'

30 seconds after his, another flare went up in answer, brighter and directly over their bow.

'Less than a mile ahead. Get ready Will. And take care out there.'

Zipping up his yellow oilskins he slipped the flare gun into a pocket and stepped outside. After the quiet warmth of the cabin, the noise of the sleet-laden wind was deafening, the temperature shockingly cold. He looped the end of his harness rope over one of the stays knotting it tight, then pulled on it to make sure it held.

Julie's voice came over the loudspeaker, 'I need to turn the lights off Will. Bang your foot on the deck if that's okay.'

'Clever girl,' he thought, stamping the deck twice. She was buying a few minutes for her night vision to return before they came up on the raft.

Another flare went up. This time Will caught a snatched glimpse of the reflected sheen of an upturned hull, gleaming shiny grey against the blackness of the sea. It was the Sea Wolf. Upside down 150 yards away. He raised the flare gun and fired the reply, aiming slightly behind the SeaBelle so as not to blind Julie at the helm. It lit up the sea like daybreak for a quarter of a mile around, and fifty feet from the overturned fishing boat, Will could see the fluorescent orange life raft bobbing violently over a foaming wave.

'I can see them, Will. I'll come up against the wind, okay?'

He stamped his foot again to signal he understood.

Julie swung the helm over to circle around the stricken vessel, then straightened her course; heading to where she had last seen the raft. They surfed down the back of a monstrous wave and as they crested its bigger brother, following directly behind, Will saw the small craft wallowing in the trough below them. The throb of the engines raised their pitch to a scream as Julie backed down hard on the throttles: swerving the SeaBelle to windward; slaloming around the Seawolf. They came up next to the raft a few seconds later.

'Let's try and do this in one go, Will. I'll put them in the lee of us. The Seabelle will shelter them from the wind and iron out the sea a little.'

He just had time to grab the stay in front of him as the engines revved and died back to a quarter throttle. One-handed: Julie spun the helm to full port – then full starboard; her other hand poised over the throttles. The cutter pirouetted neatly, sweeping across the front of the little raft which disappeared from view. Julie counted slowly. 'One thousand. Two thousand. Three thousand,' then hit the throttles – hard – unleashing the full might of both diesels. The Seabelle reacted instantly. Her bow reared up in the water, her exposed hull shuddering against the sudden weight of the waves.

Julie was ready. No longer steering by sight – but feel. The moment she felt the cutter start to drop its nose, she pushed the throttles up to full ahead, counted to two, then set them running at one third. The Seabelle obeyed: she fell back onto the ocean, spray erupting from her bow; then dug in her heels – holding a position.

Setting her teeth against the raging sea, the Seabelle went stationary, as the raft bumped miraculously against the side of the boat – right below Will's feet. It was a remarkable feat of seamanship. So deftly executed that she might have been picking up a swimmer on a choppy lake – not fighting 60 mile an hour winds and twenty-foot-high foaming waves.

The full force of the gale hit Will from behind, but the hull of the SeaBelle was now smoothing out the waves towards the little raft; taking the task of getting the men aboard from tricky, to fairly easy. Julie turned on the outside lights and Will looked down. The men were shivering in the raft, ten feet below him. One had a coil of rope in his hand. He threw it up. Will caught it and pulled the raft tight against the SeaBelle then tied it off. The cutter now closeted the smaller craft, like a concerned mother swan brooding over her wounded cygnet.

Will shouted down to the men. 'You're tied on. Cut the line to the Sea Wolf,' then he grabbed the red and white lifesaver and lowered it into the raft, waiting patiently while the first man pulled it around his waist. Leaning back, Will took up the strain, his resolve giving him strength. Hand over hand he pulled him straight up to the level of his feet, where the fisherman took a firm grip and rolled onto the deck. Getting up quickly, he stood beside Will – handing him the life ring with one hand, slapping him on the back with the other. His mood was infectious and they grinned as they lowered it back down for the next man, waiting with his hands outstretched. With both of them working the line, they swiftly brought up the others.

When they were all safely aboard, Will passed them each a section of the raft's bowline. 'Let's bring your life raft aboard – just in case.' They brought it up quickly, the fishermen lashing it down securely, before they jostled their way into the cabin.

Julie watched them step in and shut the door. 'Where's Linton?'

'He never got off the boat, Julie. He told us to get in the raft then turned sideways to the waves and rolled her.'

'You mean he was washed overboard?'

'He said he'd swim out but he never appeared,' said another man, whose nickname was "Fish".

'We didn't see him get off the boat, or get washed off. But he must have drowned by now,' added the third man, looking at his feet.

'Maybe not,' Will said. 'The boat's floating so it must have air trapped in the hull. If Linton has any sense he would wait there for us.'

'We're going to get him,' Julie said firmly. Will heard the steel ringing in her tone. He knew from past experience it was futile to argue against – not even crystal clear logic could bend it a fraction.

Julie locked eyes on the fishermen, who were gazing at her with a different unspoken thought. 'I don't care whether he's dead or alive, he's coming back with us. That's final,' Julie said forcibly, then stared straight at Will, as if he were the only person in the cabin.

'Yes Captain,' he answered her cue. 'What's the plan?'

'I'll re-position the SeaBelle upwind of the Sea Wolf and you can swim over and get him out. These men will belay you on a rope and pull you both back afterward. Simple,' and to signify an end of the discussion she turned back to the helm and tapped the throttles up.

'When the Captain's in this kind of mood, it's quicker to do what she says,' Will smiled sheepishly at the others.

They filed outside and Will stripped off his clothes until he was standing in his tee shirt and shorts. 'Fish' tied a rope around his waist then reached into the raft beside them and pulled out a rubber torch. 'Waterproof,' he said, switching it on and tying it to Will's wrist. 'One tug on the rope for slack, three pulls and you'll be back aboard before I can drink a shot of tequila. Okay?' he winked.

Will just nodded; he was sucking down deep lungfuls of air.

Julie's voice came over the loudspeaker. 'I've got her steady. Watch out for the props Will. I love...'and she cut herself short.

Without giving himself time to think about what he was going to attempt, Will climbed onto the heaving rail; the fishermen holding him upright against the force of the gale. He took one last breath, then dived as far as he could stretch from the side of the boat. The second he hit the water, Will kicked hard, knowing he must get clear of the two churning propellers. Compared to the icy chill of the deck, the sea felt surprisingly warm, and 30 strokes later his hand bounced off the hull of the Sea Wolf.

Putting his ear to the side, Will rapped on it with his torch and listened. There was a pause, then a faint thudding reverberated back – Linton was alive! Will pulled himself towards the source of the sound. A few bangs later and he had located Linton's exact position.

Turning back to face the SeaBelle he flashed his torch up and down and heard a faint cheer coming back from the men. He gave a single tug on the line and the rope went slack. Taking ten long breaths, he clamped the torch between his teeth and pushed himself away from the boat to submerge vertically. The roar of the storm cut off instantly – replaced by the quiet calm of the deep.

He found that he didn't have to move his head very far to swivel the torch in a fairly wide arc and, as the boat rocked away from him, he aimed it down to see the ship's rail shining in the dark, three body lengths below his paddling feet. Doubling over he went straight down: grabbing the rail; pulling himself around and up like a high bar gymnast. His head banged against the coarse wooden deck and he used it for balance, allowing his natural buoyancy hold him upright as he swept the beam around searching for the cabin door.

The scene the torch lit up was macabre. The natural order of things had completely reversed – causing him to double-take. Anything not attached to the boat had gone to the bottom, making the deck appear naked and barren, while anything still attached hung down limply – when it should have been hanging up. The hawsers seemed like the tentacles of some monstrous jellyfish drifting on the tide. The untidy chaos of a tangled net twisting in sartorial contrast to the straight white lines of the ropes billowing against the backdrop of the seabed, some 600 feet below. Silent and ghostly, the boat drifted hauntingly, its rhythmic lift and fall giving it life.

Tearing his eyes away from the hypnotic scene, Will swivelled his head around, searching for the cabin door. It was to his left and he dolphined over. Opening the door with one hand; using the handle to harpoon himself inside. He was urgent now. The burning sensation in his chest growing stronger with each heartbeat. Not wasting a second he swam into the cabin and went straight up the stairwell – towards the sanctuary he hoped was waiting for him at the bottom of the boat. Tilting his head back to aim the torchlight up, Will could see a mirrored surface through the gloom. Grabbing the torch in his left hand, he propelled himself up and burst into the air pocket to suck down new air. As his breathing calmed he swept the beam around, to find Linton's face grimacing at him from six feet away.

'Ahh, Linton I presume?' Will said in his best cocktail party voice.

A smile tweaked across the Captain's face. It was the tortured expression of a man in extreme pain, doing his best to hide it.

'Are you okay?' Will asked, suddenly serious.

'I think my arms are broken,' Linton winced. 'How are the others? Did you get them?'

'They're all safely aboard.'

Linton's smile broke across his face again. 'I've never lost a man to the sea yet,' he said proudly. 'Although I may be the first...but perhaps that's as it should be.'

'There's nothing like a conflict of interest to get me going, Linton, and I'm under strict instructions from Julie to bring you back dead or alive. So you're coming with, and if you've broken your arm I don't see there's much you can do about it,' Will joked, as he tied a loop in the rope floating next to him and dropped it over Linton's head. Ducking under the water, he shone the torch on the man's injuries. The weak glow revealed a horrific sight. Linton's left arm had snapped at the elbow. It was bending sideways at an impossible angle; while his right flopped lazily from just below his shoulder – dislocated.

Will surfaced and grinned at Linton. 'Nothing that a hot nurse and a case of cold beer won't fix,' he said confidently, putting as much lightness into his tone as he could muster. It was a lightness he wasn't feeling in himself. Linton's injuries meant he couldn't be expected to swim out, and he would be very hard to manage as a floating weight. They had to dive down to the cabin some fifteen feet below and the wallowing movement of the boat would make it an uneasy dive. Equally, he dare not get the fishermen to pull them out as the rope might snag and trap them under water, drowning them both.

'Okay Linton, ten deep breaths and I'm going to swim us out of here. Bite onto my shirt and don't let go – whatever happens.'

Linton nodded his acceptance through obvious pain.

'When we break surface, I'm going to hold you against the boat until we get our breath back, then your shipmates can pull us the rest of the way. Ready in ten?...Go.'

Will submerged and stepped back against Linton. Feeling the man bite onto his shirt, he positioned the torch in his mouth and swam across to the entrance of the stairwell. Gripping the guiderail with his left hand, he twirled in the slack rope with his other arm. When he had it all and the line was centred down the stairwell, Will gave a desperate push with his feet, trying to glide down to the cabin. They got a third of the way before their collective buoyancy pulled them up against the angled ceiling. They began to inch back towards the bottom of the boat.

Will kicked frantically and managed to reverse the pull, but it wasn't enough. Just as he was thinking of going back to the air pocket, Linton started kicking with him. They began to descend, slowly, but Will could feel the pain in his chest getting sharper. Flying on the wings of near-panic, he shot his hands out to the sides of the stairway and pulled them both down. It was painfully slow going. 'All or nothing now,' Will shouted to himself, following the rope which led out through the cabin door then kinked over the rail up to the surface.

As they swam into the cabin, Will suddenly felt Linton relax and let go of his t-shirt. Twisting upside down, he managed to grab Linton before he floated away. Will aimed the torch beam at the man's face: his mouth was half-open; his eyes closed; small bubbles were trickling from bluish lips and a stream of them was trailing out of his nostrils.

Will used up the last of his air to manhandle Linton bodily through the cabin doorway, then looped one arm through the man's shirt and tugged the rope three times; hoping the weak effort was enough to communicate with the men at the other end.

Nothing happened.

Forcing down an overwhelming desire to breathe, Will reached up to jerk it again, when the rope went taut as an iron bar and they began to move fast. They went somersaulting across the deck, then hit the ship's rail, painfully – exploding the air out of Will's lungs. He almost let go of Linton. Using sheer brute strength, in angry determination, Will dragged the man behind him as they streaked towards the surface with a speed that would have put a smile on the face of a waterskiing instructor. They erupted out of the water and Will dragged down a lungful of air, to feel the heady relief of the pain in his chest disappearing. The simple act of breathing had never felt so good. Panting with the sheer joy of it and elated by the speed they were doing across the surface, Will rolled Linton face up, then circled his arms around the man's stomach to hump his shoulders out of the water.

As they neared the Seabelle, Will turned his head and called out to the fishermen. They were lying on the deck – hanging half over the edge as they hauled on the rope. 'Get Linton first – he's drowning.'

Two strong hands grabbed hold of Will's t-shirt, 'No,' he shouted. 'One,' said Fish, and the men lifted them out of the water and onto the deck of the SeaBelle, in one sodden lump.

'I'm okay, help him' Will pointed feebly at Linton, then turned onto all fours to puke mouthfuls of seawater onto the deck; which instantly vanished as a wave washed across the stern. Pulling himself up the side of the cutter, Will looked back to see Fish leaning across Linton, holding the unconscious man's nose and blowing into his lungs.

A few seconds later Linton choked; coughed; then vomited up a half a gallon of sea water. To raucous cheers of encouragement from his anxious crew.

THE ELDER APE

Arriving early, she took out her key to Victor's rooms. Leah was the only student who had one. The Professor had handed over the key as though it were fashioned from freshly minted gold, saying her banging on the door had to stop: 'It sounds exactly like gunfire.' That wasn't the real reason, but she enjoyed the thought that the Professor trusted her. Going into the small kitchen in the back, she put away the ingredients for their Wednesday evening supper together.

Victor had suggested that if she were to take up her place at Oxford at seventeen, she should have dinner with him once a week to ensure everything went smoothly in her first year. They had settled on Wednesdays then carried on with the arrangement throughout her second, third and fourth years.

Leah was looking forward to the special treats she had bought for their meal – smoked sturgeon and all the ingredients for a Veal Marsala. An appropriate choice. Tonight's conversation would be conducted in Italian. The week before they had dined on spiced lamb, speaking High Arabic throughout the meal, as they batted their intellects back and forth across the dining table.

Victor had offered to pay for their meals, while Leah fetched the groceries. Initially, she had felt a little guilty in accepting his largesse but over the course of her first year she had come to realise that Victor was an extremely wealthy man. 'Though you would never guess that to look at him,' she thought.

Against strong resistance from the Professor, she had thrown out the worn corduroys and Tattersall shirts he wore day-in and day-out for the entire term, without the inconvenient interruption of a washing machine. She made him stand on the ladder which accessed the higher bookshelves, to measure the length of his leg so she could hem his new trousers properly. Previously, he had simply cut them off at the appropriate length, leaving cotton threads which eventually grew several inches long; making his trousers uneven as one leg unravelled faster than its formerly identical twin. In the end he had put up only token resistance – as near to full approval as Victor ever indulged.

At first she had believed him to be highly eccentric, but now knew better. There was a curious, chess-like logic to all of his foibles and she guessed he wore his old clothes as a form of camouflage: to wrong-foot "leech mentality", a term he frequently employed; but it also engendered sympathy in others, including those less fortunate than he. It was either that, or a hangover from his student days, when like many of his generation he had been an ardent communist.

The old grandfather clock struck the quarter hour and Leah glanced at her watch, smiling as she did; the Edwardian chiming was precisely ten minutes fast. With the exception of his lectures and tutorials Victor was habitually late, so he set all of his clocks ahead by exactly ten minutes. But this also gave him the advantage of getting people to leave ten minutes early if he didn't notify them of the fact; together with an early warning of the more control-orientated individual, who liked to arrive on time then reiterate that the tardiness wasn't their fault – the volume and frequency of their repetition enabling Victor to judge their degree of insecurity with a surprising accuracy.

'Creative, intelligent minds are often caught up by event, or other people, Leah. They are frequently late. There is no harm in being late, the crime is in not phoning it through,' he told her once. Which made Leah ask him why then, he went out of his way to broadcast his intolerance of bad time-keeping. Victor had only laughed his reply – saying nothing. Her first clue in understanding how his ability to read everyone with such succinct clarity, operated. It wasn't fruitful intuition. It was distinctly more logical.

Walking back into the main study, she caught sight of her reflection in the gilded mirror hanging over the fireplace, and fetching her bag, spent a few minutes perfecting her makeup before pulling the clip from her silvery blonde hair to let it swirl around her shoulders.

She was becoming a very attractive woman. Her large green eyes were shot with diamonds and acted as the perfect foil for her high cheek bones and full lipped, sensual mouth. She half-turned, peering over her shoulder to see how her bottom and legs looked in the light blue cocktail dress and stockings she had put on her credit card that day. As she cast a more critical eye over her reflection, an effervescent feeling of beauty bubbled inside her, causing her to smile knowingly at the mirror.

Her fresh face and seemingly innocent aura hadn't gone unnoticed by her fellow students. Leah had indulged a few of their passes; but when she told them she was committed to a career abroad and only interested in a "friend with benefits" relationship, they got angry or drifted away. That was one of the problems with the men of her age, she felt. They didn't know what they wanted, or could have, until it was far too late.

This was certainly not a fault of Victor's. The first few times they dined together, Leah had carefully monitored his speech and actions, looking to expose any hint of 'Dirty-old-man-itis', but to her relief it simply wasn't there and the relationship had blossomed along a different path: more father-daughter than professor-student. She guessed that their suppers afforded him the privacy to speak his mind without it being reported on or judged, while they gave her the opportunity to view and gain from, an astounding intellect. Several of the dons and a handful of students had queried the slightly untoward arrangement, until Leah and Victor had torched their sniffling suspicions with a similar reply, "It's our mutual love…of fine dining"; both of them taking the utmost delight in saying it in Italian. Leah anticipated their dinners together with covetous delight, and was determined no one would stand in the way of their mutual love.

Sensing the door opening, she turned to greet him.

'Buongiorno, buongiorno,' he smiled, pushing it shut. The years hadn't bowed him, he stood tall and lean, radiating an easy confidence only ever mitigated by his insatiable curiosity. Victor was a man who knew his own mind and lit his own way. His white hair hadn't thinned during the time she had known him and his hands were tapered and beautifully shaped – the hands of a surgeon or concert pianist perhaps. But his eyes moved him into the magical. They were bright, soul searching and burning with life. The green one had an unsettling habit of looking deep into her, while the blue one seemed flecked with whatever emotion he was feeling at the time. Today it appeared rather euphoric. The forty-five years between them melted away as she felt his liquid Italian pour into the room.

'I trust all is well. Care for a Negroni?' he offered, weaving his way around piles of books, heading for the antique drinks cabinet.

'Bellissimo.'

They soon fell into the easy rhythm of close friends and at the end of their meal, as she poured out their coffee, he spoke into the amiable silence flowing around them.

'Would you mind if we switched into English?' he suddenly asked.

'Of course not, but why?' she queried his unusual request.

'Because English is the most accurate medium for the topic I wish to discuss. It has more words in it than any other language we speak.'

'You mean English has a larger vocabulary.'

'Please don't be anal, Leah.'

'Oh come now, Victor. I'm not the one who spells anal-retentive with a hyphen,' Leah flipped him back with a smile.

'Precision is a weight I carry – alone unfortunately,' Victor replied, making the mark of a hyphen with his index finger as he spoke, as though he were consecrating wine in a cathedral.

'Ha ha that's funny, but I detect an ominous tone. I hope the topic's not going to be tedious.'

In an exaggerated voice, he continued, 'At the risk of bringing the ticking of the clock to the forefront of your mind, can we discuss something of particular interest to me? You can let me know if it bores you.'

'I can't hear an Edwardian grandfather clock ticking away behind me,' Leah replied straight-faced, her eyes twinkling mischievously.

Victor gave her a momentary smile before turning more serious. 'The thing is, I want this conversation kept strictly between us. You are not to mention it or discuss it with anyone. And you must never use it in an essay – even if it's one for me.'

'Keep a secret in return for an intrigue? I can't resist. What is the subject?'

'Democracy, actually.'

'Tick Tock.'

'Ha! Well it's a dirty little secret of mine but I've fought for democracy all my life and…'

'Victor, that isn't really a secret,' she interjected. 'Your work with many shades of government in seventeen countries; that you openly and frequently advise political parties in opposition is known by everyone…with the exception of a small tribe in Indonesia, and your cleaner.'

'Yes, I did rather well retaining her, didn't I? And your misplaced flattery is welcome but what I mean to say is that democracy is something I've fought for, perhaps even helped engineer for a great many people, but I'm starting to think I've made the most dreadful error.'

Sensing he was genuinely concerned, she reached out in a softer tone. 'I don't see what you mean, Victor.'

'I may have overlooked something – something highly disconcerting.'

'How ridiculous. You should feel very proud of your accomplishments. What on earth is…'

'I'll tell you,' he cut in, cocking a still blue eye at her. 'A few years back I stood on the podium with Al Gore in South Beach Miami. It was his last rally and the weekend before the Presidential elections. He was undoubtedly going to win. The two sound-bites I most remember were: "The only person who can beat Al Gore is Al Gore" and "Bush's mouth is where words go to die". They summed up the political situation perfectly. No one ever doubted Gore would triumph – he was the clear front runner. On the following Monday motored up to North Miami, to have breakfast with an old student of mine, then when I drove back I hit road block after road block. What had taken me forty-five minutes one way, took me five-and-a-half hours to return. You see it was polling day and the police had cordoned off sections of Miami to channel people away from their voting booths. I saw it with my own two eyes, and that's when it dawned on me.'

'What dawned on you?'

'That is was possible to hijack the democratic process in a modern Western country. I'd seen it before in smaller, mainly third world countries, but never in one with a free and open media. Over the following week I watched it roll out in a disbelieving daze. I knew exactly what was going on. I even anticipated the precise steps to what I sincerely hoped I was wrong about. But sure enough, it was in play. The mainstream media were focusing on the bigger picture while the local press and TV stations couldn't get a word in. No one ever thought it could happen to America – the Land of the Free. Just the possibility itself was too awful for most people to contemplate, so they simply didn't. And of course, the American's disbelief and denial that such wickedness could happen to them, was the very mechanism the Republicans were relying on to pull it off successfully. They managed the process so well that even a part of me began forming a grudging admiration for them. Ostensibly, the risk they were taking seemed substantial; but their timing was so pre-emptive and so precise, that there wasn't any risk at all,' he ended forlornly.

'I do remember hearing a few rumours, but they were only rumours.'

'All smoke and no fire, eh? Well, two weeks into a recount and those rumours gained solid ground. By the end of the first week four of them had been substantiated, attracting the interest of the national press who decided they would also investigate. To start, they began examining the same events reported by the local press and it took them three days to verify their authenticity. When they discovered the rumours were factual, they started digging deeper. A pattern of minor incidents emerged, which individually made little or no difference to the count but, when taken collectively, had enormous impact. The full extent of those incidents took a whole week to verify, but the national press never finished their investigation because the day after they started to report the tip of that iceberg, Bush suddenly announced he'd won! The timing was perfect. By then, everyone wanted a clear winner to mop up a very messy situation. The mainstream media continued to report, stoking the flames of doubt into a decent sized fire, but they were behind the curve. When the Electoral College voted 271 to 266 in Bush's favour, the media backed off pretty damn fast. 25 of those votes came from Florida. The Electoral College of Representatives had decided in their wisdom not to vote with the majority of citizens. Gore had a clear majority, but Americans vote for an Electoral Representative who is supposed to vote on their behalf, in accordance with the People's decision. For the first time in history the Electoral Representatives did not do that, and Gore lost. Governor Bush won by five votes, handed to him by the College of Representatives. That was enough for the mainstream media. They packed up to get on with the business of courting their new leader.'

'And Bush became the world's leader, with only one previous state trip abroad. China, I think it was,' Leah added.

'Here's the thing, Leah – I've met him.'

'Who, George Bush?'

'Yes but no – not that idiot. I know who put it all together. I know who planned and executed it.' He stared at her, steeling himself for his next disclosure. ' You see, I taught him. To my shame, I taught him too well. He was an Honours student here at Oxford, some years ago,' and with that, Victor got up to pace around the furniture and books in a measured gait, his head bowed. Leah recognised this as a sign of intense concentration or deep personal concern. After pausing to gather his thoughts, he aimed a low voice at the floor in front of him.

'It didn't take me long to find out who had co-ordinated it. Fortunately, my work has allowed me unimpeded access to the great, the good and the ugly. I knew the skills set required and very few possess it – thank God. I had my suspicions as to who it could be, so it didn't take me long to narrow the list down. What took far longer was getting it verified independently, before I confronted him with it.'

'And you feel...partly responsible?'

'Yes, dammit, I do!' he said angrily, throwing his arms wide then dropping them to his sides. 'Well no, not really. Oh I don't know, there is a piece of me that feels a small pride in what he accomplished and overall I'm grateful to him for opening my eyes. He proved that it really could be done successfully; executing it with an ease and simplicity that belie the complexity of the task. Luckily for us all, he put a type of corporate mafia in command – a gangster government – more interested in pursuing wealth than flexing the bicep of real power. But what if he hadn't? What if someone more Stalinesque had taken control?'

Leah gripped the arms of her chair involuntarily, as the full import of his words detonated inside her. She had spent thousands of hours with the Professor over the past four years, socially or professionally, and had got to know him well. He didn't lie, he didn't even embellish. If anything, he had an inhuman desire for accuracy that he ferociously instilled into all his students. This understanding, together with her recently acquired Masters in Political Science, gave her the insight to take in the enormity of what his simple statement actually revealed. As her thoughts raced ahead of the implications, a jagged crack tore across her perception of the world and her mind tumbled into it, recoiling in horror at the size of the void that confronted her. Using a measured voice to mask her turmoil, she monotoned, 'Stalinesque? At best it would reduce western freedom to a has-been. But if other leaders realised what they had pulled off, it could be...apocalyptic.'

'The possibility can't be ruled out. My view of the world changed with that election. Up till then I believed in pushing democracy into the world. Afterwards, I realised that democracy is also an ideal platform for manipulating the masses, to feed the hungers of a few determined men.'

'Not quite, it's not,' Leah countered. 'One man's one vote is understood by everyone. It's a concept that's hard to challenge.'

'Certainly you wouldn't want to challenge that!' He pointed his finger straight up. 'It's more subtle, Leah. They use that ideal. Hold up democracy for all to see and admire, while diluting the power of each person's vote.'

'And just how do you go about that?' Leah heard herself asking, aware she might not like his answer.

'You simply unite countries and give everyone a vote in a single government. Like say, the European Union.'

'Oh God, that does dilute the strength of each vote.'

'Indeed it does. Some years ago I and one or two others were asked to submit a government structure for the EU that would take it through the next 300 years. We put forward a concept for a strategic European Government Council. It had three representatives from each country who were to be elected by the voting citizens of each nation. The Council had a specific brief, aimed at solving our longer term problems and cutting red tape. It did not have the overreaching authority the EU holds today. The main bearings of our design were the social wellbeing of all Europeans and assistance with trade and infrastructure. Everything was going well until it was abruptly dismissed by the European élite, after interference by that cabal of bankers who privately own the Federal Reserve Bank.'

'*Privately owned?*' Leah exclaimed. '*The Federal Reserve Bank in the United States is privately owned?* But the Fed sets the interest rates and we all have debt. It provides money in exchange for government bonds, government debt, which we all have to pay for. That's terrible! It can't be…'

'It's true alright. It's privately owned by three commercial banks and a large number of occult individuals. I use the term occult accurately, because there is no official record of the Fed's ownership, while its sinister implication is just as relevant. It took me two years to dig up their names. The knowledge of who they are is one of the most disturbing things I've ever had the misfortune to know. '

'Disturbing? It's disgusting. The Fed plays the same role as the Bank of England.'

'They differ in one way. When the Fed sets the interest rate for the US, the rest of the world is forced to follow at some point.'

'That's absolutely vile. I'm horrified.'

'Are you? Welcome to the real world, Leah. A world only a few ever get to learn about.'

'But it puts the owners of the Fed in a position of enormous wealth and power. It gives them a vested interest in making the US Government borrow more – a profit motive for calamity.'

'They wield phenomenal power worldwide. Directly or indirectly, everyone works for the Yankee dollar. But the Fed doesn't only profit from calamity. It's true that when the US is at war the government is forced to borrow more from the Federal Reserve. But the Fed also profits from the rebuild after the war, via commercial loans distributed through the retail banking industry. It also profits in the good times, by providing the money with debt attached. Then they deliberately increase the money supply; causing inflation in the medium term, which gives them the excuse to raise the interest rate. We work to pay off that interest – they collect it. Every time money is released into an economy the burden of debt increases. Simply put: it's modern-day slavery.'

'I'm not sure it is the same as slavery. You must feed and house your slaves. They've found a way around that cost. We all have to support ourselves. We're all forced to borrow money to buy a house, a car, almost every damn thing. We must work to pay off that debt.'

'You begin to see it, Leah.'

'See it? It turns the medicine into a carcinogen,' Leah slapped her hand on the table in outrage.

'You can get annoyed but it won't do any good. The answer lies in the political process. Otherwise the owners of the Fed stand as inviolate as they are invisible.'

'I'm not annoyed, Victor. I feel like I've been conned. Sorry, *being conned*. I'm flat furious.'

'Then you'd better calm down because I'm sorry to say that it gets much worse. The Cabal have a grand design for the world and they are on a straight course to rule it. What am I saying? They already do. But their control isn't absolute – not yet. When they found out what we were proposing for the European Union, they stepped in and changed it. They suddenly appeared one day, the bitter sediment in the chalice of mankind: cajoling, promising wealth and power to selected leaders of Europe. They know how to tempt and they don't let anyone get in their way. So now, in accordance with their strategic design, the President of the European Union is a non-elected office, which reduces Western democracy to the same level as China. 650 million people electing 500 representatives who have even less accountability back to the people. No politician can resist that gilded carrot. It's their dream ticket.'

'Are you suggesting this Cabal are planning to finesse our control over our own destiny?'

'If you think about it – they already have. They've usurped it. By uniting large swathes of the human population under smaller government, we become much easier to control and manipulate. Our opportunity to influence or change things diminishes radically as our vote is diluted.'

'Ouch. That principle is true. The Million Man March on Washington failed to achieve anything, but when 250,000 march on Downing Street something gets done.'

'Or they simply lie about the number marching on Number 10,' he laughed. 'You've put your finger right on the button, Leah. Once a country gets beyond fifty million there's a dramatic change of control. Look at the democratic countries which are the most liberal, i.e. those furthest away from a police state. The facts strike very hard because they are all under fifty million. Look at Spain and Portugal before EU integration, or New Zealand and Australia now. Then consider America, China and Russia.'

'That's cheating a little, Victor. You're picking out countries which don't have the death penalty.'

'Not intentionally, but isn't it curious how that completes the circle?' and he glanced over at her in mid-step.

For a long moment, the echo of his reply cast a ghostly pall over both of them. Deciding to break its spell, Victor walked quickly to the dining table and reached for the decanter. He refilled their glasses in silence, draining his with a single gulp. Leah followed suit.

The smiling, contented genie of their earlier evening suddenly chameleoned into something far more sinister – Draconian. The atmosphere in the room went from chilled – to chilling...The beast had slipped into the room, to listen. Leah could see its shape forming in the ether: serpentine; sharp-fanged; exuding an aura of unspeakable power and vicious speed – omnipotent and unstoppable. She became aware of the weight of its sheer presence – a presence in which a person was reduced to mere on-off mortality. Unlike the dragons of legend this one didn't have a name. Its very anonymity helping to fuel it with unspeakable power: a nameless void with absolute control. As she saw it more clearly, the possibility slid into probability that if another totalitarian state were to materialise, it could emerge from, then take over a democratic country. Or perhaps be the result of a united Europe. The very last direction you would expect it to spring from. One of her father's sayings leapt into her mind: 'When disaster happens at sea, it often comes from behind you.' But deciding on fight over flight, she picked up the weapon of her mind and marched out to do battle with the monster.

'Victor, if a detailed understanding of the problem is more than half the solution, then what is the solution?' she asked, clicking one of her fingernails on the table in time with her words.

'Well, we have to accept that democratic countries, via their incoming governments, have a clear potential to be politically hijacked. It's already happened to the greatest nation on earth; meaning it will happen again soon and to many others. Especially now the Powers-That-Be are fully cognisant it can be pulled off successfully. They also know you can carry out the most wilful acts during your reign and get away with them clean and clear. So the proverbial cat is now out of its bloodied bag. Remember Putin's comment? "If Bush can hang Saddam – I can hang the rebel leader of Chechnya".'

'It's not only the Superpowers which have huge arsenals and the military wherewithal to carry out a leader's bidding. It's much easier to win control over a smaller country.'

'That is already the case,' Victor pointed out. 'Think Iran or any African country you care to mention. Mankind is at a crossroads, Leah. To our right, Capitalism: anything someone else has – I want. To our left, Socialism: anything I have – someone else must pay for. Freedom and harmony lie in another direction and, unfortunately, human suspicion won't permit a new direction unless it's very well signposted. The problem being that signposting takes decades and George Bush set the bloody clock ticking in 2001. The stakes are now high; the sands of time are running out. So it would be safer for us all, if governments were reduced in might.'

'Oh God, you think we've lost control of our controllers.'

'I do. The disconnect is almost irreversible – though not quite. I have a couple of ways to spike their ambition. As you well know Leah, all empires crumble eventually: Roman, Persian, British and it always turns out in the same way. They break into much smaller countries. It's as if the natural desire of mankind is for smaller governance – not larger. Once free of the yoke, people shy away from impersonalised government and demand something they have much more say in and of course, greater control over.'

'A smaller populace does have a bigger percentage of the vote per capita,' she agreed.

'Exactly. That point is well understood and kept well hidden by the Cabal at the Fed and most of our politicians – which is why they seek larger numbers of voters. That Cabal and most of our politicians crave one thing – power. The more the merrier. If you're already at the top of the pile, the only way to feed the craving is to have control of more people – which also reduces their accountability. It's the most delightful duality. The Cabal know it's a heady cocktail which most politicians will grab at, with both sweaty palms.'

'If you don't refill the glasses soon, Victor, I run the risk of making their actions seem polite,' Leah said without any trace of humour.

'A thousand pardons, my dear.'

He half filled her glass, adding a splash of soda to his own before heading off on another circuit of the room. He didn't speak again until he waded past the chess set.

'Unfunnily enough, one of the best indicators we have is that, unless it's a crisis, fewer people are bothering to vote. It's not apathy – they feel their vote won't accomplish much. Besides, where is the joy in choosing between the lesser of two evils, or selecting one minor party from a hodgepodge rabble spouting bipolar rhetoric? Once you get beyond fifty million the populace feels impotent. What isn't widely known is that the collective human mind is the most accurate computing mechanism we have. It's scientifically proven to work and it's called the "Wisdom of Crowds". In 1907 it correctly guessed the weight of an ox, while more expert opinion foundered.'

'So you think this is a trend rather than a blip? That politicians will actively seek larger numbers of voters?'

Victor looked at her sharply. 'Even at the level of company law – that is illegal. There must be voted agreement between all the shareholders of a company before any of their percentage can be diluted. Or the directors face jail.'

'Well let's not get too carried away. That's what referendums are for.'

'Supposedly, but how often is the populace denied a referendum? Or have the argument spun to them in such a way, that they will even go to war when the reason is known to be false. Though to be fair, that's not a difficult thing to arrange given today's mass media.'

Leah pushed her glass to one side. 'I know that most Americans are scared of their Government and its agencies. I'm not sure they are apathetic but they do shrug and say, "What you can do against the American Government"?'

'It's noteworthy they say that – not "Our Government". Which they ought to, don't you think?'

'Perhaps it's just a figure of speech.'

'Speech always follows thought – especially subliminal thought. It's not t'other way around.'

'Granted, but your assumption that politicians are driven by a lust for power has been known to most of us, ever since we walked out of an African rainforest scratching our heads,' Leah smiled, 'Referendums are the runaway lane for democracies, Victor.'

'In the wrong hands – a referendum becomes the opiate of the voting masses. In the right hands – it becomes the runaway train going down the track. There are many examples which prove those in power clearly understand the effects of this diluting mechanism. I can even quote them. Do you recall that after Tiananmen Square, Jiang Zemin, who went on to become China's President, said if he had to execute one or two million people it wouldn't amount to much in Chinese terms. The point being that he *could have* – more importantly – *would have* carried this out. But can you see that happening in a country of only fifty million – like Spain?'

'No I can't. Okay, so you think democracy doesn't work when a population exceeds what – fifty million?'

'I'm not saying it doesn't work, I'm saying it can lay fertile ground for abuse or takeover. All it takes is someone clever enough, connected in the right way and…motivated. Until I saw it happening to America, right in front of me, I didn't think it was possible. I had no cause for concern.'

'The Land of the Free. Free from the responsibility of controlling their Government,' Leah joked, determined to lighten the sombre mood darkening the corners of the room.

'Yes, it's a blissfully ignorant world, isn't it?'

'Ready to be gobbled up by the next greedy orator to come along.'

'One thing's for sure, the next tyrant will only get into power after a weak or despised Government. It's always been that way because people vote emotionally, not with critical reasoning, after that type of disappointment. That then opens the door for a smooth-talking bastard to step in and take over. I'm sure you know that Churchill once said "Democracy is the worst form of government – except all the others that have been tried" but what you won't know is that I knew several people who questioned him on this. They asked him what its imperfections were and he steadfastly refused to answer. Mr Churchill was not known for his silence. He could see it had major flaws.'

'Hoping as few as possible would ever learn of them.'

'I doubt he would have stayed silent, for long, if he were a passenger on a runaway train. But for now, I insist this conversation stays strictly between us.'

'Of course – you have my word. But Victor, you can't assume dilution is what he had in mind when he voiced that.'

'True, but in the established sense the power of democracy is literally dissolving. We have moved from open democracy to a post democratic era. So, what if Churchill envisaged something else? Because whatever it was, it had to be inherently dangerous or he would have explained it, non?' He sat down opposite her, clasping his hands together to hammer home his next point. 'Because Leah, I know of nothing more dangerous to the future freedom of mankind, than large populations losing control of their governments. Especially ones with overkill nuclear arsenals; several secret law enforcement agencies ready to go; and a turnkey military champing at the bit waiting for someone to lead them into a fight. Quite possibly, or almost certainly, to the unifying call for the defence of freedom.'

Leah felt the room go cold as the Dragon opened an eye. Victor had found its lair. Knowing Victor as she did, he was likely to go after it.

He wouldn't go alone. 'Supposing I share this fear with you for a moment, do you have an antidote? A cure?'

'I do. I have two. One of which will be the subject of my next, perhaps explosive series of lectures.'

'*Perhaps* explosive?' Leah repeated, aghast. 'Your capacity for understatement has no boundary, Victor.'

'Ah, so you did go over my lecture notes as I asked. I was surprised you didn't bring up the subject earlier this evening. I assumed you must have been out on the town, partying.'

'No Victor. I had to read them through three times before editing them. I couldn't stop myself. If that idea gains any momentum it will change British governance, possibly the way all Western nations are governed in future. So yes, it is *perhaps explosive* as you like to put it, but I think *highly explosive* is an inch nearer the mark. Do you really think it wise to deliver that series of lectures?'

'Given, as you so artfully put it, "my limitless capacity for under-statement", then I rather think my answer ought to be...Yes.'

'You must realise our Government will go ballistic if they ever find out what your proposing, don't you?'

He stared at her with his blue eye flashing steel. 'I do.'

'I see,' she replied cautiously. 'You do realise they *will find out about it?*'

'I want them too.'

'Is there nothing I can say to stop you?'

'Nothing.'

'Well personally, I think the concept is highly attractive. I expect most reasonable people will feel that way. So when it does catch on you won't need a fallback solution because 'We the People' is, in effect, the final solution to the political question confronting us.'

'Precisely, Leah. It is the solution to our current crisis. But it is not a solution for the ultimate political crisis.'

'I can't see how this crisis can get much worse.'

'Believe me it can.'

'What are you about to propose? A fallback solution to a dictatorship or tyranny?'

'I am. I do so hope you don't mind.'

'Mind? Of course not. But how on earth do you set about bringing down a dictatorship?'

'It's rather drastic, or as some might say – revolutionary. There is an inherent weakness in stricter regimes. In all organised societies actually – even democratic ones. I have been all too aware of it for the past thirty years and, with the exception of one other person, I've never breathed a word of it...until now.'

'I see, and the person you told is the one that put Bush into power?'

'No, no, he's not aware of it I'm quite sure. When I had it out with him I took the precaution of checking first. The only other person I ever told was my son Abdul, when he challenged me to use my skills and influence to steer world governments another way. At the time it was a path I couldn't agree to. You must understand that I was only trying to build a bridge with him. A connection that was cruelly denied us by a twist of fate in the Middle East. For a long time we lost each other and afterwards, he never really forgave me.'

'I'm sorry to hear that. But only family, good friends and lovers can feud,' Leah said resignedly.

'I have two reasons for imparting my fallback solution to any form of government. That's any form of government – extreme, or not. The first is that I do not wish my son to be the only person who knows of it. The second, is that it may become necessary to implement in your lifetime. God forbid, but I think a dictatorship will emerge and takeover the West in fifteen to twenty-five years time. The gate they will drive their iron tank of control through, will swing open as accountability to the voters dissipates: a direct result of fewer politicians representing larger groups of people. The first warning sign will be overregulation – a surge in the number of minor laws dished out. The second sign will be an escalation of police clamp-downs and the meting out of summary justice, together with the building of Superjails. The last sign will involve a rapid acceleration of military spending. Should it happen to Europe first, you will also witness the introduction of the death penalty.' He paused. 'I like to think you and I have become close. I know I can trust you and unlike my son, your heart is good. I am greatly indebted for your kindness and consideration of me, so I am sorry to burden you with this knowledge but I must – to safeguard your own future.'

'Thank you, Victor. You've been like a father to me. I can never thank you enough.'

'To the Jaws of Death,' he said abruptly, holding up his glass and smiling into her eyes.

'You'd better be twenty minutes late,' Leah replied, and they broke into instantaneous laughter, fired by the need to dispel the aura hovering in the room.

'I'm going to divulge my concept to you now…because I can see the end of my days approaching,' he held up his hand to stall her protest. 'Come now Leah, it's only fair that the Jaws of Death toast me at some point…and with their single malt, I trust.'

'Now you're procrastinating, Victor. What did you confide?'

'When talking with the Angel of Death, I imagine procrastination is quite a handy skill.'

'If you don't tell me with your very next breath, I will speed the introductions myself,' Leah's natural good humour turning up the corners of her mouth.

'There is a possibility that my son will implement what I revealed to him, and forewarned is forearmed.'

'Okay, Victor, that's quite enough. I'm touched by your trust in me, but if you don't tell me it this instant, I will scream you to death.'

'In many ways he's not unlike you.'

'Ahhhhhhhhhh.'

'Okay, calmati, calmati, I'll tell you. All societies have a deep fissure that is filled by the rule of law. The rule of law is the mortar in the house of all social order. Remove it, and you create a house of cards.'

'I'm starting to feel operatic again.'

'Alright, but the medicine has to be pretty strong to effect a cure, so what I would do is start a small war – though I'm not suggesting nuclear, chemical, biological or any medium which destroys even small numbers of people.'

'A small war? Small wars conducted against Big Brothers don't stay small for long,' Leah said earnestly. 'That risks the very apocalypse we are trying to avoid.'

'Perhaps war is too strong a word. Let's call it an attack. An attack which has no defence. To ensure it stays small, let's say you limit your force to a few.'

'Are you suggesting that only a few people could take down Russia, China or the United States? Without mass casualties?'

'I am. Of course it would have to be a new type of attack and completely original. One the world has never experienced or even imagined could happen. It would take time and careful planning, access to large amounts of money and a meticulous intellect to conduct operations...Once set in motion, it won't take long.'

'How long?'

'A little less than six months – luck depending,' he said, stroking the top of the dining table as if it were a favoured pet.

Leah leaned her elbows on the table and dropped into a businesslike manner. 'How's this? You tell me how you think it's possible to take down a Superpower with a small force in under six months, and I will put you at ease by shredding your idea.'

'Alright, I'll spell it out for you,' and to her mounting trepidation – he did. What surprised her most about his solution was that it didn't constitute an attack on those who ruled; his target was the rule of law itself, his plan was purposefully designed to reverse the 5000-year-old concept. The concept that had provided the framework for every social order of Man.

His plan would render the law obsolete – instantly – with shocking speed and assurance. In his own inimitable way he had christened his mechanism quite inappropriately, but with needle-point accuracy: "The Sword of Damocles".

As Leah listened to him explain it in detail, she began seeing why he had kept it so secret. The idea itself was terrifying enough, without his clever tweaks and practical ways of implementing it. Leah was in no doubt of the result: devastation. She suddenly realised that if his idea ever became known, there were many who would delight in carrying it out. Its originality awarding it astronomical power. No one would have any contingency for it nor could they – once implemented it was unstoppable. Ultimately, this was the reason why Victor had kept it sacrosanct. Even the original architect had no way to defuse it. The Sword of Damocles would scythe down law and order – ripping it to shreds in a few months. His plan would crush it like a butterfly caught under a train wheel. But as he repeatedly reminded her: 'Having no law is better than tyranny.'

'In the end Leah, the collective thought that rises out of my mechanism will destroy the legal system. Even the police themselves will turn against the rule of law in very short order. The Sword of Damocles will rapidly bring a populace to the point where people no longer wish to have the law in place – because it won't be on their side but against them. This will be driven by the fact that having the law operating at all will make ordinary survival much more difficult and therefore, you are better off without the law. Once that thought gains momentum – it's over. You must never forget how dangerous The Sword is, because it doesn't need a tyrant in control for it to work. It would roll out just as effectively if Gandhi himself were the nation's leader. You must promise me you will only draw this Sword if my foresight about a coming dictatorship proves correct. And only when there is no other possible alternative. I have one last request: if I am wrong about tyranny happening in your lifetime, please pass my final solution onto someone you trust implicitly before you depart this earth. Be very careful who you entrust it to. More careful than I have been.'

'You have my word,' Leah replied solemnly.

'Now I feel I've completed the penultimate task in my life – handing you this weapon. Once I have given my 'We the People' lectures I can die content,' he smiled, euphoria tinting his blue eye once again. 'Keep The Sword hidden, and understand that it is my sincere hope and wish you never have cause to unsheathe it. However, I think the chances are high that you will have no choice.'

Walking back to her rooms later that evening, immersed in her newfound and deeply disturbing knowledge, she heard a distant bell strike once; carried from afar by a thick fog which had crept in soundlessly from a cold North Sea. There was now a sharp sliver of fear in her life, but when she tried to track its source, her mind kept returning to the only other person who knew about his plan – Victor's son Abdul.

She was clear on one thing: Abdul, like her, would never breathe a word of it. Then again, if Victor was right to be concerned about his son...

But surely Victor's own son would never wield The Sword unless there was a rope around the neck of mankind. Would he? It was the one thing she felt Victor must be wrong about. At least, she hoped to high heaven and beyond all reason, that he was wrong. The problem being that in her experience, if Victor was wrong, it would be the very first time.

MONKEYING

The sun was just breaking over the horizon when he leaned back in his chair and stretched. It had taken him all week, working day and night, but he had finally finished the task. He had slept only briefly. Aided by two pounds of Darjeeling tea, half an ounce of Peruvian cocaine and four cartons of unfiltered Camel cigarettes.

He rubbed his eyes wearily. The blue one was throbbing again. Despite his fabulous wealth, Abdul knew this job was not one he should delegate, so he had written all eighteen web sites for his new 'business venture' himself. Though each looked quite different, they were remarkably similar in function. He was connecting Arabs who lived in Western countries, so they could meet online and do business, or date, or chat, or find old friends and family. Seven of the sites were dotcoms and were specifically targeted at Arabs living in the United States. There was also an online supermarket which he surreptitiously subsidised by 30%, selling the hard-to-get delicacies of the Middle East and drop-shipping the orders direct to his customers' homes. There was even a business forum where Arabs could meet and do business, and last but not least, there was an investment fund for start-up ventures.

'It shouldn't take long,' Abdul thought to himself.

He was right.

Within six months the eighteen sites were getting 25,000 hits per day between them. They even began producing a healthy revenue which he used to supplement the shops and businesses springing up from his financing, right across America.

The requests for funding new enterprises had come flooding in. Abdul examined them all. For those fortunate enough to receive his investment there was an additional requirement. He insisted on sending over a representative to work alongside them. 'He will provide assistance and the money when needed. This way there is no need for a complicated contract between us. Our word was good enough for our Fathers and it will be good enough for us,' he would say, before agreeing the investment capital on fantastically discounted terms. 'It will give the business a head-start,' Abdul explained, making sure he never met his new partners in person; stipulating they conduct all communication by phone and email, only. This arrangement is fairly common practice in the Middle East but his method differed in one aspect: he liked to pay his business lieutenants' wages out of his own pocket; not from the profit generated – the expected way. Free help is hard to refuse when you are starting a new business and most people welcomed the assistance, turning blind eyes to the fact that their companies were being closely monitored.

'As long as it's profitable and no one is stealing too much, there's nothing to worry about,' said Abdul's new-found partners. 'It's only for six months or so, while the business gets going. If it was my money I would want someone keeping an eye on it. So he reports back, so what?'

'He will be staying in our house. So we can keep an eye on him too.'

It was true that detailed reports were being sent to Abdul. He designed two databases on which he kept every piece of information he received. But one was much smaller than the other. The smaller one held the business data, while the larger one contained complete dossiers on the owners themselves: their habits; movements; Social Security numbers; family and friends' names; even the passwords to their computer systems. He also had the keys to their houses, cars and offices, duplicated; then posted on to him, secretly.

It was surprising how many different types of venture there were but when searched by category, it was noticeable that over fifty per cent were delivery companies, while only five per cent were corner shops. Abdul seemed to prefer companies which delivered product especially mainstream office items and technology. He had twenty-seven computer companies alone. All supplying their paper, ink and printers to a wide-ranging client base, including banks and blue chip companies stretching from coast to coast. There were thirteen import companies mainly handling food and seven private security firms guarding construction sites and offices at night.

He really could congratulate himself on a job well done. He had helped to birth a total of 113 profitable businesses in the United

States in a very short space of time, beating his most optimistic forecast by a wide margin.

'Phase one is now complete,' Abdul thought with satisfaction, after conducting a painstaking review of his databases one evening. Getting up from his desk, he wandered over to the tray by the fireplace of his hunting estate in Norway. 'Which means only one thing: I must take up gainful employment again, and soon.'

As he picked up a blini heaped with yellow Almas caviar, the rarest and most expensive on earth, he realised there was no better place to apply for a job than the war-ravaged streets and chaos, a few diehards still called Beirut.

UNTYING THE APE OF WAR

Waiting patiently in the heat, he glanced at the rifle on the blanket in front of him then checked his watch – 14:42. In eighteen minutes time, with a single shot, he would write a new chapter into the book of mankind. That is all it would take now – one accurate shot.

He was lying on the roof of an elevator shaft at the top of an eight storey office building, in the shadow of two large cardboard boxes he had filled with bricks. He peered down cautiously at the mêlée of cameramen and journalists who were jostling each other impatiently at the base of the steps leading up to the wide entrance of Sacramento City Hall.

Five days earlier, the laser rangefinder had given him 253 yards distance-to-target, and the awesome power of his gun meant the heavy bullet would fly virtually 'flat'; ensuring he would hit his target without having to compensate, or in sniper speak "allow for the mark"– raising his aim slightly to offset gravity's effect on the bullet. Bullets fired from a gun aimed parallel with the ground, fall at the same speed they drop from a hand; so the height of eight storeys was a blessing as the bullet's descent is always calculated on the horizontal plane – while he was shooting downhill at a forty degree angle. He didn't want to make the classic rifleman error of shooting high over the mark when aiming down at his target. In the end, he decided to use a $1\frac{1}{4}$ inch offset; then if he was wrong it would make very little difference. To enhance the gun's accuracy he had a Boss screw on the end; to the untrained eye – a silencer. It tuned the flexing of the barrel so that it always flexed in exactly the same way when fired; neatly removing the ability of the bending barrel from fractionally altering the path of his bullet. When the Remington engineers' first bench tested the rifle, they were surprised to discover it would consistently shoot a 0.5-inch wide group of three bullets at 200 yards; and given the bullet was 0.3 inches wide, that effectively meant three bullets through the same hole. High tech, state-of-the-art, the rifle packed mind-numbing punch: delivering a heavy 200 grain bullet, easily capable of felling a large elk or grizzly bear at 500 yards while only dropping eighteen inches over that range.

'That's right, son,' the salesman had said proudly. 'With a Remington 300 short Magnum, all you need do is put fur on them crosshairs at 500 – and it's down. It'll hit that son-of-a-bitch with 2300 foot pounds at that distance. Most hunting rifles max-out at two fifty.'

He was all too aware of the fact and had guided the salesman to 'find' it for him; feigning ignorance throughout the process. But the gun had an additional advantage, one even the salesman had carefully avoided mentioning: the noise it made was deafening. The sound wave would echo off the buildings surrounding the city centre for two miles, making it impossible to locate his hiding place by ear.

It had taken him two days of discreet surveillance to select his position. It couldn't be better. Not only did it meet all of the technical requirements for the shot he was about to make, but it also provided him with a superb escape route. His safe exit was the deciding factor in choosing this specific building, from a previous shortlist of three. It also enabled him to face east and at three o'clock the sun would be setting directly behind the roof he was secreted on, making visual detection by the eye witnesses around the Governor also impossible on this bright and cloudless day.

The heat was making the air suffocatingly still. Some of the reporters were holding up writing pads and umbrellas to shield themselves from the eye of the sun. He smiled inwardly. The sun had always been a good friend, a trusted ally, and he had spent most of his life in regions where this temperature was considered mild. A few of the photographers were adjusting their camera focuses, and he chuckled out loud when he realised that both he and the photo journos did have one thing in common. They would be the last people to see the Governor of California alive – through a lens.

The irony wasn't wasted on him because this Governor, like several of his predecessors, had been a movie star before stepping into the political arena. The man had lived his life in front of the lens and in a few short minutes – he would die by one. The technology that had kissed the Governor's life with fortune and fame, was the very technology that would take it away. The only thing each of them required was a good man behind the lens.

And Ali Bin Mohammed knew he was a good man.

Truly, Allah must have led him to this place in time deliberately, for without those celestial links, snapped into the tautened chain of Ali's existence, he would be leading a very different life. Surely the intervention and suffering he had experienced in his youth must have divine approval, because without this explanation, he and the rest of the world were simply rudderless ships, drifting on a windless sea of self obsession.

'It is the will of God, or I would have died before this,' Ali reminded himself.

He never imagined his life turning out in this way, but neither had he envisaged his entire family dying before he did: catapulting him out of a loving home into a brutal orphanage. Waiting motionless, feeling the tension of the coming moment draw near, his mind drifted along the switchback road of his life, over all the events which had brought him to this dividing point in the fate of the world and he knew that without each of them occurring in their precise order, he would be a doctor now as his father had always wished. Saving life – not taking it.

Ali's father had taught him how to shoot when he was still a boy. Mohammed was a respected marksman and rumours abounded that he had once shot dead four enemy soldiers with four consecutive shots – at a range of 300 yards. His father had arrived home late for the evening meal on Ali's birthday one year. A thing he rarely did on any day, believing in the importance of mealtimes as the keystone of family life. Woe betide Ali, his little brother or sister, if any of them were late for the daily ritual. Yet on this rather more special occasion of his birthday, Mohammed was late.

Ali's mother saw him coming first. She jumped up from her cushion on the floor to ladle a bowl of succulent goat stew laced with limes, hot chillies and bittersweet green dates from the tureen. A special treat in these poorer times, and the treats were getting rarer.

The memory of that day was vivid in his mind. He could still smell the aroma of his mother's stew as she spooned it onto a plate, chattering excitedly that she could see Mohammed carrying his birthday present. Ali gazed up at his mother in adulation. She was the glue and fabric of the family and never stopped working. She often shielded the little ones from their father's wrath, though lately, she had taken to exposing some of Ali's transgressions.

Two weeks before his birthday, Ali became very sure something had changed. He saw tears in his mother's eyes after she reported the rumour to Mohammed that Ali had been seen stealing bread from one of the stalls at the nearby market. Peering out of his bedroom window, he watched her run out of the farm office in obvious distress. She was covering her face with her hands while Mohammed stalked after her, grim faced. He stopped in the kitchen and bellowed upstairs that he wanted Ali in his office in five minutes.

It was true that Ali had been stealing from the market at the end of their road, but only out of necessity. His mother had been sending him out for all the groceries when she discovered he was able to get a better, often a surprisingly better price, than she could ever haggle. Ali had tried his best but the market traders eventually grew tired of his games. At first they indulged him, not because they hadn't seen those tricks before, they had. They simply didn't believe a boy of his age could pull them off so convincingly and initially, they had smiled knowingly to each other; winking their agreement around the souk at the other traders.

Ali's favourite ploy was to heap praise on the goods he needed, while lamenting that he had very little money to afford them. This was the complete opposite of the tactic employed by all the other customers, who preferred to stand around criticising and finding fault with near-perfect produce. His complimentary approach saw the traders respond with enthusiasm, driving down their price to lift a sale off such an innocent victim.

Such a positive advert couldn't be better for business. Especially when Ali would shout through the long skirts of a more discerning female clientele, 'I hope you have enough pitta left for me, after the beautiful lady has bought hers.' This often induced two, sometimes three or four hesitant women to step up to the counter as one. But after a while he ran out of ruses and the prices went back up. Worse, this happened just as his mother started giving him less money for the food.

'Times are very hard at the moment, Ali,' she said, handing over a few coins before he set off one day. 'Half the apricot harvest could fail because we cannot afford the price of water. The cost has gone up ever since that housing settlement was built at the top of the hill. Whatever money you can save us, we can use to buy more water. We will get it back ten-fold in apricots, come the harvest.' This produced a dilemma in Ali which he solved simply: he stole half the groceries. On a good day, he did even better.

With the sound of his father's bellow echoing into silence, Ali got up from his pallet bed and trudged gloomily downstairs. He could hear deep wracking sobs coming from his mother's bedroom as he passed by her door, which didn't bode well. Traipsing slowly out of the house, he took as much time as he dared crossing the yard towards the old farm building that housed his father's office. He rapped on the wooden door, hard, but the heavy cedar planks reduced his efforts to a light tapping.

'Come in, Ali,' Mohammed called out, and he went in and stood in front of his father's desk, glancing around nervously for clues to his predicament.

The room had a strong masculine feel to it and smelled of aromatic tobacco and gun oil. An old rifle stood propped against the wall by the window and a few books and strange engine parts balanced on the rough-sawn shelves. Dark magnificent rugs were spread across the floor but the years had worn them; removing their sheen and exposing their ribs in the places where the foot traffic was heaviest.

His father's voice rang with controlled anger as he shot out fiercely, 'Look at me, Ali. I want you to think very carefully before you answer. Have you been stealing from the market?'

'Yes, Papi.'

Mohammed looked down at his son in surprise. 'You do know that stealing is expressly forbidden by our own laws and those of the Prophet? What would the world come to if everyone stole everything? We would have all our apricots stolen and be forced to beg and steal for ourselves.'

'Yes, Papi. I didn't want that to happen to us, so I took some food. I stole as much as I could and gave the money I saved to Mama,' he replied proudly.

Mohammed's expression changed to shock. It wasn't what he was anticipating. He was expecting a lie. He knew that stealing and lying often shared the same dirty bed. 'I see,' he pondered. 'Well, this is still a very serious matter and the punishment must fit the crime. It is sin in the eyes of God. For His sake and yours I'm going to make sure you never do it again. Now come here and bend over the desk.'

Mohammed took down an old donkey crop hanging from a bent nail in the wall.

Svit ! He cut the whip across Ali's back, repeating in a cold metallic voice, 'You will not steal.' *Sssvit !* The half-inch thick cane sliced into him again. 'It is a sin. *Sssvit !*

Pausing to take aim with each stroke, Mohammed whipped his son mercilessly – laying each sizzling blow a finger-width apart. He worked his way down methodically, from shoulders to thighs, then stood up to get his breath back. Ali lay across the desk, gripping its sides with his eyes shut tight, but apart from an initial gasp of shock, he hadn't made a sound.

Mohammed resumed his stance. He began again on the same path, making the crop whistle an octave higher. Ali lost all self control and started screaming and bucking against the heart-stopping pain. Pinning his son's writhing body to the desk with his left hand, Mohammed carried on beating him, rhythmically, impervious to his shrieks of agony. He didn't stop until the old whip broke and, throwing it aside with contempt, told Ali to go to his room and think over the lesson.

Ali ran out of the study: writhing his hips in frenzy; clutching desperately at his back. He stumbled into the sanctuary of his room and dived on the bed, squirming and twisting in a futile bid to shake off the molten fire running across his back. Slowly, the flames melted down to a throbbing white heat, and as his ragged breathing became more even, he swore that he would never get caught stealing again. 'Never.'

He was so consumed by his plight that he didn't notice his mother glance into his bedroom before rushing downstairs and out towards the farm office. Going swiftly through the open doorway she found Mohammed upright on his knees: tears streaming down his face; his clenched fists held up to an invisible deity in supplication.

'What else could I do?' he beseeched. 'Let a stranger teach him the horror of pain? Which as God willed was my fate?'

Wrapping her arms around him, she began rocking him and stroking his hair, until gradually, his sobbing died down. Choosing her moment with care, she crooned gently to him, 'It was right for someone who loves him to teach him the horror of pain Mohammed. The world we live in is harsh and there are desperate times ahead. Some day he will have to deal with much worse. I am sure of it.' Then ever more softly she muttered half to herself, 'I just wish that Allah had blessed us with a better reason.'

Over the following two weeks, in the run up to Ali's birthday, Mohammed seized every opportunity to rebuild his relationship with his son, promising him a present he would never forget. But his father always looked deadly serious when he said it, and Ali was torn between tremendous excitement and a worrying fear. He was struck by an acute sense of dread when Mohammed stepped into the kitchen holding the present, 'I'm sorry I am late, but I had to walk a long way to get this.'

Mohammed smiled at his family lovingly then sat down on his cushion at one end of their best rug. Ruffling Ali's hair and wishing him a happy birthday, he placed the present down between them with inordinate care. Ali stared at it. Unsure whether it was good or bad; friend or foe. The gift was slender and wrapped in a blanket tied with coarse string at both ends.

'I hope you like it,' Mohammed beamed a broad smile at his first-born, showing the gap between his top front teeth – the reason he had been renamed after the Great Prophet of Islam when six years old. The Mohammed of 700 AD is thought to have been gap-toothed in the same way and it is considered very lucky in Muslims, if not tilting tentatively towards the divine.

Ali gazed at the present without picking it up: desperate to know what it was; terrified of what he might find. The present was three and a half feet long and six inches wide. 'The folds of the blanket could make a donkey whip that size,' he realised.

A few of the marks where the whip strokes had crossed were still visible; the frightful pain of his thrashing still sharp in his mind. Caught between fear and fascination, horror and hope, Ali looked down at it cautiously; as though it were a beautiful but deadly snake. 'It's a whip,' he decided, feeling his birthday mood evaporate. 'It's one of Papi's tricks to stop me stealing from the other market.' Ali had been running there and back non-stop, so his mother didn't notice the extra time he took and guess what he was up to. 'That explains why he is late. He's come from the other market, farther away. Someone must have seen me again.'

Taking a deep breath he squared his shoulders to pick up the bundle. It couldn't be a whip, it was far too heavy; and to his boyish delight he unwrapped a small rifle. It was a .243 Mannlicher, showing the signs of an active life. The ball on the end of the bolt was silvered by the three generations of palms that had slipped it home, and the wooden stock was pitted and shiny black around the grip, giving it the overall effect of a grey old man with a lopsided grin. It smelled of new engine oil and burnt cardboard and Ali mounted the gun to his shoulder. He swung the rifle around with a giggle, then aimed at his sister opposite. There was a satisfying

'Click' as he pulled the trigger.

And Mohammed went berserk.

He leapt up screaming: 'Never point a gun at anyone – ever. It doesn't matter whether it's loaded or not,' he ranted. Adding a little unfairly, as Ali didn't know how, that he hadn't even checked it was empty first. 'You could have killed Nadir,' Mohammed finished with a low growl.

Ali could feel his tears forcing their way to the surface, but instinctively knew he must not cry. Pouring weakness onto stupidity would only fan the flames of his father's fury. Getting a hold of himself, he looked straight up at his father. What he found surprised him. Instead of the burning coals of his father's ire that he expected, worry and fear shone in his eyes.

Mohammed snatched the rifle away. 'You cannot have it for a week as punishment for your stupidity. You foolish child. I expected better from you. You could have killed her.'

It was the best present Ali had ever been given, but the humiliation in front of his mother, brother and sister was making it the worst birthday of his life. The urge to cry threatened to overwhelm him again but he managed force it aside, transforming his lips into a pained smile which he hoped his father would interpret it as manly and strong.

Seeing his son was upset Mohammed relented. 'Perhaps I have been a bit harsh.' Turning to lock the gun away in the cabinet, he glanced back over his shoulder at Ali. 'At dawn tomorrow we will go into the orchard, where I shall give you your first shooting lesson.'

Ali slept in a fever of anticipation that night, getting up a full hour before first light. He heard a soft noise coming from the kitchen and crept downstairs to find his father sitting cross-legged on his cushion, the rifle mounted to his shoulder – levelled straight at Ali's nose. He froze in shock: transfixed by the black eye of the rifle barrel, which stared back its emptiness, unblinking.

'Terrifying isn't it? Now you know how it feels to have a gun aimed at you. Come sit beside me, Ali,' Mohammed said, dismounting the weapon which broke the gun's mesmeric hold, granting Ali the function of his limbs. He went over and sat on the cushion being patted by his father's right hand.

Mohammed poured out a cup of thick sweetened coffee from the pot on the tray. After drinking two cups in comfortable silence, his father said sternly: 'It is time.'

As they walked into the orchard, Ali asked excitedly, 'Papi, it's still dark. How will we shoot?'

'There are many lessons you must learn in life, Ali. Many can only be taught by Allah, all praise to His name. Today I am going to give you one of the most important lessons a father can teach his son. From today onwards you will no longer be a boy,' and with that strange statement he lengthened his stride, quickening the pace. Ali trotted alongside, as his father led them up the beaten earth path which wound its way through their twenty-acre orchard; which constituted the family's entire wealth and estate. When they were half way up the slope Mohammed halted in a small clearing in the trees. 'This place is perfect.'

It was still dark, though not black. Ali knew exactly where he was, but in the half light that precedes the dawn he could just make out the silhouette of some trees twenty paces away. The only thing he could see clearly was his father, standing on his left. Ali began wondering how he could avoid disappointing him. 'It's too dark. I'm going to miss,' he realised.

'Now watch me carefully,' Mohammed's voice resonated in the stilled mystique of the pre-dawn. 'Here are the bullets and this is the breech where you load them. This is the safety catch. Only when you are about to fire should it ever, ever, be pushed forward,' and he clicked it back with an exaggerated motion of his thumb, so that Ali could see it was on safe. 'And now for your first shooting lesson,' Mohammed said gravely, sliding forward the bolt, which eagerly chaperoned a brass cartridge into the breech.

'First, I want you to swear a solemn oath. You will swear it on the soul of the Prophet. Hold out your hands,' Mohammed ordered, tucking the rifle under his armpit. He gazed into his son's eyes as he took Ali's hands, 'Repeat after me: I will never point a gun at anyone – unless I am going to shoot them.'

Ali looked straight back at his father. 'I will never point a gun at anyone, Papi. Unless I am about to shoot them. I swear you this oath, on the soul of the Prophet.'

The gun was now pointing correctly – stock up, barrel down – as his father passed it across to him, and as his little hands took up the weight, Mohammed pulled the trigger. There was a blinding flash and a deafening bang. The gun recoiled viciously, hitting him hard under his left armpit. But although the impact helped to push him over backwards, he was instinctively set on the same trajectory – directly away from that shocking concussion. Throwing his hands behind him to soften his fall, he looked up to see his father's expression underscored by a wide grin. Mohammed's hand was gripping the rifle: his thumb on the safety catch; his finger curling tightly around the trigger.

'Never aim a gun at anyone, unless you intend to kill them. Now look down here,' Mohammed pointed his left hand at the ground. 'This is why you must obey your oath.'

Ali got up shakily and looked down. A step in front of the imprint left by his heels was a jagged hole, fully nine inches round and over a foot deep. The dry grass and soil had disintegrated completely, leaving no trace they had ever existed; wisps of blue-grey of smoke crept towards his knees, smelling of burnt newspaper.

'We will go inside and clean your gun, but before we do, I wish to ask, what is the lesson you have learned here today?'

Ali searched his frantic mind for an answer to match his upheaval. 'Is it to expect anything, Papi?'

'That too is a valuable lesson. But there is another, far more important,' Mohammed prompted. Ali looked at his father blankly, his hands beginning to quiver with delayed shock. He clasped them behind his back, hoping his father hadn't noticed.

'Listen to me carefully, Ali. This world we live in is ruled by terror. And Terror is a powerful chariot that can fly on the wind; so it comes at you – swift and silent. It has immense power because it is drawn by the Four horses of Fear. Three are stallions, one is a white mare. Two of the stallions are black as night, the other – invisible. The name of the first stallion is Fright and you just met him. He is the easiest of the Four to master. To conquer him, you only have to feel the strength inside you and his power melts to nothing. The second stallion is called Threat. He is not honest – he lies, but not always. You must handle him with great cunning for he respects nothing less. The invisible horse is the most dangerous of the four and rightly, he has no name because he is fashioned from all the evils of the world. He is difficult to see because he is a coward, so he hides, but that also his weakness. He often wears the invisible cloak of righteousness, but if you look for him with your heart, not your eyes, you will see him. You must attack him as soon you have a good chance to better him. Never hesitate, but if you cannot see a clear opportunity then you must wait for your chance, patiently. As I say, he is the most dangerous of the Four. He is extremely powerful but like all cowards, he hides behind others and gets them to do his bidding. You will often find him standing behind an army – never at the front. With him, you must always choose your moment with precision. To fight him you must use the weapons of wisdom and truth, otherwise he is immortal and cannot be killed. But fear is not always dangerous. It is not always bad. The White Mare is the fastest of the Four and she is a gift from God. Her name is Flight. You must learn to control her for she also has a weakness: she is blind. She can outrun the other horses with ease but to do it, she needs a firm hand on the reins and a clear mind that can react as swiftly as she can gallop. She is not easy to master but you must learn it well if you wish to survive in this world, because someday, you will need her speed and she will need your sense.'

The first rays of sunlight glinted over the horizon and Mohammed turned his face towards the lightening sky. 'I am going to tell you now, what you would have discovered yourself, eventually. The drivers of the Chariot of Terror are men. Never forget that – they are men. They use the Stallions of Fear to gain control over others, when it is they themselves who are driven by them. Shaitan unstabled the three Stallions into this world and Allah gave us the White Mare. The Stallions have the power to paralyse, the Mare has the power to make you fly. Fear can kill you – or it can save your life. The only time you should ever allow yourself to experience the sensation, is when you are the driver of the Chariot. You must learn to recognise the Four Horses of Fear and understand all of their moods. You must learn to shoot straight and you must always choose your moment with care. Learn all these things well and you will have nothing to fear – except the wrath and majesty of the one true God.'

Stunned, eyes wide; Ali gawped at his father; feeling his innocence draining away through the soles of his feet. When they had walked into the orchard it was a new and exciting game. Now the instant violence of the gun and the meaning of his father's words twisted together in his being; as for the first time in his life he thought about having to kill. He realised his father was preparing him for this. Getting him ready because one day, he would have no choice. He wondered how it would feel: selecting the exact moment when a person would die, watching their body collapse; lifeless. Taking the most valuable gift that God had given. But it would be an act of his own hand; at a time of his choosing. It was the ultimate act. Absolute, final control. The life or death of another human being would be his decision. His alone to make – not theirs. The heady feeling of omnipotent power streaked through him: filling the void his innocence had left behind; swiftly replaced with the unbearable lightness of infinity.

All he had to do to possess this power; to command it; to have control over life and death; was learn to shoot well.

Slowly, he became aware that he was gaping at his father. Realising his emotions were visible he quickly shut his mouth with a plop, then looked away, embarrassed.

Little Ali was eight years and one day, old.

BOOK 2

"If we compare the faults of a people with those of princes, as well as their respective good qualities, we shall find the people vastly superior in all that is good and glorious".

Machiavelli

L'APE FEMININA

That Friday marked the successful conclusion of Victor's new series of lectures he entitled 'We the People': a term he had lifted from the opening lines of the American Constitution. Leah, together with many of his students, knew Victor considered the document to be one of the clearest statements of human freedom ever penned.

The lectures had created a storm of interest amongst a wide spectrum of students and several of the dons. It was given impetus by a carefully crafted rumour, which Leah had slipped into the gossip-sphere, that the talks were seditious and it was likely Victor would be suspended for speaking out, as they constituted a direct attack on the British Government. To ensure the hall was packed to the rafters she told three selected friends she had edited Victor's lecture notes, and they must keep the subject matter secret. This worked so effectively that on the second day the firewarden asked Victor to re-locate to the 1500-seat theatre, but still had problems closing the doors on the clamouring throng trying to force its way inside.

To celebrate his success, Victor and Leah decided on a private supper between themselves. Victor opened a bottle of champagne and they toasted 'a new world,' downing their first glass in a single gulp. Victor refilled them from the bottle in his hand.

'I can understand how the second lecture drew such a crowd, but not why the first one did,' he said, crackling a crystalline blue eye at Leah.

'Then you have much in common with George Orwell's Winston Smith. You understand the "how", not the "why".'

'I see. Now I know the "who", the "why" becomes obvious. But the "how" still eludes.'

'Well Victor, I can't be certain, but there was a vicious rumour circulating that the lectures were going to propose a better system of government and were a direct attack on the present one. People were saying that you would probably get defrocked.'

Convulsing into laughter, he started shaking so uncontrollably that he spilt champagne on the table. After several moments he calmed down saying, 'Machiavelli would have envied you, Leah,' then his expression became thoughtful and he looked at her squarely. 'I hope you don't mind, but I have a favour to ask. A boon to beg of thee.'

'Ask away, Victor. I never tire of watching a grown man beg,' Leah replied, the Pol Roger '62 emboldening her risqué.

He smiled quickly as he replenished his glass. 'Most of my relatives died some time ago, Leah. My son and I fell out and besides, he's richer than Croesus so it won't be much interest to him. Anyhow, what it all boils down to is this – I'm not without some money and property and I wondered if you would consider being an executor of my estate?'

'I would be delighted…Though you're not intending to put me to work in the near future, I trust?' she asked with a flare of concern.

'At some point. Of that, you can be certain.'

'I can't imagine you dying. Who are the other executors?'

'There would be three of you in total. I doubt you'll have heard of the other two but, at one time or other, they were both students of mine here at Oxford. I know that it's a lot of extra work and nobody wants to do any real graft these days, so I have offered them each 100,000 pounds for their time and effort. I am prepared to make the same offer to you. And if you are wondering about any Catch 22s, I should mention that if you do not administer my estate in accordance with the exact instructions in my Will, you only get 10,000 each. I have also arranged for the tax on these amounts to be paid by my estate. So you will receive 100,000 pounds free and clear.'

'That's an incredibly generous offer, but I would do it anyway,' Leah replied. 'Are these instructions illegal, or perverse in some way?'

'Ha! Sorry to disappoint – but no. The only one you may have a little difficulty with is that I want all my notes, records and books destroyed. All of them – every one. If you have any other concerns, why not read the Will then give me your answer. Let me fetch it from the top shelf upon which it resides and you can go through it.' He slid the ladder along the side of the library, positioning it with care.

'*You mean burn your library?*'

'I do.'

'Why on earth?'

'Because contained therein is the knowledge of how to control mankind, and I don't want to have mankind controlled. I prefer anarchy to tyranny, as I'm sure any reasonable person does. And before you say anything more, let me add that the other two have already agreed to my wish.'

'I see. Of course I'll read it. I would be delighted.'

'Delighted with the money, rather than the opportunity to burn my books,' he chuckled, climbing back down with a thick wad of papers. After blowing the dust off, he passed them across to her.

'Here, have a read while I prepare supper.'

Leah carried it over to his writing desk as Victor disappeared into the small kitchen in the back.

'How are you cooking the scallops?' she asked.

'Coquilles Mornay à la Victor.'

An hour later he called out in French, 'How are you getting on?'

'I've finished,' she replied in the same language, walking to the dining table.

'Good, good. Then allow me to serve you the finest scallops north of Normandy... served Chez Victor,' he smiled, shamelessly plagiarising the famous London eatery in Soho. He placed a large blue and gold Coalport plate in front of her.

Four white scallop shells with a crisped brown breadcrumb top sizzled and hissed through mini volcanoes of erupting cheese sauce, scenting the room with the fragrances of white wine, nutmeg and garlic; the fresh tint of the sea drifting in the background.

'Victor, that smells divine.'

'Perhaps we should give them a moment to cool,' he suggested, knowing the anticipation was part of the pleasure.

He sipped tentatively at his Pouilly Fuissé, then asked in faultless Parisian French, 'So, what is your answer?'

'I am honoured by your offer, and will honour all of your wishes. Also, let me add my sincere gratitude for the money. Thank you. You are a very generous man,' and she leaned across the table to kiss him on the cheek.

'Thank you my dear, thank you. You are a very sweet girl. I can't tell you how delighted I am that you've accepted. Now as I always turn the other cheek, let me seal our bargain with this.' He fished a velvet jewellery box out of his pocket and held it up with a flourish, before placing it gently on the table next to her.

It was Prussian blue and worn with age. A gold motif on top of the box outlined a pair of balancing scales with a lion-headed horse in one tray and a globe of the world in the other. It was exquisitely crafted, to the point where the lion-horse seemed to flow with motion while the globe appeared to turn, whenever she looked away from it slightly. The quality of the workmanship imbued it with an ancient and classical mystique. Leah suddenly felt the wheels of her life tip, then change direction, as she reached out to pick up the box.

Opening it, she found a magnificent ring; sandwiched between soft satin folds which had yellowed with age. The ring was delicately inlaid but sturdy. A large diamond in the centre was surrounded by semi-circles of rubies and sapphires, set in interlocking half-moon shapes. Lured by its hypnotic beauty she took it out to turn it in the buttery rays of the setting sun. It had an inscription carved on the inside; a pair of iconic symbols which looked a little like Egyptian hieroglyphs, but her closer examination revealed they were not quite the same. Unable to translate them, she looked up at him expectantly.

'It's Ancient Assyrian, so the writing is cuneiform,' Victor volunteered. 'As they were the oldest civilisation that could write, it wouldn't be foolish to assume the ring is much older than the box.'

'How old is it?'

'The inscription dates from around 1500BC, but no one has ever been able to tell me its exact age. They just say that it's extremely old.'

'It has a timeless beauty,' Leah smiled, slipping it onto the middle finger of her right hand. It fit her perfectly and she gazed into the depth of the stones. The late evening sunlight seemed to pass between each semi-circle, changing colour slightly before prisming into the next, so she was surprised to discover only a single dot of white light reflecting on the bookcase in front of her: a fierce bright white centre, surrounded by the softened colours of the rainbow. She felt her sense of wonderment drop straight into awe.

'It's the most stunning present, Victor. Thank you. I shall wear it always and every time I see it I will be reminded of this moment. I would love to know what the inscription says.'

'It's hard to be certain because the Sumerians used the same icons for several different things. In my view it's the combination of the two icons which date it. Either that or they were carved on later; which is highly unlikely as we've only been able to translate that particular cuneiform for the last hundred years and the wear on the inscription is obviously older. A forger could have gone to a great deal of trouble only to have inscribed "I drink camel urine" on it, for all he was aware. What I mean to say is this,' he went on as Leah rolled her eyes at him playfully, 'only a person who knew what the inscription meant would engrave those two icons. It's the translation which leads me to think that the ring must date from a time when that writing could be understood. And that combination was used prolifically around 1500 BC. It's an excellent example of how an understanding of human nature can be used to reason out the most likely set of events, when there is a dearth of scientific fact.'

Leah knew he was deliberately lengthening the process in order to heighten the moment, so ruefully, she locked eyes on him. 'Perhaps learning ancient Sumerian would save me some time.'

'That's what I felt too,' he smiled back.

'In that case, I'll probably find some excellent reference material in those books behind you. If I dig deep enough and long enough.'

'Anything but that, I implore you. Allow me to remove the vandal of your curiosity by telling you plainly and simply...it means "One of the Chosen Few",' then he smiled broadly at the frozen look on her face, as picked up his knife and fork.

"War is a way of shattering to pieces, or pouring into the stratosphere, or sinking in the depths of the sea, materials which might otherwise be used to make the masses too comfortable, and hence, in the long run, too intelligent."

George Orwell

THE DESCENDANTS OF THE KILLER APE

The sounds of a bustling excitement bubbled up to Ali from the steps of the City Hall, breaking his reverie. He peered down cautiously, to see the waiting press corps reacting to the movement of a uniformed security guard swinging open one of the large glass doors of the entrance. A group of men and women threaded their way out in a line dressed in smart, and for California, very conservative suits. They filed down the steps robotically, forming into two orderly rows at the side of the podium, fifty feet from it.

They were under strict instructions to do so – the new Governor enjoyed having the limelight focused solely on him. On his first day in office, he had issued a memo forbidding all staff to stand anywhere near him, or wherever the cameras might pick them up, while he was photographed going about his stately duties. One of the staff loyal to the previous governor had forwarded the edict to a journalist at the San Francisco Times, which had gleefully printed the entire memo in the middle the front page. The editorial went on to describe the arrogance of the new People's Favourite, asking whether Californians were to be ruled by spin – not substance.

When the Governor finished reading the article, he flew into a white hot rage, instigating the first of his many witch hunts and firing five people on the spot. None of whom happened to be guilty of the act.

When Ali finished reading the article, he saw how perfect the man was – as a target. Not only was the Governor a bastion of American culture, a hero of war movies and a staunch Republican, but by standing on his own, could be shot without anyone getting in the way of the bullet. This had prompted Ali's closer scrutiny of the Governor's habits to unearth his weaknesses. It didn't take him long to see that the man's most vulnerable side was vanity. The

Governor liked to speak in public, and often.

'In the Muslim and Christian faiths vanity is a deadly sin,' smiled Ali to himself.

14:56. 'Only four minutes to go. It's not too late to pull out,' he thought. 'I could pack up and walk, with no one the wiser.' But he knew there were too many people relying on him to deliver. He was only a small, albeit crucial, piece of the terrifying jigsaw about to be clicked into place. With a twinge of regret, Ali dismissed the notion. His mission to assassinate the Governor was only the beginning. The real glory would come at the end when he orchestrated the fear and chaos that would bring the United States crashing to its knees in a few short months. To occupy himself for the few tense minutes before taking the shot, he allowed his mind to flicker back to when this had all started: to a terrible night so long ago but which haunted him still, as if it had happened only yesterday.

He was sleeping peacefully in his bed on that warm September evening, when he was vibrated awake by a strange noise coming from the bottom of the mud packed road which dead-ended at their home. Staring out of his small bedroom window, Ali watched it coming: clouds of dust and blue smoke were billowing in its wake; the roar of the diesel engine growing louder as it accelerated along the final 100 yards. It appeared to his thirteen-year-old mind like a terrifying monster, raging through the dark, seething with malice. Ali felt an icy fear squeezing his throat dry as it screeched to a halt only twenty yards from their home. Lights erupted from all over it, illuminating the house in a sterile whitewash, then the long barrel whirred down to level with the front door.

The commander stood up in the turret and waved at the soldiers clinging to the sides of the tank. They jumped off quickly and fanned out around the house. Satisfied his men were all in position, the commander hoisted a megaphone to his lips and a surprisingly young voice rang out so sharply that Ali could hear the strings of his mother's lute in the kitchen hum in sympathy.

'This is the Heavy Armour Division. You are surrounded and an incendiary shell is zeroed on your house. Come out with your hands up – naked. You have one minute to comply before we fire. I repeat: you have one minute to undress and walk out with your hands up. And that minute starts now.'

The officer lifted his arm theatrically and looked down at his watch. Though young, he was nobody's fool. He had seen more than his share of this hard and bitter conflict and it had made him exceedingly cautious. He knew the tactics of his enemy included hiding explosives and grenades under the long garments of the men and women surrendering, which they would detonate in a last act of defiance. The best, safest way, was to arrest all suspects with their clothes off. It made the arrests safer and took all the fight out of their civilian enemy: humbling and humiliating the men, while some of the more devout women were shamed into suicide afterwards.

Just at that moment Mohammed rushed into Ali's bedroom. 'My son, if anything happens to me you must take my place as the head of the family. Remember the five pillars of Islam? There is a little money buried under the fifth apricot tree, five rows up and five across from the ditch. Whatever happens tonight, you must first take care of our family. Do whatever these people say and above all, do not attempt anything heroic. Do this for me and if the worst happens, I will be waiting to greet you in Paradise. Remember, you must do exactly as they say. I will go out first and give myself up. You must follow with your mother, brother and sister.'

In the room next door, Ali heard his little brother start crying, then his mother telling him to hush and be brave before asking Nadir, his twelve-year-old sister, to help calm him. 'We must be brave my little brother,' Nadir whispered. 'If you are not quiet something terrible will happen,' and remarkably, Hassan's crying choked back to a low sobbing.

Anxious and frightened, the family gathered in the narrow corridor then filed downstairs to re-assemble in the kitchen. Ali watched a silent tear rolling down his mother's cheek, which she wiped away with the palm of her hand. Mohammed took her in his arms kissing her, saying, 'Shhh, Shhh my beloved. We must be strong now. As long as we do nothing to anger or provoke them everything will be alright. I will go first, then Ali. You and the children must follow.'

The tank commander's voice boomed out, 'Twenty-five, twenty-four, twenty-three.' Mohammed turned half-around to glance nervously at the two albinoed windows radiating their shadowless glare through the kitchen.

At "twenty", the soldiers joined in with the chant. Some were slightly out of tempo with the main group, sounding almost weary. Mohammed took off his nightshirt and stood by his front door, naked but proud. Squaring his shoulders he drew himself up to his full height, taking a deep breath as his hand fell on the latch. He looked back at his huddled family with an expression of deep sadness and mouthed, 'I love you all.' Then he opened the door to step into the floodlights in front of his home.

'Good,' came the metallic voice. 'Walk towards the light...Stop. Lie on the ground face down. Spread your arms and legs...wider.'

Ali watched his father obey, thinking this wouldn't be as hard as stealing bread from the market, and he began to undress, motioning at the others to do the same.

'I will go first,' Ali copied his father's lead. 'Then you Mama, then Hassan and then you Nadir. Remember what Papi said. Are you ready?' His mother and sister were holding an arm across their breasts and a hand in front of their groin in a feeble attempt to hide their nudity. Nadir stared at him – terror stricken.

The voice from the loudhailer echoed out again, 'We know there are more of you in there. Come out now or we will fire.'

'We must go,' Ali urged, trying to make his voice sound as confident and steady as his father's. 'If we obey them we have nothing to fear. You must be brave, Hassan, and not cry,' he added, adopting the same technique Nadir had used to quieten his younger brother. 'Are you ready? Now follow me and nothing bad will happen.' Ali thrust his chin out and walked into the sterile white sheet of the halogens, casting backward glances at the rest of his family.

'Good,' the voice barked. 'Put your hands up and walk towards the light. Stop. You at the front. Walk to your left. The rest stay where you are. Stop. Lie face down. Spread your arms and legs wide.' Ali dropped to his knees then flopped forward, doing exactly as instructed.

'Now you – the woman. Move to your right. Stop. Lie face down.' Ali's mother gently closed her eyes and sank to the ground in the crucifix position. 'Spread your legs– wider,' and the soldiers gave a loud jeer. Some giggled nervously. A few made ribald comments.

'Now you two – move apart,' and Hassan and Nadir obeyed.

For the first time the soldiers could see Nadir clearly, and they switched their attention to her. One, with a swagger of authority, walked towards her cat-calling which set off the rest of the pack. They laughed and cackled like hyenas: baring their teeth in wide wolfish grins; their eyes feasting lustfully on the twelve-year-old girl. Nadir dropped to the sanctuary of the soil at her feet, squirming frantically in the dust in a desperate attempt to cover herself.

The man strolling towards her was a sergeant but like all of their militia, wore no insignia to give away his rank, except a small white mark on the back of his steel helmet. He took his time getting to where Nadir lay, then stood with a leg either side of her, drinking in her nudity before placing the tip of his rifle between her legs. 'I hope you've got something explosive in there,' he called out to hoots and shrieks of laughter from the pack. 'I'd better make certain...even though I've forgotten my rubber gloves today,' he added, pulling out a thin blue pair and dropping them straight in front of Nadir's terrified face. Slinging the rifle over his back, he leaned across her and took a firm grip on each of her bare buttocks; then wrenched them apart to inspect his prize, hard-eyed.

A soundless flicker of movement caught Ali's attention. He moved his head a fraction, in time to see his father roll onto his back and kick the guard standing over him. The soldier was so engrossed in the show Nadir was unwillingly starring in, that he didn't feel it coming until Mohammed's speeding foot was lifting his testicles. There was a crunch and he bent over double, dropping his rifle straight into the waiting hands of Mohammed. Cradling the gun like a newborn infant, Mohammed continued his roll, coming up elbow on knee in the classic position of a marksman. Aiming as low as he dared at the sergeant, he gently squeezed the trigger; allowing the natural tendency of the semi-automatic to ride up through the man's body. The first bullet hit him in the thigh, the second in the hip and the next three in his torso. The last bullet found the gap in his Kevlar jacket just below his armpit. It ricocheted off the inside of his shoulder joint and took the path of least resistance: ripping through his chest cavity; tumbling through his intestines; exiting from his groin. The sergeant fell onto Nadir, convulsing and shaking his life away.

Until Mohammed fired, the other soldiers were too absorbed to notice him and it took them almost two seconds to respond. Mohammed threw himself sideways, towards the tank, then scooted underneath it. He was now behind the lights and invisible to the soldiers; some of whom fired anyway, hitting the tank and the man standing next to it.

'Turn on the rear lights,' screamed the frantic voice from the loudhailer. There was a 'click' and his father was illuminated in the open, sprinting for the safety of his orchard. He was ten yards short when fourteen soldiers fired as one. Mohammed collapsed to the earth like a rag doll, limp and still.

Glancing nervously around, Ali could see no one looking in his direction. Deciding to follow his father's example, rather than heed his advice, he jumped up and ran for the pitch black shadow at the side of the house. As he approached the edge of the light there was a shout from behind and his foot tripped on a stone. He went down hard as bullets snapped and cracked over him.

'No one move or you will all be shot. I repeat – do not move,' shouted the urgent voice from the megaphone. Ali complied willingly. Peering though half closed eyelids he could see most of the soldiers were aiming at his mother, brother and sister. Two were still aiming at his dead father and only one was pointing a rifle at him. 'They think I'm dead,' he realised, watching the man nearest him drop his gun barrel six inches and call out to the others, 'Reloading.'

As the soldier unclipped the magazine from his rifle, Ali got up swiftly; bolting for the shadow ten feet away. Shots spit up the ground around him but he jinked and swerved into the blackness; his terror gifting him speed. He didn't stop running until he reached the top of the hill where a thick bamboo hedge met a deep ditch which drained one side of the orchard in winter. Crouching behind a tree trunk, he searched back anxiously to see if any of the soldiers had followed him. His relief on seeing no one was quickly replaced by a sensation of utter helplessness. What could he do against so many men? There was only one thing that could re-balance these odds – a gun. But all the guns were locked in the kitchen, which was in full view of the tank. Then a distant bark from the neighbouring farm reminded him of the old Martini action .270 next to the window in his father's study. Mohammed kept it there for shooting the wild rabid dogs that scavenged the orchard in the late summer months.

Stealing quietly along an old path which skirted the orchard before bending around the back of the farm buildings, Ali crept up to the rear wall of his father's office; giving thanks to Allah when he saw that the window was open. Peeking inside the room cautiously, he made sure it was empty then felt under the window frame for the cold comfort of the rifle barrel. It was exactly where he remembered it and, getting hold of the end, he levered it out towards him. In the shadow of the wall he pulled down the under-lever to open the breech and saw the gleam of a bullet lying in the chamber.

Though accurate, the rifle was single shot and had to be reloaded each time it was fired. 'I need more bullets,' Ali thought, but as he was about to climb in and get them from the drawer in his father's desk, there was an unmistakeable squeak of rubber on the stone floor outside the study. He stepped back from the window as the door burst open and three soldiers ran into the room, guns in their shoulders and eyes on their sights.

Ali grabbed the rifle and ran into the sanctuary of the night, listening acutely for any sign they had seen him. The crash of breaking glass and furniture echoed up to him from his father's office and he quickened his pace, feeling suddenly sad and very alone.

He angled over towards the ditch but, preoccupied with his plight ran straight over the edge of it, tumbling down the steep bank and splashing into the pool of muddy water at the bottom. It hurt, but he hadn't let go of the gun. Terrified the noise might have alerted the soldiers, he clambered out and hurried down the old stream's course to where a large olive tree grew.

'I will have a clear view of the house from there,' Ali thought, breaking into a trot. Half way there a shot rang out, then the desperate shrieks of Hassan came ringing up to him. They ceased abruptly: cut-off in mid-scream. Hot tears sprang into Ali's eyes, blinding him, causing him to stumble over the smooth river-stones. Gasping, he forced back the tears and negotiated his way through the dark, finally getting to the base of the tree. He threw his arms around it and broke down crying – as quietly as he could.

The old olive tree had stood there for six generations of his family and had been struck by lightning when half-grown. The bolt had killed a section of the tree near the top and the seasonal rains had rotted out a hollow, in which Ali and Nadir played hide-and-seek from Hassan in bygone, happier days. He gazed up at the tree silhouetted against the face of the new moon and shook himself to will away his tears, then slung the rifle over his back and started to climb. The familiar handholds came straight to him as he pulled himself into their old hiding place. Only when he was completely hidden, did he dare to look through a small gap towards the farm buildings, seventy yards away.

The image confronting him was surreal. The branches seemed to frame a picture postcard straight from the lowest pit of hell: sent signed and stamped, by the Devil himself.

The house was ablaze. Tall red and yellow flames snaked through the roof crackling evilly, bathing the scene in an orangey glow. Hassan was nowhere to be seen and a line of men were standing next to the white picket fence which ran around his mother's vegetable garden.

Here the queue ended and Ali's lifelong nightmare began. Bent over the fence, tied at wrist and ankle to the bottom rail was his little sister, Nadir. The man behind her had his fatigues around his ankles and was rutting into her; while the waiting soldiers passed a bottle and told him to hurry up. Ali moved his head around to see through the latticework of twigs and leaves, searching for his mother; to find her lying in a pool of blood, leaking from a cavity which had once been her tender, loving face. He choked on the horror and dragged the rifle off his back to look through the scope. It placed him only ten feet away.

The man raping his sister had just grunted himself to a finish and was being pulled out of the way by the next one in line. Ali focused on the crosshairs, aiming at him. But as he did, he noticed Nadir's face in the bottom of the lens. She was looking straight at him and crying. Moving the gun a fraction, he put her lips in the centre of the lens. Nadir wasn't crying, she was repeating the same thing over and over. As he read her silent lips he shuddered violently, and his foot slipped on the branch: 'Kill me Ali. Kill me.'

Taking a deep breath to calm his panic, he looked through the scope again. There was no mistaking it. She was definitely looking at their old hiding place and those were the words. Ali looked away for a moment, thought about it, and decided he couldn't do it. Instead, he chose to shoot the soldier stepping up behind her and he wriggled himself into a shooting position. Resting the barrel on a limb, he tweaked the crosshairs onto the soldier's chest.

Then he clicked the safety catch off.

This man had been born luckier than most. He called out loudly to the others as he took out his engorged penis. It was monstrous: nearly a foot long with an angry red head as bulbous as Nadir's ankle. Large enough Ali knew, to present him with a fairly decent target. The soldier held his arms high over his head, thrusting and rotating his hips to make the monster dance. Moving next to Nadir, he slapped it onto his palm as if to weigh it, then squeezed his hand around the base of its massive girth causing the head to inflate to an impossible size.

Some of the men burst out laughing, while the others stood rooted to the spot, round-eyed in their disbelief. The soldier grinned, evilly. Satisfied he had the full attention of the others, the man stepped behind Nadir. He bent his knees slightly and lifted his aim a little, then lunged forward: pile-driving the monster deep into her anus.

And Nadir screamed. She let out a bloodcurdling shriek as it tore into her. The ear-splitting sound of her agony ripped through Ali's being: shattering his soul; making him whimper out loud in acute, physical pain.

Nadir's magnificent, chocolate brown eyes were staring deep into his, when the recoil hit him.

THE SLOTH: A BEAST THAT SLEEPS IN DAYLIGHT

Abdul was sleeping contentedly, when he was suddenly and rudely woken up by the PDA vibrating on his bedside table and crashing to the floor. Clawing his way over to the side of the bed, he peered down blearily at the screen, to see that it wasn't a call but a message alert from the London Times. He had hooked his PDA into 87 different news feeds with a small application he had coded himself; enabling him to monitor events on a variety of subjects he was interested in – and an even greater number of people. If the news wires used any of his key words in an article, he would be instantly notified. It saved him time and meant he didn't have to trawl through the newswires each day to stay on top of things. Should anything of interest hit a newspaper from Australia to Iceland, he would know about it a second later. He leaned further over the edge of his bed to read the screen in detail. It was displaying the name of his father, "Victor Simmius", and the number fourteen, which told him how many newsfeeds had written an article on the subject.

'Fourteen?' he queried, coming fully alert, 'What the…?' Anything over ten normally indicated a national disaster. Leaping off his bed he hurried over to his laptop, tapping the space bar impatiently to waken it from its slumber.

'Come on, come on,' he muttered impatiently, as he waited for the computer to boot up from standby. The moment the screen flashed on he tapped control 6, which took him straight to the English newspaper section. Choosing the London Times, his mouth fell open slightly as he read the front page headline due for release that morning.

RESPECTED OXFORD DON CREATES FURORE IN GOVERNMENT

'What's the old sod up to now?' Abdul mumbled, scanning the article. At the top was the introductory paragraph:

Highly respected for the advice and guidance he has provided to many different governments over the past twenty-six years, including our own, Professor Simmius has put forward a proposal to change our system of government. It consists of five main steps, all of which could be implemented quickly and easily. Taken together they constitute a major shift in the balance of power held by our Members of Parliament and could form a basis for change in Britain. His proposals, which have already won wide acceptance among the student fraternity already, have now started to win approval from a larger section of the British public, who are shocked and dissatisfied with Government standards.

'Blah blah blah,' joked Abdul to himself, mimicking his father.

Step One: All voting by our MPs to be made public.

The Professor recommends that our MPs would still debate issues in the established way, but declare their vote to the nation. They can vote yea, nay, or abstain, but must publish their reasoning, which would then be displayed on a variety of media – free to all who wish to look.

This is an obvious attempt by the Professor to lessen the dominance of Government Whips, who concentrate power into the hands of a few Cabinet ministers – an accepted process which the Professor thinks undemocratic. When looked at objectively, the use of a Whip does make a mockery of our democracy – metaphorically and literally. The fact that our MPs are cowed into submission at the crack of the overseers' instruction is a sad reality of our Government today: the Whips effect government by one person, enforced by a few, over many.

The professor's proposal should also stop any behind-the-scenes dealings in which our MPs frequently indulge to get their own Bills and interests through the House. This carpet-bagging malaise, a shameful and much criticized aspect of our governing process, would wither under the light of open public scrutiny: forcing Members of the House to vote with their conscience, all of the time.

Because MPs would have to justify their decision making, it should also ensure they have read and digested the issues on which they vote. This will radically change the current practice, whereby Government Whips tell MPs how they will vote and in doing so remove any requirement for an MP to wade through lengthy paperwork. The most shocking example of this malfeasance being the Maastricht Treaty, when only 34 MPs had read the document voted into law. This was the Bill that initiated the handing our self-governing power to a European Parliament.

Abdul let out a low whistle as alarm bells started ringing in his mind. Pausing to gaze up at the ceiling he bit his lip absentmindedly. 'This is out of character,' he realised. His father had never stepped up to the plate to voice his concerns in public. Something must have changed, because this wasn't his father's modus operandi – he preferred private persuasion. *What did he think he was doing?* Abdul knew how astute his father was: aware more than most of the implications of such an action. And a sensible man does not walk into a darkened cave, shouting his arrival, while the lion of British Government waits in the gloom – fangs bared and claws out.

'He's putting himself in real danger and he's too experienced not to know that,' Abdul mused. Then it struck him. The old man must be dying. 'Grief, he's got nothing to lose.' He read the next item more eagerly.

Step Two: The people of Britain to have the final say over all MPs' voted decisions.

'Whaaaat?' Abdul exclaimed.

The Professor has detailed a practical methodology to achieve this initiative, both quickly and effectively. In essence, he is proposing that our MPs would still debate and vote on an issue, but before it is passed into law there would be a short interval, during which the electorate of each constituency can also vote. He recommends that if more than 50% vote against their MP's decision – their will carries. Forcing the MP to vote with them in the final count at the Houses of Parliament. The Professor has added the proviso that this should only occur when a reasonable proportion of those citizens do actually vote. Simply put: the will of the People supersedes the decision of their MP – providing it holds the majority. To ensure enough time for this process, the Professor suggests that our MPs' holidays should be cut back to seven weeks per annum: halved.

Most legislative change is humdrum and not of interest to many, so it is likely that most people will not intervene, allowing their MPs to make their decisions for them in exactly the same way they have done in the past. However, if an issue caught the public's attention or was momentous enough, like going to war, the people of Britain would have the final say – not our Government, whose role would become one of idea creation, persuasion and rational argument.

The main criticism levelled at the Professor is that the population is not suitably well-informed or intelligent enough to make the right decision. But as the Professor points out, they will get better at it as they learn about the issues and arguments put forward by their MPs: education by example. One of the most attractive aspects of the Professor's concept is that if any voters are in any doubt, they can still side with their MP's advice and suggestion, so nothing changes unless enough people feel strongly about an issue and decide to vote on it.

In view of the high number of decisions made by our MPs which have been catastrophically wrong, morally, technically, or even borderline legal in the case of the second Iraq war, it is no longer possible to argue that the people of Britain would drop below our Government's level of incompetence.

Additionally, the voting populace will never be motivated by secret political agendas, which have tempted our political masters to go to war many times over the past six decades; either for self-aggrandisement or to harness patriotic fervour to their own Party before an election. Unfortunately this is no longer the exception, it has become the root cause for war – the overriding factor and driver behind every conflict Britain has conducted since WW2. It provides clear proof to all right-thinking men and women that our government has horse-traded our longer term interests for their own short-term gain – safeguarding our long-term interests is the prime function of any government but this is not what they are doing.

If the Professor's ideas were in place, it becomes difficult to imagine what could induce the majority of the British public to go to war, when we are not attacked first. As we now know, the second Iraq war was arranged through excessive use of government spin: stretching past breaking-point most people's belief in the honesty and integrity of Mr Antony Bliar, who many people feel should be tried for treason – possibly war crimes.

Professor Simmius thinks his methodology will also curtail terrorist activity in our country, as the militants would be attacking the will of free people, not the ivory tower of government authority. It is not hard to see that the terrorists would undermine any support or sympathy by such action – arousing the anger of the ordinary person on the street – a counterproductive step in winning hearts and minds to their cause.

This is particularly relevant, as there is now a widely held belief that the British Government was aware of the terrorist attacks in London *on the 7th of July – beforehand. This has been sparked by the knowledge of a "practice exercise" held at the same Tube stations; on the same date and at precisely the same time. Prior warnings of the massacre have also come to light from outside intelligence agencies, including Mossad. This "practice exercise" involved over a thousand people and was conducted by Visor Consultants, supposedly to gauge our readiness and response to the very attacks which occurred. This undoubtedly created enormous confusion on 7/7, as the emergency services were initially unsure if the attacks were real. It is reminiscent of NORAD conducting a similar "practice exercise" – coincidentally on 9/11 – which created so much confusion that it prevented the second plane from being located and intercepted, even though there was more than enough time to do so before it reached the second Twin Tower. This NORAD 'exercise' included the simulation of flying passenger planes into strategic buildings in US cities, and it is interesting to note that George Bush, the President at the time, said in a press conference immediately afterwards: "No one ever imagined this kind of attack could take place", even though Dick Cheney, his Vice president, was visiting NORAD on 9/11 to oversee that exact process.*

This raises the possibility that the British people have been subjected to a Manchurian Incident: so called after the Japanese deliberately blew up a section of railway track in Manchuria on 18 September 1931, which they then used as an excuse to widen their invasion of China. In view of this, the implication of terror by our own government – against us – cannot be ruled out. It promotes the idea that our political masters should have government warning signs placed on all of their literature, and any of their comments.

'Holy shit!' Abdul exploded involuntarily. 'Dad's put a noose around his own neck with that one.' There was absolutely no doubt in his mind now: his father was at death's door, deciding he had nothing to lose by speaking out. He was committing a mortal sin against the God-like power of the British Government. Abdul suddenly recalled the large number of people who had already disappeared – for doing far less that his father was suggesting. And his father was respected by many, including the students he had taught, most of whom held his thinking in the highest regard. Worse still, he was dangerously well-informed and party to a number of sinister government secrets. Secrets which could never be allowed to surface.

'If he starts rubbing the Government's nose in that pile of shite –

he's dead,' Abdul thought to himself happily, recalling the fate of many, including the famous Dr David Kelly: who managed to push back the frontiers of science by killing himself in a medically impossible manner. Dr Kelly had leaked a document proving that Saddam Hussein had no weapons of mass destruction, neatly collapsing Bliar's argument for going to war. Immediately after the leak was traced back to the good doctor, he told several of his friends that he feared for his life – not realising it was about to be cut short by his own hand one week later. Not far from his home Dr Kelly had been found dead: propped against a tree in a wood that he enjoyed walking to alone. Half a packet of ibuprofen had been found in his pocket – unused. Not something a suicide would leave behind as ibuprofen can kill. Thirteen doctors had sworn an affidavit stating that cutting the small ulnar artery in his wrist would not have killed him. While a frightened ambulance crew, clearly terrified for their own safety, had called an international press conference to tell the world they had seen very little blood around the body. One senior pathologist, more au fait with the subject of human mortality, had offered a more plausible and more rational explanation: that Dr Kelly, an accurate and learned man, had swallowed one half of the pack of ibuprofen to dull the pain of his task, and on finding to his horror that he was still alive, must have held his breath until he expired. More naturally, the autopsy report had never been released. It would not be released until 2080, while most wartime secrets are only classified for 30 years – not 70. Abdul knew this spoke volumes about Tony Bliar and his merry band of henchmen. Eloquently demonstrating through censorship, just how far they were prepared to go to maintain absolute control over their wonderfully naïve subjects. While at the same time, sending out the crystal-clear warning to the intelligentsia: Do not rub up against a person who shares his initials with a deadly disease.

Abdul could see that his father's proposals would castrate British Government control at a stroke, placing the power firmly in the hands of the British people. A wider reaching result than Dr Kelly had achieved – and far longer lasting.

He looked back at the screen as a feeling of elation began to blossom inside him; because with his father out of the way, no one alive would be able to link his involvement with The Sword of Damocles. He was certain that his father would never divulge the plan to anyone else. Abdul had seen the look in his eyes when he had outlined the concept. It was as if he suddenly realised what he had done. There was a weighty pause as he went through the possibility of his plan actually happening – registering on his face as a deep shock, followed by a look of fear and immediate regret. His father had gone to some lengths to cover his tracks, saying the idea was purely theoretical and could never work in practice. But Abdul had seen the cover come down over his eyes. He had heard the veiled pleading in his father's voice and knew he was only trying to steer him off course. There was simply no way his father would repeat that mistake. Abdul relaxed considerably before reading the next item.

Step Three: The appointment of a panel of independent experts, drawn from the professions relevant to each issue, who publish their opinion and reasoning adjacent to their MPs' arguments.

Abdul laughed out loud at the ceiling. 'Nice try, father, but if you think MPs will allow themselves be exposed for their incompetence in public, then you're sadly mistaken.' He was starting to see this was all idle suggestion on his father's part. He knew the British Government would never let that nasty little genie out of the bottle: no one enjoys being highlighted for their stupidity. Expert opinion was best kept locked in a deep dark dungeon, emerging emaciated and blinking as mere solitary opinion.

Step Four: Full transparency. All information not marked 'Top Secret' to be provided to anyone who wants to drill down on an issue.

Surprisingly, this is remarkably easy to implement as our Civil Service already carries out this function. But at the moment this information, paid for by the British taxpayer, is only available to our MPs and Cabinet Ministers.

Step Five: Fixed term parliaments. A vote of confidence in the Prime Minister to be held at the mid-point.

See editorial comment page 2

Abdul clicked over to the tabloids to assess their reaction to his father's suggestions, knowing they would be instrumental in either winning public support, or bitching them to death. The first was headed simply:

CHANGE FOR PROGESS

The five steps outlined on the front page by Professor Simmius are timely, possibly overdue. For the first time it will give people the final say over our government's decisions, with very little effort on their part. Given that only 45% of the electorate turned out for the recent by-election, there is a real danger that MPs with more extreme views and agendas will win a number of seats at the next election. We live in harrowing times.

If we find ourselves with a hung parliament, these extremists will have the casting vote on many issues. It would be foolish to think that they will not use this tempting lever of power to further their own agenda and consolidate their political base. Professor Simmius' new system provides a practical defence against this – a safety-valve approach. Judging by the way our students have publicised the Professor's views, alongside a growing number of Labour supporters and a less vocal swathe of the middle classes, who traditionally side with the Conservative Party, it appears to have struck a chord in the minds of many.

Unfortunately there are countless examples of shoddy decision making by our parliamentarians. Both by our MPs and their overlords – the Cabinet – who should know better. This refutes the belief that our government knows best – they do not.

One of the Chancellor of the Exchequer's first acts of considered lunacy was to promptly sell off more than half of Britain's gold reserve when the price was at a 20 year low, failing to realise the insurance it provides when the country is struck by adversity. Naturally he found many willing buyers. Emboldened by this success he then presided over the lackadaisical policing of the banks which required a bail out from taxpayers of around 850 billion. His argument that it was a global tragedy which began in the United States, is undermined by the 125% mortgages that ran rampant through Britain, delaying the inevitable housing deflation just before an up-coming election. This delay and over-fuelling of the housing market turned it into something far more destructive than the expected market correction. His incompetence even managed to bring the notion of capitalism itself into question. On the plus side though, the Labour party managed to win another term of office which gave them a chance to spin their way out of the debacle. If Mr Gordon Bennett was unaware that his actions would amplify the predicted housing crash, then he should have resigned for his foolhardiness. However if, as many did, the Chancellor realised what was likely to happen, then he should be tried in court for wilful misuse of a Public Office – modern day treason. The fact that he then went on to become our Prime Minister, without being elected, cannot be overlooked when the question is asked: is Great

Britain a democratic country?

Moreover, the public outrage resulting from the London terrorist attacks bolstered the Labour Cabinet's argument to fight terror overseas; their logic running counter to the fact that all of the bombers were born and brought up in Britain and only attacked us to protest against the war abroad, which they thought was being targeted at their fellow Muslims. Another terrible decision by our government, with a mislead thrown in so they could curry favour with American nationalism. A patriot being a person who loves his country; a nationalist is someone who hates everybody else's. To date, attacking Iraq has killed an estimated 2 million people. It has to be estimated because official figures are classified.

Even we, the media, will be forced into acting more responsibly because promoting wrongful ideas will directly affect our own journalists and staff. It should also reduce government spin, a thing almost unimaginable after the past three Governments who have managed to elevate their rhetoric past the point that most people consider absurd. This bent tool of persuasion has been so widely used, that most people can no longer distinguish truth from fiction – nor should they try.

Conservatives, with both a large and small 'c', know that injecting responsibility creates responsibility; conversely, instigating a nanny state creates babies. Exposure to responsibility is one of the main reasons why they send their children to private school in the first place. Which begs the question: why do Conservatives resist change? The answer does not require a degree in Political History or Economics – a rudimentary understanding of the rules of shove-ha'penny is sufficient.

What may appeal to many uncomfortable voters is that nothing changes unless enough people want to vote on an issue. Most Government legislation is fairly mundane and commonsensical, but a few things, like invading a distant country, are definitely not in this category and rightly attract people's attention and concern. As it is 'We the People' who must do the fighting and dying, and 'We the People' who have to face the terrorist repercussions in our cities and aircraft – a direct result of the foreign warfare – it seems only right that we should have a say in the matter. Professor Simmius' concept provides us with that opportunity. We believe it is now a crucial step towards restoring the health and wellbeing of our beloved democracy.

'I take my hat off to you. You're a braver man than you know.' Abdul breathed a sigh of relief. There was little chance of those ideas ever being implemented – not before another disaster or three. 'I'll be surprised if he's still alive a week from now,' Abdul thought as he went back to bed. 'Dulce et decorum est pro patria mori*, father.'

He slipped under his duvet and fell into a deep and tranquil sleep, convinced that the only way change ever occurred was when a populace was prised out of its sloth-like attitude by crying need or sheer brute force.

And he already had the neck of public apathy lying fully exposed to the executioner's blade, by another, far more powerful idea of his father's. Its razor-sharp edge was the most dangerous concept which could ever to be unleashed on organised society: the destruction of the rule of law. He hefted the weapon in his own fist, ready to strike the head from that slumbering beast of sloth.

He would bring down The Sword of Damocles on an unsuspecting, somnolent world.

It is sweet and honourable to die for your country

APING

'You've got to realise, my dear, I was old by the time I was twenty and young by the time I was forty, and youth makes the same mistakes. Unfortunately, by the time I made my biggest one I had the experience to know it really could happen. "Be sure your sin will find you out",' he quoted, shaking his fists at an imaginary heaven before collapsing dismally onto the chaise-longue.

'He really is upset,' Leah realised, and the feminine urge to soothe his pain melted into her, lending tenderness to her reply. 'What mistakes could upset you this badly, Victor?'

'It's not how many, it's the scale that counts. A big one being far worse than a few inconsequential errors forgotten in under a month. It wasn't until recently that I settled my thinking on this matter. Now that I have, I can think of only one way to prevent it from happening.' He gave a deep groan of self pity.

'Nothing is that bad. Tell me what's troubling you.'

'It's the understanding that when good meets evil it may be very hard to distinguish them. As you know, Leah, I have a son. When I was in my twenties, I fell in love and married a Lebanese anthropologist called Kamilah. She was a wonderful woman. I've never met her equal. Anyhow, she was staying at a hotel in Beirut with Abdul, waiting for me to join her there when I had finished up some work for the French Government. It had dragged on a bit, as it always does with them, delaying my arrival by a week. When I did arrive, I was given the horrific news that my wife and son were among the victims of the bombing that had completely destroyed the hotel the evening before. We found her body – not his. I searched high and low with every spare moment I had, then I finally managed to locate him in an orphanage. By then he was nearly thirteen. I recognised him immediately because he was born with different coloured eyes, like mine. I took him straight out of that dreadful place and brought him back home to London. Given the circumstances things were more than a little difficult, then I noticed a change in him. He became argumentative and moody. He began accusing me of helping the Great Satan, the label the Middle East and Asia apply to the West. I followed him one day and watched him go into a mosque in Shepherds Bush. He didn't re-emerge for five hours – longer than simple worship required. When he eventually came home I asked him what he had been up to and he flew into a rage; saying it was to his shame that I was his father and that I had helped to blow up the Middle East, indirectly killing his mother. I suppose in a way I had – though not intentionally. We tried to give them peace through democracy but the military got in the way. Anyway, not long after we got into that senseless cycle of angry recrimination and he left home to study computing in Cairo.

'Ten years ago I came across his tracks by chance. He had set up an investment fund which linked the Western banks with Hawala, the word-of-mouth banking system of the Middle East. He had just sold his company and there was a small picture of him in the Financial Times. I tried to contact him but to no avail. Then I bumped into him at a conference centre in Geneva. He was part of a delegation that was setting up orphanages in Afghanistan. We had dinner and, over the next few weeks, spent a lot of time together. I gave him a ring identical to yours – they were originally a pair. Kamilah called them her family heirlooms and it seemed right at the time he should have one. I was hoping it would remind him of his mother's tenderness and love, in the same way you do sometimes,' he said, flicking Leah an embarrassed smile. 'My son has a passion for fighting social injustice; but I realised that although we believed in the same goals, we were on very different sides of the coin. He detests the West, calling it decadent and destructive. Feelings which I think stemmed from the loss of his mother all those years ago. He put his arguments well and I indulged him. So much so, that I let my guard down. One evening we had a little too much champagne and he asked me if there was any way to re-balance the injustices of the world. Stupidly, I went and divulged The Sword of Damocles to him. He posed the question and to my aching shame, I showed him the Achilles heel of Western democracy – how easily a society could be dismantled. At the end of that evening he said he was off to Afghanistan and we swapped addresses. I've never heard from him since. I wrote to the address he gave me but all my letters were returned unopened. I even flew over to the place but when I got there, I discovered the address he gave was false. I've had a nagging concern about that last conversation. Knowing the way his thoughts and feelings run, I worry he may do something the world will regret. Abdul-Aliyy Saqr Khalifa as he called himself then, has the mindset, intelligence and the resources to carry out anything he wishes...Oh God, Abdul. My son, my own son! I should have been there for you,' he wailed, breaking into anguished sobbing.

Leah put a hand on his arm to comfort him. 'If he's your son, he can't be all bad.'

'That's precisely the problem,' Victor replied through his tears. 'When he lays down his thinking, it would persuade the most bigoted zealot that he is on the side of good and we really are the Great Satan. If he's right – we are the greedy ones; it is our ideology and way of life that will enslave mankind or destroy the planet first. And he may be right; it is probably how the meek get to inherit the earth.'

'Shia logic,' Leah retorted. 'So we all go back to living in 700 AD as they want us to. That will help feed the world efficiently.'

Ignoring her sarcasm, Victor continued. 'Back then, he predicted the exact sequence of events which have actually occurred: the fragmentation of the Middle East; the rise of the Shia in Turkey and Iraq; even the civil wars in Yemen and Pakistan and the Afghan Government being usurped by the Taliban. He went on to say that it would lead the West into a rapidly expanding conflict, uniting an ever-widening region against their common foe: you and me.'

'God. I hope he's wrong on that,' Leah said slowly.

'If the enemy of my enemy is my new friend, then it stands to reason that when the old enemy goes down, you have a new enemy to contend with,' Victor stated.

'But peace and freedom are the only reasons we fight. They fight for power, wealth and control. None of them helpful,' Leah countered.

'Ever since Kamilah died, I have dedicated my life to winning peace and prosperity for people. I fought at every turn for people's right to be free and control their own destiny. It would be hateful to know that I made one mistake, handing my own son a sword to hack to pieces the few positive things my generation did accomplish. I feel as if I've handed unto the Devil, the secret name of God.'

'Well, any friend of the Devil is a friend of mine,' Leah joked, trying to lift his mood.

'Obviously you haven't read the Tanakh, the ancient Jewish Bible. I strongly suggest you do, under the heading "required reading" if you wish to understand mankind's foolishness in detail. The legend of the secret name of God is in there. It's the ancient and widely held belief that if you know the real name of God – you control him.'

'You worry too much. The secret name of God is a myth and, although The Sword of Damocles is a scary idea, it is only an idea. A bit like having a nuclear weapon and no missile system. It would be impossible to implement.'

'Impossible?' Victor spoke softly into his lap. 'How many times have I proven the lie in that word?'

The old grandfather clock chimed the hour. Victor levered himself up from the chaise-longue to drift away from the fireplace with his head bent over in thought. Reaching a decision, he suddenly spun around to face her; his right foot cocked at forty-five degrees; his hands pushed deep into his jacket pockets. He looked at her questioningly, 'Would you indulge an old man and meet a dear chum of mine who is coming up from London next week? We could sup together next Wednesday, if you don't mind dining à trois?'

'I'd be delighted,' Leah smiled.

'His friends call him Jimmy… but his real name is James MacCack,' he said cautiously.

'Not *the* James MacCack?'

'The very one.'

Leah let out a gasp of shock. James MacCack was the head of MI6. 'Victor! You're trying to recruit me.'

'I prefer to think of it as introducing you to the God of Secrets. That is all.'

She held his gaze steadily. 'I think it might be inexpedient to turn down the head of MI6 at this stage of my career. Perhaps I'll let the two of you dine alone.'

'Nothing untoward will happen, Leah, you have my word. As long as you let your yea be yea, and your nay be nay, he will respect you for it. Besides, I'm fully aware of Jimmy's limitations. He won't do anything iffy with me hovering about in the background. Apart from anything else, you are not the only person I've introduced to him. I know several people who are now his top managers.'

'Well, if you are certain it will be okay,' she replied warily. 'I suppose it would be interesting to meet him. Very interesting.'

'All I'm asking is that you listen to what he has to say before you decide anything at all,' Victor replied, holding up his hands to placate her.

Though it appeared more like supplication to Leah.

AN AMORAL APE

The following Wednesday, Leah arrived outside Victor's study to find the door slightly ajar. She paused to listen. Victor's radio was blaring out Trad Jazz and there was an indistinguishable hubbub of a male conversation reverberating softly in the background. Without knocking, she pushed the door open and saw them sitting in the armchairs in mid-argument.

They both looked over at her, then Victor reached behind him for the dial of the 1950s Roberts radio. 'Sorry about the cacophony, Leah, I'll turn it down,' he said, as they both stood up to greet her. 'Allow me to introduce the two of you. Leah Mandrille, this is James MacCack.'

'Please,' he corrected courteously, 'my friends call me Jimmy.'

Leah went over to his outstretched hand without taking it, 'It's an old schoolboy trick to leave the door open with music playing – no one can overhear your conversation.'

Jimmy laughed. 'I was just asking Victor for his opinion on a silly little matter, but old habits you know… We were not discussing you, although you are the reason I'm here this evening,' he said in a gravelly Scottish accent.

'The silly little matter to which Jimmy refers, is he wants me to publicly criticise my proposal of "We the People". So your intervention is timely, Leah, as I was just about to tell Jimmy that I won't. Besides, there isn't an argument to refute it that will appear rational to the thinking majority. My answer is no, Jimmy. I shall not, will not, and could not do it convincingly – even if I tried.'

'You're setting the country against the Government, Victor.'

'No I am not! The Government of this country has been against the betterment of its people for the last fifteen years and I'm addressing the imbalance.'

'You're skating on very thin ice as I explained to you. You must retract those ideas and proposals or you will find yourself in very deep water, with nothing I can do to safeguard you.'

'When you reach my age, Jimmy, a swift end becomes a hope, not a fear.'

'Consider the benefits of having a powerful European Government, Victor. A bulwark of reasonable people sitting between America, Russia and China; able to wield positive influence in the world.'

'You are using my own argument against me, with one major difference. Those reasonable people are now controlled by an unelected President. A role that will quickly develop into one of Supreme Ruler, with a court of toadies sitting around the throne waiting to be thrown a morsel of power. That post is not elected by the people. I will not stand idly by and let it continue. Think of your future, Jimmy. A non-elected President sets a terrible precedent for control, and how do you reverse it? That will prove impossible, so I intend to stop it before its authority becomes absolute.'

'You must turn away from this, Victor. And you must turn away now.'

'I will turn from nothing! I will not turn from freedom and people's right to be free. They may have fooled the masses but they don't fool me. To use one of your own arguments against you, Jimmy: "All it takes for evil to triumph is for good men to do nothing". Well I am a good man and if everyone turns their back on this, we will all be turned into nothings – within a generation at most. You have children, Jimmy; think of them instead of your blind duty for once.'

'Don't do anything rash, Victor. I'm warning you for the last time.'

'Don't worry, I shall probably be dead way before I can accomplish anything.' A broad smile lit up his face. He flicked both his hands up to elicit a moment's silence, then gazed up at the ceiling beatifically – as if he had just seen an angel alighting on top of the bookcase. His smiling suddenly erupted into laughter and he bent over double, holding his sides as it roared out of him – unchecked and unfeigned.

'There is nothing at all amusing about this,' Jimmy said ominously.

'Oh, yes, there is,' Victor replied between gasps.

'Perhaps I should leave the two of you alone,' Leah offered, turning to go.

'You will do nothing of the sort,' Victor said, standing bolt upright. 'You and Jimmy are both guests at my table and we have concluded our business.'

Jimmy rolled his eyes at Leah and tut-tutted. 'Perhaps you can make him see sense. I can see I've failed.'

'His ideas wouldn't have gained any degree of acceptance if our Government's incompetence and dishonesty hadn't opened the gate wide for them.' Leah spoke quietly, torn between her loyalty to Victor and her trepidation over James MacCack's warning.

'Oh, so it's all the Government's fault is it? We do occasionally get good governments too,' Jimmy rejoined.

'Really Jimmy? Name one. They didn't accidentally leave the gates open for my proposals, as Leah just implied. Their self-serving actions and gross inability to govern has torn them off their bloody hinges.'

'Selfish and incompetent Government is better than untested change, Victor. Can't you see that?'

'Our original government system was forged in the furnace of untested change.' Leah threw the comment between them, trying to redirect James's anger.

Victor glowered at Jimmy. 'Impoverishing the nation through incompetence? Going to war to bolster a party's election prospects? Currying favour with the nationalist elements of a superpower? Those three alone do enormous damage to people's confidence in any type of government structure. I'm sorry, but the changes I put forward are necessary for the future peace and stability of our country. And as you well know, they will put a stop to the wars and upgrade the level of governance in one fell swoop.'

'You're telling me that you're doing all this to improve things?' Jimmy shot back.

'Absolutely he is, and absolutely it will,' Leah jumped in. 'People are not as stupid as you think they are, James. That argument is out of date or foolish propaganda at best. Where is the harm in having a stop-button for any extreme or idiotic Government decision? All Victor is doing is widen government control to include everyone. A far safer machine than the broken-down car we're stuck with.'

'I hope you're right, young lady.'

'It's democratic,' Leah said more firmly. 'A small step towards true democracy. When it works well we won't even need different parties, simply the best decision-makers for Government positions. I've never understood how our politicians' ability to squeeze votes out of the populace, qualifies them to head up British industry or run the Health service. When you analyze the mistakes and constant changes of policy made by our elected Cabinet ministers, it becomes glaringly obvious that my point is correct. Read a few of their published diaries and you will see them admitting it in their own ink – bewailing their lack of understanding over the complex decisions they are forced to make. It's ghastly. It happens in no other profession or industry. Candidates have to work their way up to positions of responsibility – through merit. I'm sorry to say that putting an inexperienced person in charge of vital aspects of our country has proven catastrophic. It's putting the postboy in charge of the Post Office. No wonder we're in such a mess. I fail to see how Victor's proposals are a step back from that ruination. You should brace yourself, James, because most informed people are forming a similar view…and we hold the vote.'

'If it does work out, then I suppose it might be an improvement. But there are one or two dark horses who are very upset by his proposals.'

'That's the beauty of the democratic process. The majority decide and the handful with vested interest in power must toe the line,' Leah replied.

Jimmy looked at her carefully. 'My understanding is that Victor is doing this to prevent future wars breaking out which could escalate into a wider conflict. So let me say this: wars are not always bad. They can have very positive results – look at America for instance.'

'I thought wars were simply God's way of teaching Americans geography,' Leah joked. 'Only 18 percent of them know where Afghanistan is.'

Victor stepped up close to Jimmy. 'The Americans have made a terrible mistake by attacking countries with an ancient religion, yet to have its renaissance. Very foolish. The Muslim religion is the largest on earth and borderless. Things won't go the way they did in Vietnam, Korea or Japan, I assure you. The Muslims won't give up. America's open society will become ruled and overregulated from within, as they try to prevent the slow drip of occasional terrorist attack. It will become a police state. More so than at present. Ironically, it will be they themselves who turn it into a giant prison. They will build a fortress around themselves, and self-protectionism is the first indicator of a doomed empire. The cost of building it will drive up their taxes over the medium term, increasing their costs nationally, making them uncompetitive with the trading nations of Asia and South America. The Land of the Free will be enslaved by its own fear, then crumble from within. There are countless examples of it happening throughout history. The cycle is always the same and unfortunately, the most powerful military force on earth is no defence against a suicide bomber. The same process of paranoia is already underway here. I'm going to stop it. My solution is the only practical and realistic way around the dilemma. Anyway, my proposals don't change anything unless half the country thinks something is a bad idea. If two heads are better than one, then thirty-five million heads are better than twenty Cabinet control freaks with an overriding interest in power. Look at Bliar siding with naïve American ambition. To do it, he sacrificed our country's sense of right and wrong and the world's perception of us as honest and fair. "We the People" will set that straight. It also has the potential to elevate mankind as a whole. My proposals are a positive, moral leap forward for our country. In the longer term – the world.'

'He's right,' Leah agreed. 'It will be more dangerous in the long run if we don't implement his ideas. Once they've had the wrinkles ironed out, other countries will follow our example. They always have in the past. It will put the 'fair' back into the fairest nation on earth. Imagine what will happen to countries ruled by despots. Those suppressed will rise up demanding the vote, holding control on a constant basis. It'll be bye-bye to extremism in all its forms because the majority of people are not extreme – anywhere. The majority of people prefer peace, welcome harmony, and enjoy stability. It's our leaders we must be wary of.'

'That's a very convincing argument,' Jimmy smiled in slight wonderment. 'Bright, isn't she, Victor? Let's leave this for now and let me get to know this wonderful new protégée of yours.'

'Well, it's lovely to meet you too,' Leah stepped towards him, waiting until they shook hands before hitting him with her most devastating smile. 'Let me add that while I'm flattered by your interest in me, I intend to join the Diplomatic Corps. I doubt you can persuade me to swap that for a pretty cloak and a hidden dagger.'

'Och dear me, no,' he drawled offhandedly. 'Victor told me all about your planned career. In fact, I knew your father quite well. My condolences by the way, the world is a poorer place without him.'

'You knew my father?'

'We worked on a few projects together. Initially, when I was a young whippersnapper working undercover in Rhodesia; then later, when he was our Ambassador to Egypt. Back in those days Egypt was in Africa, now everybody says it's been moved to the Middle East. And the Middle East became my brief for a while before I was turned into the pen-pusher I am today,' he finished, smiling modestly.

Much against her previous intention, Leah found herself warming to him. His self-deprecating manner was charming and she decided to go along with the civility being offered. 'There's no harm in listening, then giving him a polite no,' she reminded herself.

'That's quite enough of that old blarney,' Victor said lightly. 'You've both eaten shish kebab in its country of origin, so you both know we can't discuss these matters until after coffee,' and taking them by an elbow each, he steered them over to the dining table. 'Let's dine first. Now then Jimmy, if you will be kind enough to pour the wine, I'll do the fetching and carrying.'

After a leisurely meal they carried their Armagnac and coffees to the armchairs and couch circling the embers of the fire. Victor put another log on it, then went over to the door. Cracking it open six inches he switched on the radio set and carefully adjusted the volume. 'That should do it,' he grinned at them both.

They sat in relaxed silence, listening to Cole Porter and staring into the flames of their own distant thoughts.

Jimmy spoke first. 'You mustn't blame Victor for wanting us to meet, Leah. He always puts the principal of social good above the desires of the individual. So you'll not be surprised to learn that in his younger days, he was a raving communist,' he finished, making Victor laugh.

'Well, you know what they say? If you're not a socialist by the time you're twenty you haven't got a heart, and if you're not a capitalist by thirty you haven't got a brain. I don't mind admitting that in my youthful and somewhat zealous youth, I was a communist. It's no big secret.'

'It is according to my dossier on you,' Jimmy returned, and they all laughed. 'Seriously though,' he went on in his rich brogue, 'Now that I have met you, Leah, I find myself not at all disappointed. You have beauty and intelligence and a definite will for good. It's a rare combination. One that's sadly lacking in today's world.'

'That is common to each of us,' chuckled Victor.

'Let me add that I can think of no better way for you to help your fellow man, than by going into the Diplomatic. Especially in these troubling times.'

'There are not enough good people in the world with the will to see things through and the brains to make them happen,' Victor agreed.

'So with your permission, I would like to propose a toast,' Jimmy announced, getting up and refilling their glasses from the crystal decanter. 'To the youngest female ambassador Britain has ever appointed.'

Leah raised her glass with them, suddenly feeling numb. She went through the motions of toasting, becoming increasingly excited by what he had just proposed. It dawned on her that his toast was not wishful prophecy, it had substance attached. She had already sensed that these two men were part of a secret decision-making process which chose who did what; probably to a very senior level and well above the title of Ambassador. They were opening up their clandestine little club to her. And sister, what a club!

'James, you are so difficult to dislike that I am going to call you Jimmy from now on,' she clinked her glass on his, looking straight into his heart and adding sweetly, 'Perhaps you should have chosen the Diplomatic?'

'Aaah, ya lovely lass. But y'know, spies and ambassadors are much the same nowadays, so perhaps in a way I did. Spies don't really have wars, they observe them. And the first duty of a good ambassador is to know exactly what's going on, then report it accurately to his or her Government. In other words, all ambassadors are spies.'

'But not all spies are ambassadors,' Leah smiled.

'That, unfortunately, is true. But the lines between the two are now so blurred, that one without the other couldn't function in its present form. We are a source of information to the Diplomatic Corps, just as diplomatic staff are a constant source of information for us. And fortunately, we are both on the same side.'

'Look, Leah,' Victor leaned forward, 'I thought the two of you should meet because I am certain you will succeed in becoming an ambassador, and Jimmy is right. You will have to work with many different agencies and come to realise that any information is much better than none at all.'

'Quite so,' Jimmy nodded. 'You have been very forthright and open with me, Leah; for which I'm grateful, so I'll lay it out for you. If you help us, we in turn will help you... and we really can help you, which then helps us and so on. All you have to do is let us know if you come across anything of interest to us. I'll set you up a contact; give you a BlackBerry phone which has a secure connection to us at all times, and you get in touch if you want to. The only other thing we might ask, is your opinion on various matters from time to time. Now I'm afraid we can't pay you, and anyway, that might be foolish. However, we can offer assistance in other ways. For instance, it would be in our mutual interest to invite you to various state functions, government parties, that sort of thing, where you can make the contacts who will assist your career. Naturally, if you do hear anything interesting we would be all ears. And that's it really. There's nothing more to it.'

'What do you think?' Victor asked. 'If it's any reassurance, I've known Jimmy for twenty years.'

'I think it would be rude to say…no,' Leah replied slowly. 'I suppose if I ever heard something MI-sixy, I would want to pass it on. But you did say that I only have to pass on what I wish to pass on. Is that completely correct?'

'Absolutely. Here, you might like these,' Jimmy said, handing her a BlackBerry phone and a gold embossed envelope stamped with the Royal Crest. 'It's a little party the Prince of Wales is holding next month. Hope to see you there, eh? Although when we do meet, it's probably better if we pretend not to know each other.'

Leah looked at him carefully, reaching out to take them from him. 'Let's see. Blackberries sprinkled with sweetener. Now what possible harm could they do a girl?'

But this time, only Jimmy MacCack laughed.

THE WARRIOR APE

The big glass doors of Sacramento's City Hall swept open smoothly, flashing sunlight across the crowd; startling Ali back to his place in time. He shut his eyes and shook his head to dispel the demons which ruled his nightmare.

A large well-built man dressed in a cream coloured suit, strode into the sunshine, smiling for the cameras and waving at imaginary friends. Flowing up the steps of the podium, he gripped the sides of the lectern with his arms bent ever so slightly: a pose he had perfected onscreen while playing the role of a US President. The Governor paused for a moment, looked down on the crowd dramatically, and saw that it was good.

'Ladies and Gentlemen, Senator and Mayor, I thank you all for coming here today,' his voice boomed out of the loudspeakers. 'The wild-fires of California are the worst thing that's happened since I took office...'

It was only at that moment, mindful of the oath he had sworn to his father, that Ali picked up the rifle. Turning it onto its side, he slid the bolt back and took out the first bullet, replacing it with one standing upright on the blanket in front of him. It was an old habit he had picked up from one of his compatriots at a training camp on the Afghan-Pakistani border. Once, after hearing the frustrating click of a misfire, Mustapha had told him that if he swapped his first bullet for another, it would never happen again. Ali adopted the habit and never had another misfire; though he also took up bullet-making that same evening. The cartridge he put into the breech had taken him two hours to construct and, done correctly, would increase the velocity of the bullet by a third. He slid the cartridge home with the bolt, placed the butt firmly into his shoulder and raised the barrel. Then he clicked the safety catch off. Peering through the Zeiss telescopic sight, he first ran it over the governor, then started scoping the few buildings above him to ensure the coast was still clear. It was. Wriggling his strangely humped body around, he placed the barrel on the tripod set up in front of him and snuggled into his shooting position.

As he looked through the scope, he felt himself slipping into the zone that few marksmen ever experience. The traffic noise from below receded, as though an invisible hand were turning the volume down. A deep calm began wafting through his being, making him feel secure and safe – the way a nervous addict relaxes when the prick of the needle becomes friend. Dreamy serenity drifted softly: shielding him from his mind's constant thinking; insulating him from himself; enveloping and cushioning, 'til he became weightless and numb. With a last even exhale, his breathing slowed to nothing. A slight but firm pressure was building around his inner core, wrapping tighter and tighter, as the circular movement of the crosshairs became smaller and smaller; stiller and stiller. He felt himself cutting free of all physical sensation as he floated out on a warm sea of infinity, no longer aware of his finger gently squeezing the trigger. The world was silent. The crosshairs froze on the bridge of the governor's nose. Time stopped.

The bullet went through the barrel in less than 100 thousandth of a second. It crossed the 253 yards to touch the Governor's forehead just as Ali's brain began to register the sound of the shot. One millionth of a second later, the Governor was dead. His head vanished, exploding in a pink mist. He collapsed like a sack of water, utterly lifeless. No one was ever in any doubt as to whether the Governor had died painlessly. He had.

'Click bang done,' Ali smiled, slipping the rifle into a waterproof holder. He clipped an empty bleach bottle to it, then lobbed it into the Sacramento River flowing past the bottom of his empty office block. Shielded from view by the building, he stepped into space, plunging twenty feet through the water before floating gently back to the surface. He grabbed the gun and flipped the demand valve out of the front of his jacket. The scuba tank would easily last an hour, more than enough time for him to swim the five miles downstream to where his boat lay anchored. Sliding over the bottom of the riverbed, he allowed the current to carry him for forty-five minutes, not stopping until the GPS on his wrist gave him a position directly under his jet boat. The visibility was next to zero and he circled around feeling for his anchor. He had secured it to the boat's anchor line with a Bimini twist: a secure knot which is rarely used and difficult to tie but is also highly recognisable by touch, as it closely resembles an elongated noose. It wouldn't be wise to break surface, rifle in hand next to the wrong boat; with a couple of good ol' boys in it, asking him politely what the fuck he thought he was doing.

Feeling an anchor line, Ali made sure it was his before pulling off his clothes, tank and scuba gear and wedging them under a rock at the bottom of the river. Then he floated up to the surface wearing only his bathing trunks. Seeing everything was as it should be and no one was in sight, he stepped up the diving ladder and into the boat. Just another holiday-maker, taking a dip to cool off from the summer's heat.

He switched on the engine, pleased it started at the first turn of the key, then poured out a cup of coffee from his thermos, savouring it slowly as he waited for the engine to warm up. Finishing the cup, he pulled up the anchor and got back into the large captain's chair to ease the jet boat gently downriver. Once he had control of the six knot current, he checked the way ahead was clear before opening up the throttle to make the boat plane. At thirty-five mph he would be back in his trailer on the side of the riverbank in two hours. As the boat swept downstream he glanced down at the cold-box by his feet. Inside were two King Salmon he had caught three days ago, which should be fully defrosted by the time he reached the dock at the campground. 'Just another fisherman returning with his catch,' he thought to himself; albeit one with a very dark tan.

The only thing still connecting him to the Governor's assassination was the rifle, which he had stowed in the forward cabin in a golf bag with a Mickey Mouse sock tied over the end of the barrel. He would have all night to strip it down and clean it. Another discipline his father had taught him all those years ago. Ali hoped the old man was looking down on him and if he was, Ali knew he was smiling.

EN GARDE

Apart from his height, he was indistinguishable from the other customers in the tea shop on that hot summer's day. His fashionably long hair was combed back and his neatly trimmed goatee beard wouldn't be considered that out of place amongst the trendies of the more up-and-coming Lebanese of Beirut. Waving to the proprietor, he pointed at his empty cup then settled back into his newspaper.

'Remarkable,' the owner thought as he brought over the refill. His customer had ordered his first mint tea in perfect Lebanese, yet here he was reading an American newspaper, the New York Times which he knew was impossible to get outside of the airport, and even there it was scarce. He had managed a busy restaurant at the airport; taking over the tea house when a stray rocket hit the back his shop a year ago – killing his brother and sister. The tragedy of the loss haunted him daily, making him alert to all forms of danger and highly suspicious of anything out of true. The owner now studied his customer more closely. The man was so engrossed in his newspaper that he didn't glance up or acknowledge his presence in any way. As he poured out the mint tea for which his family's shop had been famous for thirty years, he wondered why anyone would choose to wear sunglasses in the gloom of the corner table. As the man turned a page, a shard of light sharpened the owner's eye, reflecting off a ring the customer wore on the little finger of his left hand.

'Such a ring,' he thought to himself. 'He must be wealthy. Just the kind of customer I need,' and caught up in his thoughts he overfilled the cup, spilling the hot tea which ran across the table, straight under the newspaper onto the man's lap. The customer yelped then leapt up gasping, holding his steaming trousers away from his groin. As he hopped from foot to foot, his sunglasses slipped off and fell on the table.

'You fucking fool. You are an imbecile,' Abdul swore, glaring ferociously.

Now the owner had even greater cause for surprise. The man's eyes were different colours. One was dark green, the other was the blue of the sky at midday. 'How unusual, I would not have believed it possible', he thought, and his mouth fell open as he stared into the customer's face. Abdul continued to glare at him for a few seconds longer before reaching down to pick up his sunglasses. He put them back on with a swift and deliberate movement.

The owner got a hold on himself. 'Please effendi, you are right. I am a fool – an idiot, but I am also the owner and if you will permit me, I will have the trousers cleaned right away at my own expense. As God is my witness I have never done this before. I will loan you a clean dishdash and if you can wait half an hour, your trousers will be returned in perfect condition. Please come into the back now and change. Please effendi, follow me,' he insisted, waving his hand at a door in the back of the restaurant. 'Let me introduce myself, my name is Youssef.'

Abdul glanced around at the other customers in the café; some had half-turned in their seats to witness the cause of such a violent outburst of street slang. It was out of place in this upmarket, polite section of the city. Not wishing to draw any further attention to himself, Abdul followed the owner into a small storeroom at the back, changing without saying a word and returning directly to his table. Picking up his newspaper, he went back to the obituaries section to continue the article that had caused him to forget where he was, before the fiery pain in his groin brought him hurtling back to the present.

The article was headed: "Pioneer of Modern Democracy Dies at 68", and went on to describe the life of Victor Simmius, his biological father. There was a whole page dedicated to him, outlining the extraordinary achievements he had accomplished in his lifetime and their deep, lasting impact on many Western nations. It estimated that almost a billion people had been empowered by him as he forged new political structures rooted in fairness and ownership; many of which were still in place.

A quarter of the page had been devoted to his disappearance. Victor's car had been found with the door left open, next to the River Severn by the Clifton Suspension Bridge. A popular place for those overcome by the pain of existence. A suicide note had been found in the glove compartment, apparently signed in his own hand. Various conspiracy theories were doing the rounds because his body had not been recovered. The article went on to detail the hue and cry over his death, instigated by a suspicious British public who felt his demise was a little too convenient for the Government. It had been given further impetus by a cornered Prime Minister attempting to calm the outcry but achieving the exact opposite result, saying during Question Time, 'In my opinion, Professor Simmius committed suicide in order to promote and publicise his foolish ideology and to put pressure on this Government. He will not succeed.'

'I wonder,' Abdul thought. 'I can't see that tough old bird topping himself. Maybe, just maybe, that dolt of a Prime Minister is right for once,' then realised the chances of that were slim.

The timing couldn't be better. Now no one alive would be able to link him with his attack on the United States. Notably, there was a complete absence of any reference to Victor's recent series of lectures on "We the People", but in every other way the article seemed thorough. There were quotes from several Heads of State and various illuminati, all expressing the opinion that without the Professor's lightness of touch and clarity of intellect, Europe might not have united for another generation. Both sides of the political spectrum were equally saddened by the loss, which the article highlighted at length; noting he had remained independent of any political party throughout his career; enabling him to negotiate agreement when the opposing sides felt they had reached impasse. Astonishingly, the article was in the New York Times. A paper which rarely indulges in swapping out good advertising space for lengthy obituaries on non-Americans.

When Abdul finished reading the article for the first time, he savoured it again more slowly; so absorbed that he let the tea go cold, not breaking from his delight until Youssef came back with his trousers cleaned and neatly pressed. Placing them proudly on the table he said to Abdul, 'Please, effendi. Come and change. The tea is on me.'

'That makes two of us,' Abdul joked without smiling. He folded the newspaper and followed the owner into the back room, apologising for his blasphemous reaction, saying the incident was nothing. 'No harm, no foul,' Abdul lied, pulling his wallet out to hand Youssef a 20,000 Lebanese pound note. 'Just to show you how much I enjoyed the tea,' he said, before asking if he could leave through the back door, as he was going that way and it would save him a few steps.

'Please,' Youssef replied, pulling back the bolts and stepping aside.

Walking out, they both paused to acclimatise to the breathless humidity of the midday. The back of the teashop was situated at the end of a stone-walled alleyway which snaked its way down to a busy main street. Immediately to their right was a crude but newly laid concrete stairway leading up to an apartment over the shop. Turning as if to go, Abdul suddenly asked, 'That was excellent tea, when do you open and close?'

'I open at dawn and close at midnight. I must work hard to pay the bills.'

'I understand. I look forward to seeing you again. Now please put this incident out of your mind...Oh, I see that stairway is new, did you put it in?'

'Yes, I had to. The old one was destroyed in a bombing raid last year. A tragedy which has left me alone in the world,' Youssef replied, turning his head away.

In a show of concern, Abdul put his hand on Youssef's shoulder and squeezed it reassuringly. He smiled warmly before walking off down the alleyway. Youssef smiled after him, happy in the knowledge that all was well. He could measure it by the note in his hand, 'An excellent tip,' he thought to himself. 'I must make enquiries to find out who this man is. It pays to know everything about my customers.' Because there were now two things that Youssef was certain of: his customer was obviously wealthy, and distinctly unusual.

As midnight came, he closed up his little shop and removed the takings from the till; disappointed by the meagre total of 170,000 pounds. He switched off the lights and headed to the rear exit, opening the door fractionally and peering around its outer edge to make sure the alley was empty and quiet before stepping outside. It paid to be careful at this time of night, so he always took the same precaution before venturing into the dark to go up to his apartment. Double locking the door, he heard a light scuff behind him. 'Probably a rat,' he thought, and turned around quickly, only to jump with alarm on seeing a man dressed head-to-toe in black, standing only two feet away.

'Oh it's you! Thank Allah the merciful,' Youssef exhaled, recognising the short man as the one he had spilled tea on, earlier that day.

Abdul beamed a warm smile at him, 'I thought you might recognise me.' In a gesture of reassurance he put his hand on Youssef's shoulder, pulling him onto the eight-inch stiletto in his right fist.

Holding Youssef upright, Abdul glanced around to make sure he was unobserved, then let the body slide over his knees into the deep shadow at the base of the wall.

He pulled the knife out and wiped it clean on the man's dishdash. The stiletto had done its work well – there was only a little blood. Bending down he felt for a pulse, smiling when it became erratic, then stopped. Sheathing the knife under his clothing, he searched for the wad of money he felt sure Youssef was carrying, then walked calmly down the alleyway, peeling off a few bills and dropping them from his gloved fingers.

'That's one concerned local who won't be making enquiries about me any longer,' Abdul smirked as he slipped quietly away.

News of the shocking murder was printed on page five of the Anmag evening edition, with an interview given by the local police captain saying they had found some of the money the robbers had dropped as they escaped.

'Be alert, this looks like a gang of ruthless thieves,' he warned. The police captain was also a middle ranking officer in Hezbollah, so he already knew the killer wasn't a member of any known gang. He ordered his men to look for the culprit and bring him in dead or alive. They had murdered a good man. A man who was well liked locally, which makes all the difference in Beirut.

'Be on your guard,' he was quoted as saying. 'This ruthless killer will strike again.'

THE LUNGE OF THE SWORD

Ali awoke in the hour before dawn and made himself a pot of coffee. After gulping down a cup, he poured the remainder into his thermos flask and went round to open the back of the pickup. Lifting out one of the ten-gallon containers of gasoline he topped up the Nissan, hooked on his trailer and set off towards the freeway; getting onto the i5, heading south towards Los Angeles. Nine hours later, having stopped to refill the gas tank from his own supply twice, he pulled into an RV park on the outskirts of the city and parked in slot twenty-nine, paying cash for a one month stay. Walking casually around the park he threw back the answer "Great to be here," to his new neighbour's, 'How's it going?'

Satisfied all was well, Ali returned to his trailer and stripped down the rifle again before rolling into bed and falling into a dreamless sleep. He needed to be fully refreshed for tomorrow as he had a very busy day planned.

He slept until 4:am, then got up and drove out of the campground leaving the trailer set up for his return. The traffic was thick as usual for a Friday morning and it took him two hours to get to the storage facility where he had parked his stolen motor bike. Swapping car for bike, he strapped the golf bag onto the rack behind the seat and headed towards a gas tanker depot in San Bernardino, on the northern outskirts of Los Angeles.

Like all good plans, his was simple. He would drive to his hiding place on a secluded road, shoot a tanker driver, and leave. When he pulled over and looked down at the fuel depot, he could see the line of gas trucks lumbering towards the security gates to leave the yard. The day shift had just started and Ali knew that if he shot the first tanker driver in line, nothing would leave the depot that day. He made his final checks to ensure the coast was clear then slipped the rifle from the golf bag and went through his ritual of replacing the first bullet.

The range of the shot he was about to make was 560 yards – more than enough for the surrounding hills to distort and echo the sound of his firing. The sun broke over the hillside to warm his back as the first tanker drove up to the gate and halted.

Ali centred the crosshairs on the driver's chest, then gently raised them up to where the top of the windscreen met the roof of the delivery truck. He had previously measured this at nineteen inches from the centre of the windscreen and, as the driver straightened up to go through the gate, he fired. He worked the bolt to reload, aiming at the driver of the third truck in line. The recoil thumped him again and he reloaded for a final shot before picking up the empty bullet cases, slipping the rifle back into the golf bag and driving down into the thick traffic of the 405 freeway. Two minutes later he was weaving his way through lines of cars, heading for his next fuel depot.

It was two o'clock in the afternoon when Ali parked his bike and got back into the pickup. The rifle was lying on the floor behind his heels, hidden in the golf bag with the Mickey Mouse sock tied over the barrel.

The LA Times reported the next morning that unknown gunmen had fired eight shots at three main depots: killing six, wounding one and narrowly missing another; preventing three-quarters of a million gallons of gasoline from being delivered in time for the weekend. The next day only fourteen tanker drivers showed up for work, out of a total workforce of 1800. By Sunday, panic buying and the lack of supply caused half the gas stations in LA to shut down as they ran out of fuel. On Monday, the army was escorting the tankers through streets, which had less traffic on them than people could remember for a generation. Phase Two was now complete. All Ali had to do was wait until things got back to normal, then start Phase Three.

Four days later the interruption to the LA fuel supply was over and Ali drove down to collect his bike. This time, his targets were the gas stations. He managed to create panic in the ones he shot up, aiming to scare rather than kill. He shot one person in the leg, then fired at a pump and the cashier's desk before moving on to his next target. After creating a satisfactory degree of havoc in four gas stations, he went back to his trailer and waited three days before hitting another fuel depot.

By the end of the second week the newspapers and TV networks were doing his work for him: spreading panic and fear; ensuring that very few gas stations had any customers at all, let alone staff to run them. The LA basin was brought to a near standstill as people ran out of fuel or decided it was safer to work from home until the police and FBI caught the culprits. Restaurants and bars became empty and the knock-on effect to the economy of Los Angeles reduced retail spending by a fifth.

JJ was heading the team for the National Security Agency and he soon realised it was likely they were looking for only one man. 'Thank God,' he shouted into the phone when the ballistic tests had borne out his theory. All the bullets had been fired from the same rifle – including the one which had killed the State Governor, of which a small fragment had survived intact. It was either an organised group passing around the same weapon, or one man; probably on a fast means of transport like a motorbike. JJ figured that was the only way someone could get through the LA traffic quickly enough to shoot at the different fuel depots and garages in a single morning.

JJ had done everything he could to catch the killer. At first he had stationed his agents around the depots but when the gas stations started being attacked, he switched the bulk of his force to observe them instead. Somehow, the gunman only picked out the ones he wasn't covering and he didn't have nearly enough men to watch them all. He instructed another team to comb through the traffic cameras and here he had some luck. Camera 4702 on the 405 Freeway had picked up Ali at 8:17 am. When they ran the licence plate through the DMV records, they discovered it was registered to a Mr Sanchez. JJ dispatched a SWAT team over to the address with Rawlins and three of his best agents.

Mr Carlos Sanchez had been very co-operative, but all he could tell them was that he had just returned from holiday in Hawaii, to find his house broken into and some money and jewellery stolen. Rawlins examined the bike and when he looked at the licence plate, he noticed the tax sticker from the DMV was missing. He pointed this out to Mr Sanchez, who looked at the plate in genuine surprise, saying, 'I don't understand. I stuck it on the plate myself.' But Rawlins did. The thief had swapped the plates, replacing the original with a fake, probably so he could use the genuine plate on his own machine. Without that DMV tag, the thief would have been picked up by a traffic cop within a few days.

The NSA analysts ran a very fine toothcomb through Mr Sanchez's life, finding out everything they could about him; only to discover nothing unusual at all. Nothing indicated he was the shooter or connected to him in any way.

Rawlins was certain Sanchez could not be the actual gunman – his hands shook noticeably. After checking with Sanchez's doctor, who confirmed that he had Parkinson's disease, Rawlins told JJ it was impossible for Sanchez to have made any of the shots in his condition. JJ had found one of the positions from where the shots had been taken. The range was in excess of 500 yards. Very few marksmen could shoot that well; certainly not a sick man, who couldn't hit the side of a house at twenty.

They had tracked down everyone who owned a 300 Magnum Remington, to find eight had been stolen in the past six months and ballistic tests on the remaining 384 had turned up nothing. JJ had a lot of pressure coming from on high to produce a lead, but all he had to date was a possible photo of the gunman wearing a crash helmet, which didn't even reveal the man's hair colour. He decided to focus on the motorbike itself, but had drawn a blank there also. If the image really was the gunman and he had taken Mr Sanchez's licence plate, the chances were high that the bike was also stolen.

Nevertheless, he did have a picture and the golf bag on the back of the bike could hold a rifle. JJ waited until they had chased down any purchases of the golf bag itself, which also drew a blank, before playing his last card; one he desperately hoped was right. 'If not, I'm about to send my agents on another wild goose chase,' he thought as he stepped into the press briefing room.

The murmurs subsided into an expectant hush as the newsmen switched their attention and cameras on him. This was the fourth time JJ had held a press conference in his search for the killer, and each time the number of reporters had dwindled. He had hoped to see the room at least half full. He counted heads – only nine. When hungry news reporters wouldn't travel for a briefing on the pre-eminent story of the day, it demonstrated to JJ just how pervasive the fear was, and how ineffective his department had been in dealing with the crisis.

'Thank you all for coming,' he began weakly. 'I would like to appeal for the public's assistance to locate this motorbike,' he said, clicking the screen controller, showing Ali on his bike. 'We believe this person can assist our enquiry. We need to identify him immediately to eliminate him from our investigation. It is also possible that this is the only photograph we have of the gunman. Let me add that we know the licence plate is false. This photo was taken on the nineteenth at 8:17 am, at the San Bernardino freeway ramp in Reseda. I would like to make it known that if the owner of this bike comes forward voluntarily, we will not prosecute him for using a stolen plate. We will grant him amnesty for this offence if he is not the shooter. I repeat, we will grant amnesty to the man driving this bike if he is not the gunman. Now you've all been given a copy of this picture and I have five minutes to take some questions.'

The reporters jumped up and started machine-gunning questions. After replying to a few of them, all in the negative, JJ held up his hands saying he had to get back to work. 'Thank you for your courage in coming along today,' he mumbled, feeling more than a little inadequate.

The next day Ali bought a copy of the LA Times and on the front page, taking up three quarters of it, was a grainy photograph of him riding his bike underneath the headline: 'Is this the gunman?'

'About time,' he thought to himself. After his last mission, Ali had deliberately left the golf bag on the back of the bike; which he had parked in the open at the storage facility. He had debated with himself on whether to leave the Mickey Mouse sock off the barrel, but abandoned the idea, thinking it too obvious. It was only a matter of time before one of the security guards spotted his bike and reported it to the authorities. All he had to do was sit tight for a few days, then drive into the ambush he was sure would be waiting for him. The only thing that could go wrong now was if he got himself killed.

Ali smiled inwardly. God must be preserving him for greatness. Allah could have let him get killed over a dozen times already.

THE PARRY

Two days after the press conference, JJ was jolted awake at 1:am by the insistent ringing of the phone by his bed. Picking up, he recognised Rawlins's voice on the other end. There was uncontained excitement in his deputy's tone. 'We've found the bike, sir. I'm sitting here looking at it. It's got the golf bag on the back and there's a 300 Magnum in it.'

'Thank the Lord,' JJ exclaimed. 'Where are you?'

'At a lock-up in Oxnard,' and Rawlins went on to give him the address.

'Okay, stay out of sight and get a SWAT team down there as quietly. I'm on my way. I'll be there in thirty minutes. Meantime, don't do anything to alert the gunman we're onto him. No sirens, I repeat NO SIRENS, and I want a complete radio blackout. If they need to communicate get them to use their cell phones – nothing else,' he instructed his Number Two.

'I've already done that, sir. I've arranged for them to meet at a gas station two miles away and I've told them to wear workmen's overalls. They should be here in twelve to fifteen minutes.'

'Good man, that's excellent work. I'll meet you at the storage depot in half an hour. Until then I want a constant vigil on that bike. Tell them they will answer to me from a jail cell if they take their eyes off it for a single second. No coffees and no visits to the men's room. They must stake it out quietly and arrest anyone trying to get on that bike. Oh, and Rawlins, tell them to take him alive unless it looks like he might get away, in which case they are to use maximum force – got that?'

'Maximum force,' Rawlins relished, slipping his Colt out of its holster and placing it on the desk in front of him. 'Copy that. I've borrowed overalls from the night manager. I'm sitting in his office by the gate.'

'I'll see you there in thirty minutes or less,' JJ finished, hanging up the phone and leaping for his wardrobe.

Twenty-six minutes later, JJ pulled up outside the storage depot and parked. He was wearing black jeans and a black polo neck and as he stepped into the office, Rawlins pulled out the chair next to him.

'The gunman hasn't arrived yet,' he said, as JJ folded himself into the chair. 'There's the bike, sir,' Rawlins nodded at the slot immediately opposite. 'I've got twenty men surrounding it, out of sight with guns trained and I've got four teams in plain cars, one on each corner for two blocks, with two choppers on standby only three minutes flight time away.'

'Any problems?'

'None I can think of.'

'You've done a great job. What do we know about the owner of the bike?'

'Quite a bit, sir. Seems he drives a white Nissan pickup. Looking at the keypad entry log, the bike was out of the compound on every day there was a shooting. Conversely, it hasn't been taken out on any day there wasn't one. Here's a picture of him,' Rawlins offered, passing over a black and white print taken by the security camera above the entrance gate.

JJ studied the photo closely. It showed a darkly tanned man with shoulder length black wavy hair and a full beard. He was leaning out of a white pickup as he entered his security code to open the gate.

'Here's his application form. He filled it out when he rented the space. The phone number he gave, which also serves as his private access code to open the gate, is no longer in service and hasn't been for twenty days. We've also checked the address on here – it's false,' added Rawlins, saving his best for last.

JJ looked at the form and couldn't prevent a smile breaking across his face – Mr Carlos Sanchez. Looking further down he noticed something odd. 'This rental agreement's for a lock-up. Why's the bike parked in the open?' he asked, as an uneasy feeling began to prick his buoyant mood. 'Why store the bike in the open when he could have hidden it out of sight in a lock-up? See here,' he pointed to a cross-out on the contract, 'This contract's been amended five days ago… and from a lock-up to an open air space. That doesn't make sense.'

'Yeah, that is strange. Maybe he had to move it because the storage facility rented out his lock-up,' offered Rawlins.

'Let's find out now,' JJ ordered, his sense of unease sharpening the edge of his voice.

Rawlins picked up the phone on the desk, dialled, then passed the handset across. A male Californian voice came on the line. JJ introduced himself, then asked, 'Tell me, when the outdoor space was booked, did you have any lock-ups for rent?'

'Oh yeah, we always have a few. Got twelve empty right now.'

'Are you sure?' queried JJ.

'Totally man. The dude asked for an open air space last week. Said he needed to pay less. I thought it was weird at the time. It's an expensive bike and he didn't have a cover for it. He only saved thirty bucks a month and I told him that. I thought he was setting us up for a theft claim, so I gave him a space we could see from the office.'

'Thank you. Was there anything else you thought strange?'

'Not really, but that's why it stuck in my mind and when I saw the picture of the bike on the news, I checked it out as soon as I got in at midnight to start my shift. When I realised they were identical I called the information line and reported it. I'm psyched about the reward. How do I claim it?'

'Someone will contact you. Thanks, you've been very helpful,' JJ said, putting the receiver down slowly. Now his instincts were needling him more painfully. It was a feeling he had grown to trust – it had saved his life twice. Something wasn't running in a straight line but for the life of him, he couldn't think what it was.

'Everything okay, sir?'

'No it fucking isn't,' JJ snapped uncharacteristically. 'This guy's eluded us for five weeks. No one's that lucky so he has to be smart. Blind luck would have put him in our hands weeks ago. To work around us in the way he has, the gunman must have planned things meticulously. So why park the bike in a place we would find it so easily? In fact – damn it all to hell – a place we were guaranteed to find it in next to no time.'

'Perhaps he's hiding it in plain sight,' Rawlins offered limply.

'Perhaps, but that's not what my gut is saying.'

JJ gritted his teeth, calming down a little. After a weighty silence he went on, 'I want this man taken alive at all costs. No head or upper body shots. Any man that kills him will be handing in his badge if he's still breathing after I've debriefed him – got that?' He paused. 'Maybe the son-of-a-bitch booby-trapped it.'

Rawlins picked up his cell phone anxiously, jabbing at the keys with jittery fingers. JJ's sense of unease was infectious, making him nervous. His rising tension was heightened by the knowledge that his boss was normally unshakeable. He had only ever witnessed JJ being ice cool under the most extreme pressure. This was going to be a long night. Perhaps even – a dangerous one. As the call connected to Operational Headquarters, Rawlins glanced nervously at his pistol on the desk, suddenly grateful to see it there. He reached over to slide the gun nearer, placing it with care so it would come to hand – instantly.

COUNTER RIPOSTE

Ali waited two days after seeing his picture in the LA Times, then packed up his trailer for the last time and got into his pickup. It was dawn and a Californian sun was lifting over the horizon pink and orange as he drove down to the storage facility. It was going to be another spectacular day. As Ali swung into the entrance he looked into the brightly lit office by the gate. Two men he had never seen before were sitting behind the desk. One dressed in a black polo neck, the other wearing a white suit shirt under a pair of dark overalls. They both glanced at him then looked away quickly pretending they were discussing something between themselves. Ali knew what it was. They were discussing his arrival. Winding down the window, he tapped in his entry code and as soon the gate lifted, drove in.

'Gotcha' said JJ without moving his lips, watching the car pull up next to the bike and stop. As Ali stepped out of his pickup, twenty men descended on him from all points of the compass, semi-autos and pump-action shotguns pulled hard to their shoulders.

'Freeze freeze freeze! Put your hands over your head.' A man ordered him to lie on the ground. Ali complied, then felt his hands being cuffed behind his back. He was yanked to his feet and forcibly spun around to face the man in the black polo neck striding purposefully out of the office. Stopping three feet away, JJ held up his badge.

'You are under arrest,' he said firmly, reading him his Miranda rights before finishing with his more urgent question, 'Is that bike booby-trapped?'

'No,' Ali replied truthfully.

They locked him in a white van and drove him to the police station where they strip-searched, photographed and fingerprinted him;

then told him to put on a pair of bright orange overalls and cuffed his wrists and ankles to a belt which fastened in the small of his back. 'Wait here,' said an agent, and Ali smiled for the first time that morning. There was nothing else he could do.

It took three hours for the bomb squad to announce the 'All-clear'. JJ took the call in middling surprise, which morphed his sense of concern into a more deepening alarm. Something just wasn't right. Actually, it felt dead-wrong. The rifle was in Forensics being analysed and JJ decided to wait for confirmation that it was the right gun before interviewing Ali. The call came through an hour later.

'Yes,' said the technician, 'You have a match. No ifs or buts about it. The gun that fired those bullets at the fuel depots and garages is lying in front of me. It's almost certainly the one that killed our State Governor in Sacramento,' then pausing before delivering his coup de grâce, 'Better yet, his prints are all over it.'

JJ told Rawlins to charge Ali with eighteen homicides and forty-one attempted murders, then picked up the phone and instructed his secretary to call a press conference for one o'clock; adding that she might say he had the gunman safely behind bars. 'That should ensure the press corps full attendance,' he thought wryly.

Feeling more than a little weary he went down to the canteen to snag a late breakfast. As he walked into the mess hall a few of the policemen recognised him and stood up clapping. Then they all got to their feet applauding and whooping. Standing in line at the buffet counter, the man in front of JJ picked up his tray and moved behind him with a flourish, engineering him a place at the front of the queue. Even the cashier refused to take payment for his breakfast. As he went to sit down, some of the officers made an elaborate show of dusting off a chair and polishing the table top in front of it. JJ stood on the chair and held up his hands as a hushed silence descended across the mess hall.

'Officers and colleagues, we have arrested the "Terminator Sniper". He is safely in custody. We've got the gun he used for all the shootings…and his prints are all over it.'

Rapturous applause exploded around the canteen. After a smile and a quick nod, JJ sat down to eat. He was ravenous and attacked the bacon and eggs with enthusiasm but as his hunger faded, the same uneasy feeling of disquiet that he first experienced at the storage facility, returned to haunt him; sidetracking his mood; putting a crease in his forehead. JJ went over the arrest again from start to finish.

He began seeing what was wrong. There had been no running; no shouts of indignation; no struggle; no protests of innocence – nothing. No reaction and no resistance whatsoever. Just compliance. Full compliance. Arresting Ali had been easier, and certainly quicker, than picking up groceries in a supermarket. It didn't fit the profile of ruthless assassin and cool calculating killer at all. Now that JJ thought about it, there had been no show of desperation, or even indignation on being caught either. Not on any level he could recollect. Then when they searched him, he had no backup weapon on him. 'He must know California has the death penalty,' thought JJ, but he couldn't recall any indication of fear when they caught him. 'Perhaps he's terminally ill or mentally unbalanced,' JJ murmured, making a note to have him examined by the 'Psycho' before the day was out. But if that wasn't it, what did his captive have to gain by giving himself up?

'Shit, that's it!' JJ exclaimed as he stood up to go back to his office. 'We didn't catch him – he gave himself up. He walked straight into our ambush. He knew we were there – yet he still came.' He went through the minutiae of the arrest again, to see if the facts fit his theory. They did. A little too well for his comfort.

Ali had eluded all of his clever traps for five weeks. That meant he was extremely vigilant and had an in-depth understanding of how law enforcement really operated. Not only that, he had parked the bike in the open with the gun sitting right on the back, and without that gun, he would be holding Ali for bike theft at best. He hadn't worn gloves either, leaving a perfect trail which ended at Death Row. Either his captive had become very sloppy or perhaps over-confident: his ego leading him to believe he was untouchable. But if that was true, the man should have exhibited some distress; given some protest; or at least shown some fear on being caught. In JJ's experience captives always squealed their innocence or surprise. Ali had done neither. His uneasy feeling was morphing into real anxiety. If the medical report proved Ali was sane, then he was definitely missing a piece.

'Well done,' Lieutenant Samuelsson smiled as he put his head around the door of JJ's office. 'I love it when the good guys win.'

'Yeah,' said JJ slowly, sounding a little unsure. He was beginning to wonder if they had won. 'God, the press conference,' he remembered, jumping up from his desk to hurry along the corridor, eager to tell the world the terror was over and that ten million people could go back to their normal routines for the first time in over a month. As he strode towards the briefing room, JJ hoped that this time, the damn room would be full.

"Terminator Sniper Terminated," screamed the headline in the LA Times the next morning, quoting the words JJ had used at the press conference. The paper had devoted the first five pages to the story. At the bottom of the third page was an article originally written for the Economist magazine by Dr Rubin Tamarein.

Dr Tamarein was the head of economic research at UCLA. He attempted to put some financial numbers on Ali's five-week campaign and its impact on the LA basin. He blandly noted that bankruptcy applications had increased by twelve percent from the same period last year and he expected the figure to escalate rapidly over the coming months. It was hard to ascertain the exact amount, he explained, because not all of the data was in, nor would it be for six months. He added that the total cost effect, caused by people not being able to go about their normal routines for five weeks, had yet to be realised across the length and breadth of the economy of Southern California.

However, using the computer models we have developed at UCLA, a conservative estimate for the loss is somewhere between forty-five and fifty-five billion US dollars. This will rise dramatically as more businesses collapse from the catastrophically weakened environment they now face.

He was calling on William Mann, the newly elected President, to respond to the localised economic crisis in the same way he would treat a natural disaster like the floods of Central California. The predominantly logical part of Dr Tamarein's mind headed the article accurately, though quite inappropriately: *"Economic Bloodletting".*

THE FEINT

Ali was sitting on a metal chair in interview room three, when JJ and Rawlins walked in. He didn't look up. He sat motionless. The same position he had been in for two hours: poised but unmoving. His hands were resting lightly on his thighs, his back was straight and his blank eyes were staring into middle distance at ten o'clock. JJ stepped in front of him.

'Are you are Ali Bin Mohammed?' he asked formally.

'Yes.'

'Are you comfortable? Would you like the handcuffs removed?' JJ offered politely.

'If you are going to remove them forever – take them off. Otherwise there is no need,' Ali challenged.

Rawlins jumped straight in. 'Yeah Ali, get real comfortable man, coz you're in a shitload of trouble and headed straight for Death Row. We've got the gun with your prints all over it and Ballistics have matched the bullets we recovered. You're the sniper that's been terrorising this city for the past five weeks. You killed our State Governor, and man, you're toast,' Rawlins spat out, slapping fingers into his palm to drive home each point. Everyone in the room, especially Ali, knew this was the set up for good-cop bad-cop and he switched back to staring into space. JJ and Rawlins exchanged a glance, then each picked up a chair and swung them around to face Ali. They sat down only six inches from his knees and looked at him coldly.

'Now, Ali Bin Mohammed,' JJ pronounced the name perfectly. 'We need to verify who you are and ask you some questions.'

Ali responded with a silent glare.

Rawlins pounced again. 'Listen buddy – you'd better talk to us. We've got one night with you before the spooks get here. They've got Federal Warrants for terrorism, while we just want you for plain old homicide. If they find out you're not co-operating, they're gonna arrest your ass, take you off to God knows where and make damn sure you do co-operate. So it's your choice. You decide which one you're more comfortable with. Telling us with the lights on, or telling the spooks from under a tank of iced water.'

Ali looked at him squarely. 'My name is Ali Bin Mohammed and I am thirty-one years old,' he said in good but accented English.

'Where are you from?' asked JJ, and they went through the information to confirm his identity. Ali gave his address at the trailer park. Rawlins took notes then left the room. He dispatched a forensic team over to the trailer, then tapped Ali's name into the Interpol database requesting a worldwide search.

Walking back into the interview room, he was in time to hear JJ ask: 'Why did you do it, Ali?'

'To show it could be done.'

'To show what could be done?'

'To show that one brave man can stand against many.'

'But why would you want to stand against the United States?'

'Because you make war on other countries – killing millions and destroying families.'

'So you are at war with us, Ali. Is that what you're saying?'

'No. You are at war with us!' Ali shouted vehemently, pinheads of spittle forming at the corners of his mouth. 'I am defending my people from your aggression.'

'Who are you fighting for?'

'The 24th Revolution fights for all the people and innocents slaughtered by the US.'

'Is that the name of your outfit? The 24th Revolution?'

'Yes.'

'Do you know anyone here in the US, Ali? I mean this must have taken a hell of a lot of organising. I don't mind saying that you ran rings round us for a while. Someone must have helped you. Where did you get the gun? Did someone give it to you?

'I bought it using Carlos Sanchez's ID.'

'What about the money – who gave you that?'

'The money is my own.'

'Someone must have helped you.'

'Everything I did, I did on my own,' he admitted truthfully.

'Look, Ali, you've got to give us something better or by tomorrow evening you'll be begging to tell 'Them' everything.'

There was an empty silence before their captive spoke again. 'I am not scared by your threats. But I can see you are frightened of torture. Let me tell you, there is no greater torture than the oppression and destruction I've already experienced at the hand of your country…and there are far worse things than dying,' he added, thinking of his sister Nadir; the first person he had ever killed. An act of love.

'Really?' sneered Rawlins. 'Like what?'

'When you have seen your family butchered, you die inside.'

'Okay okay, let's move on,' interjected JJ. 'How did you get into the country?'

'I walked across the Mexican border.'

Over the next two hours Ali answered all their questions truthfully. He didn't have to lie because they never asked him the one thing he would have lied about. 'Whatever happens, they must believe I am speaking the truth,' he reminded himself. He knew they would cross-check everything he told them and it was vitally important he gain both men's trust. So he told them everything – everything else. How he had hung around outside a Spanish owned travel agency until a man who looked similar to him went inside. Ali had followed, watching the man sit down unsteadily to book a three-week trip to Hawaii. He saw the man was ill because when he lifted his hands they shook violently. Shadowing him home, he was delighted to find his house stood at the end of a cul-de-sac, hidden from casual view by a high hedge. Breaking into the house when he knew Mr Sanchez was on holiday, Ali had searched through his records and found Sanchez's driving licence, noticing it was classed MI for motorbike use. The bike in the garage – a Yamaha R1. Using Sanchez's birth certificate, he swapped the licence plate for a duplicate he bought at Wal-Mart; putting the original, which had the DMV tax sticker, onto an identical bike he stole the next day. Then he purchased the gun in Mr Sanchez's name, using the man's birth certificate and the driving licence for identification. As he waited the ten day cooling-off period before the gun was handed over to him, he planned his depot attacks using the stolen bike. When questioned about why he hadn't simply stolen Mr Sanchez's bike,

Ali explained that he didn't want to alert Mr Sanchez to the theft of the bike and give the police an early lead, as they must have realised he was on a bike from that very first day, when he shot up the gas tankers at three different locations in one morning.

'And if we started looking for Mr Sanchez's bike we would have found the storage lock-up sooner,' Rawlins said, shaking his head at the simplicity of the scheme.

'I also thought that if you interviewed the owners of the bikes, Sanchez's illness would eliminate him from your suspicions, providing me with continued use of his ID.'

'That's pretty clever Ali. You're a smart guy,' JJ encouraged, trying to build a bridge between them to gather more information. Because he could no longer escape the thought that something was definitely wrong. Interviewing Ali had removed his last lingering doubt. He had been hoping Ali would tip them off to it inadvertently, but so far he hadn't. Ali was co-operating. Answering all of their questions fully, perhaps passionately, but JJ could read body language well. He knew that Ali's passion was sincere, underlining the truth of his answers. There was nothing untoward about any of his replies and there were no apparent inconsistencies in his story. Having interviewed him at length, JJ had formed the opinion that he was dealing with a very clever and extremely tough operator. His kind didn't make mistakes. Not ones as foolish as leaving the bike in the open with the gun on the back – in a place it would be found in a day or two. Worse, Ali's behaviour seemed completely rational, without any trace of the egotism he was expecting to uncover.

JJ's logic was at war with his instinct. His mind told him that it was over. But he was now sure that Ali had deliberately walked into their ambush. So something else was in play. JJ was finding it increasingly difficult, but decided not to ask the two questions which were stabbing at the forefront of his mind, promoting real anxiety in him:

Why would a smart operator like Ali allow himself to get caught so easily? And if it was deliberate, what in Hell's name was really going down?

THE DOUBLE-EDGED SWORD

Leah's BlackBerry shrilled loudly at precisely 15:00 on the seventh of July, or 7/7 as it became known to the world. Britain changed forever on that day – the same way America did on 9/11.

It was the first call she had ever received on it. She never used it herself as she felt 'They' might be listening to her conversations or reading her emails, so she had to dig deep in her bag to retrieve it. The screen showed 'Enter password' and she tapped it in. A message flashed up: *UK under terrorist attack. All agents to report in SS,* meaning 'safest soonest'. Leah hit the reply key and the screen fizzed into a video image of Steve Williams, her contact at MI6.

'Sorry to disturb you,' he started, then stopped. This was her cue to switch off the BlackBerry if anyone was within earshot and she looked around casually to make sure the coast was clear. The nearest person was 100 yards away and she clicked 'Enter'.

There has been a major terrorist attack in London using suicide bombers. We are asking everyone to provide information and spec out what could happen next. Please come home at one of the times listed below.

In her case 'home' referred to the massive stone edifice that stood alongside the Thames in central London. The headquarters of MI6 – Thames House. The taped message froze while she scrolled down the list of dates and times. 9:pm tonight was free and she touched it in with her fingernail.

Later that evening she walked into an empty elevator at the back of a supermarket car park, half a mile from MI6 HQ. Positioning her BlackBerry next to the panel of lift buttons she pressed the enter button on her PDA three times in quick succession. The floor dropped from under her as she went down fifteen storeys below street level.

This was the discreet entrance to the granite monolith and given her position as Under Secretary to the British Ambassador in Qatar, she thought it somewhat better not to be seen strolling up to the front doors of MI6, keys in hand.

Walking down the long corridor, she passed by ranks of offices and rooms. There was an air of busyness and haste in the hallways as people hurried past her with unseeing eyes. 'This has really shaken up the hive,' she thought.

Finding the door to briefing-room nineteen, she stepped into an empty room that had a desk with a file on it and her MI6 number printed across the front. Opening it, she scanned through a questionnaire asking for any information on the attacks earlier that day. She ran her eye down the list of questions then pulled out the chair to sit down. She was in no doubt that if MI6 were asking for her opinion, they must be asking everyone for anything. 'It's hard to believe a sophisticated intelligence service like MI6 had no idea this was going to happen,' her commonsense told her.

The questions included: 'Do you know anything relevant?' 'Do you know anyone involved?' To all of which she ticked 'No'. She began feeling a little guilty as she wasn't being of much help, until she noticed two questions nearer the bottom: 'What is their next course of action? What is the worst attack they could launch now?' After pausing to think about it, and with some trepidation, she decided to write down the plan that Victor had confided to her – The Sword of Damocles. It was certainly the worst attack she could imagine and although sworn to secrecy by Victor, this was MI6 – the capital of secrets, and this was a critical situation. Surely he would have approved? With her patriotism tipping the scales over her former promise, she itemised the steps of The Sword of Damocles. When she finished writing, she slid it into the manila envelope underneath the folder, sealed it, and left.

It preyed on her mind for the next few weeks. She expected them to contact her when they digested the terrifying scenario she had outlined, but no one ever did. After returning to her hectic job in Qatar she didn't think about it again for a considerable length of time, until one bright summer's morning in early June when she was arrested. She was in bed in her London flat, on a well earned two week break, when the knock on the door came.

'Madam, as we are charging you under the Official Secrets Act, I don't have to give you a specific reason for your arrest until we have you safely secure. As far as I'm concerned that means the Station.

Please get dressed and come quietly. These women officers will accompany you to your bedroom and I warn you, they are both armed and know how to handle themselves,' said the Detective Inspector, holding his badge under her nose.

They put her in the back of a police car and drove her to Paddington Police Station with the siren wailing. Here she was processed and given a pair of denim overalls to wear. Although she repeatedly asked for an explanation, the only reply they gave was that she was being charged under the Official Secrets Act and an Inspector would be along to interview her.

They handcuffed her and led her up to a cell on the sixth floor.

THE SWORD OF DAMOCLES

Ali could see pearly light tinting the barred window above Rawlins's head, heralding the dawn of another beautiful Californian day. 'It must be around 6.30,' he thought. Rawlins had been looping around the same questions for the last two hours when the door opened and JJ put his head around it to nod his colleague outside. 'Anything?' he asked.

'Not really,' Rawlins replied, 'although I'm pretty sure he's been operating alone.'

'Hungry?'

'Cut the horns off and stick a fork in its ass.'

'Let's talk in the canteen. I'll buy and you can brief me.'

An hour later they returned with a tray for Ali.

'Like something to eat, Ali?' JJ asked.

Ali looked at the tray in disgust. 'I don't eat pig.'

'Then take the bacon off. Godsakes,' seethed Rawlins.

'What time is it?' Ali asked, ignoring the tray.

'7:45,' JJ replied.

'Why? Got an important meeting somewhere?' Rawlins joked.

'Do you have a copy of the LA Times I could see?' Ali asked JJ, without acknowledging Rawlins.

'Oh yeah? Enjoy reading the papers with your breakfast, do you? Coz those days are done my friend,' Rawlins grinned.

'If you let me see the newspaper, I'll tell you why you will release me by the end of the month,' Ali matched Rawlins' smile with an equally humourless one.

'Oh God, here it comes,' thought JJ.

Rawlins leaned close to Ali, putting his nose an inch away. 'Listen buddy. Your last day of freedom was yesterday and don't think it will get any better because our convicts don't like terrorists. You're gonna get ripped to pieces way before we can strap you to a gurney.'

JJ tapped Rawlins on the shoulder and nodded at the empty chair next to him. That unsettling feeling was seeping through him again. 'You mean you want to see yesterday's paper, don't you Ali?'

'Yesterday's or today's. I want to read about my arrest.'

'Okay, if you want your fifteen minutes of fame, I've got yesterday's on my desk upstairs, Rawlins. Go get it for him. I'll wait here.'

His deputy straightened up testily, throwing back a look of annoyance as he stalked out of the room.

'Now tell me what's really going on here?' JJ probed, the moment they were alone.

'Show me the paper first,' Ali replied, pushing the breakfast tray as far from him as his chains would permit.

They sat in a frigid silence until Rawlins returned. JJ motioned him to hand over the newspaper.

Ali took it eagerly.

"Terminator Sniper Terminated" screamed the headline. Underneath was a picture of Rawlins holding up a mug shot of Ali with both hands, as though it were cup he had just won in a sports tournament. Ali glanced at it quickly, then tossed the paper aside. With a triumphant smile lighting up his face, he began:

'My name is Ali Bin Mohammed. I am Lebanese and I am thirty-one years old. When I was thirteen, I was orphaned by the Heavy Armour Division who raped my sister, shot dead my mother and father and threw my baby brother into a burning house, alive. I am not a terrorist. I am a soldier. I have carried out my mission to precise military standards.'

'Military standards? You killed eighteen innocent civilians,' Rawlins exclaimed.

'And how many innocent civilians did you kill in Vietnam, Korea and now the Middle East?' came Ali's sharp response. 'I said earlier that we are at war, but it is not our choosing. It is the policy of the USA to inflict war across the globe. Your country will now experience what you have made us live with for decades. The American taxpayer has paid for it and supported this warmongering country for generations. All of you are responsible! It is not good enough to say 'I am a civilian and had no hand in this'. I too was a civilian until my family was butchered by your allies. That made me into a fighter for my people and for all those you have crushed and oppressed. I am a soldier. The people I killed are responsible for the deaths and suffering of nations. I could have killed many more than I did. I shot three tanker drivers at a range of 500 yards, with three straight shots. I rarely miss. I only killed the minimum number to achieve my objectives. No more, no less. I am a soldier of conscience.'

'A soldier of conscience?' Rawlins repeated in disbelief.

'Nothing less. I only killed the murderers who are ultimately responsible for the deaths of millions. All of you are guilty! And I am sure you have killed people who are innocent,' Ali said to Rawlins, who gave his answer by looking away.

'So you think we're going to let you go because you're a soldier of conscience?' JJ asked slowly.

'No. You will release me because my capture is a signal.'

'A signal? A signal for what?' JJ said calmly, feeling the bottom of his world vanishing from under him.

Ali nodded at the newspaper, 'Now you have announced my arrest to the world, you have triggered the next wave of freedom fighters. Two snipers will now attack America. When you capture or kill one of them, you automatically release another two. And so it will continue...'

'You mean that because we've caught you, two more are about to start?' JJ gasped in horror.

'Then four, then eight. Then sixteen, thirty-two...'

'Fucking shit!' exploded Rawlins. 'So that's why you wanted to see the paper'

'Your own nightmare has begun,' Ali said darkly. 'When the media report the capture or killing of one of my courageous brothers and sisters of freedom, it acts as the signal for the next wave to attack. Your problem doesn't stop. It doubles.'

'How many fighters are there?' asked JJ, regaining his self control.

'About 900. But I do not know our exact number.'

'Do you know who or where, they are?'

'No. I do not know any of them – or where they are going to strike next,' he replied truthfully.

'Then who does?' Rawlins said in earnest.

'Whoever designed this plan.'

'Who's that?'

'I do not know – I have never met them. There is one more thing. Once it gets past two, the next four are suicide bombers. If you still do not agree to our demands, or refuse to release those you have caught, the next wave will firestorm your cities – right across America. They will also attack your infrastructure. So it's not just the number of freedom fighters that will increase by your efforts and captures – the severity of the attacks becomes more destructive and terrifying. Believe me when I say it is terrifying, because I have lived with it all my life. Your economy will fail and you will not have the financial means to make war. You will be stopped by The 24th Revolution. Finally and forever.'

JJ stared at Ali in raw shock. Rawlins had slumped back with his hands thrust deep into his trouser pockets, frowning. There was a tense, pregnant pause before JJ croaked out, 'How do we know this isn't simply a threat, Ali?'

'You will find out in one week's time, when two more freedom fighters commence their operations.'

'Who are The 24th Revolution? I've never heard of them before,' Rawlins asked quietly, his voice now tinged with respect.

'It is the banner we fight under. A name that will fill all Americans with fear…for much longer than fifteen minutes,' Ali smiled.

'What are these demands?' posed JJ, calmly batting Ali's propaganda to one side.

'I will ask you to take the handcuffs off now.' Ali held his arms straight out at Rawlins.

'If we do, will you tell us your demands?' JJ asked.

'Yes, on condition that you do not put them back on.'

JJ lounged back in his chair and extended his legs straight towards Ali: heels on the floor; toes pointing at the ceiling. Completely unaware that the act of showing the soles of your feet to a Muslim is insulting. He took a deep breath and let it out slowly through his nostrils – a hangover from his smoking days.

'Take them off him.'

'But sir…'

'I said take them off!'

Three minutes later, JJ ran full tilt up two flights of stairs to the office section, leaving a shell-shocked Rawlins outside Ali's locked cell with the express order that he was not to repeat anything to anyone, without his prior authorisation.

'Can you get Bruce Cougar on the phone, please,' JJ asked a secretary, trying to make his voice sound calm; then noticing with annoyance that his hands were quivering. 'And I need it on a secure line now! Top priority,' he snapped, abandoning the ploy.

'Yes sir. There's an empty office at the end of the corridor. Please wait in there and pick up when the phone rings. This may take a few minutes.'

Bruce Cougar was in charge of the NSA, and JJ's immediate boss. As JJ waited for the call to connect, he ran through his mind the series of events surrounding Ali's capture. Putting all the pieces together, he tried to see if there was anything which could add the lie to Ali's story. But his frantic mind knew the nagging doubts he had harboured over Ali's arrest, fitted precisely with a man who had intentionally got himself caught. 'Oh God, he's just the messenger and he really thinks we'll let him go. Jesus, we might have to,' he swore as he picked up the ringing phone.

Twenty minutes later Bruce Cougar clicked down his own handset with a grimace. He eased back in his comfortable office chair and put his hands behind his head. Shutting his eyes in a frown of concentration, he began analysing the information that had just been relayed to him by one of his most capable field agents. His sharp mind had the rare ability to take a complex set of circumstances and break them down into their component parts. It was this skill, together with an unswerving patriotism, which had fuelled his quick rise through the service. He had come a long way since he signed up twenty-seven years ago and he focused his entire intellect on the time-bomb that had just dropped straight onto his desk.

'There must be a flaw here somewhere,' his instincts tugged at him, while his mind screamed back "Where?" 'There has to be a weakness here somewhere,' he repeated, but invariably his thoughts kept returning to only two things: should he believe this Ali or not? And more importantly, should he alert the President to the danger?

The problem with notifying the President, was that he would ask for suggestions on a solution. Given the time frame of seven days before the next attack and his dearth of information on The 24th

Revolution, he couldn't think of any sensible course of action to prevent the next two terrorists from launching their offensives. Besides, until they did start attacking he had no idea who to look for, or even where to begin looking. Even if he put all the considerable resources of the NSA to work on this, he knew from bitter experience that without a degree of luck, it could take months to track down just one or two of them. More horrifically, when he did catch up with them he instantly released a worse attack, conducted by twice the number of terrorists; leaving him with a bigger problem to solve.

And Ali had given himself up! After eluding one of his best agents for five weeks. Otherwise they would be still hunting for him. The remaining terrorists were going to do their best not to be caught, or blow themselves up in the process. In all probability – somewhere very public: creating panic and devastation wherever they struck. As he thought it through in more detail, he began to see it as the most daunting threat he had ever come across – there was a high chance the world he knew had changed forever. He could see that if Ali's threat held true, America was never going to be the same open and free society it had been up until today. A tremor of anxiety shuddered through him. They would have to catch all of the terrorists, but he didn't know where to begin looking, or even their exact number.

Thinking ahead, he ran through his mind the scenes of sixteen terrorists unleashing their brutal attacks on sixteen different cities in the same moment: visualising the chaos and mayhem. The image alone was distressing enough, without considering the likely apprehension and fear that would grip the untouched parts of the country, when he eventually caught up with those sixteen. He could see the populace holding its breath, desperately hoping the next wave of terrorists wouldn't attack on their own doorstep. He wondered how people would feel as the sixteen turned into thirty-two, then sixty-four – multiplying the violence; pouring molten terror across the entire country. It wouldn't take long before the cities under attack blamed law enforcement for incompetence if they couldn't catch the terrorists. Meanwhile, the people living in the cities which had been spared, would begin to resent the fact that he had caught them! Especially when his arrests triggered an outbreak of violence in their own city, straight afterward. In the not-too-distant future, law enforcement was going to be detested if did do its job; and thought ineffective if it didn't.

As the unassailable fortress of law enforcement came crashing down and its previously successful way of maintaining law and order disintegrated, what would be the end result one year from now? Anarchy? His logical mind reeled at the thought and for the first time, he experienced the hapless fear of a dead man walking. Which made him focus on whether he would even be able to protect his own family in a raw, semi-lawless world. Shaking himself out of this train of thought with a healthy measure of self disgust at the speed his lower mind had abandoned its higher duty, he tried to think of a way to prevent the plan from coming to fruition. But with mounting dread, he couldn't think of any course of action to take, or even a way to stop the knowledge of the menace leaking out. All the terrorists had to do was post their plot on the web, or phone a few journalists, and the terror would spread like a plague.

The only credible solution was to arrest all the militants at once. But how do you identify a person sitting quietly at home doing nothing – except waiting to attack? It was also likely that the terrorists would be operating in cells, with none of them knowing who the others were. In which case, he would only be able to arrest those he did uncover prematurely for conspiracy – a charge he knew was very difficult to pinpoint or prove, without a tip-off or an accurate communications intercept. That was a mistake the terrorists would certainly avoid making.

'Bruce Cougar, you're caught between hell and the devil,' he muttered at the ceiling.

His only immediate hope, was the plan had been used to fool Ali into thinking there were many others like him, when actually, he was the only one. Should that prove true, it would look like he'd been sucker-punched by a lone wolf.

It was a visceral pile of reeking crap whichever side he sniffed it from, and just on a political level alone was fraught with the distinct possibility that his career was on the line if he couldn't round them all up in one go – and quickly.

Coming to a decision, he leaned across his desk and hit the intercom on his phone. The moment his secretary answered he barked, 'Get Mortimer on the line. This instant.'

Craig Mortimer was the head of Homeland Security. Terrorist attacks on American soil came well within his brief.

'Thank Christ it won't have to be me who tells the President,' Bruce said, reaching for the ringing phone.

'Hi Craig,' he began anxiously. 'Tell me something… Are you sitting down?'

KING'S GAMBIT

The White House. 11:03 am

The Oval Office seemed to shrink in size as the sixteen men and three women crowded onto the sofa, armchairs and additional dining chairs brought in to accommodate them. If anyone had put a missile through the window that morning, it would have taken out the heads of every major Agency responsible for the protection and stability of the American people and ipso facto, the free world.

The meeting had been convened at extremely short notice and twelve hours earlier most of the people in it had been unaware they would be sitting in the Oval Office at this particular moment. The exceptions were Craig Mortimer, Bruce Cougar and the President himself, William Mann. Four had flown in from holiday and some had travelled all night to answer the Presidential Decree summoning their immediate attendance. The bank of secretaries in the hall outside had worked all through the previous afternoon and evening to arrange this extraordinary meeting. Anyone who was anyone in William Mann's administration was present that morning. Among those selected were two men who held ultimate responsibility for the economic stability of the USA: Jamie Mermersetter, who headed the Federal Reserve and Joe Rantong, in charge of the Treasury.

William Mann got up from behind his desk and stood his full height. He appeared outwardly calm but his demeanour was grave and his brow furrowed with an obvious concern. He ran a hand through his short salt and pepper hair and as the doors closed, swept his gaze around the room, silently demanding their attention.

'Ladies and gentlemen, thank you all for coming here today at such short notice. I know you have interrupted busy schedules to be here this morning. I would like to say up front that I do not want this matter discussed outside of this room, without my personal authorisation.' He paused to let the words sink in, adding, 'This is to include your wives, husbands and close support staff.' He looked at them sternly to reinforce the point, then paced slowly around the desk and perched on the front edge. 'Obviously you are aware that something important has come up. Let me state that what is about to be discussed – if true,' he looked at Cougar pointedly, 'has the potential to be the gravest threat to this country since the Cold War. Now Bruce, please start us off with your briefing.'

Following the President's lead, the head of the NSA stood up. 'You all know about the sniper who has been terrorising the West Coast for the last five weeks. I'm sure you also know that we caught him three days ago. During interrogation, he told us that he is the first of many, who are already on our shores waiting to begin sniper activity and suicide bomb our citizens and cities.'

A wave of shock rippled around the room and Bruce waited patiently for it to subside. He had their full attention now – he could tell by the weight of their stares. 'I should add that we have been unable verify whether this Ali Bin Mohammed is telling us the truth, but he has said the next wave of attacks will begin four days from now and the manner in which they will take place constitutes a serious threat to our stability – if it proves true. The plot he unveiled is quite unnerving and in essence it's this: there are roughly 900 terrorists hidden inside our borders waiting to attack. Ali Mohammed was the first; every time we capture or kill one of them, two more will be unleashed to replace the one we've taken out. So catching one releases two, then four, eight, sixteen and so on.' The room had now gone eerily quiet as his audience gazed at him with mixed expressions of horror and bemusement.

'Unfortunately there is a more sinister aspect. Each wave of terrorists will deploy more extreme tactics. The next pair will conduct sniper activity, like Ali. Following them come suicide bombers, and the third wave will attack our infrastructure and set fire to our cities. We've been told they won't stop until we accede to their demands, which include the withdrawal of our forces from Afghanistan and the Middle East, and the release of all jailed Muslims. Not just from our own jails but from Israeli, British and anywhere else they are held. This request is impossible to effect quickly enough to prevent further bloodshed, even if we decided to go along with it. Additionally, the signal to release each wave will be delivered by our own media as they report on any captures of these men; who incidentally call themselves The 24th Revolution.'

'Men? You mean terrorists, Bruce,' Simon Bernstein, the Secretary of State said accusingly.

'No he doesn't.' William looked at him sharply. 'And let me make one thing clear to all of you. I don't want any of you using that term while this thing is rolling out.'

'With all due respect Sir, *that is what are they are,*' Bernstein argued.

'Listen to me carefully,' William said. 'More than half the world thinks we are evil crusaders. And one man's terrorist is another man's freedom fighter. We will not raise the stakes to that level. We will not glorify or deify them with that title and status, which at the same time will raise the level of fear among our own citizens. We are not going to award them with a title that begins with 'terror'. They are criminals – only. The last thing we need is people thinking they are being 'terrorised' by 'terrorists'. I trust I make myself clear. Now Craig, perhaps you would fill us in with your assessment,' he finished, walking back to his chair.

William stole a glance at each of them in turn, trying to gauge their immediate reactions. All of them had political backgrounds and were used to the unexpected in most of its forms but clearly, this had them all shocked to the core. Some had their mouths pursed shut and all of them were wearing expressions of horror and disgust, or perhaps… 'It's raw fear,' he confirmed to himself. As he looked at each of them, he tried to spot an expression that was calm in the vain hope they might have a ready solution to the problem. But there was no one. Not a single person sat unmoved as the ramifications of what had they had heard went in deep.

Craig Mortimer stood up as Bruce resumed his seat. 'Bruce Cougar apprised me of the situation as soon as he found out about it yesterday. As well as the details he has outlined, there is another point for us to consider. Whether we accede to these demands or not is probably academic, because this plot may be designed with a more subtle goal in mind: to sow fear among our citizens and stop them going about their normal activities. This will cause acute financial withering followed by instability, something Ali Bin Mohammed has more than proved to us in LA already. Their hope is that they will cut off the oxygen which sustains our might – namely the financial wealth which backs our strength. Without that, we will be forced to withdraw from most of our global military strategies anyway. This will hand them what they are really after – whether we like it or not. Tragically, there is a precedent for us to compare this with. When the Washington sniper and his seventeen-year-old accomplice started shooting, it shut down an estimated 25% of our retail market in three cities and, as most of you are aware, 65% of our economy is retail based. It appears that Ali Mohammed achieved an even greater scale of disruption and although the final figures will be impossible to determine for a while, it looks like he shut down nearly a quarter of the economy of the LA basin and probably about 10-15 percent of the economy of Southern California during his campaign. Most of the dollars there tend to be spent six times before falling into a savings account, or coming out of circulation in other ways like import, so the total effect of his destruction is likely to be in the fifties of billions. If this strategy of theirs works in the way they intend, by stopping people going about their normal lives, or impacts consumer spending significantly, then by the time the seventh wave start attacking us – only sixty-four people – we will have lost close to quarter of a trillion dollars; raising our gross national debt while reducing our overall wealth. A net loss of half a trillion, possibly in less than four months.'

William held up his hands to quell the storm of protest and violent exclamation erupting around him. 'Please, ladies and gentlemen. Please...Thank you. Allow me to add: this assumes we catch all thirty-two of them, plus the previous sixteen, eight, four and two. It also assumes they only conduct sniper activity and we know that is not their intention. Obviously, ladies and gentlemen, this is not sustainable for us. Even if we put the army on the streets of our 220 cities and manage to contain their activities – a highly theoretical step at this stage – the interruption to our citizens going about their lawful business will be substantial. In reply all this enemy has to do is wait, before springing up again wherever they see opportunity.'

The moment he finished everyone began talking at once with the exception of the President, Bruce Cougar, Craig Mortimer and the Federal Reserve Chairman who was hunched over with his hands clasped in a tight pyramid over his nose. He was staring into space, immersed in his own train of thought. Noticing Mermersetter's poise, William asked, 'What is your view of the financial implications of this, Jamie?'

The room went deathly silent as Mermersetter sat back to find the stony looks of everyone in the room switching onto him. 'My view, Mr President, is the financial costs Craig estimates are wrong, and by a long way. If, and I say if, we have to face this kind of organised campaign, the effect on our Stock Market, coupled with a possible run on our banks will cause a dramatic fall in the dollar. That in itself will be closer to three trillion without factoring in retail spending. But countries have been at war before and survived, think of Britain during the Blitz. We have excellent computer models to help us cope with this. In theory, our country will not go bankrupt if we put in place the various controls and measures we have at our disposal. However, we have one unique disadvantage – our size. The biggest threat to the stability of a nation is the inability of a country to feed its citizens. On balance we are consumers not producers, hence our gross national debt rather than surplus. Our other Achilles heel is that all commodities are valued in dollars and if the dollar slips in value, then in simple English we will have to pay more for the oil, food, clothes – everything that we import. This will cause inflation and the supply of goods will become very costly, very quickly.'

'I mentioned our size. When a person buys a packet of Twinings tea in California, it is distributed from a logistical centre in North Carolina. In fact, all food and most other goods tend to be distributed from centralised warehouses and delivered across vast distances. Unlike say Britain, where all goods are within a day or so's walk, we face a situation where a breakdown of our logistical networks will cause a glut of milk in some areas and a complete absence of it elsewhere. The process to change this will take time. Even if we imposed effective Government control on distribution, all the terrorists – sorry criminals – have to do is sabotage our road and rail networks and we would be unable to feed a vast number of people spread across the 5000 miles of our continent.'

Joe Rantong, the Treasury Secretary finished off for him, 'He's absolutely right. And hungry people get desperate within a very short period; say a month or two at most. We can expect widespread unrest at best, and full scale rioting at worst. And unlike any other modern country – most of our citizens are armed.'

Quickly, William spoke into the vacuum his Treasury Secretary had created in the room. 'I am chairing this meeting and I will conduct things my way. Firstly, I will take questions, then we will discuss any ideas or solutions I hope some of you may have. After you leave, my office will allocate tasks to you all – tasks which you will prioritise. Now then, who wants to go first?'

'How did they get in?' asked the Secretary of Defence.

'These criminals look Hispanic. Ali told my agent he walked across the Mexican border.'

'Is there anyway to track these…people down?'

'It's virtually impossible if they entered illegally.'

'Do we have any profiling on them at all?' asked the Secretary of State.

'Not at this stage,' Bruce responded. 'The problem I face is the populace becoming increasingly disillusioned with law enforcement as the violence escalates. And we can't arrest anyone if we don't know who they are. We won't even know where any of them are going to strike until they actually start attacking.'

'That's the devilishly clever piece of this plot,' William agreed. 'We could end up arresting a lot of innocent people if we are not careful, and that will start to undermine a major tenet of our justice system. Innocent until proven guilty.'

'That's quite correct, Mr President. We are in the invidious position of having to find anonymous sleepers who will not show their hand until it's their turn. Only then do we get a chance to track them down, and when we do catch one the problem doubles. We could be locking down one city, to find thirty-two attacks springing up in others 2000 miles away. It's a nightmare scenario. The knowledge that more chaos and destruction is waiting just around the corner will eat away our citizens' morale in a very short period. It will draw a blanket of cold fear across the entire country.'

'What worries me the most,' William added, 'is when I consider the citizens of an untouched Seattle desperately hoping the militant in Dallas isn't caught, in case the next wave of attacks starts up in their city. If we don't catch them, people will die and we will be viewed as ineffective. And if we do catch them even more people get killed! It won't be long before anyone's desire to have the law functioning at all gets undermined.'

'Someone or some group must have organised this. Can't we track him or them down? Get the names of these criminals and round them up?' suggested the Secretary of State.

'Ali was first contacted on the web in a chat room,' Bruce answered. 'Afterward all contact and arrangements were conducted by post. Neither of which are easy for us to pick up on, or track.'

'Is it possible they are all Lebanese?'

'Given the sweeping demands from Ali, it's probable that they're from a variety of different countries. During the last five years we have arrested and are currently tracking Canadians, Bosnians, even Swedish and Danish Muslim nationals, who can enter our shores very easily via our visa waiver program.'

'How did Ali elude our security agencies for so long?' asked another, and the questions went on for forty-five minutes until William stood up abruptly. 'Okay, we've identified the problem areas, now I'm open to a few suggestions – anyone?'

'Well, if they are going to use our media to signal the release of each wave, why don't we censor it?' the Secretary of Defence posed.

'That's not a bad idea,' Bruce agreed.

William looked over at him. 'The problem I have with that, is I feel we should warn our citizens they are being shot or blown up, so they can get out of harm's way. Even if we do restrict reporting, what's to stop witnesses blogging, emailing or simply telephoning the details to each other? Remember, there are only six degrees of separation between anyone and everyone in the world. Witnesses, police, fire crews and the rest, will notice in a very short time that the attacks are not appearing in the mainstream media, then realise we are covering it up. That will put massive pressure on this Administration, accelerating the mayhem. I also happen to believe that the unknown promotes fear.'

'Unfortunately you're right, Mr President. We can't censor effectively even if we wanted to. People might accuse us of assisting the efforts The 24th Revolution if we don't warn the inhabitants of a particular city they are being attacked,' agreed the Secretary of State.

'Okay, if we can't censor all reporting, then what about some?'

'All well and good, except that risks prolonging this attack. Also, we will have to record some captures or the Government could fall through perceived incompetence. Then when we do report our successes we trigger the next, even bigger wave.'

'What about their guns and explosives, can we track them?'

'There are 280 million guns here at the moment – so that's just a bigger haystack to go needle-hunting in,' Bruce replied. 'I do have a team looking at explosives but there's nothing to stop The 24th Revolution stealing them, or using commonplace items to manufacture bombs, like fertilizer, sugar and diesel fuel, as Tim McVeigh did. Even gunpowder can be bought off the shelf at any Wal-Mart.'

'Then we must concentrate on the source,' Bruce suggested. 'Go for the person or people who organised this and get them to tell us who their operatives are.'

'I agree,' William smiled for the first time that morning. 'I want you all to co-operate with any requests from Craig or Bruce, both of whom I would like to remain behind if there are no further ideas,' he asked hopefully, to be answered by an icy silence freezing over the room. 'Okay, my office will be in touch with each of you specifying your individual instructions before the end of the day. Send in anything you might turn up. Thank you for your time and assistance,' he said, bringing the main meeting to a close.

They filed out of the room in a stony silence as William sat down.

Leaning his elbows on the desk, Will spoke in earnest. 'I want you to talk to your opposite numbers in every country where you can be sure of co-operation and secrecy. I've already spoken to the leaders of Britain, France, Germany and Japan, who have assured me they will fully co-operate with your Agencies. Now is there anything my office can do to assist you?' he asked.

To the requests for finance and other resources, William simply said 'Granted.' After waiting a few seconds, he got up from his chair and paced slowly round to the front of his desk. They looked up at him hopefully and with good reason; he had come a long way, from humble beginnings, to the highest office in the world. All of them were aware of his abilities. They were substantial.

During his meteoric rise in the election the previous year, the press had picked over every aspect of his background, unearthing a highly unusual past. His alcoholic father had died in a gambling dispute one week after he was born and his mother never remarried, working as a cleaner and babysitter which left little time for him and his sister. It seemed he had taken on the role of father, holding two and sometimes three jobs at a time. He did not stay in any of them long and always picked widely different job types. One newspaper noted that he hadn't duplicated any type of work although he had held twenty-six different jobs by the time he was eighteen.

Picking up from where his father left off, he started gambling and invested half his earnings in the Stock Market, giving the rest to his mother. He did moderately well against a background of Market turmoil and very well when things stabilised. Just before the Stock Market crash he had liquidated his entire portfolio and used the money to buy his mother a small house beside a river, which flowed into the Atlantic nearby. He went there regularly and was often observed fly fishing its banks and the adjacent shoreline, with more than one paper recording that he returned every fish he caught, even the keepers. One reporter had questioned this action, stating it was un-American to throw back a good fish dinner and asking how a "wuss" would be able to control the military if he became President. His published reply had been that it was "a fair trade"; he taught fish about hooks in return for the thrill of the ensuing fight, ending with the question: 'Which would you rather be? A fish caught by me or a fish that has yet to be caught?'

In a small harbour up the coast, he had fallen in love with his wife Julie who had captained a small lobster boat. They were inseparable and had two children.

Just after his eighteenth birthday he had been awarded a scholarship to MIT for building a crude but functional electron microscope using the metal-working tools in his high school projects lab; finishing the unheard-of feat in thirteen months. When he had been handed the coveted scholarship in front of a packed student hall, the Dean presenting it made the comment that in twenty-two years he had never heard of any effort quite so magnificent or difficult, as the building of such a complex machine to win the prestigious award. William's reply had become legendary and was still quoted at MIT. Walking nervously up to the microphone stand he said shyly, 'Thank you. Without this scholarship I couldn't finish my studies as my family is poor. But I didn't build the microscope to win this award. That idea was recommended to me by my physics Professor, after I had it working.'

The Dean had leaned in towards the microphone encouragingly. 'Then what was the reason?'

'The reason I built it, was so that I could study things that are very, very small.' And the hall had exploded in loud cheering and applause, with some of the students clambering onto their chairs, whooping. It had taken the Dean a full five minutes to regain control of the hall.

He went on to study astrophysics and nuclear chemistry and was awarded a Professorship at twenty-seven. He then taught for nine years before taking a senior post at NASA. By the age of forty he had woken up the sleeping giant, focusing it on long range probes designed to gather information which would enable satellite stations to be set up on distant planets in the future. A strategy he frequently referred to as "The Second Small Step for Man". He had been offered the position of Director of Operations by the Director himself, who told him he would be willing to step aside, but instead William had handed in his resignation, saying his work there was complete. He took a directorship at WHO. It appeared he was frustrated there, finding the promised assistance by governments rarely forthcoming and he left after only eight months; taking a senior position at a Wall Street bank, which he left three years later to start his own management practice. After five hectic years he sold the business for thirty million dollars and announced his interest in running for the Presidency. He was derided by both parties, so he ran as an Independent. What neither party knew, because William never told them, was his campaign war chest of 450 million dollars – garnered from clients whose businesses he had radically improved, several of which were large media organisations. He had campaigned on "Building a Better World", and when he stood in front of the American people and spoke of his vision for both them and their fellow man, they saw the essential truth in his words and realised the wisdom of his global thinking. What began as a small but loyal following, rapidly escalated into a movement which had broken attendance records at the voting booths. Already in his short term of office he had gained the respect of Republicans and Democrats and had developed a reputation for galvanising people; sending them in the direction they should be going while ensuring their personal fiefdoms were very secondary to their public service.

'I did say that I have spoken to the leaders of several other countries. You will find the doors of their co-operation wide open to your Agencies. For possibly the first time in history we all have unanimous agreement.' William smiled at them momentarily before unleashing the brilliance of his mind.

'What I am about to tell you must be kept strictly between ourselves. As you know, part of my job includes hearing about plots and attacks coming at us almost daily. They no longer keep me awake at night but this one did,' he stared down at them, 'because I find it wholly insidious and evilly clever. When I heard the tapes of Ali's interview, I was struck by how easily he had divulged this plot. By his own admission he wanted us to know an attack was coming – the point being that an enemy doesn't normally forewarn its opponent of an attack – which means it could be a bluff. They want us to believe they are blackmailing us into doing what they want; holding us to ransom against the price of financial stability and the openness of our society. But I don't think that is their real intention at all. This has been put together for another purpose, not three to five years of poverty and hardship. We survived the Great Depression and we will survive this,' he said forcefully, the strength of his conviction harnessing their thoughts and emotions to his rationale. 'To me, this attack seems wholly designed to spread fear itself – not kill as many of us as possible – or they would have attacked as each cell or individual got into position. Oh no, they've waited until they are all in place, risking detection in the process, which means they all think this plan is worth waiting for. All of them – every last one. No exceptions and not a single pariah cell stepping out of line and letting rip. We must be extremely wary of the mind of this enemy for that single reason. This person is able to control large numbers of individual cells through his ideas alone, and that elevates his abilities to an almost prophet-like status. They also say they will only attack when their turn is announced, and the signal for them to strike will be delivered by our own media. Curious that, because our media is also the voice and barometer of our free society.'

'Yes Sir, and in addition,' interjected Bruce, 'they are turning our law enforcement into the vehicle that drives the attacks, instead of it stopping the bloodshed.'

'Quite so. This plan is a horribly creative way to spread panic and fear; to do something longer lasting and far more destructive than a more traditional attack. I believe it has been designed and implemented for a different purpose. I don't think they are trying to destabilise our country through financial mayhem, though that is an inevitable by-product. I think they are using our media and police to attack the very foundation stone that mankind has built on – right across cultures and for countless centuries. Because if every time law enforcement catches one of them, the problem then escalates, it won't take long before people start thinking of law enforcement as the cause of the problem, not the cure. And not long after that, gentlemen, our citizens will begin hoping and praying the police don't catch any of the culprits if they can't round them all up in one go. As our people become increasingly restricted and their lifestyles become ruled by a desire to live in peace and be left alone, they will either turn on each other, or start understanding, then empathising, and eventually siding with their opponents' ideology. They will do this, just to put an end to the violence and chaos. I trust you know that the winning of your enemy's mind and will is the ultimate victory of any combat. I believe the real intention of this plot is not to release jailed Muslims – that is just a symbol of their victory. Their real intention is to destroy the one thing that civilisation has relied upon since Gilgamesh. They are attacking the very thing that has delivered our past freedoms and is intrinsic to the future prosperity of mankind. They are attacking the rule of law. I believe that is their real target and if we can't find a way to stop them, they are likely to achieve their objective.'

He walked back behind his desk and sat down before saying, 'Gentlemen – this is one battle that we will not and cannot, afford to lose.'

'Do you really think the stakes are that high?' Craig asked.

'I'm in no doubt our enemy does. And if you mean the future stability of mankind co-existing in an organised and law-abiding way, then yes, that's definitely on the table. Imagine what it would be like to live without the law. That situation is only a short step from people wishing it was no longer in place. Ask the people of San Francisco how they feel about the police catching a militant in New Orleans when it instantly triggers sixteen attacks in their own city.'

'I agree, Mr President. They are trying to reverse a process that people have relied on for centuries. There's no doubt that any police successes will be feared after a while and the world will change with that.'

'Indeed. Their real target is the fundamental principle behind having the law in place: i.e. to stop the violence. Now the law will exaggerate it! Well, I for one gentlemen, will not let that happen.'

'Yes, Mr President. It does have the potential to bring about a lawless world. Once this concept is seen to work or cause a degree of hardship, any dissatisfied group can copy it. Sadly, we've inherited more than a few of those. A large number of which are home-grown.'

'I'm just grateful they made the mistake of saying roughly how many they have against us,' William said. 'It makes me think that whoever designed this plan doesn't want to cause worldwide instability. They only want to harm us.'

'We must put this down hard, Mr President! The copycat syndrome can't be underestimated. If anyone duplicates this, we can expect them not to tell us the number of attackers they have. Then the fear would linger on, even after we'd arrested them all.'

'And if anyone follows that lead, Mr President...'

'So we all understand what we are up against here and why we cannot afford to fail. The fabric that holds our world together is in danger of being ripped to shreds.'

'What would you like us to do?' Bruce asked simply.

'The solution is clear,' William replied. 'We must find the person who put this together. Don't announce you are looking for one individual.

However I'm fairly sure you are or we would probably have heard something about this by now. I want you to focus your efforts on finding him or her. By all means use your spare resources to round up these criminals, but you won't get them all in the next couple of months so I intend to organise the contingency for that myself. You will concentrate on apprehending the person who is behind this plot. And when we catch him – alive if at all possible gentlemen – we will hand him over to an internationally convened court and apply the full rule of law to him, then send that message back through the media. These people are really attacking every one of us, in all four corners of the globe. If they succeed, they remove the safety and security of the law. But if we can find the person responsible, we have been handed the perfect opportunity to unite this world on a common platform of peace. Now I've got a speech to prepare in case Ali's promise holds true. It could be the most important speech any American President has given since '61. Don't waste a single second. Find him and bring him to justice…preferably alive.'

As they got up from their chairs in preoccupied silence, he added, 'Oh, there is one more thing…I want to interview Ali Bin Mohammed myself.'

With a small sense of satisfaction, William saw that for the first time that morning their objections were unified.

'You can't glorify these criminals with a meeting, Mr President,' Craig exclaimed.

'You're right,' William agreed. 'So why don't I go disguised as someone else?'

'Why, Mr President?' Bruce asked. 'If there is anything you want to know I will get it for you.'

'I need to understand precisely what type of person we are up against. I didn't get that from the tapes of Ali's interview, so I have no choice but do it myself,' William replied, cleverly sidestepping his real reason for wanting to go.

'It's a very unusual request, Mr President. It would have to be conducted with the utmost discretion.'

'It sure as hell will be! We certainly can't walk him up the White House steps,' Craig said angrily.

'You're right. I think this is one of those odd occasions when the mountain must go to Mohammed,' Will said half to himself, but concluding the matter for them all.

THE WHITE QUEEN

There came a sudden, electrifying sound of keys clinking outside her cell, then a clang as the door swung open and a senior policewoman Leah had not seen before, stepped inside. 'I'm the Head of Public Relations. I have come down here personally, to apologise to you,' she said, lighting a beaming smile on Leah's face.

The officer handed over the box containing her clothes, led her to an interview room and asked her to change. 'Please leave the prison overalls here and I'll be back in a few minutes,' she said, exiting the room without locking the door. Returning a few minutes later, she escorted Leah down a long corridor maintaining a constant stream of excuse. 'I'm so terribly sorry. There was a genuine mix up and the arresting officer thought the charge was real. I trust we treated you well and you weren't too inconvenienced. If there is anything else you need please don't hesitate to ask, but I hope we can draw a line under this. It was a genuine mistake.'

Leah was so delighted to hear she was getting out, that she pushed aside her indignation and readily agreed to it being an end of the matter.

'Thank you for your understanding. There is a car waiting to take you back to your apartment. Please follow me,' she said, guiding Leah towards a bank of lifts.

Eight floors down, the doors hissed open on an underground car park with a white Jaguar saloon parked directly in front of them. The rear door was open and Leah could see the dark outline of a man inside, while the chauffeur standing on the far side of the car was studying her every move with a hawk-like expression. His coiled menace appeared very SAS, and he didn't get the door as she stepped up to it.

Bending down to look in the back, she recognised the man inside with mixed feelings of shock and relief. It was Jimmy MacCack. He was staring at her with a stark look frozen on his craggy features. His unblinking eyes and stern countenance told her that she wasn't out of the woods yet. It spelled trouble. The kind that went way past the boundary of a limited friendship.

'Forgive the inconvenience, Leah. But this is the only way we can pick up our agents quickly, without the other side thinking we are chums,' he said in a deadpan voice.

'What the heck is going on?' Leah asked, shutting the door behind her, looking at him as openly as she could.

'You know full well what's going on, Leah,' he replied coldly.

'I do? Then perhaps you can remind me.'

A serpentine smile sliced across his face. '*Are you telling me don't know why you're here?*'

'Yes Jimmy, I am. And this had better be good, because I can feel my diplomatic skills disappearing fast,' she answered, matching his stare.

'The attack on the US of course! You know all about it. And don't even think of lying to me, Leah, because I can always tell.'

'*Attack?* I give you my word that I don't know what you're talking about.'

He suddenly went completely still in his seat, staring at her fixedly for half a minute. Then he spoke unexpectedly, 'Ali Bin Mohammed.'

Leah looked back at him, nonplussed.

'*Myeee God,*' he drawled slowly, 'you really don't know. I'm sorry Leah, but I had to see your answer for myself,' and he raised his right hand, revealing a small pistol that had been hidden from her view by the flap of his suit jacket. He dropped it casually into the holster under his left arm, with a nonchalance that implied he was only tucking a handkerchief away. Turning away from her, he spoke his next words to the window. 'Leah, do you remember that brief you wrote, way back on 7/7. Two, four, then eight terrorists being released in co-ordinated waves?'

'Of course I do. Why?'

'Because it's happening right as we speak. So I think it only fair to warn you that you are a suspect. Actually, you are our prime suspect.'

'*Your prime suspect?* That's ridiculous, Jimmy. Why would I tell MI6 about an attack I was going to carry out?'

'Och I know,' he said resignedly. 'That's why I wanted to see your answer myself. The Prime Minister gave the American NSA access to our low level files. They discovered your brief and when they found out what you did and where, they asked us to pull you in for questioning. I'm sorry for the inconvenience, but I have no option in the matter. My hands are tied tighter than a Bishop's in a brothel.'

'That sounds refreshing. So to play ball with the Americans you arrested me, which also puts a nice safe distance between Leah Mandrille and MI6, if it does turn out I am the culprit,' she said quietly, but with the bell of accusation ringing in her tone.

'Precisely. I'm not going to fob you about Leah; but this situation is desperate, and desperate situations allow for any, that is any measure.'

The tension drained out of her. Now that she knew what this was all about, she relaxed. It was a complete misunderstanding she realised. All she need do was prove her innocence, which shouldn't be difficult, before going back to her apartment for a long hot bath and a glass of chilled wine. But deciding to match his technique for getting at the truth with her own, and with no feelings of remorse – he had set the bar by having her arrested – she chose to serve it up raw. 'Jimmy?' she said sweetly, 'You do know the plan wasn't mine?'

'Really? Then whose is it?'

'It was Victor's.'

He jerked in his seat. Then shot her a startled, questioning look.

And Leah set him up. 'He only told one other person, a man named Abdul-Aliyy Saqr Khalifa...' waiting pleasurably before launching her missile. 'Who happens to be his son.'

'Good God Almighty,' he exploded. 'You mean this plan was all Victor's idea?'

'He called it The Sword of Damocles.'

'*The Sword of Damocles?* Christ, he understated that by a wide margin,' Jimmy blustered, annoyed partly with himself but mainly because Victor had never seen fit to entrust him with the concept; while obviously being more than happy to have him face it.

'Rather a worrying thought knowing Victor was the architect, isn't it? Well I thought it was, which is why I only told MI6 about it, not another living soul. So drive me back to my flat, Jimmy, and I'll think no more about it.'

'I had absolutely no idea. Unfortunately your brief didn't get the

161

corrrect priority. If I had only known it was a plan of Victor's, things would have been different, but there were so many briefs then and…'

'You simply couldn't process them all, could you?' Leah finished for him. 'Well that's one good thing, providing you're certain no else one else has read it. That should have been a left back there, Jimmy.'

Ignoring her comment, he glanced down to pick a minute piece of fluff off his knee. 'Where is this Abdul-Aliyy Saqr Khalifa?'

'I've no idea. I've never met him,' she said truthfully, going on to recount the story Victor had told her about his son and the tragedy of his early life.

'This is more serious than I first thought,' he murmured after she finished her monologue. 'I was rather hoping the terrorists were bluffing on some level.'

'I think you should assume they are not.'

'I suppose we would find out soon enough – the attacks would stop after a few arrests.'

'Where is this happening, Jimmy? I haven't heard a whisper about it.'

'You know that sniper they caught in LA?'

'No, not personally.'

'I'm glad to hear it. Keep this to yourself – he was the first. The first of 900 more's the pity. He told his interrogators that two were now out on the loose – that their number doubles each time the US security forces catch one; and more perplexingly, the severity of the attacks increases once the Americans hit four, then eight arrests. To add insult to injury, the publicity of the arrest itself is the trigger for the next wave to launch. It's the most destructive, poisonous thing I've ever come across. God, and I thought I'd seen it all. What the hell did Victor think he was doing? Telling anyone about this? He's blasted a bloody hole in the dam wall. The idiot!'

'What are their terms?' she asked casually, deliberately switching his train of thought onto another track.

'Standard revolutionary bollocks. Withdraw from all conflicts, liberate Palestine, free the resistance fighters. All the usual tripe and quite impossible to effect. After all, Israel's got the bomb and they haven't – QED.'

'How on earth did they get as many as 900 to sign up for this?'

'As many as 900? Gimme a break lassie. In any given week I could get more than a thousand in a single mail-shot of Kabul, Yemen, Islamabad, the list is endless. As long as you choose the hair colour black and you can pay well, you could have thousands to pick from in under a month. No, my guess is he's recruited small tribal groups of fighters. Quicker that way and if you split them up, you are assured of their loyalty to the cause. So no, the issue isn't recruitment. It's how did he get them in? Homeland Security is pretty good these days. They should have found three or four trying to sneak in and started looking further. I'll bet you a pound to a penny they didn't come in on visas. Semitic people look much the same as Mexicans to your average border smuggler. Now what else can you tell me about this man Khalifa?'

'There was a picture of him in the Financial Times when he sold his company. Victor said Khalifa was the name he was using, I'm sure he did,' she replied, feeling a warm glow of excitement as she followed the scent of her memory; in the heart-warming conviction that the head of MI6 was now firmly on her side.

'If he has half the capacity for reason and intelligence that Victor had, we must tread very carefully indeed. Christ, Victor, why didn't you let me know about this?' Jimmy gritted his teeth, leaning back in his seat and speaking in an airy tone, 'You're going to find out about this all soon enough, so let me tell you what I know so far. It turns out that the Terminator Sniper they arrested in LA four days ago, revealed a plan identical to this…this Sword of Damocles. He was the first and if he's right, two more will start attacking before the week is out.'

'This is a very dangerous mechanism, Jimmy,' Leah said, deciding to give the knife a twist. 'Victor had no solution for it. No way to stop it once it started.'

'Shit! Then no one does. I had the Prime Minister breathing down my neck yesterday morning, squealing: 'What if this happened in Britain?' He couldn't believe we had no contingency for something like this, especially as it turns out we'd had the detailed plot in our possession the whole time. The problem was, no one bloody read it. It was just filed. I suppose I should be grateful for that small mercy, though the bad news is that it had a low clearance level. It's possible a number of people could have seen it. I've got a team working on that now.'

'So that's why I never heard anything more about it. I was surprised, to say the least,' Leah remarked pointedly. 'I also found it surprising that you had no idea 7/7 was coming.'

He gave her a severe look, raising his finger and jabbing her in the arm. 'You're not cleared to that security level, Leah. Don't ever mention that again. Not to me. Not to anyone – ever.' Then he glanced away quickly, placing his hands on his knees, gripping them tightly.

'I do see your predicament. Jimmy. You could hardly tell the PM you had the plan in your hands the whole time,' Leah said, pulling out one dagger, stabbing him with another. She was enjoying herself.

'It never looks good when an intelligence agency can't piece together its own intel but in truth, it happens all the time. We are simply swamped with information, most of which is rubbish or deliberately designed to mislead us. We can't be expected to know everything, all of the blasted time.'

'I see. So what you mean to say is that I'm in the doghouse because MI6 didn't read a report I submitted to them. Now that's pushing the boat out a little far. Even for you.'

'The world we live in is upside-down, Leah. Perhaps the remainder of your intel can help us right it.'

'Did you turn Victor's world upside down, Jimmy?' she knifed him again. It had the delightful response of making him squirm in his seat.

'If you mean did we cause his disappearance? The answer is no, definitely not. The last thing we wanted was to raise his profile alongside that 'We the People' sedition; having him die under suspicious circumstances. Now every bloody journalist is shrieking it from the roof tops. No, if I had my way he would be very much alive – quieter all round. Look what it's done. There isn't a single person I know who hasn't asked me that same damned question, and the press are having a field day promoting his ideology. It's my belief he did it deliberately. For exactly that purpose.'

'You think he killed himself, just to publicise his ideals? You've been in the job too long, Jimmy.'

'We never found his body did we? He could have faked his own death to put pressure on the Government. I promise you this: if he's done that, I'll take the utmost pleasure in strangling him with my own bare hands.'

'I'm sorry, Jimmy, it's just that... Oh, I don't know. Of course I'll help but I'm a diplomat, so there isn't much I can do.'

'Fortunately there is quite a lot you can do. The only way to show the Americans it was a complete oversight, is to let them interview you and determine your, and therefore our, complete ignorance of the matter.'

Leah couldn't resist: 'Don't worry, Jimmy. Convincing them of MI6's complete ignorance shouldn't be difficult. But you do mean interview – not interrogate?'

He rolled his eyes at her. 'Just answer their questions,' he pleaded. 'Let them do some checking for a week and this will pass. Now, as I am not without some small influence, you will be staying in a beautiful country house, complete with hot and cold running servants, and everything you could wish for to make your stay as pleasant as possible.'

Then letting out a raucous guffaw, he nodded his head at the driver. 'Actually my girl, I even got Parker to pick up some personal items for you. Toiletries and clothing from your apartment. Don't worry my dear, because you won't even know he's been in the place. Will she, Parker?' he harrumphed, his eyes twinkling merrily at the vicious jibe. To round it off perfectly, he flashed her that thin-lipped reptilian grin again and patted her knee like a lecherous uncle. 'Care for a Scotch?' and he reached over for the cabinet between them.

'So it was you who had me arrested,' Leah confirmed to herself. 'You needed time to have my apartment searched uninterrupted. And the bastard's got the gall to tell me!'

'Make that a large one, Jimmy,' she demanded authoritatively, 'And I think it's only fair to warn you – if I find anything out of place I will call the police.'

'No need, dear girl, no need – we've already done that for you. MI6 is completely thorough when it comes to looking after our government staffers.'

'Chin chin,' he smiled, clinking his glass against hers.

PAWN EXCHANGE

Leah was exhausted. She had been awake for twenty-three hours straight, answering both the American agents' direct, oblique and occasionally ludicrous questions. They had been polite but firm, and she had been co-operative and equally firm. The questions surrounding her love life were a bit of an imposition but she understood their relevance and anyway, there wasn't much to tell as she was really married to her career. They feigned surprise on hearing how many lovers she'd had, while having so few longer term relationships.

'It's just that you're a very attractive woman, Miss Mandrille. We can't understand why you haven't found your Mr Right.'

Leah had replied wickedly, 'I simply haven't met him yet...unless he's one of you two gentlemen,' crossing her long legs and smiling sweetly at them, which produced a highly satisfactory lull in the proceedings. It did give her a little joy thinking about one or two of her old flames having their lives carefully unpeeled by one of the most terrifying agencies on the planet. But she was quite sure their investigations wouldn't find anything – there was nothing there to find. Certainly not in her own life and she doubted there was anything subversive in her former lovers. In her high-flying career it didn't pay to go out with bozos, crooks or anyone shady; and her job had forced a nomadic lifestyle on her, making flings more attainable than permanent relationships. Unlike most modern women, she believed that men were for procreating and protection while women were for nurturing and support. The two only mixing well when you added chemistry; a subject which had always been her weakest. She knew she wasn't alone – the divorce statistics said much the same thing to her mind; and her mind was exhausted. 'This really is a fantastic house though,' she thought, trailing her hand along the oak panelling as she went up the staircase to her bedroom. Once inside with the door shut, she undressed and stepped under the shower. After turning it hot and cold twice she collapsed on the bed, still damp.

The sun was streaming through the leaded glass windows when she awoke. She stretched luxuriously and rolled over to see what time it was. 'Wow, I've slept for twelve hours,' she thought, noticing a tray next to her watch, bearing a full tea service. Reaching up, she felt the blue Wedgewood teapot. It was cold. 'God, I'm naked. I wonder which one of them volunteered to bring me up tea? I hope it was JJ, and not that psycho Rawlins.'

Getting up, she showered again and dressed leisurely. There was no rush. She knew the agents had more than enough to check her out thoroughly, so it was only a matter of waiting for them to verify what she had told them was true, then apologise to her, before possibly asking for her help. Because reading between the lines of their questioning, Leah realised she was their only decent lead.

It had been more than delicious to hear Jimmy saying at the outset in his severest tone, 'I'm convinced she's one of us, so let's get this charade over with quickly, shall we? Then we can all move on to catching the person who is really behind these attacks. Make no mistake about it, when your boss gets here tomorrow I will be telling him exactly the same thing, in no uncertain manner,' he barked, wagging a hairy finger of warning at the two American agents.

'Oh God,' she groaned. There was only one way the river of her life was flowing – downhill. The problem she had with side-stepping all responsibility was also the one thing she had deliberately withheld. Leah knew a senior man was arriving to interview her today. She would decide then whether to mention it, as she wanted to assess him herself, first. She hadn't written it down in her 7/7 report or even discussed it with Jimmy, intending to do that only when she was exonerated, because it was also her last ace if things went awry. Her trump card was the secret motive behind the attack, and she thought it better if only a few knew about it. Including those on her own side; especially them, she felt.

After putting on her makeup she wandered downstairs, scenting the delicious smell of cooking bacon which led her to the kitchen. Pushing the swing door open silently, she saw JJ at the stove, wearing jeans and a white tee shirt with the black outline of an oversized finger pointing to his groin and the words "I'm with stupid" written across the chest. She experienced a momentary shock of surprise to see him so casually dressed. It altered the impression she had formed during her interview; his dark suit and garish tie had lent a sinister aspect to his presence which now vanished completely, making him appear humane, almost studenty. 'Perhaps this is all part of the process,' Leah thought, deciding to proceed with caution.

He was moving around the stove with a cat-like grace, a lightness that complemented his athletic build. A lock of blond hair had fallen from the side of his head to touch the corner of his mouth, casting a shadow over his nose and exaggerating the angular profile of his face, leaving only his dimpled chin visible. He hadn't shaved and she could see the spikes of his morning beard winking at her in the yellow light of the gas burner. Overall, he looked damned fit and more than a little devastating.

'Hey. You're up, Leah. I was just fixing a Californian breakfast sandwich. Want one?' he asked, without turning his head to look at her.

'What is a Californian breakfast sandwich?' she replied stepping in, unable to prevent a furtive glance at the bulge the finger was pointing at.

'It's bacon, avocado and tomato, lovingly sliced with no egg. Here have this. I'll make another.'

Pulling out the nearest chair from a breakfast table that would have seated twenty in comfort, she sat down and took a tentative bite. 'Mmmm... This is sublime,' she said through her second mouthful.

'Yup, we don't get bacon like yours in the States.'

'Really? What kind do you have?' she invited, enjoying his attention.

'It's the same as your streaky bacon but without the meat,' he laughed. It was a delightful sound, heart-warming and infectious.

'I wonder how old he is?' she thought. 'He looks just a little older than me, probably early thirties,' she guessed correctly, watching his loose-limbed form making up another sandwich. There was no harm having an ally, and nothing wrong with an attractive one. 'A particularly good looking one,' Leah mused, deciding to go to work on him. 'Sooo, how long will it take for you to realise I'm a good girl?' she asked provocatively.

'Why? Not enjoying your gilded cage?'

'Actually, I'm getting to like it almost as much as this,' Leah waved the end of her baguette at him. 'But I'm a free spirit, so even pampered containment feels a bit like jail.'

'Jail? Lock me up and throw away the key,' JJ said playfully, offering his wrists to her then pulling out the chair opposite. 'Leah, my boss is coming to interview you today. With what you've told us and that glowing reference from Mister MacCack – terrifying man by the way – I imagine he will feel pretty relaxed about letting you go home.'

'*Home?* Do you really believe that?' she queried, unable to hide her disbelief.

'Well...'

'Yeah, I thought not.'

'You're in a unique position, Leah, and we need all the help we can get. We also need it soon and there's no doubt you can help us. Question is – will you?'

'You might think it rude if I refused,' she said resignedly.

'Sure. We might think you were one of 'them' instead of one of us. Anyway, you could still be the mastermind behind this. You knew about the plan way before it started and no one else but Khalifa did. So you say. For all we know the two of you could be in on this together. You keeping a watchful eye on us, playing wounded ostrich, then reporting our progress back to him. It wouldn't be the first time that's happened.'

'Whatever, JJ. I'm not going to dignify that with a reply. Instead, let me say that Victor was very good at keeping secrets. He only told the two of us – I'm certain. And believe me, apart from MI6 I didn't breathe a single word about it and you can guess the reason why. I can't be absolutely sure it isn't someone else but Abdul Khalifa should be treated as a priority. You know...'

'You know what?' he nudged gently.

'Victor was nobody's fool. He never said a single word he didn't mean or hadn't carefully considered beforehand. So if he told me about this plan – which could give away his only son – he told me for a reason,' Leah said, trying to demonstrate her innocence through implication.

'Sure he did. He told you so you can help us stop this maniac son of his. Think you can?'

'I don't know. Maybe. One thing's for sure – I can't while I'm locked up here,' and she studied him closely to gauge his reaction.

'Okay, okay I surrender,' JJ held up his hands. 'Between you and me only, if my boss thinks you can help us he might release you straight away. That's what I'm recommending in my report anyway.'

'Thank you JJ, I'm grateful. Do you know him? Know him well?'

'Yeah, I guess. We work closely. He gives me some pretty serious cases to work on, as you can see.'

'How about personally? Do you trust him?'

'Absolutely. With my life.'

'Then let's hope he realises I'm the help, not the hindrance.'

'I think he will. Well, I hope he will. And I also hope he assigns me to the rest of this case,' he said, flashing an infectious smile at her before taking a massive bite out of his sandwich, conveniently preventing any more questions.

Later in the day, as the peacocks outside began calling the other birds to roost, JJ finished briefing Bruce Cougar on the results of his interview with Leah. At the end, he volunteered his opinion on what they should do with her.

'Let me get this straight,' replied his boss. 'We've got a person who knew about this plan in detail and you want me to release her before we've checked her out thoroughly? If I could predict the future that well I'd be in Vegas right now. The answer is no way – so get over it.'

'Why not interview her yourself, then decide,' was all JJ could offer in return.

'Don't worry I intend to. March her in would you?'

After an hour of answering his insightful and deeply probing questions, Leah looked up at him suddenly. 'Can we talk alone?'

'Sure.' Bruce motioned JJ and Rawlins out of the room.

'No one knows what I'm about to tell you. I didn't write it down in the brief I gave MI6 and I think you should treat it in the strictest confidence.'

'Really? And just what might that be?' Bruce asked cautiously, having already formed the opinion she was extremely bright: capable of making a strong ally or a formidable opponent.

'It's the reason for this attack. What it's really designed to do.'

'Uh huh. And that is?' he asked slowly, remembering the promise of secrecy he had given to his President, forty-eight hours earlier.

'Well, anything they ask for to stop the attacks is a ruse to disguise their real intention. And even if you grant all of their demands, it won't stop The 24th Revolution because they have no intention of stopping. At best they will pause for a little gloat, then issue a brand new set of demands. This plan is solely designed to cause anarchy, by shattering people's faith in the rule of law. If every time you catch someone the number of attacks rises dramatically, it won't take long before a large section of America starts thinking law enforcement's role is amplifying the violence, not stopping it.'

'Okay, hold it right there. Did Professor Simmius tell you this?'

'He did. He said it was the sole reason for engineering the attacks in this way. He believed that within six months people would turn against the rule of law, wishing it was no longer in place. This won't happen initially, it will happen gradually; gathering momentum as the police successes ratchet up the chaos. And a lawless society is ungovernable, uncontrollable. It loses all direction and cohesion, reducing its citizens to the level of independent, self-serving survival. You're on a downhill slope with a tipping point, that once passed, will prove very difficult to reverse. I want you to understand how dangerous your situation is, because this style of attack has the power to take the United out of the United States. People will form themselves into smaller and smaller groups for mutual defence. Cities will turn into ghettoes. Towns will have barriers put up around them. Each surviving group will be guarded by its own townsfolk and most Americans are armed, so they already have the tools at hand. When this gets a full head of steam, it will wind back the clock of civilisation fast. It only takes one town in an area to throw up a wall and the others will follow – immediately afterwards. 'Gated communities' will become an understatement worthy of Victor Simmius.'

'We share the same concern. Do you think Khalifa knows this?'

'He must. I think we should assume the worst and pray for the best, don't you? Now please, if I was the mastermind do you really think I would alert you to this?'

'That's a pretty good point. I don't mind admitting that when James MacCack told me Professor Simmius was the architect of this shit pile, it made my hair stand on end. I don't suppose he offered a way to defuse it?'

'I asked him the same thing but he didn't have a solution. In his view, once this idea leaped out of the box he thought it was unstoppable.'

'Dammit to Hell. We can't think of a way to fight it at ground level either. Look, I'm in a tricky position with you, Leah,' he said, walking over to the window to gaze out across the moonlit parkland. He suddenly turned around, staring at her hard. 'Would you be willing to help us?'

'I can try but I'm not trained for it. So I strongly recommend you pursue all other options available.'

'Of course we will. But I can't let you fly out of here free as a bird until we've checked you out a bit more. However, there maybe another way. I could release you into JJ's custody and you could both make a start together. It also has the advantage of not having to ask your employer, Her Majesty's Government, officially for your help. That can take time and the second pair could start attacking tomorrow, so we need to get moving. I could simply okay it with James MacCack, which shouldn't be difficult – I already know he wants you out on the hunt for this, this... man Khalifa,' he corrected himself, narrowly avoiding the term 'terrorist'.

'That might work because I've no spy training as such. I don't even know how to use this BlackBerry properly,' she replied.

'I can reassure you there. JJ is very resourceful. He's professional, resourceful and highly competent – one of my best. He's so solid that the only people who know what his initials stand for are me and his parents. And one more thing, Leah: we don't call ourselves spies we are agents. Now tell me, if I go along with this, how would you go about tracking him down?'

After discussing it in detail for twenty minutes, Bruce stood up abruptly. 'Let's get JJ in and tell him your idea,' he said, walking towards the door before turning to her with a thoughtful look on his face. 'One last thing Leah – JJ has smarts. He might have worked out the real reason for this attack but in case he hasn't, let's not keep him awake at night, okay? I think it would be a lot safer for the world if we keep that part strictly between ourselves,' and without waiting for her reply, he opened the door and shouted down the corridor. 'Come in JJ, I've got some news you'll wanna hear.'

Over the next hour they fleshed out her idea in more detail and identified the teams that would support them in the field. Then JJ and Bruce Cougar's cell phones started ringing.

'I see ... when, where? Uh huh.' They both clicked off looking anxious.

'Well? What is it?' she asked.

'Leah, someone shot dead the Mayor of New York fifteen minutes ago. Another sniper in Miami has just killed the Chief of Police. Both incidents happened at almost the same time and both gunmen have got clean away. We can't be sure as yet, but this could be the beginning of the second wave.'

JJ insisted on driving them back to London that evening.

'I like the idea of you being in my custody,' he smiled at her, holding open the door of the Audi and waving her inside with a theatrical sweep of his other arm. Leah knew he was telling her where his first loyalty lay, but that he wasn't going to behave like her jailer which technically, he now was.

'It's odd to think he will shoot me without hesitation if he ever suspects I'm siding with Khalifa,' Leah thought, looking at him less objectively again. The understanding didn't lower his appeal. 'Watch yourself girl, this one's on the list of untouchables,' her common sense warned.

'In view of what we are working on together, I think we should maintain a strictly professional relationship at all times,' she shrilled uncharacteristically.

'Right on,' he replied silkily, shutting the door and going round to climb behind the wheel. 'So let me tell you my immediate duties. I will deliver you to MI6 HQ tomorrow for a week's training, then we fly to Beirut to interview the people at Ali's orphanage. My suggestion is that we travel together, but pretend we don't know each other. That way, you can look for Abdul Khalifa without anyone knowing I've got your back covered.'

'You mean: got my back in your gun sight.'

'Leah, I want you to know that I have orders to take you in, or down, if you even hint you're not one of us. It's professional not personal, so please be careful. The stakes are very high and I wouldn't hesitate.'

'Thanks for your honesty, but I'd sussed that already. Don't worry, I know I'm clean and you will too when we catch him. Sooo, where are you from in the US?' she asked, trying to stabilise the conversation.

'I grew up in a place directly above the centre of the earth,' he joked. 'Agent's Rule number one, Leah: no personal questions.'

'That's a pity. I was going to ask you what JJ stands for.'

'That's the beauty of rule number one. It neatly cans the mundane,' he flashed white even teeth at her.

'Yes sir, and that's also the difference between a spy and a diplomat,' she reminded herself gratefully.

'Whoa, that's one hell of a lot of books,' JJ exclaimed, as he walked into the living room of her Kensington apartment. 'I've never seen so many outside a library. Sure the floor will take the weight?' He looked around himself in disbelief, then turned over the cover of the book nearest him: "The Philosophy of Plotinus". 'Wow, some of these are ancient.'

'Oh they're nothing really,' Leah replied casually, putting her hand on his to close the book. 'I rescued them from Victor's library and I haven't been here long enough to have more shelves put up – that's all,' she said offhandedly, watching him pick up another volume entitled "Nietzsche's Moral and Political Philosophy". Leah spoke more forcefully, 'Some are very valuable and shouldn't be handled without gloves. So if you don't mind…'

After dinner in her flat and an early night, they got up and drove the short distance from Kensington to Vauxhall, driving into the supermarket car park to use the discreet entrance of MI6. Leah led them through the maze of corridors to Jimmy MacCack's office. Arriving at the security desk guarding the floor she flashed her ID. 'We're here to see Mr MacCack.'

'He's expecting you both. Please come with me.' The guard ushered them up a long flight of stairs, stopping in front of two tall oak doors. He tapped on one and they heard Jimmy's unmistakeable voice call out 'Come'.

His office was spacious, almost the size of a tennis court with a picturesque view of the river Thames flowing sedately past the building, and very little else. Three-quarters of the floor was covered by an ornate Persian rug, which had the unusual characteristic of being only black and white. At one end stood a large bookcase, but apart from these his office was spartan. Space and minimalism had been welded together *in extremis*, each locked in uncomfortable harmony with the other, making the experience of being in Jimmy MacCack's office as focused and as daunting as possible. There were no pictures on the walls and no personal effects which imparted a sterile atmosphere that was most unsettling. His office was barren, open and weightlessly impressive.

Jimmy was sitting behind a green onyx writing desk with nothing on it but his clasped hands. He got up to greet them and introduce the other person in the room. 'Hello both of you, this is Paul. He's the living version of 'Q' in the Bond films, but far more dedicated and with absolutely no life outside the Service – which makes him quite perfect for us. He's come up with a crash course for you, Leah, so I will hand you into his loving care without further ado. Normally the course takes a month but as we only have a week, I've told him to dispense with lunch. Don't worry, my dear. A smart girl like you will pick it up in no time,' he said, dismissing her with 'Please wait behind, JJ.'

'If you would kindly step this way,' Paul invited, walking her towards the door. Outside with the soundproof doors shut, he asked, 'I notice from our log that you haven't used your BlackBerry much. Am I right in thinking you don't know how to?'

'Well, I know how to use it for reporting in,' she responded weakly.

'Ahhh, it has many more functions than that,' Paul replied, stopping outside his office. 'Here, let me have it. This attachment on the front can open any lock, electronic or manual. It also has a permanent tracking device. I'll show you.'

He spent the first half of the day teaching her its many functions, which were impressive. After four hours she could feel her attention span waning and in an attempt to lighten his robotic technodrone, she asked him when she should put the vanilla in?

'*Vanilla?*' he questioned.

'Yes, when it's baking me a cake,' she smiled.

'*You do know these cost 40,000 pounds each?*' he said, deadly serious.

The second half of the day was a crash course on basic spy craft; how to follow a person or spot someone tailing her. But the most exhilarating part came that evening: gun training at the shooting range in the basement. JJ was there to greet her.

After watching her shoot five rounds from the Smith and Wesson .38, he gave a low whistle. 'Not bad, where did you learn to shoot like that?'

'At a ladies' finishing school…in Zimbabwe.'

He laughed then turned more serious. 'Come on, Leah. How did you learn to shoot that well?'

'My father taught me, then he asked me to teach my two younger brothers.'

'Ever shot a live target?'

'Not yet.'

'Ha! The first time it feels completely different. The second time it's just like target practice.'

'Thanks for the tip. I'll try to forget it when the time comes.'

'And always count the number of shots fired by you and him. Then reload when you still have a bullet in the chamber. That way, if anything happens while you're reloading...'

'Yeah, it's just target practice,' she said squeezing off another clip, making the bullseye wink at them, then disappear.

'How did she get on?' Jimmy asked, when they delivered her back to his office at the end of the week.

'Excellent,' Paul answered. 'I wish we had more like her. By the way, has she signed for the BlackBerry?'

'No, I did. Now will that be all, Paul?' Jimmy said sharply, before turning to Leah and JJ, 'Here you two. These are your papers and travel documents. We decided to use your own identity, Leah, then if anything happens we can scream blue murder that one of our brightest diplomats is missing. Works a little better than telling them one of our agents is missing, don't you know. Now, I don't want you doing anything risky, Leah. You're simply not trained for it and besides, if anyone is going to get killed that's what JJ's for. But if things do spin out, you are to follow his instructions to the letter. And JJ, let me just say that if anything happens to her while she's in your care, I would like you to report it to me in person. Senior NSA agent or no, matters very little to me. Now good luck both of you. Let me wish you very good hunting and be careful out there. Scotch anyone?'

'I think you should pour yourself out a large one, Jimmy,' Leah said offhandedly, trying to make the remark sound ordinary.

'I see. Paul, give JJ a quick tour of your department would you? Come back in half an hour.' He waited until they had both left the room before padding over to the bookcase and pulling open a drawer at the bottom. 'Now what's so bad that I need a large scotch to hear it?'

'Are you convinced I'm onside, Jimmy?'

'Course. Though I'm never a thousand percent certain of anything. Why?'

'I told Bruce Cougar there was no solution to this; but since then, I have thought of a way to slow them down.'

'Really? How?'

'You're not going to like it much.'

'Try me.'

'It will give you cause to doubt me.'

'If you don't tell me now, I'll have greater cause for doubt, so it's up to you.'

'Okay, but don't say I didn't warn you,' and she took a deep breath. 'The chaos and panic will really start to bite when The 24th Revolution get to the third and fourth waves – suicide bombing and attacking infrastructure. That's far worse than one or two people getting shot each week. Let's face it, disabling the rail networks would be far worse. The consequences terrible. As a result, the terror and panic will spread rapidly, over a much wider area.'

'*What are you suggesting, Leah?*'

'I think you should tell the Americans not to go after those second two terrorists.'

'Whaaaat?'

'It will buy us time to track down Khalifa, or whoever is behind this and put an end to it. Assuming that's even possible.'

'You want me to advise the US authorities to let those two maniacs carry on shooting?'

'Yes, I think you should.'

'I'll pour, while you give me one good reason. Soda or water?'

'Straight up if you don't mind, Jimmy.'

'No Scotsman ever minds hearing that from a pretty girl.'

'I'm charmed, Jimmy, but I'm also quite serious and I've got three good reasons, not one.'

'Shoot. My apologies. That's an unfortunate idiom given the circumstances.'

'Idiom? Idiot with an M is closer,' Leah thought, saying instead, 'The principle reason is: the more we catch the worse it gets. So in the interests of damage limitation we only get one good chance to slow them down drastically, and it's by not capturing the first pair. Because when the Americans do catch up with them, the increased ferocity of the attacks will spread greater fear and panic. Secondly, we need to buy ourselves time to track down Khalifa while we minimise the mayhem. And thirdly, we have to react somehow in order to regain any degree of control – however small.'

'But we would be handing two assassins a free pass to kill innocent civilians.'

'I'm aware of that.'

'I should probably have you arrested for just thinking it, let alone saying that to me.'

'I really am onside, Jimmy.'

'In a way I suppose you must be. Unless you are in cahoots with Khalifa and you've only two more terrorists to deal out.'

'It occurred to me you might think that. Unfortunately, there is nothing I can do to make you a thousand percent certain of me. But think it over it would you? Because I feel it's the right course of action and it should reduce the body count.'

'You don't see it, lassie. The President is the only person who could sanction that type of order. He risks being vilified or worse, if it ever got out that he'd told the security services to back off. It risks political suicide, probably jail and possibly worse than that. After all, he would be handing those two shitheads a free rein to murder.'

'Don't think I haven't considered it, Jimmy. But it's a lot better than four, then eight, then sixteen, and you don't need that many men to firestorm a city if you approach it in the right way.'

'Really? How would you go about firestorming a city, Leah?'

'God, I don't know. Wait for high winds maybe?'

'Shit, Leah, you're not in on this are you?'

'No, Jimmy, I'm not.'

'Mother-fucking bastard this is a nightmare!' he exploded, losing control of his temper; draining his Scotch in single gulp. Then shrugging his shoulders, he resumed more evenly, 'I suppose I should thank my lucky stars this isn't happening on my patch.'

'Jimmy, if we don't stop the person behind this, or find a way to break the plan, it's only a matter of time before it does happen here. Let's be honest, there are plenty of dissatisfied groups who would love to try it on if it works out in the way it's designed. So we must do the opposite of what our enemy expects, whenever and wherever we can, or this will roll over us all like a tank. Remember Jimmy, Victor was the architect. Don't underestimate the danger we face. That will add to the problem.'

'There's no doubt their objective is to blow up the legal process. And if the Americans go along with your suggestion, they are doing Khalifa's work for him. Because ultimately, you're suggesting we suspend the rule of law for those two bastards.'

'Exactly, Jimmy, I'm suggesting you suspend it. Not stop it altogether which they are planning on doing.'

'Hmmm, point taken. I suppose there's no great harm in putting the idea to Bruce Cougar. I could leave it up to him to suggest placing the President of the United States on the side of the killers for a while. Because that's what it boils down to, isn't it?'

'Maybe. It depends which side you approach it from. Why not tell him it will protect a greater number of lives from harm and hardship? I mean, it's the odd shooting once or twice a week or cities in ruin. A revolting choice but an obvious one. Think about what's going to happen when they start suicide bombing and burning down buildings.'

'I haven't been able to think of anything else these past ten days. You've not discussed this with JJ or anyone, have you, Leah?'

'No. I really am onside, Jimmy. Now you must decide whether you are on-message,' she added, aware of the risk she was taking in making this dangerous man bend to her logic.

'I'll mull it over, I'll mull it over,' he repeated, ambling over to the window to gaze down absent-mindedly at the thick brown river below. It was flowing like effluent on an inevitable course to its final objective.

And only a fraction beyond his own doorstep.

'The Americans want me to transfer you over to them, Leah. *They think*, that because the attacks are happening on their patch it shouldn't come under my authority. *I think*, you've just furnished me with the reason why I won't.'

QUEEN TAKES PAWN

William Mann stepped out of his armoured limousine and walked through the back entrance of the makeup studio, to be warmly greeted by José Colobian. The renowned make-up guru was known as the "best in the business", or as many preferred it: "unfortunately the best in the business". He often freelanced his skills to disguise agents for the CIA and NSA and he looked William up and down for a full minute before deciding to: 'Go really, really fat.'

Rounding on his two assistants, José shrieked in a tone reserved by Lady Macbeth for doing her washing, 'Fetch me the paddink, darlinks,' he commanded them both imperiously; shooing them away with the hand movements of a ballerina and one last screech, 'Fetch unto me the padding, this instant!' over their disappearing backs as they scurried into the hall-sized wardrobe, returning moments later with mounds of it.

'Not all those you silly things. Just get me the biggest. Really, Mr President, a simple thing like that. I don't know what the world is coming to.'

'I hope I do,' William smiled at him.

Twisting an extra whine into his high pitched voice, José shrieked out again, 'And hurry up you two, you're keeping the President waiting.'

Turning back to William he struck a pose: right hand on cocked hip; head tilting slightly to one side; left hand swinging limply in the breeze. 'You just can't get the staff these days. I don't know what I'm going to do with those two.'

'I'm sure you'll come up with something,' William smiled again. 'Don't worry – there's plenty of time.' He was starting to enjoy this show.

'Here then,' José said, twisting William around by his shoulders to face a long dress mirror. 'Wave a fond farewell to you.' Peering over the President's shoulder he added, 'Take a good long look dearee, because the next time you see yourself you're gonna know what eating hamburgers and drinking a bottle of scotch-a-day for a year looks like.'

'Is that all it will take?'

'It will…if I add a street fight to that slobby lifestyle,' José replied, taking William's jacket.

At the end of the process, José swung the full length mirror around with a grand theatrical flourish. 'Ta-Dah!' William stared at his reflection, not recognizing the 300lb man looking back, while the disfigurement aspect made him appear ghoulish.

'Did a Stephen King movie once.'

'One? I'm surprised you didn't do them all.'

'Trust me, William,' they had been on first name terms from the beginning of the performance José had woven around them as he stuck, greased and prodded the President's hands, face and neck for three hours. 'A nasty scar like that draws the eye away from everything else. So don't be surprised if he stares at it pet, okaaayeee? Just make sure the lighting's not too strong and you'll be the happiest ugly in town. Now I'm sorry it took longer than you planned, so off you go Mr President…. and try not to sweat, there's a dear.'

As William strolled purposefully towards his car, the three of them leaned out of the window to watch him go. 'He was such a nice man. He can come round and get my vote any day of the week,' José said mincingly, turning to his ménage. 'Why can't one of you two, be like him?'

'Fetch me the paddink, dahlink,' camped one of them to the other. And a stilled moment later, his assistants doubled over in fits of uncontrolled giggling. Then completely overcome, they convulsed onto all fours, slapping one hand down repeatedly, in perfect time to their screams of hysterique.

As the full-length version, with shocking close-ups, played across their minds.

REMOVING THE BLINDFOLD

Reclining in the back seat of his armoured car, William knew they had achieved the impossible. They had left the West Hollywood make-up studio, crossing LA to the Orange County lock-up, into which Ali had been secretly transferred, in under forty minutes. The motorbike escort running relay in front of them, blocking off the junctions and waving them though the lights, was the principle reason but even so, it was still impressive. For the last five minutes they had been pushing against rush hour traffic already at a standstill, and they hadn't gained much headway.

'How far is it to the jail?' William asked his driver.

'About a mile and a half, Mr President,' came the chauffeur's quick response.

'Okay, give me the directions and you can drop me off here.'

'The jail is the other side of Downtown, Mr President. You can't just walk through that! The Secs will go nuts.'

The Secs, pronounced sex, was the tag his predecessor's teenage daughter had innocently applied to the security services; though once she had seen their pained expressions she had used it more ruthlessly. Somehow, it had gained a wider acceptance then a more generalised usage, as it seemed to bestow a romantic power on the life and death danger of guarding the President. Besides, if you were the Sex you were the best – and they are.

'I'm in disguise and I want to try it out on Joe Public before I meet Ali. So tell the outriders to disappear, then you can casually pull over and drop me at the kerb. And tell the Sex they can trail me on the condition I can't see them.'

'I'll try Mr President, but they aren't going to like it.'

'Then tell them I'm in no danger unless they are spotted.'

182

'I can, but it won't make any difference. Would you mind telling them that yourself, Mr President? They won't take it from me.'

'Certainly.' Will picked up the telephone in front of him. 'And give me your pack of cigarettes would you? I'll replace them later.'

'Certainly,' repeated the driver, pulling out his pack of Camels. 'I didn't know you smoked, Mr President.'

'I don't.'

'Here's some matches.'

'That's okay, I won't need them.'

Stepping onto the pavement at the northern edge of Downtown Huntingdon Beach, Will glanced around to see if he could spot any of his guards. To his delight, found he couldn't see any of them; up, down, or across the street. They were there though, he knew, but following his instructions to the letter. 'They really are good,' he thought to himself, lumbering towards the bright lights shining out of the cafés and bars three blocks further down.

He began studying the people walking past him to see if they could read his disguise, but instead of looking back openly and smiling a greeting in the normal Californian way, they glanced at him then dropped their gaze furtively; in exactly the same way he had noticed the British doing. 'I must look terribly ugly or a little scary in this half light,' he thought, feeling a lot more comfortable with his anonymity. Swerving on impulse, he strolled into a bar and went up to a man sipping beer and smoking on the patio outside. Fishing out a cigarette, he asked for a light in his normal voice.

'Man, what happened to you? Lose an argument with a train?'

'Afghanistan,' replied William, humbling the man.

'Sorry to hear that. We should never have gone in the first place.'

Just at that moment two drunk twenty-year-olds, their arms locked around each other's shoulders for support, staggered out of the bar singing. Seeing a fat man smoking and blocking their exit, one of them shouted, 'Out of my way you fat fuck.'

His companion dived on the bandwagon eagerly. 'Yeah you fucking slob – and you're smoking. Gotta hang onto that oral fixation, eh peeeeg? You need some exercise. So get me a brewski you fat slug,' and he kicked him lightly on the buttock.

What happened next, William later described to Julie as "like a watching a wraith materialise". As if out of thin air, an agent stepped smoothly and soundlessly in front of William, grabbing the man's calf as he swung another belated kick at the presidential backside. Holding it calmly in the crook of his left arm, his right hand snaked out like lightning and took a firm grip on the other man's throat, then squeezed. Both drunks stood completely immobilised and without taking his eyes off them, the agent said good-naturedly, 'Heard you served in Afghani, man. I was there too – Special Forces. Don't like to see a former military man unable to enjoy a quiet beer. Guess it's your choice – what shall I do with them?'

'Oh, they're just drunk kids – they don't know what real fighting is,' William replied, matching the man's even calmness.

'It'd be wrong to just let them go, Mr P...' the agent said, stopping himself in time.

'Maybe you're right. Okay, tell them to strip down to their boxers. Then they can get a little exercise themselves – running home.'

'You heard the man,' said the agent in a voice which didn't invite further discussion. 'Strip off those tee shirts and jeans. And the shoes.'

'No, please man – I went commando this evening,' squealed one, hopping.

'Me too,' added the other, rubbing his throat.

'You haven't earned the right to use the name commando,' replied the agent. 'Tough. Just make sure you run as fast as a commando can and you'll be fine.'

William and the agent watched them scamper off naked, covering their groins with their hands, their faces a bright cherry red as they tried to negotiate a packed Downtown without being seen. William and the agent burst out laughing together as they watched them run slap into a cop, walking round the corner of the next block.

'Thanks,' William said to the agent. 'What's your name?'

'Langer, Sir.'

'Fancy walking down with me?'

'I'd be honoured, Sir.'

'Hey, who the hell are you?' asked the man who had given William a light, but they had already walked away.

'He doesn't know who I am, Langer.'

'No, Mr President and he never will. Even I had to get you pointed out to me.'

'So it really works.'

'Yes, Sir. It really works.'

'Then let's go get a beer after I've interviewed Ali Mohammed. I never get the chance to be ordinary these days.'

'Mind if I bring along another agent, Sir? He's very good in a bar.'

'You mean very entertaining, or good in a bar fight?' William studied the man closely. Langer chose not to answer. 'Wow this getup really is that bad, huh?'

'Let's make sure we pick the right bar, Mr President.'

'Sounds fair. You choose and I'll pay – how's that?'

'Now that's something I can definitely work with, Sir.'

When they arrived at the police station, Bruce Cougar was there to greet them. William went straight up to him, 'Hi Bruce.'

'Who the hell… Oh, hello, Mr President. Come with me. I've got Ali downstairs in an interview room with three of my best men.'

'It's okay,' William replied. 'I want to interview him alone.'

'Impossible. I can't permit it, Mr President.'

'Okay, how about Langer here? He can look after me. Don't worry he's pretty handy.'

'Hi Alan,' Cougar greeted Langer. 'Long time no see. How's tricks?'

'You two know each other?'

'Special Ops Afghanistan, Mr President. Must be five years ago now, isn't it?' Bruce asked.

'Five or six.'

'Think you can handle it?'

'One man? Sure.'

'Yeah, and he looks completely ordinary – no offence,' William added.

'None taken, Mr President. It's the reason I got this assignment.'

'Say nothing, okay?' The agent simply nodded. 'Lead the way, Bruce.'

'Here, take my gun,' Langer said to Cougar as they assembled outside the door of the interview room.

'If it was anyone else I'd make you carry it,' Bruce replied, taking it from him.

'How reassuring you're on my side,' William remarked.

'Always was and always will be Mr...Smith,' he adlibbed quickly, as the door opened and Cougar's three agents filed out. William put a restraining hand on Bruce's arm, motioning Langer in first.

Following him in, William shut the door with a bang and looked across at Ali. He was sitting on a steel chair dressed in orange prison overalls. His hands were cuffed to a leather belt around his waist. Looking down, William could see Ali's feet chained to the legs of the chair, which had been bolted to the floor.

'Hello Ali. I'm Mr Smith.'

Ali held onto his expression of aloof boredom for a moment. 'Course you are.'

'I'm here to interview you on behalf of the President. I report directly to him.'

'I've told you everything.'

'Yes, you have. You've been extremely co-operative. Here Langer, take those cuffs off. Leave the leg manacles on then we can all relax,' William said, pulling up a chair to sit facing Ali six feet away. The agent did so without hesitating and took up a position mid-way between them, slightly off to one side. Ali didn't even rub his wrists. He dropped his hands straight onto his knees, then looked carefully at William.

'It's your level of co-operation which makes me think this is all a bluff,' William leaned forward in his seat. 'Okay, maybe there's a few of you out there, but if there really were 900, it would be better if you didn't tell us your intentions, and maximise the advantage of surprise. But you want us to know everything, don't you?'

'The 24th Revolution is not bluffing.'

'How can you be sure?'

'You'll find out soon enough when fires rage through your cities. The same way they have raged through mine for ninety years.'

'Hmm, I see,' William replied dubiously, letting his disbelief hang in the air. 'Why are you called The 24th Revolution?'

'Because there have been twenty-three great revolutions which have changed the world. One of them was your own civil war.'

'And you're the next "glorious revolution" I take it?' William responded in a voice laden with sarcasm. 'The trouble is Ali, you need a lot of people to make a revolution and I don't think you've got them.'

'It doesn't just stand for that!' Ali shot back angrily. 'It also represents the number sequence of the first two waves of freedom fighters, two, four...'

'Exactly,' William cut in. 'It's not called the 2,4,8,16 Revolution is it? I think you've been fooled, Ali. You've been misled into giving up your life for the foolish fantasy of someone else.' William leaned further forward to underline his next point. 'Because I think you've only got six or eight at the most,' and he looked at Ali intently.

And Ali didn't blink.

Continuing his tack, William asked, 'How would you feel if I was right?'

'I am disappointed there are only 900 against you. There are many more who would gladly sacrifice themselves for peace in this world,' Ali sneered, returning William's glare. 'It's nothing new. Fifty-five million people died in World War Two, for exactly the same reason.'

'How noble. I want to believe you but I'm having trouble. What's the real reason for you adopting such an inglorious name? I mean The 24th Revolution? It's a name that lacks punch. It doesn't have the quite the same impact as the Black September Group, does it?'

'I was told that in the space of one day – 24 hours – we would change the world. That once the power of this attack was understood, the world would never be the same again.'

'Who told you that?'

'The person who recruited me.'

'And who is that?'

'I don't know. All contact was made remotely.'

'Did he have any additional message? One for the President's ears only?'

'Not that he gave me. What other message do you need to stop attacking other people's countries?'

So it is a man, William thought. 'Let me ask you this,' William continued, 'if we let you go, would you give me your solemn oath as a devout Muslim, that you will never take up the gun against us again?'

'Only if you can swear the same oath in return,' Ali replied. 'And as you are not a Muslim, I might have trouble believing you. I was promised these manacles would not be put on again. Yet here I am chained. It is you people who cannot keep your word. You people who start the wars. Now you will be stopped.'

William paused, looking away for a few seconds. 'You're a clever man, Ali. Why did you do this? Was it revenge for your family being killed?'

'That was my detonator. I hope any decent man would fight back after seeing his family brutalised and butchered. Now I represent all the families that you and your allies have killed and dispossessed for the last ninety years. And a century of it is enough. You must be stopped! My brave brothers of The 24th Revolution will end it.'

'When you say it that way, it does sound like there's quite a number of you.'

'Take your pick from half the world,' Ali replied. 'I was lucky to be chosen because I have special skills.'

'And they are?'

'I learnt English at an orphanage in Beirut and I'm an excellent shot.'

'Okay, I've heard enough,' William got up swiftly, walking to the door. He knocked twice and it swung open instantly. Before stepping out of the room he turned back to Ali.

'I'm sorry your fractured life led you to this, Ali. I'm sorry, because I understand what made you act. But if I were in your shoes, I would not have carried out what you did. Above all I'm sorry because we will never let you go. The ordinary man in the street would never understand it. Ultimately though, you made the final choice that was instrumental in your ending up here, and when we stop The 24th Revolution you will come to realise that choice was wrong. At least I hope you will, because salvation is the only way you will get to paradise after what you've done. You have sent your own tragic pain into many other families. And you more than anyone must have known the suffering and trauma it would cause. Remember, under Sharia Law you would already be dead. Either way you have failed the test of forgiveness set by your God. I hope He shows more mercy than you. An eye for an eye might be one of your beliefs but it will never be one of mine. I can't find it in myself to wish you luck, so goodbye.'

Bruce was waiting for him in the corridor outside. William walked him straight out of earshot into another room. 'You're looking for a male, I'm certain. Not just because he said it, but because he didn't want to divulge it. It's even likely that Ali knows him – without actually knowing it's him – if you see what I mean. Because the man who recruited Ali knew him pretty well before he made contact. He knew exactly how to turn him on.'

'You got all that from that, Mr President?'

'I got much more.'

'What else, Sir?'

'Possibly the most alarming message any President has ever been given.'

'What message, Sir?'

'That's for me alone to know – so don't trouble yourself,' William replied enigmatically. 'Treat him well, Bruce, because we've got everything we'll get from him. But above all, treat him well because if Ali is a terrorist, then as the President of the United States, I am also a terrorist. Certainly I must be to the families we are inadvertently bombing this evening.'

Bruce maintained his blank expression. He was going to listen to the tapes of the President's interview with Ali again – but this time forewarned.

Turning to Langer, William said, 'Come on, Alan, let's go get that beer. I could really use one.'

The agent quickened his pace to draw alongside his President, who was striding purposefully out of the police station.

'But surely, Mr President, we can't be the terrorists because we're the good guys, right?'

'That's exactly what they think as well. The problem being that we took a war into their homes and they simply retaliated. Now pick a bar would you? My suggestion is the nearest one.'

'The nearest one it is, Mr President. Mind if I register off duty and call my colleague?'

'Go right ahead. And as we're both officially off duty, call me Will for the rest of the evening would you? Or I'll stop buying.'

'Certainly, Mr Pr...Will,' he replied, smiling nervously at the natural mistake.

'And thanks for handing me that John Doe "Mr Smith" back there. You definitely owe me a beer for that one,' replied the President of the United States of America.

CASTLING ON THE KING'S SIDE

Back in his office, Bruce Cougar flicked through the channels to CNN in time to catch the President's televised broadcast.

President Mann was seated behind his desk in the Oval Office, looking the epitome of a leader and statesman. Pausing, he looked steadily into the camera before beginning his address. 'My fellow countrymen and women, I am here to inform you of a grave threat to our security. One that began with the Terminator Sniper who was a member of a group which calls itself The 24th Revolution…'

Bruce puffed his way through a cigarette without taking his eyes from the screen.

'…there are only 900 of these criminals against us. Nothing compared to a united front of 270 million Americans.' It was an excellent speech; designed to unite the nation against the trial they faced; neatly swerving around the chaos and destruction about to crash into them like an underway aircraft carrier laden with bridge spares.

'We must be vigilant and stand against this evil foe as one. I urge you to rise to your patriotic duty and show these monsters the might and greatness of the American people! Our understanding of what is good and true each of us knows well; it will act as our beacon to guide us. We must not fight each other. That is what this enemy wants. To fight them we must go about our normal lives in the normal way. If we do that, we have nothing to fear.'

He suddenly stopped speaking, and got up sedately from behind the desk. Standing to one side of the chair, William shrugged off his blue suit jacket and folded it neatly in front of him. Dressed in a white shirt and blue silk tie, he put his hands on his hips and levelled his eyes straight into the camera. 'Today, I have told my security staff I will not wear a bullet-proof vest until every one of these criminals has been brought to justice. I stand with you. I urge you to come together. And together, we will fight them. Unified, we will knock them aside like a leaf blown on the wind. We are the greatest nation of earth. They will find out the hard way that no one goes up against the American People. No one and nothing affects us. We are concerned, but we are not afraid. I call on you to be vigilant. I call on you to help our emergency services wherever you can. We shall overcome them by going about our lives in the normal way. God bless us all.'

Bruce Cougar felt like standing up and applauding. 'Thank God this didn't happen when that bozo of a president was in office,' he murmured to himself. For the first time in two weeks he felt his hopelessness lift a fraction, as he realised that his President was going to get them through the coming crisis by leading from the front. 'He's good because he's so damn smart,' Bruce thought, feeling a glimmer of hope catch inside him. He glanced over at the chair in the corner of his office, where his own Kevlar jacket was thrown. 'Guess I won't need that heavy old thing for while,' he smiled.

'That was a magnificent gesture darling, but I'm not sure it was a good idea,' Julie said to Will later that evening, after watching his speech on television.

'I thought about telling you, but I knew what your reaction would be.'

'Well, if you're not using your bullet-proof vest, then perhaps I should borrow it – for the sake of the children.'

'I know, honey. But I have to lead by example and the bar is set high. Don't worry, it's shaken up the Sex so much I've never felt safer. I hope they do try it on, I'd like to watch what happens.'

'If you do get killed, don't think heaven or hell will be able to hide you from me.'

'Ha ha! That's why I love you so,' Will hugged her to him, planting a kiss on her upturned forehead. 'Do you remember that time we went round for dinner at Alex Spyder's? The first time he suggested I run for office.'

'Of course I do. Why?'

'Do you remember that conversation after dinner, about needing to make our country less vulnerable to becoming someone's personal kingdom?'

'Sure I remember.'

'Well, it would make that less likely if we handed over more Federal authority to individual States. Like giving them the power to decide whether to provide troops for a war,' William said wistfully.

'But you both agreed it was purely conjecture. That the powers behind the throne would never permit it. It would upset the religious right who believe they are God's chosen people, superior to all. It would reduce their overall authority.'

'I know, but I think this attack may hand me the perfect opportunity to steer things that way.'

'You're incredible, Will. You're under attack. People will be battened down in their homes too terrified to step out the door, and you think it's a good idea to hand more authority to States with no previous exposure to it?'

'I may have no choice. It's the only way to fight an enemy operating from within. Ultimately, all the attacks will occur at a local level and we must respond in the same way. It's the only defence that has the teeth of an attack.'

'If we were organised locally, I suppose our military would know the ground as well as The 24th Revolution,' she replied, realising the decision he had to make.

'The question is – how much authority do we give them to begin with?'

'Why don't you tie that in with the voting system, Will? You believe in democratic principle – use it. Why not tell the State Governors that when you are satisfied efficient voting channels are in place for 90% of their citizens, they will be given more authority?'

'That's a superb idea. The funny thing is, I've just been reading about that same concept… You should be on my staff.'

'I am, Will. I work for free that's the only difference.'

'That makes all the difference. It requires a lot of thought but in essence…it truly is a great idea. It will also empower the individual. Now that we are under attack my authority over those Republican fanatics in Congress is absolute. I could order each State to install that new internet voting system I saw last month and add a cell phone voting system. That would make it easy for people to vote, comment and suggest ideas.'

'And more importantly, the citizens of each State will control their State's decisions.'

'It's a wonderfully altruistic and employable idea,' Will smiled. 'If we empower the people directly, they will enrich themselves. It's only when responsibility is removed from a populace they become poor, hungry and dispossessed.'

'How true, darling. And of course, there is another advantage.'

'Go on.'

'You could sign the Global pollution agreement. If you give States more self-responsibility, it won't take long before they start producing more of their own goods. We wouldn't need to transport them so far.'

'Grief, that solves another problem I face. Mermesetter is worried that when The 24th Revolution start cutting the rail lines and blowing up roads, we won't be able to provide enough food to everyone.'

'Individual States understand their problems better than anyone. If they have more say and greater authority over themselves, they can act more efficiently. They will target their own needs and shortfalls with greater precision. They can solve their own problems quicker than any outside agency could ever do, and it will provide more employment at a local level. There is one problem though. It will downsize quite a few large corporations. Think you can handle them, Will?'

'I'm not sure. They wield a lot of power and influence. Collectively, they control my office.'

'Then don't tell them. Push the vote through using the military argument you mentioned. Then it will follow.'

'That's clever.'

'It's odd to think that you and this Khalifa are both after the same end result in a way. He wants to stop us attacking other countries and you want to stop a future dictatorship from taking over here.'

'The really strange part, is that I wouldn't stand a snowball's chance in Hell of handing more power to individual States without this attack. I can't ignore the military advantages of defending ourselves locally – that would be wrong. And I daren't let the military loose on our home soil with only a few generals to control them – it's too dangerous. We need more checks and balances or I risk some terrible repercussions. Imagine if one general decided to implement his own private agenda; our country would turn into a dictatorship.'

'Break it up then, Will. Give States the ability to vote on their needs;

but make sure it's the citizens of each State who have the vote, or you will create another set of oligarchs. Transparency will improve because people will have a vested interest in making sure there's no financial misappropriation of public money, so it will also reduce corruption. When you are confident proper voting is in place, you can give each State executive power over very small units of the military. Start small and manage the voting process well. The majority of people are good. They will do the right thing. Keep the bulk of the military under your own control and if anyone steps out of line – use it.'

'That's how our country was originally designed to operate under the Constitution, so it's not a new idea. Actually, it worked extremely well for 120 years, until it got bent out of shape by a few bankers and a number of giant corporations.'

'Well, it's a big decision, so why don't you sleep on it, Mr President?' Julie said, lowering her eyes and taking his hand to lead him upstairs.

He awoke the next morning with the sun streaming through a gap in the curtains and an equal feeling of beaming contentment. He knew it was right to allow individual States to organise their own defence, and have a small military force placed at their disposal to begin the process. 'I can use that tempting carrot of power to ensure they are held in check by their voters. It will only take a nudge from there to get them to vote on whether to send their own troops off to a distant war, at the whim of some future President.'

He trusted the people of his land, for it was their land too. In truth, more theirs than his, he felt. Reaching over, he pressed the intercom switch on the nightstand next to his bed.

'Yes, Mr President,' came his secretary's voice.

'Sammy,' he whispered. 'Cancel all my engagements tomorrow and get those people with the internet voting system in for a full demonstration of the product. Invite the usual great and smart to attend would you, and also phone Charles Slovak, the director of NASA, and ask him if he'd be kind enough to attend. I'd like his view. I think he's fly-fishing in the Bahamas at the moment, so you might have to send a helicopter, together with my apologies.'

'No problem at all, Mr President. Is there anything else?'

'Yes. Invite every State Governor and Vice Governor to a formal dinner at the White House sometime next week. No wives or husbands and a fully sealed room, okay? Tell them to come with their thinking caps on and their notebooks in hand. No alcohol until the end and make the meal simple but nutritious. They are not coming here to enjoy themselves, they are coming here to work. And you can mention I said that if you like.'

'Consider it done, Mr President. Anything else?'

'Yes, I think I will have breakfast in bed this fine morning. Tea for me and coffee for Julie. Make it the chef's monster plate because for some reason I'm ravenous.'

'Just give me twelve minutes, Mr President.

'Make that an hour would you?' he instructed, and turned onto his side, propping his head on one hand. He glanced down at his wife's sleeping form then nodded his head slightly, smiling as he stroked her back. He was still smiling when their breakfast trays arrived an hour later. Waking Julie, he sat up and held his orange juice up to hers.

'I think we should toast the Founding Fathers of our great nation. They are going to get their original wish back.'

'I see,' she said, clinking her glass against his. 'In that case, you'd better leave me your bullet-proof vest.'

'Now don't start worrying about those right-wingers in Washington, honey. I've just worked out how to sell it to them so they won't even feel the knife go in.'

'Really? I love it when you attempt the impossible.'

'Nothing is impossible when you approach it the right way. I've got a military report on my desk saying we need to co-ordinate our fight locally, to provide a swifter and more accurate response to the attacks. Those Christian extremists in Washington love a fight, especially when they think it's against another religion. They won't be able to resist. I can see through their uncharitable hypocrisy like a pane of glass. They're going to hit that bait – hard.'

'You're incorrigible.'

'Not really. But when something is meant to be, everything becomes very easy. That's one of the ways to determine if it's supposed to happen.'

'Providing your heart is good and your intentions are honourable,' Julie added, picking up her knife and delicately buttering a croissant.

'Names are very important to people. So I'm going to give my Bill a name that will remind everyone of what was meant to be – not what it's been turned it into.'

'Oh?'

'I'm going to call it the Constitution Bill. That's really what it is – a Bill to reinstate the original concept behind the Constitution.'

'Goodness, Will. You don't let a crisis go to waste, do you?'

'Never have and never will. It's the reason I was promoted so quickly at NASA,' Will said, smiling his delight at her.

FIGHTING FOR POSITION

JJ and Leah checked into the Beirut Hilton an hour apart. The white colonnaded hotel had taken six years to rebuild after the bombing in '83. Most of the delays in finishing it had been wrought by the iron pendulum of war swinging through the centre of Beirut with a repetitiveness that had inured the world to the city's strategic importance. At the time of its refurbishment in '89, the hotel was considered a pinnacle of modern style and luxury, but now had the tired look of an old warrior who has seen it all, been through too much, and had to fight off too many people.

Their pre-booked rooms were on opposite sides of the corridor on the same floor. Contrary to what most people see in movies and on television, the rooms of operatives on critical assignment are never booked next to each other, but opposite. If one person is compromised or attacked, the other has the option of flight or fight, coming out of their room to a turned back.

After taking a long shower to cool off from the oppressive summer heat, Leah changed into local dress and tied a white cotton scarf over her head. She carefully tucked all her hair out of sight so she wouldn't draw undue attention to herself amongst the mainly Muslim population of the city. It is customary in the more liberal society of Beirut for women to wear only a headscarf, though a few of the more devout from West Beirut still wear full abayas – an over-garment stretching from head to toe. This less extreme covering of her head was all she needed to blend in. At worst people would think she was from the eastern sector, or Christian quarter of Beirut.

JJ had phoned her, departing fifteen minutes earlier so he could get into a position to keep watch. Like all good plans theirs was straightforward. She would go to the orphanage and ask about a cousin of hers – Abdul – who had stayed there thirty years ago, and

197

see if they could provide any information to help locate him. The only lead they had was Ali and Abdul both spending time in a Beirut orphanage, and while they didn't know which one Abdul had stayed in, she did have the address of Ali's. In a few minutes she would be standing where Ali had spent his teenage years and hopefully, pick up some scent of their quarry.

Leah was going to ask the staff for access to any records they held which might confirm Abdul's presence there. If she discovered it was indeed the same orphanage where Victor had found his son, she would have proved a direct connection between Abdul and Ali and, more importantly, they could be certain the mastermind behind the attacks was actually Abdul. Once she had authenticated the link, JJ would take over and get the Lebanese Government to hand over all the information on everyone and anyone who might have come into contact with him.

It made sense to her that orphanages provided fertile ground for Abdul to harvest recruits for his terror campaign. Most Middle Eastern orphans have little or nothing to lose and harbour a deep-seated suspicion, bordering on hatred of all things Western, who are largely responsible for their predicament. She didn't imagine Abdul had recruited his entire force from this one orphanage, but if she could prove he had sourced one person from there, they would then examine all the orphanages Abdul had worked with or provided money to, when he was going through his charitable phase.

The moment she notified Bruce Cougar about Abdul's knowledge of The Sword, a team of NSA analysts had scoured every friendly database they were allowed to access, together with several searches conducted under absolute secrecy, without the relevant Governments' knowledge. The highly classified C13 section has some of the best hackers in the world at its fingertips; many of them choosing to work for the NSA or the CIA, rather than face lengthy jail sentences.

Apart from the Financial Times picture, which was over ten years old and only depicted a bearded man crossing a street in Geneva, the NSA team had been unable to come up with a single picture of Abdul. And this picture was shot from the side, at a range of 150 feet. It didn't reveal him well enough to even form a rough composite of his face. The only identifying characteristics they were certain of, was Abdul was very short and thin. By comparing his size with other objects in the picture, they had verified his height at between four foot eleven and five feet tall.

Drawing a blank with the picture, the NSA analysts had tried to follow Abdul's financial trail; but he had taken the money from the sale of his company in bearer bonds and cashed them all over the world during a nine month period. When they attempted to trace this cash, they found it too had vanished. The analysts were surprised. It was impossible to hide seven billion dollars they argued, but Leah knew why they couldn't trace it. Abdul had made his fortune dealing with Hawala, and was using it to hide his fabulous fortune. Certainly his connections with the system were more than excellent. It would have been effortless for him to arrange and Hawala had the delightful bonus of presenting a firmly closed door to the West. She knew it operated partly on a verbal basis, so there were no databases to search through, while the use of a different set of names guaranteed anonymity. This is one of the main tenets of the system: the reason it has survived unbroken and unchanged for a millennium. Even a Russian banker would be cowed by the wall of silence and subterfuge standing in the way of anyone looking into Hawala's dealings or clients.

Walking across the lobby, Leah went up to the hotel concierge and gave him the address of the orphanage, asking him to call her a cab. The taxi driver told her it was market day there, and it would be quicker if he dropped her at the end of the closed-off street, letting her walk the remaining distance. After a mad dash through the horn-blasted streets of Beirut, she climbed out of the cab into a world very different from the tired luxury of the Beirut Hilton.

It was hot, loud and intensely busy. Hundreds of people were shouting and bustling, backed by a line of brightly coloured market stalls stretching all the way down the ancient walled street.

Leah ambled casually though the centre of the market, heading for a dogleg turn she could see at the far end. The houses there were larger, and she assumed it must be where the orphanage was situated. Weaving her way through the throng, she looked around for JJ without spotting him once.

As she walked around the corner of a giant ten-storey house – Leah met with a shock. The next building was a smoking ruin. She confirmed it was the correct address before turning her attention back to the remains of the old orphanage.

It looked like a meteor had hit it. The previously whitewashed walls were blackened with soot and only half standing, while the remains of roof tiles were strewn among the debris, orange and black. Here and there tendrils of smoke snaked up lazily, to be cut off by the light morning breeze.

Stepping onto the buckled metal doors which had once guarded the two-acre site, Leah tried to read what had happened. The devastation was obviously caused by fire which had raged through the building unchecked. To her left, she could see scorch marks stretching onto the roofs of the adjacent buildings, leaving gaping holes which had been hastily covered over with blue plastic sheet.

'Coincidence?' she wondered. 'Definitely not.' What are the chances of the orphanage burning to the ground at roughly the same time Ali had been caught? 'Minimal', she thought.

She began looking at the destruction in more detail. In the far corner, she could see twisted metal boxes sticking out of haphazard piles of burnt brick. She teetered over for a closer look and drawing nearer, realised they were the remains of old filing cabinets.

The first thing she noticed was that all of the drawers were open. Someone had deliberately pulled every drawer open before the flames had consumed the orphanage otherwise most, if not all, would be shut. It couldn't be looting afterwards because some of the paper would have survived. But none had, and her closer inspection revealed extensive flame damage inside the cabinets. All the drawers had been pulled open before the fire started; meaning only one thing to her mind – arson. A tremor of anxiety ran through her with the thought that it could well have been Abdul – in person.

Leah knew that burning down an orphanage in Beirut comes under the "lynching by angry street mob" category, and she wondered if it would even be wise to attempt to pay someone for such wickedness. 'Not in Beirut,' she murmured. Abdul was a highly skilled computer programmer, so he wouldn't take an illogical risk. Besides, what if the person he deputised had stayed there; or had a friend who was given sanctuary at the orphanage? Even if he brought in someone from outside Beirut, what if they'd bungled it? Or caught red-handed and pleading for their life, shouted out his involvement. 'This is the hand of Abdul,' Leah reasoned. 'Just asking someone to carry out this evil would be inherently dangerous here.'

The thought struck her that not only was she standing where Ali had spent his formative years, but where Abdul had been creeping about only a few days ago. A ghostly hand took hold of her. She glanced around nervously, half expecting to see Abdul standing among the devastation. To her relief she saw no one, not even JJ.

In her mind's eye she could see how it must have gone down. Abdul had opened all the cabinets before setting them alight and she began looking for solid proof of her theory. It didn't take long. In the bottom drawer of the second cabinet she found the unmistakeable carbon outline of a match. 'Abdul must have walked down the line of cabinets, squirting accelerant onto each set of files, then reversed his steps – tossing matches into the open drawers,' Leah decided. 'Then he probably stood right here, making sure his handiwork was nicely ablaze before exiting quietly.' Having spent nearly a year at the orphanage, Abdul would know exactly how to get in and out without being seen.

Leah let her instincts loose to try and pick up some sense of him and a numbing fear grabbed her by the throat. Standing among the burnt bricks and ruination, she could feel a dark malignance thickening the air around her. 'This must be what hell feels like,' she thought; as her instincts began tearing at her to run back to the market. Pushing aside her intuition, she wandered around the rest of the site. After ten minutes spent kicking over ash-strewn rubble and tiles, she realised the fire had been thorough. 'Well at least we're on the right track,' she thought. But the disappointment of having her suspicions confirmed, without leaving a clue to follow deflated her mood. Somewhat bereft, she tripped, stumbled and nearly fell onto the main street, grateful to put the sights and smells of that reeking destruction behind her.

Back on terra firma, Leah wound her way through the busy market stalls and, as she walked past the third one in line, a man began waving and shouting at her. It broke her train of thought and she glanced over at him. He was looking straight at her; exhibiting a great deal of excitement. She pointed a finger to her chest, then walked cautiously towards him.

'Dear lady, a moment I beg of you,' the man entreated, as she approached his jewellery stall. He was gargantuan. Six-and-a-half feet tall with a large bushy beard flowing down his chest onto his massive sromach. He was flapping his arm up and down and his hand looked odd – making her focus on it. When she got to front of his stall she saw that both his hands were prosthetic. The pink plastic fingers had faded to a light brown with age and strangely, all the fingers and both thumbs were covered in rings. Some had four or five squeezed onto a single digit. They winked and flashed at her in the bright sunshine.

'Dear lady, I see you bought that ring,' he said, pointing his arm at her right hand.

Leah looked down at the ring Victor had given her. 'My ring?' she asked, confused.

'Yes, I tried to buy that ring last week but the lady would not sell it to me. How much did you pay? I will pay whatever you wish for it.'

'You mean you tried to buy this ring last week?' Leah repeated.

'Yes, from the lady at the orphanage. I saw her go in wearing it and I asked her if she would sell it to me. It is one of a kind and I would very much like to own it. How much did you pay? I will double it and give you a handsome profit.'

Leah stared at him; lost for words; trying to get her mind around what he was saying. Mistaking her pause for refusal he went on, 'You see I have no arms. I like to wear the good rings myself, to take my eyes from these ugly things. Please dear lady, will you sell it to me? I have never seen a ring so beautiful.'

Slowly the lights went on in Leah's mind. It was an unusual ring but he was wrong about it being unique. There was another one identical to it worn by Abdul, or perhaps he had given it to a wife or a girlfriend.

The vendor waddled around from the back of his stall. Moving awkwardly, he squeezed his massive frame between a gap in the stalls, then stepped into the shade under the front cover of his booth. She gazed up at him as he towered over her. 'May I hold it?' he asked, holding out his hand, his breath smelling of garlic and cumin.

'Here,' she said, twisting it off her finger and placing it on his plastic palm. 'Are you sure it's the same ring?'

'Let me see... Ah yes, there is the inscription. It is truly wonderful. Very old. What will you take for it?'

'Well...' and she let the word hang in the air as if undecided. 'Who was wearing it?'

'She is a small lady, not as kind as you,' the vendor grinned black teeth at her.

'And you say she works at the orphanage?'

'She said she was from the main office. I saw her inspecting the damage after the fire destroyed the building. I think she wanted to see if anything could be salvaged but the fire was very fierce. It burned everything. Now there is nothing left, as you can see,' he gestured with his other arm. 'It is a great pity. For many poor children it was their only home. I often see her going into the building. She helps the orphans.'

'And she was wearing this ring?'

'She let me see it but would not part with it for any price. She used the excuse that it was a gift from her late father. How did you obtain it, dear lady? If you bought it I will double what you paid.'

Ignoring his request, Leah asked, 'What is her name?'

'I did not ask but you must know her, surely? For you to get this ring she must know you well. She said no price would part her from such an heirloom. Ahh, perhaps you stole it; or found it, eh? I don't care how you came by it, and I am a most generous man. What will you take for it?'

'I cannot part with it. I would like to see this other ring if you say they are similar. How do I find this lady?'

'You must go to the main office of the Lebanese Orphan Mission at the end of the next street. She must work from there. It is not far, maybe a ten minute walk. Now please, name your price.'

'I'm sorry,' Leah replied, 'it's too precious to me.'

'I understand, it is exceptional. If you ever change your mind please come and find me. I will pay a better price than anyone, as Allah is my witness. When you see the other lady please remember me to her. I am always here on Wednesdays. My name is Hakim. Everyone here knows me.'

'I will remind her of you, Hakim. How will I recognise her? You say she was small. How tall was she?'

'Oh, not as high as this,' he held a plastic arm across his chest, squashing the bottom of his magnificent beard.

'God, that's about five feet,' she thought. 'Did you notice the colour of her eyes, Hakim?'

'That I cannot say. She wore sunglasses and a burqua. She is a good Muslim woman.'

'*Sunglasses and the ring?* Got him!' Leah thought excitedly. 'Thank you Hakim. If I ever sell my ring it will be to you. You have been very helpful,' and she turned away to walk a few steps up the street, then pulled out her BlackBerry. In her excitement, it took her three attempts to hit speed dial 1 properly.

'Wassup?'

'JJ, I've found him. He's working at the Lebanese Orphan Mission. Where are you?'

'I'm in the coffee house opposite. I can see you. Remember your training. Don't speak English on the phone in public. Go back to the hotel and I'll meet you there.'

Safely back in her room, she relayed what Hakim had unknowingly revealed. Her rapid-fire energy was infectious and JJ began pacing up and down as he considered their next move. 'Did Hakim think you were Lebanese?'

'I think he did. He only spoke a local dialect to me and observed full Arab custom when speaking to a Muslim woman. He even thinks I live in Beirut. He said he was always there on Wednesdays, as if I could pop back anytime and sell him the ring.'

'If your accent can fool a Lebanese street trader, then you can fool anyone. In which case we have a choice. We could whistle up the cavalry and storm the place but that will tip Abdul off, if he's not there at this precise moment. So, how do you feel about stepping into the lion's den to see if he's there? You can leave the BlackBerry on speakerphone and if anything happens I will be with you in sixty seconds. If you get a visual on him, just turn it off and leave. If you don't come out in two minutes, I will come to your aid. Think you can do that without being unmasked?'

'Well, Abdul doesn't know of my existence. I could change my story to one of concerned philanthropy and offer them some money to help get the orphanage rebuilt. That should guarantee I meet with him or rather, her.'

'Okay. Let me report this in to HQ, then we'll head off down there. Same as before – I'll go first. And Leah, better take that ring off before you go, eh? An oversight like that might be very hard to explain to your boss. I'm keen to avoid upsetting him.'

Arriving at the door of the building an hour later, Leah pressed the buzzer on the speaker panel. A woman's voice answered, 'Yes?'

'Oh, hello. I saw one of your orphanages has burned down and I wondered if you needed funds to rebuild it.'

'Do you have an appointment?' came the metallic voice.

'No.'

'Moment… Please take the lift to the second floor,' tinned the voice as the lock release buzzed. Leah pushed the door open, whispering the translation into her bag, 'Lift to second floor, JJ.' As they agreed, there was no response.

When the lift door slid open, she saw a man standing in the hallway wearing a black suit and a welcoming smile. He couldn't be Abdul. He was too tall and too old – six foot and sixty, if he was a day.

'I am very pleased to meet with you,' he said courteously. My name is Sameh Douroucouli. I am the Director of the Lebanese Orphan Mission. Please come this way.'

He led her down a long corridor into an office at the end.

'Do you have a bathroom I could use first?' Leah asked.

'Please, I will show you.'

The moment she was safely inside, Leah whispered into the phone again. 'I'm with the Director on the ocean side of the building on the second floor. North-east corner office, but he's not Abdul.' She flushed the toilet and waited a few seconds before stepping back into the unlit corridor to follow the Director back towards his office.

'May I ask your name?' Sameh requested.

Leah was glancing into the offices trying to spot Abdul and startled by his question, said the first thing that came to her. 'I am Alima Adara Khouri,' she replied, kicking herself the moment the name fell from her lips. 'The wise virgin Khouri? Dammit that's an oxymoron,' she cursed herself, and in revenge her mind threw up the image of a woman torn between belief, desire and curiosity. Leah bit her lip to suppress the mirth forcing its way to the surface.

'So you know all about the fire?' he asked.

'I certainly do,' she said straight-faced, desperate to prevent laughing out loud at his unintended double entendre. 'I was shocked when I first found out about it. I hope no one was hurt?' And as she heard the words tumble out, she couldn't hold it down a moment longer. Spluttering, she bent over to laugh a cough into her hands, then gave full vent to her feelings.

'Are you all right?'

'Perfectly, thank you,' she choked, calming herself forcibly. 'It's the pressure of my situation,' she realised; that lightening sensation of stepping onto soft, dangerous ground.

She fought for control over herself as he continued none the wiser. 'I thank Allah the Merciful that the fire started in the records office and there was plenty of time to evacuate the children before it took hold. If it had started anywhere else, the outcome would have been more tragic.'

'Well, that's one good thing,' Leah replied. 'I'm here to make a donation to help you rebuild it.'

'Thank you. We have a small budget and there are no spare funds. May I ask what figure you had in mind?'

'Well,' she replied, hesitating. 'How much will it cost to rebuild?'

'Madam, that is most generous! I do not know exactly the amount, but it will be in the region of a hundred million pounds,' he said, posing the huge figure as a question.

'I must speak with my husband, but that may be possible.'

'Of course, of course,' Sameh said with delight. 'Would it be possible to meet him? Who is your generous husband?'

'He prefers to remain anonymous with his charitable gifts but I think he will approve of this one. You see, my husband is an orphan and spent two years there when he was younger. He asked me to find some of the people he befriended there. When I saw the fire I knew he would want to help, so I called by your office. You say it started in the records office. Did you manage to salvage any of the files? He would like to contact some of the boys he knew.'

'I'm not sure. Forgive me, but I have only been here for two weeks. I took over from my predecessor when he died in a car crash recently. Another tragic waste,' the Director replied.

'How terrible. I was told that two people from this office went to see the damage, the day after the fire,' Leah ventured, pushing the conversation onto the path of her real enquiry.

'No, madam. I have been very busy relocating the children. I did take a look myself but the destruction seems total. I will check for you, but to my knowledge no duplicate records were ever kept. We may have lost that information forever.'

'That is a great pity,' Leah said with sincerity. 'I was told these two people work here and inspected the site. Do you think you could ask them if they managed to salvage any of the records?'

'I'm sorry, madam, I sent no one down there. You must be mistaken.'

'How strange. Well perhaps they went on their own initiative. If I describe them, could you double check for me? I know my husband would be very grateful if they did manage to save anything which could help him locate his old friends.'

'Certainly. What do they look like?'

As she outlined the rough description Hakim had given her, the expression on Sameh's face fell into a glower of annoyance. 'Is this a joke?'

Reinforcing her lie she continued, 'That's what I was told. A short man and a small woman. One of them had different coloured eyes. Surely you must know them, even if you have only been here for a short time.'

'The person you are describing is Mr Guenaan, my predecessor, and he died in a car crash three weeks ago.'

'Oh, I'm most dreadfully sorry. Perhaps the man who told me was confused about when he saw them. Are you quite sure there is no one else who might fit that description?' she asked limply.

'I've heard there are a couple of small villages in the north where people have different coloured eyes. They say they are descended from Alexander the Great who camped there after a great battle. He was supposed to have the same characteristic so it is not unheard of; though I myself have only seen it once. In Mr Guenaan's personnel file. He was 5 feet tall and had those same coloured eyes.'

'A picture? May I see it?' she asked, risking all.

'I suppose there is no harm.' He picked up the phone and spoke into it. 'May I offer you some coffee?' he asked as he replaced the receiver.

'No thank you.'

'While we wait, may I ask the name of your husband?'

'Yes, it's Ashraf Khouri.'

'He must be a very successful man to be in a position to help us,' the director said in a tone laced with suspicion. 'Do you live in Beirut?'

'Not any more. My husband is a busy man and often away on business. We live in several different places.'

There was a knock on the door and a woman walked in with a brown folder. She went over to the director and whispered to him hurriedly as she put the file on the desk. Douroucouli's expression changed to a look of bemusement. He opened the file – it was empty. 'This is most strange. I looked at Mr Guenaan's file when I arrived here two weeks ago. I put it back myself. I was trying to find a clue to who his benefactors were, some of the donations were large. But there was only a copy of his employment contract and his picture. I don't understand this,' he slapped the file with the back of his hand, 'everything's gone.'

Leah understood it only too well. She knew there were several American agencies that would have paid handsomely for that picture. Probably more than the Lebanese Orphan Mission had received in its history to date. Masking her genuine disappointment she said, 'How inconvenient. Perhaps it's been misplaced. I'm staying at the Hilton for a week so if it does turn up, perhaps you could phone me there. I will speak to my husband about our donation next week.'

'Thank you. You are most kind. Believe me when I say we need all the help we can get. Your donation will help many poor orphan children. I will see if we have any duplicate records and call you. Your donation will help us a lot more, if it comes soon,' he emphasised.

Leah stepped into the lift feeling distressed, partly because she knew the trail to Abdul had petered out, but mainly because she had lied to this kind man: raising an expectation she knew would be unfulfilled. Damn. She was beginning to dislike the role she was playing in order to carry out this assignment – it was making her resent herself. For the first time she felt a flare of anger towards the man she was hunting. 'How dare he burn down an orphanage to cover his tracks! How dare he put me in a position where I have to lie!'

Stepping into the hot sunshine, she headed for the line of waiting taxicabs at the far end of the market. As she walked towards them she noticed Hakim sitting outside a coffee shop, deep in conversation with another man; his massive bulk overflowed the chair, rendering it invisible. The person next to him was counting through a thick roll of money which had just been given to him by Hakim. He was doing business in the timeless way of the Arabic world – cash. Judging by the amount, he must have had a very successful day's trading in the market. Hakim lifted one of his arms in greeting.

'Dear lady, where is your ring?'

'Oh, I left it in the hotel safe.'

'For a bad moment I thought you had sold it,' he said, placing his plastic hand on his heart in a mock show of relief.

208

'No, Hakim, if I ever decide to sell it, I will come to you first.'

'You are wise to be so careful. There are many thieves here. The owner of this teahouse was stabbed to death last month, for a paltry 170,000 pounds.'

'Hakim, are you certain you saw the lady after the fire?'

'Of course I am sure. I see you come from the direction of the Mission. Did you meet her and pass on my message?'

'No. She's not there any more.'

'Huh,' and he looked away, bemused.

'Was there anything else you can remember which could help me find her?'

'No, no. She was wearing a white abaya. I didn't even see the shoes on her feet. Tell me,' he asked, changing the subject, 'do you live in Beirut?'

'No.'

'I'm surprised – your accent is local. What is your name, dear lady?' he asked, trying to build a conversation which she was not in the slightest mood for; he was lining up on another beseeching request to sell him the ring.

'It's Leah Mandrille,' she replied, thinking: 'Damned if I'm going to lie to two people in one day,' and she waved him goodbye as she went up the street.

He called after her, 'The blessings of Allah be upon you. I hope we will meet again and you will let me buy your ring. Do not forget me. I will beat any price.'

'I won't, Hakim, I won't. Goodbye now,' Leah called over her shoulder as she made her way to the line of cabs, shimmering in the heat haze of the still afternoon.

When she closed the door of her hotel room, a feeling of melancholy pervaded her and she went over to the minibar and poured herself a glass of wine, taking a large gulp. A gentle knock on the door was repeated twice: JJ. Leah let him in and offered him a drink.

'Are you sure?' she asked when he declined. 'You may need one. It appears our bird has flown. I think Abdul set the fire then went back afterwards disguised as a woman, probably to make sure it had destroyed all of the records. He was the Director of the Orphan Mission until three weeks ago, when he faked his own death in a car accident. At some point after that, he stole his personnel file which had his picture inside. He probably still has keys to the building and just walked in one night.'

'Damn, he hasn't made a single mistake. Maybe our trail has come to an end,' JJ said morosely.

'Yeah, maybe, but I now know roughly what he looks like. I told the Director I was looking for a man and a woman in case Abdul worked there as a woman. I guessed his beard and well groomed hair, and when I mentioned the colour of his eyes the Director recognised him immediately. He used an alias there. He's probably got a host of different identities.'

'Don't let a little thing like false identity get you down. What name did he use?' JJ asked, picking up his Blackberry.

'Guenaan.'

JJ tapped it in and went over to the minibar to fetch a beer. Fifteen minutes later the PDA buzzed and he looked at the screen. 'Whoa! A man named Guenaan boarded a flight to Cairo twelve days ago.'

'Guenaan is an unusual name and Cairo is where Khalifa went to University.'

'Let's haul ass to Cairo. If he paid for his flight with a credit card it will give us his bank account and we should be able to track him through that. I'll get our team on it while we fly over. By the time we land we should have some idea where he's holed up.'

It was raining in Cairo when they landed that evening. A summer storm had swept down from the Black Sea, picking up moisture as it drifted over a warm Mediterranean, then the frazzling heat of mid-afternoon had triggered its payload over a parched northern Egypt. An NSA agent from the Cairo office held an umbrella up for them as they climbed into a dishevelled Mercedes Benz with an orange taxi sign on the roof. The hood was a faded yellow and seemed to blend in well with the patched up and broken down buildings around them.

'Best camouflage we could find for a car. There are 3000 cabs in this city and most of them are German made,' the agent said, noticing the silent mood of his two passengers.

'Did you get a bead on his bank account?' JJ asked him.

'Yeah, we did,' he replied, gloomily.

'And?' Leah and JJ chorused.

'The visa card was only used on three consecutive days. The last time, when he arrived in Cairo twelve days ago so we have no idea where he is at the moment. We've searched every record and database in the Middle East but it's like he suddenly stopped living. The address on the credit card is for a house in Beirut owned by a blind man. He was paid 100,000 Leb Pounds cash, probably by Guenaan. We're asking around at hotels and guest houses here, but the locals don't like to play with us so I doubt they will tell us much. You've probably wasted your time coming over,' he added, in a voice tinged with envy. The agent obviously didn't like being stationed in Cairo and he smirked as he glanced in the mirror to watch their expressions deflating. Leah caught his vibe instantly.

'He's probably got several different aliases and we've no idea what they are,' JJ said. 'He could have flown in, switched identities, then flown off the same day. For all we know he could be anyone anywhere, right now.'

'Maybe, but Victor told me Abdul went to university here. He probably has friends and associates who will help him. I bet he's hiding in familiar territory while his campaign in America rolls out. Don't ask me why, JJ, but I sense he's here.'

'I'd like to get him alone for an hour,' the agent drawled in a deep-south accent.

Leah ignored the spurious comment. 'What do we do if we find him, JJ?'

The agent didn't let up. 'We handcuff him upside down to the ceiling and force him to tell us who he sent over. Then we round up every one of those SOBs and fry their ass,' he grinned with relish.

'What if Abdul won't talk? Anyway, he's not going to remember all 900 in detail is he?' she reasoned, deflecting the idiocy of his redneck solution.

'You're right and time's on his side,' JJ agreed. 'The longer he holds out, the worse our situation becomes.'

'Our real mission is to find the terrorists in the States,' Leah stated firmly. 'Abdul can't possibly remember them all, so he must have worked from a list at some point. We need to get him and that record. He studied computer science so it's probably on a computer somewhere.'

'Wouldn't that be a gift?' JJ smiled. 'If he bought a computer with that alias we can track its chip number when he goes online. We can get a pretty close fix on that computer, and him with it.'

'Do you have a list of purchases on that card?' Leah asked the agent.

'Yeah, we do. I'll drop you at the safe house and email it when I get back to the office.'

'Nice,' replied JJ.

'Nothing about this man runs in a straight line. We've got to start thinking like him, not us,' Leah pointed out.

'Let's see what he's bought on that credit card. Maybe we can identify something that will lead us to him. Even if it's just a lifestyle choice or two, it will help us lock in.'

'Yes, let's go through that list,' Leah agreed. 'There's a good chance he's still here. If I were him, I would hide in a place I know well. That's why he stopped using the credit card, JJ! He was already set up here.'

'That makes sense, but there's one thing which doesn't,' JJ pondered.

'What doesn't?'

'We know Abdul's got one alias which means he's probably got others, so why did he leave Beirut using the name Guenaan? Why leave a mile-wide trail to Cairo?'

'But he didn't really leave a trail, did he?' Leah said, twisting the ring on her finger. 'If it hadn't been for that street vendor, we would still be in Beirut clutching a big bag of nada.'

'Yeah, I suppose,' JJ agreed. 'Let's hope our luck holds.'

'When we get hold of him, I want to interrogate him alone,' the agent smiled, making JJ and Leah look away to stare at the rain sluicing down the windows; the steady thump of the wiper blades counting out the seconds of their impatience.

Pulling into a driveway, the agent turned around in his seat. 'There's the house. It's a four bedroom paradise. The keys to the jeep are in the kitchen drawer and your new papers and credit cards are here. Sign here…that is, if it's not too much trouble,' he added testily.

They did so in silence, then got out and walked up to the house. The agent put the car into gear and accelerated away with a screech, without saying goodbye. 'Arrogant English bitch. I'd like to handcuff her upside down,' he muttered as he sped away.

'Hotdam, if this is his idea of paradise, I'd hate to see his version of hell,' JJ exclaimed, kicking a pile of rubbish towards a corner of the living room.

'It rather lacks the old world charm of an MI6 safe house, doesn't it?' Leah grimaced.

After a microwaved meal, which JJ dug out of the freezer from a solid block of ice, he perched on the greasy brown couch and pulled out his BlackBerry. The list of Khalifa's purchases had arrived and they pored over them together. It showed sixteen transactions made over a three-day period. On the first day Abdul had bought a few items in Beirut; on the second he had bought the plane ticket and lunch at the airport and on the last day he had used it only once, in Cairo. Among the Beirut purchases was a 562 dollar item from ComputerCentre – Abdul had bought an HP G60 laptop.

'Sweet! We've got a hit,' shouted JJ ecstatically. 'We can get the unique chip number from HP and see where he's been on the web. When he gets online again we can pin him. I'll set the hounds on it while we grab some sleep.'

'I hate to party-poop, JJ, but this feels a bit too easy. My alarm bells just went off.'

'Really? Damn, I hate it when that happens. But my bells are silent. I think Abdul's luck just ran out. He's made a mistake. All criminals slip up eventually. Their ego leads them to believe they are clever enough to fool anyone and it insulates them from reality. Nine times out of ten they simply underestimate their opponent.'

'I hope you're right, JJ. But my instincts are saying – be careful. Very careful indeed. We're up against a first class mind. Let's make doubly sure that our egos don't walk us into a trap.'

READING THE BOARD

Sitting at his desk in his apartment, three storeys above the weary streets of Cairo's slum district, Abdul trawled through the news wires on Google expectantly. It was the sixth time he had done it that day. Once again, he was surprised to discover the Americans still hadn't arrested his second two snipers. Leaning back in his swivel chair he looked up at the ceiling with a frown; his lips tightening into a thin line of anger. 'This is way too long for those two imbeciles,' he thought.

During the extensive recruitment of his fighting force, he had realised early on that there was a weak link in his chain, and it was language. Potentially, he had tens of thousands of willing fighters in Asia and the Middle East to choose from, but he had only selected those capable of passing themselves off in America unnoticed. The biggest barrier to that, had been selecting people who could speak reasonable English or Spanish. Once the attacks started to roll, he knew the American populace would become ever more fearful and increasingly more suspicious of their neighbour.

Abdul had solved the problem in two ways. By recruiting fighters who were fluent and by including two individuals who should stick out like Martians; thus turning his weakest link into a point of some considerable strength. He had deliberately chosen one particularly incompetent pair and placed them as his second wave of fighters. His logic was simple: they would be caught after two or three missions; releasing the next, more terrifying wave, in a shorter time scale than the security forces were anticipating. He knew that Ali had subtly educated America's law enforcement to expect each wave one month apart, which was way too long for his patience.

Now that Ali had demonstrated to a fearful American public what one man could achieve in five weeks, it made the severity of attacks by the next pair less important. In order to build the level of fear into a tsunami of terror and crush America, it was vitally important the third and fourth waves were released quickly. And the third wave couldn't get going until these two had been captured, or better yet to his mind – killed.

'Now that Mann has told the world everything, those two idiots should have been picked up the moment they bought a pack of cigarettes,' he murmured. 'Those two must have acknowledged their weakness and hoarded supplies beforehand.'

The shooting of six officials was truly excellent work, way past his expectation of them, but they were now delaying his overall strategy and he wanted the plan to run on his schedule as it scored a beautiful double whammy against American law enforcement and he prided himself on efficiency.

'What's taking them so long to find those two idiots?' he wondered. 'Unless the police are deliberately holding back. But only the President could sanction that type of order, and the political risks of issuing it are high – mortifying even,' he grinned. It was bound to come to light, and a war-torn country is not the best place to go begging for forgiveness and understanding.

Immersed in his thoughts, Abdul reached across the desk for an ornate silver box and poured out a long line of glinting powder. As the Bolivian flake sharpened his mind, a vulpine leer spread across his face. 'If they are holding back from catching those two, it means the President of the United States is helping me kill his own citizens! What a crying shame we'll never meet, we would have got on like a house on fire,' he laughed out loud at his gallows humour. This was a moment worthy of a more sophisticated celebration. He picked up the phone and hit the intercom button.

'Hey, girls, bring me a bottle of the '62 Cristal and an ice bucket.'

Deciding to balance things more evenly, he tipped out a second line and snorted it up through his other nostril. Then he sat in the chair with his eyes half-closed, and let his mind loose.

'Someone must be advising the President. Now I wonder who came up with that defence? Can't be a member of the security forces with their one-track MO of catch or kill. Definitely not a politician – too selfless. I must make a few enquiries and find out who it is. Not a bad try person X, but I'm afraid I must put a stop to your little game.'

There was a knock on the door and he waited patiently while the girls fussed over him and poured his champagne. 'Later girls, later. I'm devilishly busy at the moment. Come back in half an hour and you will both get my undivided attention, I promise,' he said, smacking a pert buttock to elicit an excited squeal as they scampered out of the room.

'Let's see...What to do? What to do? Can't let it continue,' he smiled, picking up the bubbling glass in front of him. 'It deserves an equally clever reply or a swift response...or perhaps both,' he debated with himself pleasurably.

For a few minutes he considered switching his plan around another way, but he knew that in order to cause countrywide chaos it was imperative to have the President deposed and arrested at the end of the process – not the beginning. Besides, he didn't have the hard proof he needed to guarantee impeaching the President at this precise moment. Then it suddenly dawned on him that he and William Mann had effectively swapped sides. And if the President was letting him kill US citizens unhindered – he should become the hand of justice.

'Who's the terrorist and who's the law-abiding citizen now, Mr President?' he laughed with delight; flipping open his cigar case; selecting a Davidoff No. 4 to christen his new-found power.

'Master Mann appears to have usurped my own position, so I must step into the breach to protect and serve the American people. It will make some muck-raking journalist a bit of a star, but it's not a perfect world...not yet,' he thought, logging on to the internet using his 1998 computer: the last ones ever manufactured without a numbered chip; tracing them is impossible when the web connection is routed through fifty ISPs simultaneously.

After logging off, he refilled his empty glass with the delightful knowledge that he must have his enemy pretty rattled for them to imitate Winston Churchill, who on discovering that a blanket bombing of Coventry was imminent, didn't publicise it, as it would have tipped off the Germans that their Enigma code had been broken. The fact he had achieved a similar result, with only three men, made him feel unusually high, before a more sinister thought came round to haunt him.

'The only reason the American President would take such a reprehensible course of action is if he needed to buy some time. But buy time for what? They must assume the cells are operating individually with no connection between them, so rationally, holding off can only serve another purpose: they need time to hunt me down,' he grimaced, pouring out another line.

Covering one nostril with his index finger, he bent over the desk to vacuum it up, then sneezed twice and picked up the phone again.

'Hey, girls, give me an hour would you? I need time to think.'

Two men, thought to be responsible for the recent spate of shootings were arrested this afternoon, following a tip-off to the Washington Post that they were hiding in an apartment on the second floor. Over 100 officers from the NYPD and three SWAT teams surrounded the building in Downtown Manhattan. The men were caught after leaving through a side entrance and attempted to bluff their way through the police cordon. Police have charged both men with the five shootings in New York and the murder of the Chief of Police in Miami.

A bomb disposal team spent two hours in the apartment before forensic teams went in to conduct their analysis. Eight rifles, an assortment of handguns and ammunition were discovered hidden under the floor.

As they were led away, one shouted to reporters that another wave of four extremists will attack us before the end of the week. Speculation is mounting that it would have been better to suppress this information and there is an unsubstantiated rumour that the next four terrorists will use more drastic methods than the bullet.

Sales of guns, ammunition and Kevlar jackets have sky-rocketed, selling at ten times the price they would have achieved only a month ago. The apprehension now gripping the country is making people stockpile food, while gas stations are reporting shortages as people fill up containers to minimise their number of trips in future.

President Mann has appealed for calm, saying there is a greater statistical likelihood of being run over by a farm tractor than being killed by The 24th Revolution, but most people are ignoring his plea.

Panic broke out at 7am this morning at the Chicago Union train station, after a loud bang caused passengers to stampede for the exit. Four people were critically injured and an elderly woman died when she was crushed against a wall as two hundred commuters panicked and fled platform 5. Rail chiefs have apologised, their press spokesman saying the noise was made by two trains being coupled together.

The number of false alarm calls reached a point last night where the emergency services would not respond unless they had independent confirmation that a genuine attack or emergency was taking place.

People everywhere are waiting to see where they will strike next. Some churches are holding services and prayers that it will not be their own city that is attacked. Senior clergy have criticised this, calling for compassion and prayers for all those affected, rather than praying for the attacks to occur elsewhere. They have called this behaviour un-American and a meeting has been convened to formulate a moral response to the crisis.

QUEEN'S DEFENCE

JJ awoke to the timeless sound of the muezzins calling their flocks to morning prayer. He grunted and rolled over to look at his BlackBerry. Opening up his email, he went straight to the ones from Head Office and was disappointed to read that there was no trace of Khalifa's laptop ever being used on the internet. 'NUS purchase' seemed far too simplistic a message to announce a dead end. He got up resignedly and went into Leah's room, tossing his PDA onto the pillow to wake her.

Leah looked at it. 'What does "NUS purchase" mean,' she asked.

'Not Used Since. It's normally used for credit cards against a date, but in this case it means he hasn't used that laptop on the web.'

'He must have bought it for a reason JJ. If it wasn't to get online then it's for something else.'

'You think that's where his list of terrorists is, don't you?'

'Well it has to be for something and who wouldn't use a laptop to hop on the web? If he hasn't gone online then it's for another purpose, and I doubt anything is more important to him than that list right now. So yes, I bet it has his list of terrorists on it.'

Leah looked at the PDA again, noticing the Cairo purchase – 12106 Egyptian pounds at Karida's Belly Dancing and Cabaret. 'JJ, we're looking for a short man carrying a laptop, with a penchant for prostitutes.'

'What does that word mean?' he asked, putting his finger under the charge.

'It means "entertainment",' she translated disapprovingly.

'That's one hell of a lot of entertainment,' JJ said wistfully. 'You're right, Abdul's been whoring. It's too much for dinner and dance.'

'JJ, if we catch up with him, I think it's vital we get that laptop. Without that computer all we get is a culprit with no guaranteed way to track down the terrorists. Nice to have him, but it might not stop the bloodshed.'

'He can tell us where it is when we catch him.'

'If we take him alive, but what if one of your gun-toting buddies kills him in a fit of patriotism? We must make sure we've got that laptop before we call in your boys with their hardware. Capiche?' she said forcefully.

'Okay, we'll try and locate it before we move on him.'

'There's no possible way he could remember all 900, and he bought that laptop just before he went to ground. I'm certain of it, JJ. We must locate that laptop before we jump.'

'Okay, but if we can't verify where it is first, I'm not going to risk losing him.'

'No, but we must try for both. What if he kills himself before we get a chance to interrogate him? There's not much point in finding a door you can't open. If Victor had the suicide gene then so does Abdul. There's a lot of evidence that suicide runs in the family... think Kurt Cobain,' Leah added.

'Yeah, okay. Well, I guess the only leads we've got, are his interest in prostitutes and his love of a fine lunch. Maybe I should become a patron of the better bordellos Cairo has to offer, while you stake out the restaurants. Unless you'd like to swap me,' he suggested, flashing a little-boy grin at her.

Walking into Karida's later that evening, the first thing that struck him was how luxurious it was. Stepping off the rain-washed street on the edge of Cairo's slum district, JJ was expecting something far less sumptuous. Its quiet opulence was further exaggerated by the rain storm which had cleaned away the layers of summer dust and grime on the dilapidated buildings outside, exposing their huge cracks and peeling plaster. A glaring reminder of the poverty endured by the families inside.

With his feet sinking softly into the plush crimson carpet, he walked up to the large mahogany desk and asked the overly made-up girl where the bar was.

'Amorrican?' she purred in a soft Egyptian accent.

'Sure am. Just got in,' he said looking around.

'To drink here, you must be accompanied by one of our hostess.

Drinks are fifty pounds each, and house minimum is 3000 pounds. Here is list of our girls and here is one of our boy companions,' she smiled, handing him two crimpled laminated sheets. As he took the battered menus from her, he kicked himself for not wearing gloves. He ran his eyes over them. Twenty-five eager expressions smiled at him eagerly, as enticing as stale beer.

'Do you have any girls that speak English as well as you?'

'Some does, but I think you like Resolin best. She very nice and from Croatia so her English is very good,' she said, tapping a bell on the desk.

'Okay, that sounds excellent. I was supposed to meet a friend of mine here at the beginning of last week but I didn't arrive in Cairo until this morning. You may remember him. He's about this high, well cut hair and a light beard, with one green and one blue eye?'

'Many men comes here, I cannot remember all.'

'I understand. Perhaps this will help?' He peeled off a hundred dollar bill from his money-clip.

'Let me think a moment. Yes I remember now...he is here last week. A very generous man – he left with two of our girls.'

'We've always had the same tastes. Can I have them as my companions this evening?'

'This is impossible – they have not returned,' she replied, looking a little anxious.

'I see,' he said handing over the note. 'Did he leave in a cab?'

'No – he want to walk. Not a good idea in this part of city. If you speak with him, ask the girls to call me. I am worried.'

'I'll come back with him another time. If he returns, give me a call,' he handed her his business card with another hundred dollar bill folded on the top.

'Thank you. I will call you when he return again.'

'And I'd like it to be a surprise. So don't tell him I was here,' JJ passed her another two bills.

'I understand, sir,' she replied, slipping the money under her skirt, glancing furtively behind JJ. 'Please come back soon,' she called after him as he strolled back towards the entrance. Safely outside, he walked around the corner and stepped into a darkened doorway to call Leah.

'I'm pretty sure he's close by. He left here with two girls and he walked. It's good in one way, bad in another. If he'd gotten into a cab we could have traced the address.'

'Almost as though he knew that isn't it, JJ?'

'Yeah. He would have stood out a mile – travelling late at night with two hookers in tow.'

'Where did they go? Have you asked the girls?'

'That's another thing. They haven't returned or called in. Even the Madam's freaked.'

'He can't be far away. How do we find him?'

'Stake-out. If he walks around this part of town with a laptop he won't be hard to spot. We'll start first thing tomorrow.'

'Why? Planning a little more research first?' Leah asked, annoyed with herself the moment she said it. There was an unmistakeable twang of female jealousy in the tone.

'No, I'm coming straight home to you. Unless you think I should?' he teased.

'I don't think the US taxpayers would approve.'

'You mean you don't approve.'

'Stop messing around and come straight back. And don't wake me unless it's life or death,' she shouted, clicking off abruptly.

'Damn, where did that come from?' Leah thought, flinging her Blackberry at a cushion on the bed.

SWAPPING PIECES

Following JJ's suggestion, they both set off for the slum district which also houses the largest souk in Cairo. Leah dressed in a chador and a black headscarf without the veil, because JJ insisted she shouldn't wear one. 'How the hell will I know it's you?'

'But I want to look for him without being seen,' she pleaded, as a small tremor of fear butterflied in her stomach. 'We're stamping on his turf and something feels wrong, JJ.'

They stepped out of their cab a few blocks from Karida's into the narrow maze of alleyways that circle and weave around the slum quarter. It was grim. Grey faded walls bulged over the narrow streets and an open sewer was running down one side of the uneven pavement.

'Smell him?' JJ joked.

'With his wealth, Abdul would be safe anywhere in Cairo; so why choose here?' Leah asked, wrinkling her nose in disgust.

'Why indeed,' JJ responded, knowing Abdul would become invisible among the sea of humanity hurrying about its business.

After spending the morning familiarising themselves with the network of streets and alleyways, they started to realise the hopelessness of their search.

'There must be five thousand people in this one square mile,' Leah sighed. 'This isn't working.'

'Yeah, let's split up. Why don't you wait in that coffee shop opposite Karida's and I'll stake out the archway over the main entrance to the souk.'

'Deal. But I feel like I need a shot of white lightning to wait around here for any length of time – not coffee.'

'Pretty bad, isn't it?' JJ nodded at a lump of human sewage boating down the open drain between them. 'Call me if you spot anything,' he called back, striding towards the souk.

She found her way back to the café on her second attempt and sat down outside; drinking in the warm sunshine as though it were antiseptic balm. Just as she was lifting her third cup to her lips, a low voice behind her said, 'Don't move. I have a gun on you. Point-blank.'

Startled, Leah froze. 'What on earth? Who are you?'

The voice chuckled. 'I have many names. Let's suppose I'm the person you and your American colleague have been asking around for.'

Realising it was Abdul, Leah struggled to stay calm. 'What do you want from me?' her voice trembled.

'A little patience and your power of reason for the time it takes to drink our coffees. This may be the only chance we get to chat without Copus Interruptus.'

'Chat? Why?' She asked, trying to claw back some control over her panic.

'Why? That is my question. Why are you hunting me, Leah? Yes I know your name, who you are, what you're both doing in Cairo. An associate of mine has been trailing the two of you around all morning. You see, I too have a support network, but unlike your military resources mine is made up of concerned citizens.'

'Count me firmly among them,' Leah stated with feeling – her fear turning to anger. 'As a citizen myself, I'm concerned you've launched a horrific nightmare on the world, Abdul.'

'Evolution and progress do not happen without change, Leah.'

'Evolution and progress? You risk taking us back to the dark ages. You could unhinge people's perception of the rule of law and send the world spinning into anarchy.'

'Oh come now. People prefer to be in organised groups. They like being part of a structure, so after a little freefall a better structure will emerge. If you think about it rationally, the law was designed to help people live together in harmony – without fear from a few. It used to be controlled by the people, and therein lies the problem.'

'What problem?'

'I see from your ring that you knew my father well, so you probably know the answer to that question. You must be extremely bright for him to have given you that gift because he didn't tolerate fools unless they were politicians. Whatever else your relationship involved I can only guess…Ah haa! All becomes clear to me now. It was your idea not to arrest my second two snipers – am I right?'

'My relationship with Victor wasn't like that at all, Abdul. In a way, you and I are more like brother and sister.'

'So it really was your idea. I congratulate you. It was brave thinking and cost me a few days.'

'Victor didn't want his plan implemented unless a dictatorship took over. Why are you going against your father's express wish?'

'Largely because I agree with him. The dictatorial and gladiatorial foreign policy of the West must be halted or the world will fall into enmity and chaos – or worse. There are many more people living under the Western yoke than there are holding it in place – so God speed the majority. Anything less, seems a little unfair.'

'How vainglorious of you, Mr Khalifa.'

'Alright, let's cut the bullshit,' Abdul replied earnestly. 'I'll tell you what made me act. Democratic freedom has been caught, chained and sold down the river. It's being manipulated to quench the thirst of the few who crave ever more power. Certainly in Russia and China and even in America under George Junior. Several bankers I used to spar against in the US are bleeding democracy out of the European Union right as we speak. When I was selling my company, they asked me to join their clandestine Skull and Bones fraternity. Mr Bush is a member of that select club…There's nothing quite like sitting alone in the dark for three hours with only a human thigh bone and skull for company, to really focus your mind on what life's about. It doesn't answer the "why" but it sure answers the "what". I went along to their private little island in the St Lawrence river out of curiosity, then decided it was safer to organise my own disappearance rather that put them to all that trouble when I turned them down. Democracy is dead. As dead as those bones I sat with. They killed it a long time ago. All that's left is an involuntary twitch of its corpse.'

'Democracy is dead? It's not dead, Abdul, and it's worked well for the last 2,400 years.'

'Foul! What society has had real democracy in the last 2400 years? Not one. The irony of democracy is that it was invented by small warlike bands to make them fight as one unit, instead of individually, the noblest form of human conflict. Think of the knight engaged in single combat: extremely powerful but against numbers he will always lose.'

'Democracy is the only mechanism which supports the greater good,' Leah said firmly.

'Democracy can work well, providing people maintain control of their leaders. It disappears when the voting population exceeds forty or fifty million, mainly because the more reasonable citizens start feeling they have lost their influence and stop voting. If you don't believe me, look at the percentage drop in the voting public against the number of citizens able to vote. More and more people are not voting. Many actively refuse to do so, thinking their individual voices are being drowned out by the greater volume of voting citizens.'

'You're picking out the faults and conveniently ignoring the good. Democracy is a trusted concept. A belief that has stood the test of time.'

'Time? True democracy was killed in Greece a few hundred years after it was born. Ever since, the notion of democracy has been commandeered by powerful men then used as a platitude to disguise their real intent – which is greater power coupled with less responsibility for their actions. Originally democracy was invented by pirates. It was used to great effect for thousands of years. Why do you think it came out of Greece? You think that mere coincidence? It emerged in Greece because there were a large number of pirates operating among its plethora of islands and inlets. Pirates used it to great effect there, then everyone was forced to follow their lead as it became the only way to defend yourself and survive in that region. That's why it spread so quickly. Pirates developed a code which unified them, ensuring they attacked as a single force, which gave them a fighting edge. Then everyone had to adopt it to defend themselves and survive and Hey Presto! Democracy was born. Those pirates unified themselves by voting for their captains and had a single code they all agreed on. Pure democracy is virtually identical to that original pirate code. Is that is what you choose to base your "rule of law" on, Leah?'

Leah hunched her shoulders, '*What is going on here?*' she wondered. Abdul was using her own weapons against her, while she was playing devil's advocate. Devil's advocate against the devil himself. She decided to take the gloves off to test him. 'Our laws have been developed over many centuries and most people prefer it that way.'

Abdul laughed. 'Most people are too blind, too lazy, or too ignorant to look at the past and transpose it onto the future. The democracy you so love and admire has disappeared completely. It no longer exists. It's an empty shell which modern politicians hold against people's ears, telling them they will hear the sea.'

'No, the beauty of the democratic process is it prevents extreme forms of government.' Leah fought back.

'It's supposed to but as you well know, that's not reality. Our leaders manipulate democracy to win control, then force their own private agenda down everyone's throat. Many of our leaders can't even wait that long. They use violence and intimidation to win power. For example, how about a hero of modern democracy? Aha! There are so many to choose from. How about the great Nelson Mandela? Thousands died at the hand of his officer wife Winnie, whose preferred means of political persuasion was the rubber necklace – possibly the most horrific death ever devised. Oh yes, I can see how motivating the game is, but I hope you're not going to add that being torched is the will of the people. I tell you, even pirates wouldn't have put up with having a couple of car tyres squeezed over their arms and set alight. But Nelson's party, the ANC, carried it out for years. You know, it's not the fire eating through your sides which kills you. The heat makes your brain expand before mercifully, your head explodes like a grenade. People scream right up to that point.'

'I don't believe Nelson Mandela gave orders to use the Rubber Necklace.'

'Don't think that after the first few rubber necktie parties he didn't know all about it. And he certainly didn't choose to stop it. When he could have so easily – with a single word.'

'That can't be true. When election time came, millions voted for Nelson. They wouldn't have done that if they thought he was a murdering thug.'

'How delightfully naïve. The ANC weren't the only black political party in the running. I assure you, when the time came to vote for Mandela – it was a no-brainer.'

'Okay, what about the real despots? Hitler and Mussolini.'

'Yes, and they were both democratically elected. Hitler was another who used intimidation to win control. Most people think Hitler,

Mandela, and Bush W in another way, are the exceptions. I hope you aren't one those made foolish by altruism. It would lower expectation of you, Leah.'

'The system enables us to vote for our leaders and change them if they run amok.'

'They do run amok, don't they? That's because we hand them four or five years of unfettered power. Modern democracy is a contradiction in terms. People vote once every four or five years then surrender to the king's rule. And it doesn't have a good track record for delivering the best leaders of a nation. Those who get in are ruled by fear of attack or driven by a lust for power, or both, so they frequently go to war. That's without mentioning the gleeful feeling they experience when they implement the momentous – however stupid it is. Our democratically elected leaders are governed by those base motives. Often with appalling results.'

Leah's informed mind knew the points of his argument were correct. And she wasn't born to that belief – she had studied politics in depth. But countering this, Abdul had loosed the Sword of Damocles on the world. She decided to change tactics. To put him on his back foot she needed to raise her game and she went on the offensive. 'Okay Abdul, if you have a better suggestion, then what is it?'

'It's democracy. But real democracy. There is still a piece of me that is my father's son.'

'Real democracy? What's that?' she feigned, hoping against hope it wouldn't be the same as her own beliefs.

'As I said, it works well when politicians can be held to account by their voters. This vanishes when the voting populace becomes large. The public may not realise that, but our politicians know it well. I find it no coincidence that they all push hard for bigger numbers of voters. Take a look at the European Union. They've put 300 million voters under one government roof.'

'But there is a safety aspect, Abdul. A united Europe won't war with itself.'

'No, it simply wars with someone else. It doesn't stop war, Leah. It's far more dangerous in the medium term. It creates a base from which the few can effect their own agenda, without the inconvenience of having to answer to their citizens. Our leaders understand this. They know the individual stops bothering to try and change anything when confronted by a hundred million voters.

Think of it this way: if modern democracy is such a saviour then one day we will have a united world, with one Government representing all nations. Interestingly, that means that if Europe and America voted one way, their votes won't equal half of China's – which has two billion citizens. So in a united world democracy, China rules forever. I can't see the average Midwestern American farmer tolerating democracy in that situation, can you?'

Leah picked up the coffee pot to pour a fresh cup. She used the movement to camouflage her other hand sneaking towards her BlackBerry.

'I've never killed a woman before. I wonder if it feels different from killing a man.'

'Sorry.' She put her hands where he could see them.

'Allow me to finish. Look at the frustration of the majority of reasonable people with the first American President of this century. When he was elected for his second term, it boiled down to 180,000 bozo farmers in Ohio choosing the leader of the most powerful nation on earth. In doing so, they handed power to a fool and dictated the future fate of the world. Hardly something that most people agreed with. That's what I call usurping democracy and look at the end result – an idiot in charge. A dangerous idiot who went on the record saying he believes in the "End of Times", then promptly set the two greatest religions on a collision course which will take at least a hundred years to resolve. That's reaping the rewards of old school democracy alright. My God, what it's really done is achieve feudalism on a scale this world has never had before. Even when it became obvious to most people around the globe that he had barefaced lied, what did they do? What could they do? Nothing. Not until his reign of global terror was over.'

'Exactly. His reign was over and he had to step down.'

'But he was a religious fanatic. He left behind a hundred year religious war.'

'You're perpetuating the myth by saying that, Abdul. We've no proof it will continue for that long.'

'But the fighting does continue. Even now it's killing thousands of people a month.'

'It will resolve itself because people have a desire for peace. Peace goes hand in hand with democratic principle.'

'I'm sorry to inform you, Leah, the argument that old school democracy prevents war is idiocy. The wars just get bigger and more dangerous. As they get bigger, they become harder to stop. Tell me, which country is at war with the most other nations, and which has it been for the last hundred years?'

'It's the USA. But only because the leading nation of the free world must also police the free world.'

'And you think that's why they went to war with Iraq, is it? To police the world?'

'I don't know the answer to that, truly I don't.'

'I don't much care what it was either. If I did, I would have sent way more than 900 over. I'm only interested in stopping them fighting other nations. If I wanted to take it further and put them down harder, I could have done so with ease. With surprising ease actually – there are many that hate them to the point of sacrificing their own lives. The USA are the warmongers of the world. They have destroyed more foreign families than any other nation on earth.'

'They are carrying the brunt of the burden by keeping the world free. Don't you see that?'

'I'll tell you something I heard rather than saw. It was an epiphany for me. I had dinner with the governor – make that the ex-governor of California – when all that WMD crap was being spoon-fed to the populace. At the end of the meal, one person told an old joke about George W Bush and Dick Cheney in a restaurant, planning the second Iraq war. It was late and the owner asked them if they could leave as he was closing up. George said, 'But we can't leave now we're planning to invade Iraq and the lives of millions of Iraqis are at stake.' Dick Cheney said, 'Actually that's two million Iraqis and a blonde.' The owner asked them, 'Why are you going to kill a blonde?' and Dick turned to George saying, 'You see, I told you no one cares about two million Iraqis.' That's when I realised something had to be done. The joke had been updated but there is no real humour without some basic truth. Americans don't care how many die – providing it's not one of them. They are certainly not as democratically minded as I am. Perhaps I care a little more than they do, or I might have set about destroying them completely. And don't think I didn't consider it.'

'So you want to reduce their ability to conduct war. That seems noble but your method is wholly misguided to my mind.'

'They can't go on dictating their self-serving feudalism to the world.

It has to end for mankind to progress to the next level. If they have their balloon deflated enough to ensure they stop their killing around the globe, then that's enough for me. So Leah, what would you fight for?'

'I would fight for freedom and peace.'

'So we are the same.'

Leah's breathing stopped in her throat. 'Look, Abdul. You're a very accomplished man with vast resources at your finger tips. Why not enter politics and fight for the changes you want?'

'I did consider it, but it's the task of many lifetimes and we only have twenty years at best to straighten this out before real mayhem erupts. This way is more certain and much, much quicker. Besides, in the true sense of the word I am fighting – probably risking my life in the process – for a real, more modern democracy. I don't see you out there sword in hand.'

'The pen is mightier.'

'Tell that to the American, Russian and Chinese military.'

'Okay, but you can't justify your means. You're risking too much on one turn of the wheel.'

'Tell me another way then.'

'Is that all it would take to call off your attack?'

'That is no longer possible.'

'Then there's not much point, is there?'

'You still don't see it, do you?' he said sadly.

'Democracy is fair and a good way to control our leaders,' she replied, suddenly aware that her repetition was weakening her argument, but she was desperate to find a point to undermine his.

'The formula is simple, Leah. No war in history has ever taken place without a strong, charismatic or religious leader at the helm. I'm not suggesting we should completely do away with the captain, but his role must change to controlling those around him. He in turn, must be controlled by the People. To win power, every single leader plays the separatist card. African leaders use racism. Conservatives use social distinction and selfish reward. Socialists use wealth imbalance. Religious leaders use the mislead of God, when by definition they are invoking his good looking counterpart. Handing politicians unfettered control of a nation for four or five years causes wars, financial hardship, social separation and racism – every evil there is in the world. Unlike our current, old school electoral system, pirates could mutiny at a moment's notice and their captain knew this. It kept things in check and filled one of democracy's biggest holes.'

'One of the holes? Name another Abdul,' Leah challenged, feeling confident of her argument for the first time.

'I don't have time to name them all. So perhaps I should choose something relevant to you… how about hung parliaments in your beloved Britain? They are often born out of a crisis. Just when a country needs clear direction to get itself out of the mess created by the previous democratically elected government's incompetence, the people are rewarded with a hung Parliament. The different parties then spend their time bitching at each other instead of getting the job done.'

'Yes, and the more extreme parties with only a few seats end up with the casting vote,' Leah found herself agreeing.

'Exactly Leah. Hung Parliaments are the tyranny of the minority. If you want to hand power to small bigoted factions, there's nothing like a crisis followed by an election to really cement it in place. It becomes the worst of all worlds. Alternatively, look at Barack harnessing the power of the Internet to garner 500 million dollars for his election campaign. That's what people can achieve en masse. That's what can happen when ordinary people have a say.'

'Oh God, I know…and when he did get into power, Obama had his hands tied by the Republicans in Congress. The will of ordinary people was smothered by their control.'

'Indeed it was. Good old fashioned democracy – chugging along at its very best – in quite the wrong direction. Republicans are ruled by fear. They're terrified of an attack on America. They know it will reduce their power, wealth and influence, so they panic and send their military overseas to do their dirty work. They attack other countries with the idea of keeping the wolf at bay, but it also prevents the development of peaceful co-existence. It hands their victims a uniting grievance, creating two opposing sides. The smaller one then becomes bigger and more deadly. Al-Qaeda's most effective recruiting sergeants were the two burning Bushes, democratically elected and handed a four and eight year reign of global terror. George Senior funded and trained the Mujahedeen in Afghanistan, out of which Al-Qaeda emerged. George W attacked a Muslim country, probably for its oil reserves; the fool not realising that the Muslim faith is borderless. He united every one of Islam's extreme factions against the West, when before, they were happy wrestling with each other. Although the groups were many – they stayed small. Look how the attack on Afghanistan united the region against the West. Now extremist Islam rules an enormous region and when the Taliban take over Pakistan, they will have the Bomb. They're half way there now. Personally I think George Junior knew exactly what he was doing – he was an extremist Christian himself.'

'Yes, and Gordon Brown thought it was a good idea to hand the Taliban supporters 87 million pounds to try and turn them, which they used to buy arms. His naïveté beggared belief,' Leah said resignedly.

'Yup, and he slimed his way into power without being elected. Look Leah, there is another way to use democracy without these antiquated aspects and pitfalls. The people of the Western world are more educated now than they have ever been. They are better informed and they like peace. For the first time in the history of Man we have a way to vote collectively on issues – the internet and phones. It's no coincidence that Europe was united by a few politicians at the same time the power of those two mediums was becoming self-evident. The idea of using efficient communication to win control over our leaders was starting to develop in people's minds. The oligarchs' solution to us having that power was to increase the numbers of voters – so they united Europe. They fast-tracked it. It's one thing to organise that kind of change in Britain using the Net to vote more frequently – quite another to organise that change across the different languages and cultures of Europe. That's how the European élite, together with the real men of power in America, prevented it from happening. They fought fire with fire. But the élite were not satisfied with that, so they put in fail-safes to guarantee their autonomy. Now the President of Europe is a non-elected office. Find me the democratic principle in that, Leah? Government is no longer on the side of the People. It is on the side of Government. They are supported by a broken electoral system which is dangerously out of date. 350 years out of date. I intend to bring it in line with 21st century technology and harness the power of peaceable, reasonable people. My goal is to create that platform. But I can't make an omelette without breaking eggs.'

'But where is the omelette, Abdul?'

'Ah, a George Orwell question, I might have guessed. The omelette is people being able to vote on issues, via the internet and mobile phones. The internet also allows for an in-depth critical examination of any and all ideas. If 25,000 people argue a policy is wrong or stupid and provide sensible reasoning – people take note. In reality, it isn't as popularist as you imagine. Effortless, accurate, mass communication wasn't around when Mr Orwell said "show me the omelette". Personally, I think he would have approved. I think he would have run down to the chicken coop before breakfast and slapped the pan on the stove himself.'

'Damn,' she thought, 'Orwell would have been up with the dawn for those eggs.'

'Think about it, Leah. My political process is exactly the same as a court and a jury. The citizens of each country are the jury, so no change there, and MPs become the legal council. Are you saying you don't believe in the method used to determine guilt or innocence, Leah? Because my process is exactly the same as the one which supports, maintains and delivers your sacred rule of law.'

Leah went silent, sipping at her coffee as her mind raced. His reasoning was distinctly unsettling. She had never supposed his intentions were based on the side of righteousness, and worse, his solution wasn't only possible, it was both feasible and pragmatic. She recalled what Victor had told her about his last discussion with his son. What were his words? That when good meets evil, it may be very hard to distinguish them; if you asked which culture was more likely to usurp the earth's resources or enslave mankind first, the Great Satan could well be the Western nations. She knew if everyone had the ability to vote frequently – things would change. And Abdul was right about the majority wanting peaceful co-existence. Switzerland suddenly flashed into her mind. The country which had the most frequent voting system had also been neutral for the longest period. Switzerland had never attacked another country. Not bad, considering that two world wars had raged around it. She imagined it starting in one country then sweeping across the world. It was an exciting idea. An ideal which matched her own. She decided to push him once more to find out if he was telling or selling. 'Look Abdul, I knew your father well. He fought for democratic principle all his life. You're trading a tried and proven system for the distinct possibility of anarchy.'

'But Leah, I do believe in democracy. I just want the "For the People" and "By the People" elements to which Lincoln referred, reinstated. We can do it now. We have the means at our disposal.

The "Wisdom of Crowds" is a scientifically proven concept that works. Try and get 30 odd million people in Britain to vote for going to war. It's not possible when they are not attacked first. Then ask yourself: who would want to attack an enlightened, tolerant, peaceful country? Anyone doing that will lose the PR battle instantly and the leaders of the aggression will fall. They won't be able to sustain their militant impetus because the warrior faction is always in the minority. Most people, everywhere, like peace. The warmongers are outnumbered thousands to one.'

'So how are you going to achieve that with an attack on the US?'

'Oh I will. Just watch me now. You're clever, Leah. I can see why father gave you that ring. He must have thought highly of you.'

'You don't really know do you?' she pushed, hoping that by challenging his reasoning he would divulge details of his plot.

'Let's just say that I still have an ace or two to play. I'm sorry, but I'm not going to forewarn you of my plan to get us there.'

'Do you really believe that by wreaking havoc on people's normal existence, you can break down the might of the USA?'

'I do. They will be forced to form themselves into smaller and more accurately governed groups.'

'You really believe the US will break into smaller entities as a result of your attack?'

'They have no choice – it's the only way they will be able feed themselves. The lines of supply will break down, forcing people to find food and provisions on a more localised basis. Most of California's milk comes from Wisconsin 1,500 miles away. When that changes, it will create massive employment locally at the cost of a few faceless corporations. Not all bad, eh? The controlled fear that is about to hit them will lead to a low-key chaos and radically reduce freedom of movement. And hungry people become resourceful, quickly. They will form themselves into smaller, self-governing groups to service their needs. States, I think they're called.'

'Why America? There are bigger and more dictatorial Governments in China and Russia.'

'Indeed there are. Well for a start I'm lazy and America is the easiest one to attack. Secondly, when my plan does pop their bubble, it will stop the religious war of Christian against Muslim from going any further. Not much glory in attacking the weak is there? Unless you're Western I suppose. And thirdly, I am attacking those other two Superpowers; because when I succeed in the US, someone is bound to implement the plan in Russia and China. They in turn, also become targets of my attack.'

'People will be too terrified to go to work, Abdul. The lines of supply will rupture, leaving each State to fend for itself to feed its citizens. Is that what you want your success to look like and history to remember you for?'

'Actually, that will do me nicely. When that does happen the real targets of my attack, or I should say – my far-reaching goal – will have come to pass. I'm going to take the might out of the oligarchs wherever they are. As a knock-on, the might out of any dictatorial government so they can't do any more world harm. My objective is nothing new. Have you read the American Constitution? I mean the original one drawn up by the Founding Fathers?'

'Of course I have....' and her voice trailed off as she realised his point.

'The original has been radically altered by amendments. A process that was ratified by Congress. The original idea was that each State would provide the military personnel for national defence. The concept behind it was that the President has the power to go to war but each State had to provide the forces after a vote among its own citizens. I know that California and most of the coastal states would have voted against sending any of their troops to Iraq. Even New York State was against that war and it houses the highest percentage of Jews in America. See what I mean about "By the People, For the People"?'

'There's no doubt he would have had difficulty initiating his war under those rules,' Leah said resignedly.

'Indeed he would. But in its current form, the Constitution allowed him to go to war in return for a few lies and a lot of fear he spread about WMDs. Even when it became apparent he'd misled the world he still maintained his office. After all what can one individual, voting once every 4 years, do against the US Government?'

'There isn't much they can do.'

'True democracy, Leah. Brought up to date in a modern world. Now that's worth fighting for, don't you think?'

'So you intend to engineer a greater good by launching a terrible fear on the world. But in the process, you risk undermining the rule of law forever.'

'Nothing is forever, Leah, we are both intelligent enough to know that. As I see it, we both hold the long term safety and freedom of our fellow Man at heart. You think it can be arranged peacefully, while I, together with all leaders, think it must be fought for. It's only in the method, the medium to deliver those freedoms, on which we differ. Personally, I don't think the outmoded structure of democracy has any chance of getting us there. It hasn't done so far, and there's now a real risk of world destruction and tyranny attached.'

'Where is the risk if people unite peacefully, Abdul? As they have done in Europe.'

'I'll tell you. I'll tell you exactly how it will happen and it will take place within the next generation. Which means your children will have to face it, if good people like you sit back or persist in employing non-effective methods. You know about Hungary? Right as I speak, tens of thousands of ordinary citizens are holding rallies dressed in Nazi-style uniforms. They have an extreme right wing agenda and they've already singled out the Romanies as their anti-Christ. Then there's Poland. It has one of the most brutal police forces in the western world, where kicking down your door and beating you senseless is considered the standard way to arrest a suspect. Combine that with a man who knows how to snip away freedom, and you've got the perfect formula for the slippery path to tyranny.'

Leah seized her chance to score. 'Eastern Europe has had little time to develop and mature. They will calm down and become less extreme under the influence of the more mature cultures of Western Europe.'

'Ah, like Denmark, France or Britain perhaps? Let's see. Denmark introduced a law in 2009 so the police can arrest anyone demonstrating peacefully. The French use a law to arrest anyone without a valid ID; they can also seize their victim's home and possessions. Then there's the British. Demonstrators have been arrested and charged. They are no longer permitted to complete their march if it is considered embarrassing to the Government. They are crowded into areas which are blocked off, and held there until they lose interest. In several recent demos people were attacked and killed by their own police. Seeing the pattern yet? Add to that a European President who is like say, Idi Amin, General Pinochet, Omar al-Bashir, Robert Mugabe, Hitler or even the boy Blair, and it becomes obvious what will happen. The laws for controlling the populace are already in place, Leah – put there by our democratically elected leaders. Add someone who wants to feel his power and we've got a problem. An irreversible problem.'

'That last assumption is far-fetched, Abdul.'

'Is it? I find it difficult to name any large population where it hasn't happened. Take a look at George W implementing Homeland Security. He raised the flag of fear to remove *habeas corpus* and many other basic freedoms from the Constitution. More obviously there's Putin in Russia. Then consider mankind's history. It's brimful of examples: Stalin, Atilla, and every single Chinese Head of State – whether supposedly communista or feudal lord. Every politician wants to rule the World, Leah. They all climb the ladder for one thing only, and they literally get away with murder. The murder of their own people first, their neighbour second. It's far-fetched to think it won't repeat itself.'

Leah sat staring sightlessly at the people passing by. The thesis for her Master's degree had been 'The History and Politics of Eastern Europe'. All Abdul's points were cast-iron fact; and she had never considered a President of Europe using the internal forces already at their disposal. He was also right about history repeating itself. Anyone betting against that – lost. Her mind was spiralling into quandary; caught between the knowledge that his argument was correct, and her instincts screaming that the end never justifies the means. 'But war is often considered a just means, which is as bad as you can get,' she thought. The weak have always been ruled by the strong. But being strong did not mean you were bad – she was inherently good. Why should the power-hungry, the evil, the stupid, have all the power? Another comment of Victor's came to her: "There are not enough good people who have the brains to instigate change and the will to see it through".

She suddenly saw it. It blossomed in her like a scorched lawn kissed by the summer rain. To create positive change the strong – people like her – had to act; not sit on their hands. They had to stand up and play a part, or risk relinquishing control to the darker side of Man. A feeling of inordinate strength radiated through her. She herself, could create change. She had the intellect, the ambition, the training and a few bonus cards: her good looks, empathy and social skills. Victor had told her she would have to rely on many different agencies and she held the belief that you should never stop talking to the other side – no matter how loathsome it was. And Abdul didn't even fit that category. It appeared that he was fighting for freedom.

'Dammit, Abdul. You're a hard man to ignore.'

'Domesticated animals are the easiest ones to stalk, Leah.'

'The problem with war is that it drops the future of mankind into the control of second and third rate minds.'

'I think we have much in common, Leah. Look – why don't you join me? I could do with a person as bright as you and only the two of us need ever know. My intentions are honourable. Perhaps a little forward-thinking but that's all. I will speed up the advancement of mankind – not hold it back. It's unfortunate I have to use such drastic means to get us there, but if you want to crack a large nut you need the right sized hammer.'

'But there are peaceful ways to instigate change,' Leah countered.

'Funnily enough, if there was a peaceful way to go about it I think most reasonable Americans would welcome my end result. Unfortunately, they are so fearful of losing their top-dog status that there isn't another way left open. If things progress they way they were going before I stepped in, think of the eventual show-down they would have had with China. If nothing had been done, the US would have continued to vent its paranoia creating wars in distant lands – like a child with a shiny new toy to play with. Especially now there's a law protecting the entire administration from any and all wrongdoing, providing they are at war. Courtesy of George W.'

'Yes, that is a very dangerous law.'

'Excellent euphemism. It was implemented by Georgie Boy to include all of his staff. It wasn't reported on any US media network and most Americans are unaware of the change even now. He did it mainly to ensure that he couldn't be prosecuted for torturing suspects. I heard they used razor blades on men's testicles – pretty effective on the guilty. After a moment or two, I imagine they all pleaded guilty as loudly as they could scream – even the innocent ones. It's no small wonder he consistently refused to give out any detail on how he interrogated his suspects. I noticed he always crossed his legs when refusing to answer that question. And Blair must have known about it too. If not, he is guilty of the most heinous incompetence. Makes you wonder who the real terrorists are, does it not?'

'I know, I know. If a president wishes to remove any accountability for his actions in Government, he simply engineers a war.'

'You're bang on. And zero accountability equals absolute power. Instantly granted providing you're at war. Even George realised the advantages and let's face it, he was not the sharpest knife out of the drawer.'

'I accept that your intentions might be positive. You would have created more fear and panic if you hadn't told the US how many terrorists you had sent in.'

'Absolutely correct and quite wrong, Leah. Because they are freedom fighters – not terrorists,' and he laughed out loud at the clear and indisputable point it lent his argument, knowing it would be the statement of any reasonable person oppressed by a greater force. Which he now realised, included the high-minded morality of Leah.

'Okay, supposing I am convinced, what do you want me to do?'

'Write your phone number on the paper napkin in front of you and I will be in touch.'

'Call me old fashioned, Abdul, but I don't give out my phone number to a man pointing a gun at me.'

'You don't expect me to hand over mine?' he joked.

'If you want my help, you'll have to trust me sooner or later.'

'Trust takes time, Leah.'

'Okay. I'll trust you first. I'm going to turn around. You can shoot me, but I won't be much use to you dead.'

'Okay. Then turn around.'

Without hesitating, Leah swivelled in her seat to look straight at the source of his voice. In complete shock, her mouth fell open involuntarily. Instead of the man she was expecting to see, there was a black-robed woman in a full chador, wearing a light face-veil.

Khalifa sat motionless. His left hand resting on the tabletop, his right underneath; holding the gun. She could see the glinting outline of a pair of mirrored Ray-Bans reflecting a sterile glare back at her. His unwavering stillness made him appear robotic and although she was quite used to seeing people dressed in this way, the knowledge of what lurked beneath his disguise lent an aura of menace to his appearance.

Leah stared at him without breathing; mesmerised by his mannequin-like stillness. He suddenly reached up and lifted the veil. Slowly and deliberately, he took his sunglasses off, letting her see into his eyes which instantly arrested her own. They glinted like diamonds. But the burning coals were ice cold and had the terrifying look of emptiness at their core. 'If the eyes are the windows of the soul – this man has no soul,' Leah realised, the thought allowing her to return to herself. She forcefully broke his gaze by looking away; to find the waiter standing next to her, asking if she would like another pot of coffee.

'Yes, I will have another,' she said, summoning the courage to face Abdul a second time. When she eventually resumed eye contact he had put his sunglasses back on. She was met by her own reflection. It looked startled and fearful.

'I wear them as a social nicety, as my eye colour seems to have a rather daunting effect on people,' he said carefully.

'It's not the colour,' Leah thought, standing up to swing her chair over to his table, using the action to compose herself. 'I didn't believe you when you said it was impossible to end your attack on the US.'

'Nether did I,' Abdul replied evenly.

'If you call it off – I will help you. I will help you take down more dictatorial Governments but not the US. That must stop.'

'That would be a more dangerous game to play.'

'It depends on who we target first.'

'Who would you target first, Leah?'

'Russia. It has an enormous number of dissidents already. Russia is bound together despite different languages and cultures. Traditionally though, they were separate independent societies. With the right timing and co-ordination we could have people voting for their own smaller governments within a year.'

'I agree with your timing but not with your target. China is the place to start. It's averaging sixty riots a month in the countryside, which are being put down hard by their military. All we need do is move the insurrection to the cities, then boom!'

'China would involve too many deaths. I can't go along with that.'

'True. China has a love of capital punishment and mass execution. The beauty of attacking America first is that it demonstrates the phenomenal cutting power of The Sword of Damocles to the rest of the World. It sets a perfect precedent that will terrify the leaders of stricter regimes. A smart dictator will hand the vote to his people pretty fast, or he runs a substantial risk of losing his own life.'

'Are we back at square one then?'

'I'll swop China for Russia if you throw your hand in with mine.'

'That's tempting, Abdul. Call off the attack on the US and I will.'

'All well and good, but I can't stop it instantly. Then again, how do I know you aren't bluffing? Let's face it, we've only known each other for twenty minutes. I think you're setting your price a little high.'

'Okay, call off the attacks on the USA early. You've made your point. Then I will help you.'

Abdul chuckled to himself. 'You have a deal Miss Mandrille, but you must be patient. It will take time and I need some assurance of your loyalty. I'm not convinced I have it.'

'I was your father's protégée. I helped him edit his last series of lectures on "We the People". If you read that series of lectures you will know that when it comes to Russia, I'm already onside Abdul.'

'I know all about them. Since he went and topped himself, who doesn't? Look, write your phone number down and I will be in touch. Then get up carefully, turning only to your left, and walk to the Ladies without looking back. Wait inside for five minutes. Forgive my caution but like many women – I don't enjoy getting fucked on a first date.'

'One last thing Abdul.'

'What?'

'You burned down an orphanage. You must pay for it to be rebuilt or count me out. 100 million Lebanese pounds.'

'I've already arranged for 250 million. Trust me, it will cost around 150 and the excess will effect immediate assistance. Now, do we have a deal?'

'...Yes, we have a deal Mr Simmius,' and in rising excitement, Leah got up and did as he instructed, but only waited in the toilet for one minute. Walking quickly to the front of the café she glanced up and down the street, but he had disappeared into the endless mass of people streaming along the busy thoroughfare. 'There are advantages to being short,' she thought, feeling a strong desire to stamp her foot in frustration. Instead, she pulled out her BlackBerry and clicked speed dial one.

'JJ,' bounced back his reassuring voice.

Three storeys up, on the top floor of the building opposite, one of the girls handed Abdul a cup of mint tea as he sat down to observe the street below. He watched Leah pacing up and down as she made her call to JJ.

'Pity. What a pity. Now I will have to destroy you too, Leah,' he thought, turning to the girls. 'Pack your bags, we leave here tonight.'

EN PASSANT

Christopher Childs was a very precise man. He had a perfectly functioning and beautifully formed loathing of all things he considered imperfect or inferior and happily, they were legion. He won a doctorate in mathematics before deciding on a career in the logical discipline of law. A natural progression to his mind: the mental precision needed for legal documentation reassured him. He found it effortless to switch his clinical mathematics for a more verbal logic, while thinking it no small coincidence that the number 1 and the letter I required identical strokes of his pen.

He had changed his name to Christopher Childs after qualifying as a criminal lawyer at Columbus University – the same year his father died. He didn't want his father to feel his shame so he waited patiently until that moment, telling his small circle of friends he was changing it because of the bigotry and intolerance associated with his Arabic one. Privately however, he simply never liked the old man and changed it because he wanted to expunge his father's memory from the earth – waiting until he died as he had always been a little scared of him. It was a small, but deeply pleasurable act of revenge, and well worth his patience. Besides, he would breeze, his new name was better suited to his profession and he had been forced to change it to avert people's racist preconceptions – beautifully implying that it wasn't his fault.

In truth though, he hated the name he had been born to because he assumed that was the reason why everyone treated him differently; conveniently shutting out the realisation that the precision he so loved and admired, others felt was stilted. So he carried on blindly measuring everything. Priding himself on his ability to work out the truth in a case – and the likelihood of winning it – by using logic and advanced mathematical principles like chi-square correlation techniques; whenever the opportunity arose. If he had monitored

245

his speech with the same objective approach, he would have discovered that 'I' and 'idiot' were among his most frequently used words; which would have surprised him greatly, had he taken a moment to consider what that truly meant.

One of the by-products of his linear thinking was that he was always on time and insisted on a similar punctuality in others. This trait had led to his subordinates and colleagues awarding him the nickname 'Clocker Chris', which wasn't quite as affectionate as he considered it to be, but then, a wider understanding of human nature was not something he could ever be accused of.

His first wife was born Christian but became a Muslim out of love for him, even though he no longer practised his faith. His life was so precisely organised and pre-planned, that when she announced she was pregnant he had flown into a rage which as the years went by, festered as a well-hidden anger and deep resentment towards his wife and son. And all because the birth wasn't timely. At least, not according to his schedule. He wanted to have a child three years later, when they had some money saved and he would be less inconvenienced by the intrusion. The untimely arrival of his son annoyed him so much that he policed the boy – finding fault at every turn. He never missed an opportunity to chastise.

When his wife tried to demonstrate Western tolerance to the boy, in combination with Muslim doctrine and beliefs, Christopher spotted it and became even more incensed.

His logic so ruled his mind that compromise was alien to him, even though he could express the concept as an algorithm, which he often used for negotiating difficult plea bargains. There was a right and wrong in everything and he was the only person who had the intellect to understand that. Christopher was the keeper of the gates of precision and, as far as he could see, the only one capable of the responsibility.

When his wife died of a brain haemorrhage five years later, she left her son defenceless and more tragically – loveless. Christopher remarried and had three wonderful children; presenting him with a new way to vent his spleen on the boy: he openly flaunted his love for them; turning his back on his firstborn, whom he openly despised. This alienated the boy, who wandered into his teenage years with well-rounded sense of bitterness and isolation, until in his mid-teens, he found solace in the needle and set about destroying himself with a determination that should have impressed his father. 'I knew he would go down the drain,' Christopher thought, upon discovering the fact.

'I felt sure he would turn out this way,' he confided to his few friends, without noticing that some of them also thought it was inevitable after witnessing his constant berating of the boy. But 'chicken or the egg?' is not a concept which can be expressed mathematically to provide a conclusive result. So he simply locked away the idea in his box of 'foolish little things' that he kept firmly under the bed of his better self – then dismissed it. In this way, he removed his unfathomable fear of anything he couldn't pin down with accuracy.

In keeping with Christopher's two-dimensional view of the world, when he did lose a case it was never his fault or the fault of his mathematics – it was someone else's stupidity or an unforeseeable event. A mantra he had to repeat time and again without ever suspecting the true common denominator.

He had chosen the legal profession not just for its logical sanctuary, but because he loved to win an argument. Certainly, he hated to lose one. There was nothing he enjoyed more than roasting the dove of someone's imagination on the burning flame of his logic. He never realised that the oldest portion of man's brain is reptilian – the part which enables logical thought and the low level cunning of survival. This would drive him to prosecute successfully even when he knew the person was innocent. 'That is the function of the law,' he would say as he congratulated himself on a job well done. For in keeping with reptiles, he was happily devoid of conscience and consideration for anything he didn't enjoy, benefit from, or own.

Christopher glanced at his watch as he poured himself a coffee in the kitchen, noting he had exactly four minutes to drink it down before leaving for court that day. He was eagerly looking forward to this particular morning in the San Francisco Court of Criminal Justice, as it was judgement day on a case that had come to the attention of an incensed public over recent months. Most people didn't feel that the woman he was prosecuting should be executed for killing her husband, while the tyrant slept off another night of alcohol and abuse. In Christopher's view, she had murdered her spouse in cold blood and must pay for it accordingly. That was the beauty of his mathematical thinking, it was delineated; so perfectly pure and, as straight as a falling suicide. Better still, it made events inherently predictable through calculus; enabling him to shut out the occasional twinge from his higher mind without pain. Christopher always felt it was safer to stick to his maths than reach for the esoteric pinnacles of compassion and acceptance.

'I would've had this in the bag months ago under Sharia law,' he lamented, picking up the large box-briefcase he had packed meticulously the night before. An efficiency he had carried out every day of his working life.

'Don't forget to collect the kids from basketball tonight,' his wife called down the stairs in Arabic. 'The auditors are coming in today to file the tax return, and it always drags on till late.'

'Of course I won't forget,' he shouted back, angry at her reminder. It seemed to imply that he was as stupid as everyone else and he wasn't – he had his degrees in mathematics and law hanging in pride of place in the hallway to advertise the fact.

Double-handing his black briefcase into the trunk of his car, he was mildly surprised by its weight. 'I did a great job squeezing all those briefs and papers in last night – I bet I need the lot today,' he thought as he clambered behind the wheel.

Arriving at the courthouse, he parked in his allocated space in the underground car park and took the lift to the main floor. In this way, he didn't have to fight through the jeering crowd which had taken up residence at the bottom of the courthouse steps.

At first, he rather enjoyed the notoriety that his position as Assistant DA and Chief Prosecutor afforded him in this case. With news reporters fawning over him, sticking microphones under his nose to beg him for comment. But as the case neared its climax over the past few days, the crowd had become increasingly belligerent and Christopher had been jostled and shouted at, with one woman grabbing his arm and tearing the sleeve of his Armani suit in a desperate attempt to make him listen.

'No comment! Now let go of me or I'll have you arrested,' he snarled before stalking off; checking his watch to see he had lost three minutes from his busy schedule. That was all it took to upset his orderly life. 'A gaggling group of idiots,' he thought, lengthening his stride to make up for the unexpected delay.

Striding into Courtroom Four that morning, he placed his briefcase on the table in front of him and sat down. Unlike his associates, he was in the habit of leaving the large black case on the table; taking out the relevant document as and when required. It was a show trick designed to impress the jury and cower the defence council, who knew how difficult it is to be that efficient. Each time he put his hand in the briefcase, Christopher would allow an expectant hush to fall across the courtroom, before pulling out the correct document with a flourish and quoting from memory – without ever referring to it for a prompt.

As the second hand on the clock above the judge's chair clicked to ten o'clock, the court usher called out, 'All rise for Judge Sarkwood in the case of The People against Jane Marshall,' and Christopher stood up and made a show of swivelling his briefcase around; positioning it precisely in the centre of his desk.

'Before we proceed, do you have the submission documents with you?' asked the judge in a bored manner.

'I do – I have them right here, sir,' he replied, leaning over to release the two fasteners of his briefcase, which sprang open with a satisfying double thump. Pulling up the large flap across the top, he looked inside to retrieve them. In shocked surprise he saw that instead of his papers there was wiring and a battery, surrounded by marzipan with nails stuck in it. As his mind computed what it must be, he opened his mouth to scream out his terror. One second later it detonated in a monumental explosion.

Had he still been alive, the perfect timing of the bomb would have impressed Christopher, without him once realising that his robotic thinking had engineered the highly predictable lifestyle that killed him: his foundation stone / his headstone. But he, like everyone else in Courtroom Four that day, was either killed instantly or died a few seconds later when the roof collapsed.

The news reporters outside rushed to transmit the tragedy to the world, as the CCTV footage of the courtroom revealed the first American-born Arab to become a successful suicide bomber. Over the ensuing few days they combed through Christopher's personal life, coming quickly to the conclusion that he had carried out the bombing in revenge for his son's overdose; deciding he blamed the decadent standards of Western society for the decline which had caused his son's death. Even the terrified reaction he had shown on opening the briefcase had been clearly identified as a last scream of angry defiance.

'The first suicide bomber of The 24th Revolution' and 'The first Muslim suicide bomber born in the USA,' they chorused in their news coverage to the world. Which would have eased Christopher's lifelong frustrations immensely: he always wanted to be a number one.

'He certainly won't be the last,' Abdul smiled, reading through the news reports before deleting Christopher's real name from his database:

Click.

CROSS CHECK

They both waited in a fever anticipation for Abdul's call to come through. After the first week, JJ began thinking Abdul had changed his mind, but Leah felt certain he would phone, insisting they wait patiently in their hotel without 'Chasing around like a dog after its tail. Let him come to us, JJ,' she had to repeat, almost daily.

She had told JJ everything about her meeting with Abdul. Everything except the agreement she had made with him – the bargain they had struck. Towards the end of the first week, Leah also started wondering if Abdul had reneged on their deal. She wasn't convinced he would keep to their pact and the terror attacks in the USA were on the increase – in both number and ferocity – with four suicide bombers venting their horror on two packed shopping malls, a nightclub in Dallas and the San Francisco Courthouse.

Moreover, JJ seemed unsettled by Abdul's attempt to recruit her. He questioned her in depth about it more than once, with a lull in between to see if the answers she gave back were identical. Towards the end of the second week, Leah felt relieved she had kept their agreement secret. One dangerous ally seemed enough, without adding JJ to the list.

But there was a price attached. It smacked of betrayal and she started to feel a little guilty by not telling him. What stopped her was the clear belief that if JJ ever thought she had teamed up with Abdul, in any way whatsoever, he would shoot her dead in a heartbeat. And arguing that she was fighting for the world's best interests would not convince a bullet from his gun. She wracked her mind for a solution to the dilemma, but without one that would guarantee her safety, she thought it better not to divulge it – hoping against hope that Abdul would end his attack. How long could it take him? Assuming he wanted to, and that option was subject to the law of diminishing returns.

Eventually he did phone, but they had to wait two weeks before her BlackBerry announced the anonymous call. He didn't say his name or use hers. His well-manicured voice said only, 'Meet me where we first met one hour from now. If you want to stay alive, be sure you come alone.'

This sparked a heated debate with JJ, who wanted to send in a team the moment he showed.

'He knows who you are and that you're after him, JJ.'

'That Madam in Karida's must have tipped him off. You should have let me pull her in.'

'If his information flows through an intermediary or more likely several different contacts, Abdul will see it coming. He'll be long gone before you can kick down any doors and we can't afford a single mistake.'

'The pig of it, is I can't be sure of the local police and military here, and I don't have nearly enough men to guarantee a sure-fire capture,' he said resignedly.

'Yup, and if just one of them gets spotted we lose our connection to him and with it – our advantage. Besides, JJ, if he wanted to kill me he could have done it already.'

They finally agreed on a compromise. She would go to the meeting with her BlackBerry on speakerphone, while JJ shadowed her from two streets away; allowing him to react instantly 'if anything spins out'. His last comment was designed to remind her of Jimmy MacCack's express order, that when danger loomed, she must follow JJ's instructions to the letter.

Arriving at the rendezvous, she was relieved to see her old table empty and sat down and ordered a pot of coffee; paying the moment it arrived. Half an hour later she was about to order a second when her BlackBerry vibrated an incoming call. She put JJ on hold and pressed answer.

'Walk to the northernmost part of the souk and meet me there,' came Abdul's distinctive voice before the line went dead.

She clicked over to JJ and told him the new meeting place.

'I'll parallel you two streets away. Go slow, okay?'

Leaving what she hoped was a memorable tip, Leah got up and

meandered slowly down the busy street towards the market. Arriving at the right area of the souk she wandered up and down the stalls, trying to look calm and ordinary while her heart pounded to a very different rhythm. 'So this is what it feels like to be bait,' she shivered in the hot sunshine.

On her fifth circuit the BlackBerry vibrated again.

'I see you are alone. Do you know the Luxor Hotel? Meet me there. Room 216.'

She knew she wasn't that far away, perhaps a fifteen minute walk at most. Returning the BlackBerry to her bag she rummaged around, pulling out a pair of sunglasses, using the subterfuge to say, 'JJ can you hear me?'

'Just, wassup?'

'He's in the Luxor Hotel, room 216. And someone's watching me.'

'OK. Go there but wait in the lobby. Don't, I repeat DO NOT go up to his room. If he comes down, stall him. I'll re-position the team.'

'How long will that take?'

'We'll be in place in less than twenty.'

'I'll be there in twelve or fifteen.'

'It will look bad if you don't make it on time. If you need me before we are in position just click the BlackBerry off, okay? And Leah, don't go anywhere with him – understand?'

'Don't worry, I won't.'

Making her way slowly to the new rendezvous, she was suddenly overtaken by the same ghostly feeling she had first experienced in the burnt ruin of the orphanage – the iggerley sensation of someone following her. It felt like Abdul in person. Her vulnerability shrieked out warning and she flickered her eyes around nervously, unable to prevent herself from looking back twice. She began studying the reflections in the windows of the shops she went past, but couldn't spot anyone trailing her, tall or short.

Mainly to compose herself, she focused her mind on the coming meeting. An unsettling instinct was crying to be heard, shouting that something was wrong. 'This is a little too easy,' she thought, and the alarm grew louder. 'Think girl,' she told herself. 'What if it's another test?' Abdul had already sent her to two meeting points – why not a third?

As she stepped into the cooler air of the hotel lobby, it struck her that this could well be a foolproof test of her loyalty. If Abdul was not in room 216, JJ bursting into the Luxor with ten armed Westerners would be witnessed by everyone in the vicinity, let alone the twenty people drifting about the lobby itself. 'Christ, it might even make the local evening news,' she thought. If this was a set-up, they would have nothing but embarrassment to show and when Abdul discovered her betrayal, he would come after her.

Caught in a crossfire of indecision she set all of her intellect to work; desperate for a clue that would reveal the correct course of action. 'It's the damned delay,' she realised. 'Why did he wait so long to call? It doesn't take two weeks to set up a meeting. Abdul knows this city well, so there must be another reason for the delay.' Making up her mind, she walked determinedly past the reception area to the lifts, as though she were already a guest of the hotel. Once the doors closed she relayed her decision to JJ. 'I'm going up to his room, JJ. Don't talk or you will get me killed. Just listen.'

'Dammit Leah, I told you to wait downstairs.'

'Stay silent and stay back – I know what I'm doing.' Another whopping fib she told herself.

Arriving outside room 216 she tapped on the door – nothing. She knocked again louder, listening acutely for any minute sound. After one more go she could sense the room was empty. Her first instinct had been correct and she pulled out her Blackberry.

Positioning the front of her PDA directly over the keyhole she selected the 'Key' option. A small silver balloon disappeared into the lock, then a hissing sound announced it was inflating properly. A few seconds later the BlackBerry tried to rotate and the lock clicked. The screen flashed 'unlocked' as a shoof of air sucked the metallic balloon back into its compartment. Pulling down the handle, Leah pushed open the door, waiting where she was before stepping silently into the room. The air inside was completely still but laden with the scent of expensive aftershave. It smelled fresh, no more than half an hour old.

'He probably made his last call from right here. Perhaps he hasn't bailed, maybe he's coming back,' she hoped, sensing the complete opposite.

Walking around the end of the bed, she spoke to JJ again. 'Call it off. I'm in the room and he's not here. It was a test, JJ. There's a chance he'll return.'

'Shit, Leah, we're arriving outside the front entrance.'

'Wait there and don't show yourselves.'

'It's too late for that – a cop's coming over to us…. Shit.'

Leah read the room quickly. The bed was unslept in, but showed the wrinkling of someone sitting on the end. A small black wire snaked out from under the bed to the wall socket by the nightstand. She bent down to investigate, then let out a squeal of delight. Blinking at her from the darkness was an HP laptop. 'JJ, his laptop's here. He must be close. Disappear – I'll wait in the lobby.'

Later, as the sun was casting long shadows across the marbled foyer of the Luxor, the girl behind the reception desk was becoming increasingly suspicious of her.

'Are you sure your husband is coming?' she asked Leah for the fifth time. 'Why don't you let me check you into a room and you can wait for him there in comfort?'

'No, no… No, you're right. Do you have a room on the second floor?' Leah asked, walking over.

'Certainly, let me see. Room 220 is free.'

Going back up to room 216, Leah unlocked the door then locked it behind her, 'He must have spotted you, JJ, or he would have called me by now. What shall I do with the laptop?'

'Grab it and leave. I'll meet you out front.'

'Take it? That's a giveaway if ever there was one. What if he sends someone for it? He'll find out I'm against him as soon as the cleaner gets here tomorrow.'

'Okay, plug in your BlackBerry and download the data to Head Office. You know how to do that, right?'

'Yes, JJ, I just look stupid.' Unfastening the Ethernet clip from her BlackBerry, she plugged it into the port on Abdul's laptop.

As the computer booted up from stand-by, it found the additional hardware of her PDA and connected to it five millionths of a second later. Immediately, the laptop received a file that took over the Windows operating system source code, handing her full control of the keyboard. She typed in her user ID and password, then ran a de-encryption program to get around any security he may have put in the way. Satisfied she had done everything correctly, she clicked "Download to server".

She was now connected to an S11 military-class satellite which bounced the signal to its neighbour on the other side of the world, which beamed it down to GCHQ Cheltenham at just under the speed of light. "Big Brother 1" – a Cray Supercomputer – the most powerful electronic processors ever built, hooked in to receive the data; sending it straight into a secure vault to prevent the spread of any hostile viruses. A sensible precaution as there had been countless cyber attacks on the secretive system from the first day it had been switched on. The giant mainframe is one of four Crays which are connected to each other in parallel. Collectively, they are referred to as 'The Brotherhood' by the 260 technical staff who support, maintain and develop their programming. The "Brotherhood' represents a substantial portion of GCHQ's information capability; which is both phenomenal and highly classified.

For several minutes, Leah watched the screen flashing "Running download" in electronic green, then went back to the door to make sure it was locked. 'I'm getting panicky,' she thought, suppressing an urgent desire to bolt from the room when she pulled the handle down.

Twenty-three minutes later the screen changed to "Download complete" and with a haste borne by the fear of being caught in the act, Leah disconnected her BlackBerry from the laptop, slid it back under the bed and ran for the door.

Back in their safe house she watched JJ accessing the data Big Brother 1 had processed and pronounced virus free.

'Sweet! We've got them all, Leah' he grinned ecstatically. '917, including Ali and the first two snipers. Names, money spent – the lot…No pictures though, huh.' And he looked up at her, puzzled.

'What? What is it?' Leah asked, picking up on his concern.

'When you were up there, did you take a shower or something?'

'Are you kidding? Of course not.'

'What were you doing up there for half an hour then?'

'I was downloading the data. Why?'

'Because this file should have downloaded in two minutes. Definitely less than five.'

'Well it damn well didn't, JJ. It took that long while I sat watching the blasted thing and counting the seconds. I'm not doing that again in a hurry I can tell you. How big is the file, anyway?'

'Only three megs,' he said, studying her more closely.

'Only three? I suppose that is odd, maybe the connection was slow.'

'Yeah, maybe it was,' he said, making a note to check the line's baud rate as soon as he was alone. 'I'm sure you're right. I'm getting the hunt on for these men... and women,' JJ said with surprise, as he scrolled through the list of names.

'This is off limits to hotel guests,' the cleaner said angrily. 'How did you get into this room, it's lock...' were the last words the Luxor Hotel janitor ever spoke before the point of the stiletto punched through his diaphragm, slipping on without resistance to sever his heart. After wiping the blood off the blade, Abdul stood up, shut his laptop and placed it carefully in an expensive leather briefcase. He attached a heavy veil around his face then slipped a pair of brown calfskin gloves over his hands.

Cracking open the door an inch, he checked the coast was clear by standing stock still and listening for the count of twenty. Satisfied the utility room was empty, he walked out of the cleaning cupboard to the service elevator and went up to the fourth floor. When the doors opened onto an empty hallway he stepped into the customer lift next to it and pressed 'L' for lobby.

'I'm going straight to L,' he smiled as he pressed the button.

A warm inner glow of satisfaction suffused his senses, making him smile broadly under his disguise. He hadn't felt this good since he sold his company for seven billion dollars – not even that amount of money would have purchased the password information in his briefcase. 'Thank goodness for wireless internet protocols,' Abdul grinned as he strolled away from the bright lights of the Luxor; heading towards his second apartment. Hidden among the dark maze of streets in Cairo's slum district.

DISCOVERED CHECK

By the evening of the following day, JJ's mood had turned black. With good reason. He had received two emails from Head Office; and from a professional point of view the first was terrible, while the second felt even worse. He had grown extremely fond of Leah, so to find out from the log of her download that she should have been in and out of that hotel room in under ten minutes, pointed at betrayal.

He had discovered that both their BlackBerrys had the highest communications priority. Meaning they would enjoy the fastest connection to the servers that the laws of physics would permit, with the Ethernet link adding the only restriction. And he knew Ethernet connections were fast, extremely fast. They would download a 3 megabyte file in the blink of an eye. So what the hell had she been doing up there for twenty-three minutes?

When he picked over her actions in detail, he began to see a common theme. Leah had deliberately disobeyed his instructions not to go up to Abdul's room, and he only had her say-so that it was empty. What if it wasn't? Twenty-three minutes was plenty of time to update each other and didn't involve the risk of communicating by phone or computer; either of which would leave an electronic trail of their duplicity. Mouth-to-mouth was the safest, quickest way. Then more perplexingly, Abdul had got clean away. But they had been concentrating on the people going into the hotel, not so much on those leaving it, and all because Leah had said Abdul wasn't there. Leah also knew when he was arriving with his men. She had asked him 'how long' and he had told her! Then just as they were about to storm the place, she instructed him to stop and 'disappear'. Conveniently, it was only after that, Leah said she would cover the lobby. For all he knew they could have had lunch in the restaurant together while he and his men waited outside in the heat, panting.

Something was definitely amiss and he fought with himself on whether to challenge her over it, but knew that if she was working with Abdul, it would inevitably tip him off. Abdul would simply vanish and he had no guarantee that Leah had the right intel to locate the terrorists. It was a futile gambit. So instead, he decided to monitor her future actions more closely, while saying nothing.

The frustration of being forced to keep his suspicions silent had deepened his sense of anger – not triggered it – the first email was responsible for that. His NSA colleagues had scoured every database in the USA for the remaining 914 terrorists and had come up with a big phat zero. There was no record of any of them entering the US and, with the exception of Ali, no record of any of the names being used for driving licences, social security cards or anything a person would need to operate in the States. It was puzzling – unless it was pap. For all he knew she could be laughing her pretty head off inside, as she sat opposite him plastering that look of concerned worry across her face to mask it from him. Shit!

It would be much easier if he didn't like her so much. The combination of her possible betrayal and the thought that he might have to harm someone he really liked, was unnerving. Topping all this, his radar had been picking up her desire for him. He had been secretly hoping their relationship would blossom in greener pastures when this mission was over. Shit!

The bitch of it, was that Leah could carry out anything she set her mind to. Perhaps the signals she had been sending out were all part of a ploy to win his confidence; providing her with enough elbow-room to operate in comfortable ease. He looked up from his BlackBerry, wondering if she would read the suspicion in his eyes.

'What is it?' Leah asked, sensing his mood.

JJ locked eyes on her. 'That list you downloaded isn't going to help us. Apart from the first three terrorists none of the names connect to anyone in the US. If it were five or ten of them I could accept it. But 914 hiding anonymously in the US for the past six months? Hey honey, that's 904 too many...' and he let his voice trail into deafening silence.

'Well, Abdul has forged identities, he probably handed them round.'

'Maybe, but we should have some trace on a few of them: a car accident; a hospital record; some damn thing. Anyone setting up that many false IDs over a short period would stand out a mile. There are behind-the-scenes checks and cross references on all

US visitors and residents that make it a lot trickier to get around than we let on.'

'Do you think it's a false trail then? Is that what you're saying?'

'Maybe. What do you think?'

'I think the list is real or it wouldn't have Ali's name on it. Abdul must have seen you coming and discarded the laptop. He probably thought it would make him stand out as he left the hotel.'

'Possibly, Leah, possibly,' JJ replied, not liking her answer one bit. If they were operating together it was going to be very hard to catch her out – but he was determined to try. Sharpening his voice to the razor edge of accusation, he took a long clean swipe at her. 'Why didn't you alert me when Abdul first made contact at the café? All you had to do was click one button and this would be over now.'

'I told you, JJ. The Blackberry was sitting on the table. He saw me trying and warned me off. Christ, this is unbelievable. Talk about no good deed going unpunished. You really think we're in cahoots? What's changed, JJ? Don't you trust me?'

'Leah, my father taught me never to trust anyone saying "trust me".'

'God in heaven, you really don't. Do you?' she fired back, her temper starting to blaze. 'What a bloody nerve! You take that back right now or I'm resigning this instant. It's not my country that's under attack.'

'What's wrong, Leah? Scared I've rumbled you? Coz if I have, I know why you'd like to bail. Maybe you should, it might save your skin.'

'Oh very cute, JJ, very cute. Now why this sudden change of heart?'

'Perhaps you've had a change of heart,' he accused angrily, kicking himself the moment he said it.

'What? Hang on a second. Let's calm down and be rational. Let me get this straight. You think that because the list is a dead end I've teamed up with Abdul? Well for one, he's very astute so I'm not surprised he's running rings around your security agencies. And for two, why would I tell you he had made contact with me? Eh, JJ? Then lead you straight to him?'

'That's true I suppose,' he admitted grudgingly. 'It would be easier for you both to operate in concert if you didn't report the contact.'

'But I did report the contact, didn't I?'

'Yeah, you did.'

'It's not just that, is it? Now come on, JJ, What's really going on?'

'Shit, Leah. I don't know. I want to believe you but the facts speak otherwise.'

'Facts? Facts plural? What facts? I thought you were accusing me because you can't trace any of them. What else is there?'

Radiating repressed anger, JJ jumped up from the sofa. He went over to the kitchen drawer and pulled it open. When he had hidden his gun in it earlier, he had spotted a half empty packet of Camels. He took them out and lit one. It was his first cigarette in eight years. He took a long pull, stepping to his right before turning around to face her.

'He's left that drawer open, next to his right hand,' Leah realised with a shock. She knew JJ was precise in everything he did, so the drawer was open for a reason and it wasn't the cigarettes – the pack was sitting on the counter next to him. 'He's left it open because he's got something in there he needs,' she thought, glancing at his shoulder-holster on the kitchen table. It was empty. 'Oh my God! Right this second girl, provide him with clear proof of innocence – he's lining up on you.'

Cupping his chin in his left hand, JJ looked at her hard. 'Okay Leah, take these facts out for a spin. I ran a check on your data download and I've got the log of your connection right there,' he stabbed his finger at the BlackBerry on the sofa. 'Take a look yourself. Then tell me why a three meg file took you half an hour to download.'

'I didn't know it was only three megs till you told me, JJ. How was I to know it was all text? I couldn't see what I was downloading because there's no read out on the screen when it's sending.'

'True, but that doesn't explain your twenty minutes to do it – Honey,' he spat the word at her, making it sound anything but sweet.

'Let me take a look.' Leah's hand trembled slightly as she reached to pick it up. JJ saw it.

'I don't understand this either. So you think I was up in that room with Abdul and warned him he was about to get busted?'

'You had plenty of time to update each other and to maintain your cover with us, you downloaded a list of people that wouldn't help us one bit. In fact, it was probably designed to mislead. You simply leave the connection open while you have your nice little chat, then click off when you've finished updating each other.'

'You'd have heard us talking JJ. The connection to you was open.'

'That's why you booked another room, Leah. You had your chat in there.'

'I booked that room because it was the only way I could get back up to the second floor. The hotel receptionist had pinged me.'

'Smooth. You've got all the answers haven't you?'

'Oh that's neat, JJ. Very neat. And who led you to him? Just suppose you are right and he was there? Why, JJ? Why would I take such a risk?'

'I don't know – I really don't. But as you say he's very clever and he's running rings around us – and so are you.'

'What? Running rings round you?'

'I can't believe you just said that! I mean you are also extremely clever. Abdul is Simmius' son. Your admiration of the man who cooked up this poison is blindingly apparent. Working both sides of the fence, who the hell knows what you and Abdul could get up to together.'

'Look, JJ, the sorry truth is that I was terrified of being caught in his room downloading that data. I sat watching the screen bleeping 'Running download' for the longest half hour of my life and a micro second after it finished I ran full tilt out of that room. I don't know why, but it really did take that long.'

Her course was now set, she realised. There was nothing she could do about it. She could never risk telling JJ she had cut a deal with Abdul. And the bastard had set her up. But why? Suddenly, the call she made to JJ after Abdul left the coffee shop flashed into her mind. Also, she had come out of the toilet sooner than instructed. If Abdul was watching her, he could have heard her reporting the contact to JJ – an unlikely act of a friend, bearing all the hallmarks of a foe. 'That's it,' she thought. Abdul had seen her, probably overheard her, then set her up against her own side. The irony of her situation only heightened her sense of alarm. Abdul was sweeping her from the board. Using JJ's hand to do it for him – his hand was three inches away from doing it. Desperate, Leah looked up to see his sharp eyes boring into hers. He was on fire inside but holding it in check – just. He looked like a predatory cat in the moment before it pounces. Amped up. Rock still.

JJ took a long pull on his cigarette then stubbed it out. He only spoke two languages well – English and body. While there are many lies spoken in English, he knew that for anyone but an accomplished actress, body language spoke the truth. Her flash of anger seemed genuine and her emotions were in the correct sequence for someone who was innocent – which surprised him. What he was seeing and hearing was wrestling with the unassailable logic of her guilt.

Without turning his back on her, JJ reached down for another cigarette; lit it; then resumed his analysis. For a person with nothing to hide she was exhibiting a high degree of nervousness, but that could be expected if she had worked out her predicament. Equally important, she hadn't altered her story to satisfy his implications, and easy explanations made him distinctly uneasy. This gave him a glimmer of hope that she could be innocent, but outweighing this were the hard facts of her download and the time she had taken to do it.

As he slid the ashtray nearer with his left hand, he realised he couldn't take the chance that his instincts were right, and the facts were wrong. The stakes simply were too high. The country he loved was being attacked by terrorists – leaving no room for error on his part. And his gambit of silence and careful observation had failed. Leah now knew he suspected her. If he let her live, she would warn Abdul: putting him on his guard; making him much harder to catch. JJ took a last pull on his cigarette. He stubbed it out half smoked, using the action to memorise the exact position of the gun with a camouflaged glance. 'I'll do it so fast she won't know it's coming. Then it's over,' he decided, steeling himself for the dreadful task.

Leah watched him: her trepidation turning to terror. She had to find a way out of this maze and judging by his cold demeanour, she had to find it fast. Unable to prevent her nervous fixation with the drawer, she stood up quickly: tearing her gaze away; forcing a smile onto her face. Putting an expression in her eyes she hoped looked like openness and honesty in equal measure, she steadied her voice. 'Just listen to me, okay? We can work this out.'

'Be my guest because I would like you to. I really would but I'm struggling. I warned you the stakes are very high, Leah. I don't have the luxury of error.'

She could see only one way out. There wasn't time for considered reasoning – JJ was about to make his move. It wasn't a 24-carat argument, but it was nearly golden and if she polished it with conviction it might throw enough doubt into his mind and buy her some time. Taking a deep breath she lined up the pieces in her mind, then looked straight into his withering stare. 'Okay, JJ. I can't prove my innocence to you – but I can disprove my guilt.'

'This better be good.'

'Just listen to me, okay,' Leah said earnestly. 'Everyone knows how long it takes to download a couple of meg on the internet these days, it's common knowledge that it doesn't take long. So anyone but a complete bonehead would expect a dedicated secret service satellite connection to be fast... Si?'

'Si. So?'

'So if I was up to no good in that hotel room, I would also know the size of the file. And even if I didn't, Abdul would – he's a computer expert. If we were allies he would protect me, his asset, and warn me to leave earlier – am I right?'

'Maybe.'

'So if one of us knew the size of the file was small, only three megs, then he or I could expect it to relay fast. Being as smart you think we are, we would also know you would find it suspicious I had been up there for that long; so neither of us would have stayed up there for twenty-three fucking minutes, JJ,' she raised her voice, allowing herself to lose a little temper, hoping it looked like righteous indignation. 'I would have come out of that room much sooner or risk getting rumbled by you. And as you say – I'm not stupid. Not that stupid. So if I had teamed up with Khalifa, I would have been out of there in under ten minutes…. Capiche?' she added, trying to ratchet down her argument.

'Not bad. I hadn't considered that.'

'The question still remains, JJ.'

'What? Your collusion?'

'No, why did it take that long?'

'I've no idea. You?

'I'm not a technician but I think we should find out.'

'I suppose. My apologies Leah. I'm sorry I doubted you,' he said resignedly, but the atmosphere between them was still sour with the stink of mistrust.

JJ was not entirely comfortable with her reasoning. Not comfortable at all. 'I'll wait a little and see if she steps out of line,' he decided. 'If she puts a single toe over it, my solution is justified,' he thought.

'Okay Leah, I'll get someone to look into it. I'm off to bed now. I'll do it in the morning, first thing,' he said angrily, slamming the drawer shut and stalking off towards his bedroom. Something else was bothering him: he wasn't completely sure that disproving guilt was as solid as the proof of innocence. His foot caught on the carpet with the thought, making him stumble as he made his way to the bedroom.

'He's not going to say goodnight,' Leah thought. Anxiety draining out of her.

JJ banged the door shut, then locked it. For the first time.

'Thank God I didn't tell him everything,' Leah breathed out, as she took three steps towards the drawer, without making a sound.

PERPETUAL CHECK

Less than a mile away, Abdul leaned forward in his hand-tooled leather chair and spun himself around in ecstasy. Even after three months of careful testing he knew there were flaws in his programming. Not flaws, but assumptions he had to make about the security software at GCHQ. The trick was to let them walk you into their computer system, holding the vault doors open and escorting you in. He wanted access to the database: ultimately, the download of his data led straight to it. No scrabbling around searching once he was in the system, that would alert the electronic hounds of security in an instant.

He had been driven straight to the treasure trove – chauffeured there.

Granted there was an algorithm or two in the way, but in the end his data had to go into the database, with him, cloaked by his dormant programming, right alongside. It really was the most incredible high and definitely worth the risk he had taken.

'No, it was a calculated risk, using my calculations,' he smirked knowingly.

He had to be in close proximity to the sender, that had been the only drawback. But once Leah had typed in her password – he had it too! The minute fisheye lens of the camera in the laptop with its light disabled, showed her blurry fingers typing it in. He received it a millionth of a second before GCHQ did – sent by the wireless card connecting straight to his computer in the basement of the hotel. Five floors beneath her in a dead straight line – the reason he had picked room 216.

Leah hadn't only downloaded a list of terrorists. A complicated string of one section of the data was tripped as it went through the security software. What started out as seemingly normal raw data, mutated each time it was examined: a hundredth of a second after the relevant examination had cleared it; passing it to the next virus program which didn't look for the same problems. Problems which were only created by the virus examination itself, causing a portion of the data to morph into an All-Seeing-Eye.

'With a bit of luck Leah will be dead by now,' Abdul thought.

Either that, or she was safely on her way to the States, hooded and chained to the inside of a private jet. All he had done was lower the priority of the programs operating the download function in the laptop. To make sure it took longer than expected, he had also implanted a small routine which channelled most of the CPU recourses away from the programs sending the data. Just for fun, he had tested the individual parts of his set-up without seeing how long the data transfer took – betting with himself that it was twenty-six minutes. Twenty-three would do it though.

'Unless JJ is a complete fool or in love with her,' Abdul mused. 'If he is in love with her he should be nicely fucked up by now. Either way there's trouble at mill,' he laughed. He had killed two birds with one stone. It was admirable. Worthy of his high standard of efficiency. And extremely satisfying.

He had spent the last five hours waiting for his data to be transferred to SCOPE: the amalgamated database of MI6, GCHQ, the police and MI5. The collective law enforcement computer system for the entire UK. It was one of the things Abdul had gambled on, and his gamble had paid off. The terrific high he was experiencing was a direct result of his entry into SCOPE. He had watched the screen on his Apple with mounting excitement, as he saw that SCOPE had exactly the same security programs and protocols that GCHQ had put in the way. He had worried about it endlessly, but his understanding of the British mindset, combining with the knowledge that GCHQ housed some of the most technically advanced programmers in Britain, made him believe they would almost certainly be the ones recommending the security software for the SCOPE system.

'If it's good enough for the boffins at GCHQ, then it's definitely good enough for us, old boy,' Abdul mimicked a haughty rendition of an upper-class English accent. 'No point in gallivanting around reinventing any new wheels, and it might save us a bob or two, eh what?'

He was tired; physically, mentally and emotionally. Twenty hours was a long time to work without a break, but then he'd had a little help from Charlie, 'And not the one that runs the chocolate factory either... or then again, perhaps it is,' he smiled, hoovering up another line of the crystalline powder, only to cough a laugh which turned into full scale hacking. Calming himself, he wondered how to celebrate his hard-fought victory.

'I know,' he thought, clicking onto the Times website and looking back a week. 'Yes, there it is.'

A young, name-seeking Foreign Secretary was prodding the Russian Bear with a very uncomfortable stick. Obviously on a bull's rushed charge for the Prime Ministership of the UK. 'If the unctuous prick can sow a little more fear and discord, he might even get there,' Abdul thought to himself. 'Huh – fear! He doesn't know the half of it. The self-serving moron shouldn't be allowed to play on this level.' This was going to be the perfect ending to an exhilarating day.

The British Foreign Secretary must have assumed that his government position would underwrite his naïve antagonism, lending it a weight and substance it should never have been granted in the first place. However, the idiot was creating a very real danger, in the very near future.

'Only a fool sticks his dick in a hornet's nest. Well, perhaps the bumptious pipsqueak isn't as unaccountable as he thinks.'

With relish, Abdul typed in the man's name to bring up his file in SCOPE. 'Sooo, let's see... What to do, what to do... Ah perhaps itinerary? Hmm. Stayed at the Gloucester Hotel three months ago. Wife not present. Went to bed 23:43. Appeared sober. No calls, mobile or hotel phone... submitted agent 107712 at 00:09. Perfect.'

'Okay then, I'll write another report. Backdate the clock first, copy that date across... Now, let's write instead that he was visited at 22:43 by a blonde, unknown, twenty-five-year-old woman.' He paused. 'No, better make that two women. That's far better suited to a British public hell-bent on schadenfreude. Screams of delight were heard at 22:54... they were obviously his, te dum te dum te dum... and they left room 322 at precisely 23:41. Abdul's eyes blazed with rapture.

'Change the agent's number to this dead one here. Save. I'll flag up a request.... Better go full search I think, and run a full background check on him as well. Triggered by... this program. Now!' he exclaimed, rubbing his hands together. To savour the moment, he slowly elevated a stiffened index finger, holding it poised on high before swooping it down to dive bomb the enter button, activating "run".

Abdul hated many things the British upheld. He was bitterly aware of their national identity from first-hand experience of it in his teenage years and as a consequence, Abdul knew that the country of rules, roles and ritual would turn viciously on anything they perceived as different from their norm – en masse. He was now using their own energy against them, to his complete advantage. The culture which took inordinate pleasure in saying 'No, Won't and Can't', was about to say 'Yes We Can' to him – in no uncertain manner.

What was it his father used to say? "Ignorance is bliss" that was it. But he knew that when it came to the British denial of anything different, it became evilly spiteful. He saw the pleasure they received from pointing the finger so vociferously at their victims; awarded greater impetus by the vain attempt to camouflage their own secret faults and desires; fuelled by the terror of being similarly exposed and unified by the rest of the herd, bleating in chorus. Abdul was hypersensitive to the hypocrisy of the banal – it was always the same: ignorant, transparent, and underwhelming. 'A glance at the headlines of one of their tabloid papers – the litmus paper of all societies – is an effortless way to monitor their MO, and anyway,' he grinned, 'their self-frustration will only exaggerate their anger. There's no way the British have attained that level of enlightenment and acceptance, so it should work effectively, and fast.'

It was the most delicious irony he had ever tasted. The beauty of it being that the average British Bulldog would consider it "quite proper" to tear the Foreign Secretary apart – as painfully as possible.

'Only those frustrated with their own failings and faults, seek vicarious revenge through schadenfreude,' Abdul thought, swivelling himself around in his chair again. Then in shocking mockery of a sailor's accent, he spoke his next words to the computer screen.

'Ha, ha, me hearties. Let's see if he lasts the month out – shall we boys?' He broke out laughing and coughing as he clicked 'log off' and reached over for his pack of Camels.

However the real irony to it, was that Abdul was doing exactly the same as the British – separated only by the degree of their denial. Perhaps not shunted by the same shove of insecurity, but definitely with the same elasticated pull, of pure malicious pleasure.

The SallyMarie an ocean going oil tanker, exploded at 7:20 this morning, moments after leaving its berth at Corpus Christi Texas where it had taken on 400,000 tons of refined gasoline.

According to eyewitness accounts, the tugboat pushing the fuel tanker away from the dock exploded at its bow section, rupturing the double hull of the tanker and igniting the fuel in its forward hold. Seconds later the tanker exploded in a gigantic fireball, showering burning fuel over the main depot 200 yards away which set fire to six storage tanks.

The fire spread to the main facility and thirty minutes later, two of the burning storage tanks exploded. A firestorm is now raging out of control with firemen struggling to contain the blaze. Early reports indicate the refinery may be allowed to burn itself out.

The heat from the burning fuel is so intense that police have set up a cordon five miles away. Corpus Christi and an area up to twenty miles from the blaze are being evacuated. Eric Hammers, a police spokesman, is asking everyone to leave the city, as toxic gases are being blown into the heavily-populated zone by the steady onshore breeze.

Flames 200 feet high can be seen up to ten miles away. People are panicking and abandoning their cars as they try to flee. It appears the city will be deserted by nightfall. The number of casualties is unknown at this time, but is expected to be high.

The harbour office has issued a brief statement saying the tugboat and ship have sunk in the harbour, blocking the cut to the sea. Their account states that at 7:15 am, the tugboat Big John and its sister ship Little John, went to turn the SallyMarie away from its berth and push it out to sea. As Big John moved the tanker with its snubber (a front bumper backed by a steel plate) a small explosive charge detonated. Explosives may have been placed inside the snubber and, as the tugboat was exerting a considerable pushing force at the time of the explosion, nearly all of the charge would have been directed into the hold of the tanker.

One eye witness said the initial explosion was enough to send Big John back fifty feet, destroying its bow. It sank moments later. The SallyMarie took 24 minutes to go down after erupting in a series of four explosions.

This could be the work of The 24th Revolution. The harbour master, Jimmy Simmons, said he watched the tragedy unfold from his office and it was 'definitely no accident'. Since security measures have been reinforced at all fuel storage depots for the past few months, it is worth mentioning that the registered berth of the tugboat is in a different section of the harbour, not subject to the same level of security.

CHECKING IT OUT

The tension between Leah and JJ dissipated as the first week ground into the second. The atmosphere between them thawed and was nearly back to where it was before her data download; though there was still the occasional whiff of an unanswered question, hovering in the air between them.

Leah had staked out the coffee shop during the first week without any sign of Abdul, but had to abort this strategy when the proprietor asked her what she was doing in his coffee shop each day – without an escort. Getting up from the table, she struck a pose. Throwing her right arm across her breasts, Leah put her left hand in front of her groin and with her lips pursed shut, shook her head in universal 'no'. This action demonstrated that she was a pious Muslim woman, and sent out the accusation: "Are you a religious man?"

Religious Muslim men do not abuse virtuous Muslim women as it is considered a direct insult to the Prophet. Her stance is an effective dissuader in the Middle East. This style of rejection invokes such a powerful reminder of Mohammed's teaching, that it has been known to stop a rape dead in its tracks.

Maintaining her haughty demeanour, she paid and left without saying a word – the act of a worthy Muslim woman exiting with her full dignity; leaving the owner mortified by his zeal.

When JJ lifted an eyebrow on hearing her explanation of why she had to stop her vigil, Leah had countered, 'I could hardly turn round and say I was on stake-out for the US Government, JJ.'

The boredom of non-eventful repetition fuelled their edginess as the trail to Khalifa convincingly petered out, though it was slightly mitigated by an email from William Mann. It wasn't sent directly to them. Bruce Cougar had forwarded it to JJ.

Please pass my sincere thanks to the agents in pursuit of this dangerous criminal and let me add the gratitude of all Americans.

The information they obtained on the 914 criminals has not yielded any direct results, but it has alerted us to the size of the task and the type of action we must undertake.

Most of the problems in tracking the militants are the result of previous inadequacies in Homeland Security. I have taken all the necessary steps to rectify the issue. They are now in place, which means their efforts have had a tremendously positive impact, contributing greatly towards ensuring this atrocity cannot occur again.

If your agents require any assistance from my office, or have any opinion or advice not known by me, please tell them to request or state whatever they think appropriate.

Once again, I applaud your efforts They must involve considerable risk. I would like to offer your agents lunch at the White House when they are next in Washington, hopefully with their task completed. Good luck and thank you.

William Mann

'Wow. I've only heard of a dozen or so agents who've been invited there before. That's quite an honour,' JJ said, passing his PDA across.

'It's good to know our efforts are producing some results.'

'It sure is. But it's only fair to warn you that unless we get our "task completed", I don't think we get to go to the White House.'

'You don't need to tell me that – I've got a day job, remember?' Leah said, and JJ burst out laughing. It was refreshing to hear him laugh again. It was the first time he laughed since he had taken up smoking. JJ pulled out a Camel from his pack, then replaced it unlit.

'There is another bonus,' he said, frisbeeing the packet into a wastepaper basket in the far corner of the room. 'If I read this right, and certainly as far as my boss is concerned – We – that's you and me, are now working for the President of the United States. "Any assistance from my office", "any opinion they have". Interesting, that. Do we have an opinion?'

'You mean like everybody has one, or relevant to Abdul?'

'You know exactly what I mean. Christ, Leah! This is the President. The leader of the free world. Nothing's sacred to you is it?'

'Oh JJ, please lighten up a little. If I was Abdul, the one thing that would give me immeasurable joy, is you and me fighting each other instead of teaming up against him.'

The full truth of her criticism went through him like a spear. He knew it was him who had initiated the harsh words every time they had fought recently. JJ was finding it hard to balance his true feelings for her, against the secret fear he still held over her possible betrayal. He had been unable to prevent himself from lashing out. But her last statement dissolved his last doubt. Not only was it the natural logic of friend not foe, but she had said it with a conviction impossible to fake.

'You're absolutely right, Leah. Perhaps I owe you an apology.'

'Still wondering whose side I'm on, aren't you?' she said sadly.

'Not any longer I'm not. So help me God but I truly believe you are on ours. Will you accept my deepest apology for ever doubting you?'

'Gratefully accepted,' she smiled into his eyes. 'Was it something I said?'

'Let's just say it wasn't something you did…honey.'

And she leaned forward for his kiss.

Eventually they slid in to a dreamless sleep, completely satiated, but it had taken three bouts of passionate lovemaking before they floated into its soft cotton clouds. The first round was intensely physical, the second ran around the perimeter of their emotional boundaries while the third was tender, almost non-sexual; their bodies entwining as one. Each seeking a higher connection with a deeper bond.

JJ awoke first and stretched, feeling a momentary shock of surprise when she nuzzled further into his chest half asleep. He wasn't used to waking up with someone else in the bed and his smile grew broader as the memory of their previous night came flooding back to him. Leaning over, he gazed down at her in a sense of wonder. The place they had touched was deep inside both their hearts. Their small sounds and murmurings easily understood as they poured into the calm and infinite lake, where only souls freed of the weight of mortality are normally permitted to roam.

For the first time he understood why the French call it 'le petit mort';

that perhaps there really was a God after all. His discovery of this new and timeless sensation seemed more powerful and yet more fragile than anything he had experienced in his life.

He watched his hand gently stroking her hair, concerned only that he might wake her, knowing that even if he did, he was unable to stop. She murmured something unintelligible and to his amazement, found he understood their meaning without hearing the precise words. He offered no reply – it needed none – and carried on stroking her softly before stealing out of bed to make her breakfast.

Looking around for his boxers, he found them by the door and slipped them on. The room looked as though it had hosted a St Patrick's Day party. The chair at the end of the bed was on its side, bedclothes were strewn across the floor and a pair of feminine knickers were hanging by a thread from the mirror. He followed the trail of their abandoned clothing downstairs and into the living room, where it ended in a small heap by the sofa. His detective eyes flickered over it, recalling the minutiae forgotten in their passion.

'You don't have to be a rocket scientist to figure this one out, Einstein,' he joked, as he pushed open the kitchen door.

They spent the rest of the day in bed: making love; sipping wine and snacking. As the dusk deepened into the gloom of evening, they lay back on the bed, enveloped in a dreamy silence and gazing into the middle distance of the same thought.

JJ voiced it first. 'What are we gonna do now?'

'You mean given the choice of rooting through the sewery slums of Cairo looking for Abdul, or staying in bed with you? Mmmm. Let me think about that,' she teased.

'Think we can do both?'

'We can do anything we set our minds to, darling.'

'Yeah, I suppose we can.'

'You know there isn't much we can do about him right now. We've got no idea where he is and less idea who he is,' she posed.

'Maybe we should take a little time out. Go on a trip or something.'

Leah sat up bolt upright. 'Have you ever been into the desert, JJ?'

'The desert? I was thinking of a pampered week at the Four Seasons Hotel in Santa Barbara.'

'That's schmaltz JJ. But the desert – that's real. It has a strange and wonderfully sad beauty.'

'Strange? How can countless miles of sand be strange?'

'Time in the desert is measured in miles – not by grains of sand.'

'I see,' he said, half-following.

'I've never felt so free and so awed by anything else. There's nothing quite as beautiful as watching the dawn paint the night sky with colours you've never seen.'

'Colours I've never seen?'

'Okay – ever seen red fade into green without pink or yellow in between?'

'Can't say I have, no,' he replied slowly.

'No eternal reward will ever repay us for forsaking the dawn,' she quoted. 'Please let's go, JJ – it'll be a blast. There's a jeep in the garage and all we need for a few days is water, food, a tent, and about 200 condoms.'

'Leah, if you ever go into business I want to be your first backer.'

'Deal.' Leah exclaimed, in the knowledge they were going.

'I can probably get everything we need from our NSA office, here in Cairo,' he mused.

'Yeah, we should let them take up the strain and track Abdul for a bit. We've earned a break and if they find out anything they can call us using the Sat connection on our PDAs. We don't have to go far.'

'How far?'

'Far enough so there's no surface light to interfere with the night sky. Say a day's drive.'

'You mean about a hundred miles, don't you?'

'That's what I love about you JJ. Even when you haven't done something before, you somehow still get it.'

'Right on, honey. Now slide over here,' he said, reaching across for her.

The Director of Operations at the NSA office in Cairo was far less relaxed about Leah and JJ's holiday excursion. He was beside himself. He had just finished reading an overnight report on how six suicide bombers had detonated themselves in shopping malls in Houston and Dallas, together with the shocking news that the refinery in Corpus Christi had burnt to the ground.

'You can't go walkabout in the Sahara at a time like this.'

'There's nothing we can do until you get a bead on Khalifa. I'm sorry, but until you get something concrete we're out of the loop for a few,' JJ stated flatly.

'What if something happens to you guys out there? It's a desert! It's fucking dangerous if you don't know what you're doing. Shit, they'd skin me alive if anything happened to you two. No, I'm the one that's sorry because the answer is no way.'

'Not according to the President.' JJ said, producing a copy of his 'thank you' email. He had been expecting this reaction and had printed off a copy, which he intended to destroy the moment it had served its purpose. 'We're only going for four or five days. I want food and water for two people for a week – and none of that field-ration crap either. Here, I've made a list. I'll come back in hour and if you can't get that organised, I will be forced to express my concern as part of my opinion on your operation. To the President himself.'

'Smoked salmon? Champagne and a gas cooler! This is the Cairo NSA office not a Chicago Wal-Mart. How the hell am I supposed to get all this together in an hour?'

'You could try casting spells,' JJ said evenly. 'Let's just say that it's a test of the logistical competence of the NSA office in Cairo, because I can feel a very uncomfortable opinion forming.' JJ looked down at his watch pointedly, then levelled a cast-iron stare at the man.

'Okay, okay, but come back in four hours. Then you can drink your damn champagne cold.'

'That's the problem-solving approach I really admire about our Cairo office. Okay, four hours it is. I can't tell you how relieved that's making me feel,' JJ said as he went over to the shredder. Just as he was about to leave the office he looked back at the Director, 'Better make that Scottish smoked salmon, would you?'

Now it really was a test.

A FRIENDLY GAME

The desert changed JJ. The way it changes anyone venturing into its black and white reality for the first time. His perception of it subtly wavered, then altered in shape as he realised how much was going on around him. Small things, like a puff of wind heralding the onset of the soft sundowner breeze which blew for the last hour of daylight, or the formation of a tiny mound of sand a his feet, warning of a scorpion. In the desert, awareness of the smallest of events, the tiniest of things, can separate life from death. Slowly, JJ began seeing the desert as beautiful and fair.

Brutally harsh but fair. Treating all people equally, regardless of creed, colour or status but in return, it takes anyone who is ill-prepared, unlucky or alone. This is, and always will be, the unchanging price of its ticket of entry. Its non-negotiable bill of fare.

When travelling in the desert – you pay attention. And when you sleep in the desert – you pay attention; even when you think you are paying attention it still might not be enough, so you listen for the small ticks of sound in the heat; watch carefully for the slightest of movements; paying the utmost heed to the minuscule. To the things that don't matter when you are anywhere else. This is how you survive in its baking bosom, because no one has ever found another way and lived to recount it.

The desert plays to its own rule and sets the standard high. But for those fortunate enough to experience the wonder, the rewards are immense – though subtle. In the desert only the sun marks the time and a thought as tiny as eternity becomes symmetric, as you begin to see that it is the only thing which trails no tether. The desert is vibrant, yet it is still. It lives, but is not alive. The countless miles of sand are vast but we see only a fraction at a time. It is equally magical and deadly in the same moment. The desert is a reflection of space – on earth.

They drove out heading due west from Cairo, running parallel to the coast and ten miles inland. The first seventy miles were paved road which deteriorated dramatically after fifty and eventually the worn tarmac disappeared altogether. Here, they decided to stop for lunch. JJ led Leah to the back of the jeep to get their lunch out of the small trailer they were towing.

'Grief, JJ! What happened to minimalism?' Leah exclaimed.

'There wasn't enough room for it.'

'That's funny,' Leah laughed.

'Miss Leah Mandrille, you are a guest of the American Government for the next week and we are a generous nation.'

'Generous? This is staggering. Here's me with my small backpack and fishing rod and you with a.... What is that thing anyway?'

'It's a propane fridge.'

Leah laughed uncontrollably. 'Damned civilised, JJ. That's damn civilised.'

'I admire restraint, providing it doesn't go too far. And at the risk of asking a stupid question, why are you packing a fishing rod in the desert?'

'To catch fish for our supper, my love. Why else?'

'In a desert?'

'If you think I'm camping out in this shade-less void when there's a perfectly good beach over yonder sand dune, awaiting my pleasure...'

'We've got GPS, we can go anywhere. And it'll be a lot smoother than this,' he agreed, pointing at the beaten track running on from the pre-war tarmac.

'It sure will. Cooler too, and we can swim. I think this is a champagne moment, JJ.'

Popping the cork and filling two plastic flutes with the amber liquid, she held hers up in salute then dribbled a little onto the sand. 'It's a toast my father used to make whenever we went sailing. It's an offering to the Gods and it brings good luck,' she answered his questioning expression.

'Only Leah Mandrille could offer sacrifice to Neptune in a desert,' he laughed. Then suddenly feeling superstitious he copied her lead.

'Listen, JJ,' she said, cocking her head slightly.

'What? What is it?'

'Absolutely nothing. But if you listen again tomorrow at midday or maybe the day after, you will hear it.'

'What? The echo of you laughing at me as I try to hear sounds in this emptiness?' he laughed, sweeping his arms at the horizon.

'No, honey. You will hear the hiss and click of the heat rising silently through the air.'

'Oh, God. I'm going into Nowheresville, with a mad Englishwoman who hears sounds in the midday sun.'

'I am mad, for you,' she said wrinkling her nose and leaning in to kiss him.

After a prolonged, initially hurried siesta, spent on a blanket which Leah insisted they spread out in the shade of the trailer first: 'I don't like counting my lovemaking by grains of sand,' she countered, when he suggested doing it bare-assed on the empty road, they set off. JJ swung the wheel over, aiming the jeep north, towards the coast. Three slow miles later they reached the edge of a dead flat saltpan, marked by conical piles of shiny crystals darting silver and pink shards of light at them. JJ pulled over and walked to the edge of it, testing the hardened crust with the toe of his boot. It seemed firm enough.

'What phase of the moon are we at, JJ?' she shouted over from the front seat.

'Waning,' he replied, getting back into the driver's seat. 'Why?'

Pulling out her BlackBerry, Leah GPSed their position and copied the coordinates into memory before pasting them into Google Earth and selecting "satellite view". 'Okay, we're eight miles from the ocean and that's a salt pan. So at full moon the tide comes up and the salt pan sucks in the seawater from the coast, turning the ground under the top crust into ice cream. My family got stuck in one in Namibia. Luckily, the moon's waning so the tide will be at its lowest. It shouldn't be a problem.'

'It felt solid enough.'

'That's exactly what my dad said.'

'Right, I'm changing into two-wheel drive. It's two for in and four for out.'

'What a clever chauffeur,' she smiled.

'Yeah, and I'm going to pump another ten pounds into the tyres first, so gimme a minute, okay?'

'Why? I thought you were supposed to let them down?'

'Amateur camper thinking, honey. My way, if we do get stuck I can let them down for more traction and back us out. We might need it if we end up in that ice cream of yours. Besides, the harder the tyre the sooner we will find anything dangerous.'

'Ooh, you're so smart. Can I drive, darling?' she asked, exaggerating a sugary voice.

'No way. If there's going to be any shouting and screaming done, I want it directed at me,' he said, climbing out of the jeep.

Driving at a low five mph, JJ was paying attention. Staring fixedly out of the window, he slalomed the jeep through the gaps where the crystals were thinnest. Weaving like this, it took them two hours before they climbed to the top of a 150 foot sand dune and JJ stamped on the brakes, stopping them abruptly.

The sun was just beginning to set, bathing the green apple sea below in a softened light of burnished bronze. A steady breeze was blowing offshore, picking up the surf, lifting the waves higher before they crashed onto the sand frost-white, a hundred yards away.

'Hotdamn, this is gnarly.'

'And we've got it all to ourselves, JJ. There's no one within 100 miles of us at least,' Leah said excitedly.

'Let's set up camp and go for a swim.'

Lying beside a driftwood campfire later that evening, JJ gazed up at the deep blue of the star-studded night sky doming overhead, untainted by any manmade light. He had never been fortunate enough to witness the full glory of a naked universe.

The line of the horizon ran around him in a circle making the earth appear two-dimensional, as though he were looking at a jet-black cardboard cut-out. The stark outline was saw-toothed on the desert side and bent slightly over the sea: a strong black line with bluish infinity a pixel above. He became aware of the earth turning sedately on its axis as he watched the dark line of the horizon descending through space. He suddenly pictured himself travelling on the small ship of his planet, rolling purposefully through the heavens, and it humbled him to know how small his ship was against the gem-littered void, and how infinitesimal a part he, in turn, must be. All held together as one, with everything connecting to all; though his mind told him the distances were vast and the links between, invisible. Watching him closely, Leah saw the moment his wonderment slid into introspection and rolled over to him. 'You've never really seen the earth, have you?'

'No, I'm a city dweller. At least, I was.'

'It can make you feel tiny the first time, but it also makes you realise how lucky we are to be here. Even if it's only for a few fleeting moments.'

'It's so big, Leah,' JJ threw his arms wide, staring at the panoramic splendour in disbelief. 'When I try to imagine it going on forever and how many galaxies there are, it makes me feel so...infinitesimal, so inconsequential.'

'Nothing about you is that,' Leah laughed, cupping him with one hand, pushing him back over with the other. 'Let me show you the best way to travel through the heavens, darling,' she murmured, twirling her tongue across his stomach then sliding it further down.

They rose with the dawn and JJ stirred up the coals of the fire to make a pot of coffee. It wasn't until they waded into the sea, hand-in-hand and naked, that he finally spoke. 'Let's swim to the reef and back. The workout will do us good.'

'Race you there,' she smiled, and dolphined under the next wave, coming up in a strong crawl to swim for the boom of the reef half a mile away.

JJ grinned with delight as he watched her lithe form slipping through the waves. 'God, how I love that woman,' he said, diving in after her.

Deciding to camp where they were for a few nights, JJ unhitched the trailer and refilled the tank on the jeep before offering her the keys. 'Winner's privilege,' he smiled.

'You might need your seat belt for this ride, honey.' Driving the section of hardened sand twenty feet up from the furthest reach of the waves, Leah gunned the jeep down the beach, changing into fourth gear at fifty-five and whooping.

'Yehaa! Put the pedal to the metal, honey,' he shouted as the speed whipped the air over them, flattening their hair and buffeting their bodies. After the enclosed fetid streets of Cairo, it felt like freedom.

They dined that evening on cold cuts of smoked salmon and beef, to the echoing silence of deep night amplifying the sounds of the shore. He broke their harmony softly. 'Tell me about your ring.'

Leah recounted how Victor had given it to her and how their relationship had become almost father and daughter towards the end. She joked about how maddening he had been when she tried to find out what the inscription on it meant and finished by telling him that it was ancient Assyrian.

'Huh, that's interesting. I shouldn't really tell you this. I live in Santa Barbara and there's a Sumerian stone in the museum there. It has carvings on it; icons more than hieroglyphs and it's part of a series of stones that tell a very strange tale.'

'Tell me this strange tale,' Leah said dreamily.

'You want the long or the short version?'

'Oh definitely long…and slow,' she purred, stretching luxuriously on the rug.

'Like a well fed lioness. All supple strength and dangerous beauty,' he thought, drinking down her fire-flickered form.

'Well it goes something like this. Some Gods came down from the heavens, choosing the area which became Assyria – roughly where Iraq is now. They came here in search of gold to take back to their home in the heavens, as they needed to sow it in their atmosphere to save their planet. A planet with two suns, no less. Not long after they started mining, the younger male Gods, who were doing all the digging, mutinied; saying the work was too hard and they wouldn't carry on. The King God immediately sent for his chief medical officer, who was a woman, ordering her to make him workers or in Assyrian – "dams".'

'Oh, like Adam in the Bible.'

'Yup, except this writing predates the Bible by 2000 years.'

'Huh, that is curious.'

'Yeah, it becomes more than curious. The medical God goes into a "birthing shed" and combines the essence of the most advanced creature on earth with an egg from one of the younger female Gods.'

'Whaat?'

'Bizarre, non? And there's an extraordinary level of detail in everything described. For instance, they mined the gold a long way from Sumeria; they got it from southeast Africa. In fact all of the legend has a surprising accuracy, most of which we've only realised is correct in the last thirty or forty years. Anyways, she makes mistakes at first and describes what they were. She discovers that an egg from one female God transferred into another has a much higher success rate – which is true of surrogate mothers. She also describes adding a copper solution to the pot she mixes the egg and essence in. Which is a little unnerving, because when you do that to test tube fertilisation the take-up rate increases a hundred-fold and we still don't know why.'

'What were the mistakes?'

'Oh, two heads no arms, that kind of thing. Quite a few half-beast, half-Gods. Nothing she was happy with. If you take a look at a couple of Assyrian statues you get the idea.'

A sudden gust of wind blew in from the sea, fanning the embers of the fire and bellowing the flames higher before flattening them off with a roar. Sparks streamed from their snaking tips as liquid fire then went dancing across the dunes in rivulets of red and gold, dissolving into nothingness with a 'crack'. Then the wind ceased as suddenly as it had come, and the flames resumed their more gentle waving at the stars.

'Please continue,' Leah said in a hallowed whisper.

'Sooo…Eventually, she makes a dam which meets her approval. She walks into the king's court, holding it up for all to see and announces: "I have done it, my hands have made it".'

'*My hands have made it?*' Leah repeated.

'That's the quote. The King God is pleased, so He orders her to start full production right away and within no time, the dams are proving so popular that the birth-mothers rebel, saying they won't give birth to "those monsters" any longer. The King decides his medical officer must make the dams so that they can breed, which is very disconcerting. We've only known for the last fifty years that clones can't reproduce.'

'Good Godsss,' she laughed. 'That's remarkable.'

'Innit?'

'And how old do you say this stone was?'

'It dates from around 3000 BC. So it's 5000 years old.'

'Grief, the Old Testament is 3000 years at most.'

'Yup. Even the word Eden derives from Sumerian. It means plateau or plain.'

'This is hard to take in.'

'Think so? Then you better get a grip your belief mechanisms because it gets a lot tougher from here. Maybe I should stop. This can offend some people.'

'Don't you dare stop.'

'You sure? I've seen people spark out over this. I've seen two good Christian souls get violent.'

'Go ahead. Please.'

'Okay, she goes back into her birthing shed and operates on a dam, extracting his essence from a bone in his chest and somehow, she produces a female to go with her male.'

'That sounds like the Genesis story of Adam's rib.'

'Indeed, and the best DNA in the human body is in the spine marrow,' JJ added.

'Uh oh, I can see why some people get upset. Then what happens?'

'The ending, which is rad. The dams can now breed. They breed rapidly and in next to no time, the Gods have enough gold to take back to their Home in the Heavens and save their atmosphere. But meanwhile they are stuck with a problem. As they are leaving forever, what are they going to do with all the damn dams? The King feels it's a decision that should be taken by all the Gods collectively. So they hold a vote on whether to leave them alone or destroy them. The count is split, with the King having to cast the deciding vote and what He does is pretty strange. He thinks about it for the time of one "sun cycle" and against mounting opposition, proclaims they will leave the dams behind alive, but give them all different languages first.'

'Why?'

'So "The dams will always be fighting each other", is the carving on the stone.'

'Makes a horrid kind of sense, doesn't it?'

'I had the same thought. And let me add one thing.'

'Go on.'

'All of the senior Gods are distinguished by unique icons which identify them individually. And you'll never guess what the chief medical officer's icon was? The one who did the essence mixing in those jars?'

'Surely not?'

'Surely yes.'

'You mean the two serpents entwined around a copper rod? The ancient medical symbol?'

'The very one. That symbol originates from Ancient Sumeria, not the Far East as many believe. And the shape of two twisted serpents is a double helix – the same shape as our DNA string. Stranger yet, she is always depicted with jars or pots around her and you'll never guess where her birthing shed was.'

'Not Africa? Please don't say Africa.'

'South Central to be precise.'

'That's extraordinary. How come I've never heard about this before?'

'The stones were discovered in the late nineteenth century, but they weren't translated until the early 1920s and at that time, most people thought it was ridiculous – they had no idea it was possible, so they dismissed it as the fanciful legend of a fairly primitive race. Fifty years later it took on a whole new significance but by then, the religious powers were making sure the focus stayed on the Dead Sea scrolls, not on the source of all religious belief. Because the Assyrians were the first. Even Buddha came a long time after.'

'You're not making this up are you?'

'No. I'm not. It's God's truth. Pun intended. It's written in stone over 5000 years old and I've seen one with my own two eyes,' he said, reaching around to scratch his back.

'As a political science addict, there is another strange aspect to that story,' Leah offered. 'All societies then were feudal. Extremely feudal, so the idea that lesser Gods could refuse a direct order from their King is not a natural idea for an ancient society. Add the concept that women could refuse a male edict and it becomes radical in almost any era before 1890s America.'

'Whoa, I hadn't thought of that.'

'To my mind, it's more than strange. Especially as it was carved on stone, because in any other society right up till recent times, those thoughts would get you executed for treason or heresy.'

'Yeah, that is odd because nothing happened to them or the birthmothers, and the King had to find another way around the problem. I suppose that is an unnatural thought for an ancient society. That's clever, Leah.'

'It's highly unlikely someone of that era would even think of it, let alone decide it was a good idea to print it.'

'I had another thought about it as well. If their planet was in trouble and you could program DNA, which you undoubtedly could if you had the ability to travel across the heavens, you might leave the dams behind for another reason.'

'Which is?'

'What reason?'

'Backup. In case the God species was wiped out by its dying home planet.'

'Uh Oh, all they would have to do is program the DNA to become more godly and less apey with each generation.'

'Yup, and if you do that you're not faced with the guilty feeling of leaving anyone behind. You would also know the Dams had the power to progress and could break out of here eventually.'

'Well if God is like us, then we must be like Him. So He must be able to experience morality and guilt, because I don't think many animals have a concept of morality. It's one of our main separators.'

'It starts to make a lot of sense when you ask why the ageing gene in us is switched on. Our reproductive cells don't age, so ageing is not inevitable. By having shorter life spans you get more generations per millennium. Your creation becomes more godly, more quickly,' JJ stared into the fire.

'That's true. Scientists believe the first person to live to 200 years old is alive right now. Perhaps that's why we die then,' exclaimed Leah. 'What a neat explanation for why a supposedly kindly God puts everyone through the fear and pain of death.'

'If you programmed the DNA so that the godly genes become more dominant while the monkey genes diminish, you might need a lot of generations for that DNA to fully evolve. Against that coming to fruition, is the reality that if our species expands across the planet too rapidly then we eat ourselves out of home or destroy the planet and perish – way before the godly gene has a chance to mature.'

'Well, if the King had first-hand experience of the atmosphere failing on his home planet and the destruction it causes, that would definitely be on his mind,' Leah agreed.

'You know, there are only a few things that are common to all religions. One is the belief that we are created in God's image. Well there's a way to do that and it's through DNA. Even we can program it, so for space travellers to splice in their own genes with an indigenous species would be a slam dunk.'

'You also buy substantially more generations if there's a lot of warring and killing going on. Maybe that's why He needed to give us different languages, JJ. Perhaps He required a large number of generations for His grand design to materialise.' Leah said excitedly.

'Right on. All they had to do was program their own genes to become more dominant with each generation, knowing that the killer aspect of chimpanzees, who share 98% of our DNA, will add more than a few generations to the ticking clock of a finite planet resource. Having different languages has separated man from his brother throughout history, with any difference providing a root cause for war. There's no doubt that mass killing adds a lot more generations per millenium, so you have a better chance for your own genes to fully evolve in a set time period. Especially when you know there's a max-out to the number of people our earth can support.'

'When I was a child, I used to wonder what earthly good diseases did. I couldn't help but think that if there was a kindly God, He would never have permitted them to exist. But if you need a lot of generations to properly evolve, you tilt things firmly in your favour by releasing a few viruses,' Leah winked.

'Yup, even cancer, which is a type of self-destruct mechanism for cells at a molecular level, suddenly gets a worthwhile explanation. Because if you were aware of certain types of evolution going counter to your genetic design, or if you knew there were dead ends or even dangerous possibilities to your designed evolution, you simply full-stop them by programming in a self-destruct mechanism at DNA level. Cancers work that way…. That's only a hypothesis to consider, it shouldn't be treated as fact,' JJ added.

'Yes, I'm not sure I can go along with the cancer argument, but the rest is a little too much for coincidence,' she said, feeling the connections and pieces fitting perfectly in her mind.

'Maybe viruses, illness and disease were not enough to guarantee the number of generations He required. Maybe that's why the King God had to think about it for a sun cycle. Which incidentally, was a year not a day, in ancient Assyria. That's a hell of a lot of thinking for an advanced being or God. It must have been a bitch of a problem.'

'Well, thank heavens the birthmothers rebelled,' Leah smiled, looking up at him through half-closed eyes.

JJ leaned over her and threw a log on the fire in sheer delight, followed by another in complete abandon. And as the divine madness of their lovemaking reached its crescendo, they called out to the heavens the secret name of God – together.

And had Charles Darwin been able to observe them at that particular moment in time, he would have been highly impressed by how single-mindedly they set about procreating the species. But although he got close, he wasn't blessed with an understanding of DNA and never knew how easy it is to program. Or that the fastest and most powerful computers ever designed and built by Man are chemical computers – not too dissimilar from ourselves.

They are programmed and provide their results by utilising the natural functions of DNA.

After breakfasting on bacon, eggs and cornbread the next morning, Leah went to the back of the jeep and unclipped the spade clamped to the rear door. Picking up her rod, she led the way down to the beach, as a buttery sun peeped over the horizon.

'It's not about catching the fish, JJ. It's about catching the bait,' she whispered, handing him her rod. 'Bingo!' she exclaimed. 'See those small holes in the sand? There's gold in them there 'oles – watch this.' She drove the spade into the sand and began digging in earnest, then picked out a lump of wriggling goo and held it up in triumph for him to see. 'Sand bugs – the second best bait on a beach.'

'What's the best?' he whispered back.

'A prawn,' she replied, stepping closer to him so he could watch her half-hitching it to the shank of the hook with a few expert twists of the line.

'Neat,' JJ said. Leah slipped him a knowing look as she took the rod back.

On her second cast, the rod arched over and the line fizzed out as a fish turned on the bait, leaving a large swirl dimpling on the surface as it shot away. Jerking the rod up twice to set the hook, she threw the bail arm over to let the line run free then waded back to the beach, flicking her long legs over the top of the waves and yelping with excitement.

Back on firmer sand she slackened the drag on the reel, then squeezed the bail arm back over to get control of the streaking line. The spool spun wildly, shrieking its distress, and the rod thumped twice as the fish shook its head in the deeper water towards the reef.

Unable to throw the hook the fish glided to the surface: swimming in a wide arc around her; showing a dorsal fin and black-tipped tail at the front of its V-shaped wake. It was a strong fish. Three feet long, probably eight to ten pounds in weight. Leah applied more strain. The fish jumped clear of the water and porpoised away in a series of leaps and dives, flashing bright silver scales at them in the pale light of the dawn. The reel sang out again as it dived below the surface, stripping out her line in long lunging runs as it bored for the cooler waters of the deep.

Stealing a quick glance at her reel, she was surprised to see only a third of her line left – shrinking rapidly. The fish was swimming straight for the sanctuary of the reef, but she would run out of line long before it got there. The option of holding on to the monster while doing nothing else, was being stripped away by its powerful run.

Decision time: if she tightened the drag too much or too quickly, the fish would snap her twelve-pound mono like cotton. But in a few seconds she would have no line left, losing the fish and her tackle. She reached around for the dial on the back of the reel and clicked the drag tighter, lifting the rod high over her head to gain maximum elasticity against the torpedoing fish.

Leah saw how underpowered she was with her small spinning rod and freshwater reel. It was evident the fish had sensed it too. There was no choice now, and she risked two more clicks of the clutch. A last resort to halt its mad dash for the reef. The rod bent over with the strain and Leah grunted with the force the fish exerted, fighting to keep the rod tip high. The steady ticks and long shrieks from the reel telling her that the fish was winning.

'All or nothing now,' she shouted at JJ, locking the spool and lifting the rod back behind her shoulder. The torsion made the line sing out its agony, going from a deep bass hum to the sharp-pitch dinging of a violin string; but slowly, the leviathan slowed down. Then the rod snapped up straight and the line went slack.

Changing her grip, Leah started to wind the reel frantically. She had turned the fish and free of all resistance, it was streaking back towards the beach. Unable to pick up her line fast enough, Leah hopped back up the shore and was rewarded with a satisfying thump as they joined in battle once again. For the first time she had control. She waded back into the ocean, winding steadily.

The fish suddenly rose to the surface, thrashing the sea into foam, then rolled onto one side. Gently and smoothly she began winding it in: holding the rod up to bend its head out of the water; sliding the fish across the surface towards the rolling surf between them.

As it entered the back of a huge wave racing in from the ocean Leah stepped back, guiding it over the white foam, using the lift and momentum of the wave to run the fish onto the exposed sand to her left. Fish and wave crashed onto the shore as one; then the water sucked back into the sea leaving it flipping on the beach.

They ran over to it and gazed down in wonder. It was magnificent. Full-finned and bullet-shaped, with bright silver scales flashing like mirrors in the sunlight. 'Nearer ten pounds than eight,' Leah thought, as she examined it more closely.

'Wow,' said JJ, impressed. 'What kind is that?'

'It's some type of sea bass and they're really good eating. We can bake it on the fire in fresh seaweed. It's the most divine meal.'

'And sushi for lunch, eh? You've caught enough to feed a small tribe.'

'We'll chill it down in that outrageous fridge of yours and ceviche some in lime juice and salt. There is a problem though, JJ.'

'What's that?'

'I can never bring myself to gut them – would you mind?'

Over the next few days the bud of their bond blossomed. On the evening of the last day, in the deep stillness of the desert night, they sat in front of a roaring fire watching the flames dance, mesmerised by the copper red and gold of the glowing embers. Sitting under the canopy of stars, they bathed in a tranquil sea of infinity while their emotions flowed between them, colouring their hopes and dreams.

They fell completely in love. Not the ecstatic dizzying spiral many mistake it for, but a soaring euphoria secured by the steel ropes of trust and understanding: steel halyards, which they each now anchored for the other, more important person in both their lives.

They sat in an easy silence as the dusty jeep bounced its way back onto the first paved road they had seen for a week. On the third day of their trip, JJ had phoned the Cairo office; to be informed of another nine suicide bombings and no breakthrough in the hunt for Khalifa. Thinking they both needed a relaxing break, he didn't trouble Leah with the intel. Instead, he decided to stay on: stretching out the water, travelling at night, sleeping through the fierce heat throb of the day. It was the gas getting low which made them reluctantly break their camp on the eighth day. They left before dawn to make the long drive against the sun in a single day.

With the shadow of the jeep stretching ahead of them that evening, JJ nudged her awake.

'We're here Leah…but I can't see much point in staying,' he winked, as they merged into the clotted streets of Cairo.

'Yes, if Abdul had any sense he would have left Cairo by now. I wonder where he went?' Leah returned the wink. There was mischief in her eyes.

'Probably somewhere pleasant. Warm rather than hot. Perhaps a little more Western but still Mediterranean?'

'Like say, Cannes or Nice?'

'Spanish food is better. I'm sure Khalifa knows that too,' he smiled.

'Here's an idea then. Let's look for him in Spain. How about Barcelona? I've heard the mountains of Montserrat are stunning.'

'Never been.'

'Me neither.'

'Got your passport?'

'D'oh. I'm a diplomat. Take your best guess.'

'Wherever you go – I follow. You are my desert. So then, straight to the airport? Passing Go without the 200 dollars?'

'Is that your considered opinion?'

'God, it so is. I never want to see or smell Cairo again. If the pyramids weren't quite so heavy, they would have been shifted elsewhere by now.'

'Yes. Anyone who doesn't understand "cutting off your nose to spite your face" hasn't sniffed a Cairo slum.'

'Or understood the pain of the Sphinx,' JJ said wryly, swinging the Jeep across three lanes of traffic to take the airport road away from the city centre.

CASTLES BURNING

Almoyd picked up the phone on its third ring. 'Our Price Office Supplies. This is Al, how can I help you today?'

'Hi Al. Ben here. Have you processed that order I gave you this morning yet?' Ben was the chief buyer for Standard Western Bank and one of Our Price Office Supplies' biggest customers. Almoyd liked taking care of him personally.

'It's being loaded as we speak,' Al replied. 'Why?'

'My mistake, Al. Could you add another twenty boxes of twenty-four-inch printout paper? Sorry to mess you around but I've just been told our data centre in Wilson is down to its last box.'

'Sure thing. Is that green and white, or plain?'

'Better make it twenty of each.'

'Okay. I'll have to run down to the warehouse and put it on myself. Let me put you on hold while I call down and stop the truck leaving.'

'Thanks.'

Al hit the hold button, then wandered over to the coffee machine. The truck was scheduled to leave in two hours but Ben didn't know that, while Al knew his client would be grateful for the extra effort. It was little things like this which had enabled him to charge a bit more than his competition. Something he had learnt from the man who had helped him start the business eighteen months earlier, when he lent Al 90,000 dollars to set up his company. 'Never say "yes" when you can make the client feel obliged to you,' had been one of lessons the man had repeated. 'Especially when you hear a price you like. Don't agree immediately; pause and sound worried, as if they've got the better end of the deal.'

Unhurriedly, Al went back to the phone and tapped the button next to the flashing red light.

'Hi Ben. Yeah, that's okay. The truck was just about to leave. I've got to run down there now and load it myself, or it won't get delivered today. One of our loaders is off sick and we're really busy,' he lied smoothly.

'Thanks a lot, Al,' Ben said. 'I owe you one.'

'No problem. It's all part of our superb service. Anyway it's not your fault we've got a man off sick today. Gotta run now, bye.'

Al pressed another button and heard the gruff voice of his cousin answer and the sound of a forklift truck whirring away in the background. 'Hey Mustafa. Chuck another forty boxes of twenty-four-inch printout paper on Standard Bank's delivery will you? Twenty green and white, twenty plain. It's for their data centre in Wilson.'

'Shit, Al. I've got three trucks leaving in the next hour.'

'Well don't forget, I told them I was loading it myself.'

Mustafa chuckled. 'If you want to be certain, maybe you should come down here and do it yourself.'

'Don't be ridiculous. I'm far too busy getting the orders which keep you employed,' Al said good-naturedly. 'Don't forget now Mustapha, Western Bank is one of our best clients.'

Al put the phone down and leaned back in his chair. He sipped at his coffee absentmindedly, staring out of the window at the space-age looking tower which broke the Seattle skyline. His attention switched to a pretty girl in a light green dress walking past his window.

'Life is beautiful,' Al thought to himself. 'Perhaps I'll get a round of golf in this afternoon at that new course they've just opened.'

REUTERS NEWS FEED

Seattle on fire.

Fires broke out at 27 buildings in Seattle this
morning. They appear to have started at a similar
time, around 2am. Five of the fires have now spread
to adjacent buildings and firefighters are being
called in from as far away as San Francisco. The high
winds forecast earlier are hampering their efforts
and there is a substantial risk they will spread
across a wider section of the city. Standard Western
Bank's skyscraper in Wilson has burnt to the ground.

Early reports indicate the fires broke out in the
store rooms and data centres right across the
Downtown district. So far no one is reported injured.
Police are instructing everyone to keep out of the
area and make alternative arrangements.

Because the fires started in the early hours and are
in close proximity to one another, they managed to
take hold and spread before firemen could adequately
react. A police federation spokesman, speaking 5
minutes before this report, is saying a firestorm
could sweep across the west side of the city.

 Most of the houses in the affected area are old and
constructed from timber. They are particularly
vulnerable to the cloud of sparks being driven
towards them by the gale-force wind.

MELTDOWN

Sergeant Gibbern couldn't believe what he was holding. It seemed too small and too simple to have engineered such devastation. Yet it had, he was in no doubt about it.

Sergeant Gibbern and Lieutenant Reese's routine patrol had become one of national importance, when in the thin dawn light they spotted two electricity pylons lying on their side 2,500 feet below them. They banked over for a closer look and after reporting in their findings, were ordered to fly the line north and send in a more detailed report.

They had been flying along the power line for over an hour incredulous that what they were seeing was real. Every eight to ten miles, two, sometimes three of the metal giants had crashed to the ground: dragging their wires with them; setting fire to anything that would burn. It was risk from the flames that forced Reese to land on the uneven surface of the newly ploughed field, which for the last ten minutes he had been trying to avoid, preferring to land on the more even surface of the many corn and grass fields common in this part of America.

Gibbern spoke nervously into his headset mike. 'Lieutenant, you'd better come take a look at this.'

Reese, alerted by the worried tone of his Sergeant's voice knew something was very wrong. He decided to switch off the helicopter before walking the 200 yards of sticky earth to his co-pilot.

Whatever had rattled his sergeant had to be pretty startling, Gibbern had a well deserved reputation for being calm and steady. His rock-like demeanour was good to have next to you in a fight, and his call sign was a direct extension of that – "Polar Bear". Big, solid and normally – ice cool.

Reese's concern made him lengthen his stride over the ridges of loose earth. Getting closer, he tried to make out what his Sergeant was holding. It looked like a wooden box, about the same size as a 1000-round 50mm ammo container. 'What is it, Gibbern?' he asked in the commanding snap of a senior officer. It was clipped short, designed to get immediate control.

Gibbern offered it to him like a butler handing over a breakfast tray. 'Look – this is all it is.'

Peering inside the box, Reese saw a crude machine. Though he recognised each of the five component parts instantly, he couldn't fathom their relevance. Held in position with metal straps was a windscreen-wiper pump with a digital timer wired to it, a new car battery and a large glass bottle. A revolving lawn irrigation sprinkler had been bolted to the top of the box. Sticking out of its nozzle at the front was a foot-long glass tube which tapered to a point – a chemistry pipette. The bottle, pump and rotating nozzle were connected in series by a thin glass tube.

Then the penny dropped. 'What's in the bottle, Bear? Any idea?'

'No, and I wouldn't like to guess,' Gibbern replied, putting it down carefully – it looked like a homemade bomb. 'Can't be a bomb with a sprinkler on the top, right?' he asked hopefully.

'Dunno. Stand back 100 yards Sergeant. I'm going to examine it and relay my findings to you. And Bear? If anything happens to me, you will report my findings to HQ before aiding me in anyway – Okay?'

'Yes sir,' Gibbern replied, adding, 'Good luck, Simon.' Turning away he scrabbled across the slippery field to get clear.

Lieutenant Reese took out his Gerber multi-tool knife, pulling it apart then squashing it back together, leaving the pincher-nosed pliers extended.

'Okay Bear, I'm disconnecting the digital timer from the battery,' Reese spoke into his helmet mike, his voice quavering slightly. 'Cutting the negative wire in three, two, one.'

But nothing happened except the digital timer going dead. 'So far so good… Cutting the positive in three, two, one… Okay, I've disconnected the battery and I'm taking it out of the box… Now I'm going to unscrew the cap on the bottle – anticlockwise… Got it,' he finished, gingerly lifting it out, ensuring the glass tube that went through the top of the cap had no resistance and never once touched the sides of the bottle.

There was a droplet of thin clear liquid hanging from the end of the tube. Reese sniffed at it tentatively. He knew the sharp smell instantly. It was strong acid and he tore his face away, sneezing twice.

'It's some kind of acid. Maybe battery acid. Come on back, Sergeant.'

As Gibbern walked underneath the downed pylon, he pointed up at the metal leg fifty feet above him. 'Yeah there it is, I can see it. That leg's been cut, see that shiny line? The other two legs are bent over but they're still attached to their base. Must be really strong acid to eat through the whole leg.'

'It doesn't have to be strong, Bear. Not if the sprinkler was set to squirt a fresh line every five or ten minutes. 24 hours of that and sulphuric acid will eat through half-inch steel plate, *no problemo*. Better spark up the chopper while I bring the box. You fly us back – hot extraction – and I'll report in.'

As he swivelled across his pilot seat, Reese felt the helicopter lift suddenly and allowed its upward momentum to sit him down with a satisfying bump – the natural trick of any veteran of two tours of duty in Afghanistan. He looked over proudly at his Sergeant. Bear wasn't wasting a second.

After reporting in his findings and ETA, he turned to Gibbern. 'All they've done is swap the plastic parts for glass. It's hard to believe that 80 bucks at a hardware store and an hour's work can take down the whole fucking grid.'

'The bummer of it is: no pylons – no power,' replied Bear.

'Yeah. And no power means no gas or water,' Reese added grimly.

Precisely at that moment, 2,300 miles north at the opposite end of the power line, the senior technician at the Lake Superior power station shook his head in disbelief. He had been eating breakfast before heading off to work when all the power had gone out. It had taken him two hours to fight his way through the heavy traffic to the power plant, as all the traffic signals were dead.

He was looking at one end of the main grid: a 2,900 mile backbone supplying electricity to a third of the country; named affectionately by the staff "Pipeline 1".

Towering above him were the massive ceramic connections which should have been ten feet around but were now the size of a bicycle wheel, while what did remain was blackened past recognition.

Sections of four-inch thick copper plate had fallen to the floor as a greeny-white powder and there was an overpowering smell of electrified metal in the room, reminding him of the train set he kept in his attic at home. After taking a look at the devastation in shocked silence, he turned to the assembled technicians gathered behind him. 'What about the switching stations and their relay electronics? Anyone know?'

'We're trying to get through to them now. It's not easy because the landline phone system is out, so we've had to use cell phones. The back-up generators for the phone masts only have another twelve hours to go before they run out of fuel. It will be difficult to get more diesel into them without any electricity. We should go on the basis that is all the time we've got before we're incommunicado. The cell phones are the only comms we have right now, and we don't have all the numbers.'

'We need to check on those stations right away. Anyone got through yet?'

'Yes sir. We've got through to eighteen.'

'And?'

'All the switching relays, circuit boards and their connectors have gone. They've vaporized, same as these,' the technician said morosely.

'If they're all out at once…Shit, we don't have that many spares. What a freakin' mess. Anyone got a best guess on what happened? Anyone?'

'It looks like some pylons went down every three or four miles along a 150-mile section of the main backbone. Some of them must have gone down simultaneously – earthing together. The sudden loss of resistance sucked a gigawatt down Pipeline 1. That surge jumped the breakers and relays so hard that it waterfalled into the next station, then the next. We still don't know how far up the spines it's gone but we can expect most of them to be shot to pieces.'

'You mean the spines or the stations?'

'I hate to say this, but seven of the stations are reporting that it's both.'

'What? I suppose a gigawatt would do that. Shit me, how did all those pylons go down at once? Must have been one hell of an earthquake.'

'No, we think it's sabotage. Probably The 24th Revolution. And it looks like they picked out the pylons on the angle points. The larger ones which allow Pipeline 1 to change direction. Those bastards have cut our strongest supports.'

'Jesus H Christ. They're a nightmare to reinstate They've shut down our grid for a month at least. Anyone told the police?'

'Actually, sir, they and the air force are providing most of the info I've just given you.'

'Okay, I want a planning meeting in my office in five minutes. And can one of you rig up a generator so we don't have to work by candlelight tonight? Okay people, now jump to it,' he said, clapping his hands to instil even greater urgency.

BREAKING THE SWORD

After three weeks spent eating Spanish food and flamenco dancing at night, coupled with the diminishing number of calls received from Head Office during the day, it was becoming increasingly obvious to both Leah and JJ that Abdul had vanished without trace.

One evening, sitting next to a crackling log fire on the patio outside their rented villa, nestled deep in the Catalonian mountains outside Barcelona, they watched an ochre red sun setting on the horizon as a waxing moon climbed the sky. They were so lost in their own thoughts, neither of them spoke. They were resigning themselves to Abdul's escape. He had got clean away, and each couldn't help wondering if the buck should stop with them. Of anyone, they had been handed the best chance to get him. Leah had even sat three feet away from him but in the end, all they had was a big fat nothing to reward their risk and effort. If it was anyone's fault it had to be theirs, and they each struggled to come to terms with the fact.

A meteor streaked across the heavens, the silver line of its passing slicing right across the face of the honey coloured moon. As its glorious destruction flashed into the void, Leah's mind started down another track.

'There must be a solution to The Sword of Damocles somewhere,' Leah thought. 'Nothing is perfect, including the perfect plan, so if we can't catch Abdul, how else can we stop the attacks?' The thought gnawed at her and she reached over for the bottle of iced Monopole wine to refill her glass.

Glancing up at the night sky, she saw another streak, then a third. The earth was passing through the Perseid meteor belt and they had decided sit outside and watch the cosmic display. After a minute spent in anticipation of seeing another meteor, without one appearing, the same thought returned to circle her. 'There's no such thing as the perfect plan.'

Leah went over everything she could remember from that very first night, when Victor had outlined The Sword of Damocles to her. She wracked her memory for anything he might have given as a clue to defeat it; but in truth she knew, he had stated the complete opposite. 'It's the idea, Leah, the idea that you can no longer live your life within the law and survive in comfortable ease. At first people will assume it only affects others. Then it will happen in their own city. Then to somebody they've heard of, then to someone they know – with law enforcement escalating the chaos on every step of the way. And remember: once this idea jumps out of the box there are the copy-catters to consider.'

Victor even believed that once his idea had been placed in the public domain, it was bound to happen at some point. That is why he had kept it so secret. The reason he thought it so inherently dangerous. No, there was no clue there. She had to resolve this on her own.

'Start with everything you know and break it down into its component parts,' she reasoned to herself. 'Number one: the scheme is designed to use fear rather than brute force, delivered by the rapid increase in the number of attacks and the knowledge that another, far worse attack is coming. Number two: once they have all come out and been caught, the attacks stop. Number three: you can't arrest someone if they haven't done anything and you have no way to locate them.'

The only one that hinted at a possible solution was number two. They needed to arrest them all at the same time. A wonderful idea – but how? Because no list meant no one to arrest. It was also likely that none of the terrorists knew any of the others. Yet somehow, she felt there had to be a way.

'If we could get them all to attack at once, we could scoop the lot,' she spoke into the dark.

'What's that?

'Eureka, JJ!' Leah said, jumping up and deliberately throwing her glass into the fire in excitement.

The wonderful sound of it smashing brought JJ fully alert. 'Eureka?' he questioned. 'What are you thinking? Dammit Leah, what are you doing?'

'If I can get them to all come out fighting at once, you and your merry men could round them up in one go.'

'Sure. But how do we do that? Stick an advert in the New York Times?'

'Don't be facetious, darling. It's obvious, don't you see?'

'No I don't see…How can you…?'

'Get them to all attack at once?' she finished for him. 'But if I can, then it's over – right?'

'Absolutely. It would reduce them to their number only and remove the slow poisonous drip of their attacks at a stroke. But how on earth do you get them to all come out at once?'

'I'm not sure….well, not completely sure. Let me think about it.'

'*Whaaat?* I know you better than that, Miss Leah Mandrille. Tell me what that razor-like mind of yours is slicing open.'

'When you think about it, each terrorist must have a number. A sequential number between 2 and 916, right? That's the only way each of them knows when it's their turn to come out terrorizing. A code or any other arrangement stands the risk of being uncovered if we caught one of them alive. Even if they used different codes, or public media like newspapers to communicate, there would still be a risk of us discovering it and breaking it, or a chance we could interrupt it. The only sure-fire way is to give them each a different number. A sequential number. Anything else is risky or lacks basic co-ordination.'

'Of course that's what they're doing. They simply count the arrests or suicide bombings in the media, then when their number comes around they up and start destroying. And there's another reason it has to be that way. If they were relying on any other method and one of them was incapacitated by an accident or simply got sick, he might not be able let the next one in line know. That would disrupt the smooth roll out of each wave. Anyway they are almost certainly operating without knowing who any of the others are.'

'Precisely, so they each have a number. A sequential number. But what if you're number 64 when 125 arrests are announced in the media? And you know there should only be 32 before it's your turn? You would think you had missed your go and if you're a terrorist, keyed up and raring to go and suddenly find out you've missed your turn, you might want to play catch-up. Correct?'

'You would think the Government had suppressed the news coverage then released the information as a small Pyrrhic victory.'

'An obvious ploy on our part and one they could expect. They probably have a contingency plan for that.'

'Leah, in war that contingency is always fight, flight or hide.'

'It's not going to be flight or hide, JJ. I know the Semitic mindset well. They will all come out fighting.'

'But if they do, then we've also got something to shoot at. And there's only hundreds of them against 270 million highly-motivated Americans who are desperate to put an end to all this. God Leah – they wouldn't last a week. I think we should consider relaying your solution to the President.'

'Is that your considered opinion?' she joked.

'Let's put it this way – I'll do the dialling, while you...'

'Do the talking.'

Overhead, the meteor shower intensified, streaking the sky with its magical splendour; but neither of them noticed as they hurried into the villa to make the call.

It took twenty minutes to get through to the President, with four different people coming on the line before JJ recognised the well-broadcasted voice on the other end.

'I think it would be better if you spoke directly to the brains of our outfit, Mr President. Her name is Leah Mandrille and she's a Brit.'

'I know exactly who you both are. Please put her on.'

'Hello Mr President,' Leah said, feeling a little anxious. She hadn't fully composed her thoughts or finalised her thinking.

'It's a pleasure to speak to you, Miss Mandrille. What have you got for me?'

'I may have a way to break their spell, Mr President.'

'Go right ahead.'

'Well, they are using the media as a tool to phase the release of each wave of terrorists...'

He jumped straight in. 'Leah, I'm not going to suppress our media in return for a poor shot at wrapping this up. And anyway, the days when this office could effectively squash information went out of the window with the Net.'

'I understand completely Sir, but that's not what I'm suggesting – nor would I.'

'Forgive me, but Bruce Cougar told me that it was your idea not to pick up those two snipers. I'm still feeling a bit sensitive over their last victims.'

'For what it's worth Sir, Khalifa told me that it set him back a few days, so it did delay the next wave.'

'It was the right course of action at the time. I just wish it wasn't sitting on my conscience. Please continue.'

'Well Sir, what if we were to announce more arrests than there actually are?'

'Go on.'

'If you were a terrorist waiting for your turn, when it suddenly appears that you've missed it, what would you do? Err, Mr President,' she added to JJ's quick frown, her diplomatic training forgotten in her excitement.

'Having gone to all that trouble, I would come out fighting anyway. Mmmm, I see what you mean but there's a problem which goes with that.'

'What problem, Mr President?'

'In order to publicise fake arrests we have to broadcast fake attacks. Which means I become the terrorist of my own people in the truest sense of the word. I would be scaring the citizens of say, Chicago, when in reality there was no attack there. Think of the turmoil that will cause... the doubt it will sow in people's minds about the integrity of my Office.'

For any political leader, Leah realised, it was a dangerous course of action to implement. It also occurred to her that he had probably considered this solution, then dismissed it for exactly that reason. Perhaps he was still holding out for a lucky break – like her and JJ coming through with Abdul's list of terrorists. If that was the case, what he didn't know was preventing him from doing something which might work. Leah knew the Abdul trail had gone cold, meaning there would be no list; which made her idea the only decent alternative, unpleasant though it was. It presented her with a dilemma as well. She could inform the President they had little chance of getting the list, not a particularly career-minded choice, or persuade him to a new course of action. Possibly the only one left.

Taking a deep breath she gave it her best shot. 'Newspapers print yesterday's stories, Mr President. All I'm suggesting is that you print tomorrow's today. Because those attacks will happen at some point and given the choice of being killed in the future or scared now, I would choose the latter of those two evils, Sir. I also believe that most people will welcome any attempt to put an end to all this.'

'Print tomorrow's stories today? What a stunning way to guarantee the silence of the large number of people who would need to know and be involved. That's the problem I've always had with this idea. Print tomorrow's stories today? Damn, I like that, it might ensure everyone kept it secret. If the people involved believed that what they were falsifying was inevitably going to happen to them, we could probably execute it without any leaks. Because if there was one single leak, Leah, everything would fall apart including this Administration. And I can't risk that, it would accelerate the chaos. The country's stability is incredibly vulnerable at the moment. Things changed drastically when they took down the power grid.'

'I understand. I hadn't considered that side to it, Mr President.'

'It's curious y'know, Leah. Everything about this plan turns things on their head. Normally any media platform which could write about the future would be hailed as a godsend. Still, it's an interesting idea. Maybe it is a Godsend after all.'

Changing the subject abruptly he went on, 'I imagine the hunt for Khalifa must be at a pretty low ebb for you to be presenting alternative strategies. Am I right?'

'Unfortunately you are, Mr President.'

'I see. Print tomorrow's stories today, eh? It has real merit. Let me think it over. Meantime, let's keep this firmly in the family shall we?'

'Absolutely, Sir. It's not Britain that's under attack.'

'Quite. I imagine my office has your direct number?'

'Yes it does, Mr President.'

'I'll be in touch. Thank you. And thank JJ for me would you?'

Two days later JJ received an email from Head Office titled "New Assignment".

You have been appointed to the President's staff. This will take effect from midnight EST. You will report directly to his office as a special advisor to a team being set up to fight and apprehend The 24th Revolution. Your rank has been upgraded to Major, with an annual salary of 82,362 paid monthly. New credit cards for expenses will arrive tomorrow UPS, tracking number 12373, together with instructions on how to proceed.

Half an hour later, Leah also received one.

Her Majesty's Diplomatic Corps has been requested, via the Prime Minister's liaison, to extend to you the invitation of attending the President of the United States as a special envoy attached to our Embassy in Washington. This post is commensurate with the salary of an Assistant Ambassador, although your title will be Special Diplomatic Envoy. We understand that this highly irregular circumstance results from a personal request made by the President of the United States to our Prime Minister.

Trusting you won't be too inconvenienced, please confirm your willingness to accept this new position by sending back the form below at your earliest convenience.

Leah punched the air in delight and passed her BlackBerry over to JJ.

'When I look at mine then read yours, I nearly wish I was British.'

'We're separated by a common language alright. They say the same thing but mine seems somewhat more...'

'Yeah, somewhat more,' JJ said, closing the gate on that line of conversation as he reached into the fridge for a bottle of champagne.

'To our promotions, darling,' he shouted, as the cork bounced off the ceiling.

'I suppose this means we get to meet him.'

'Get to meet him? As from midnight tonight we both work for him. The folks back home would be ecstatic if they knew. It's a crying shame they never will.'

'You know what this means, don't you?'

'Yes, he's going to implement your solution.'

'Do you think it will work, JJ?'

'It might. I mean it should. I mean it will, providing we get all our ducks in a row and maximise our luck.'

'What if Abdul has already thought of it and come up with an answer?'

'Unfortunately for Abdul and his crew, they only have two choices if anything goes wrong at their end – fight or hide. If I read it right, they will prefer to go out with a bang.'

'Leah Mandrille – Saviour of the free world. I like the sound of that,' she smiled.

'It's better than Miss Assistant Ambassador.'

'So what do I call a Major?' Leah asked cleverly. She had been trying to uncover what his initials stood for and he had steadfastly refused to divulge it.

'You call me Major JJ.'

'I can't call you that – it sounds like a sex toy,' she pushed.

'Yeah, it does a bit. Cool name, huh?'

UNDERMINING SOCIETY

REUTERS NEWS FEED

The source of the muted explosions heard late last night in San Francisco and Washington, has been traced to the underground sewer networks of both cities.

Two 30lb propane gas cylinders have been discovered in a tunnel beneath Fulcrow Street in San Francisco. Their taps were turned on, the bottles were empty and a car fan and battery with a digital clock wired to a car coil and spark plug have been found stuck to the wall of the tunnel with expanding foam. Inspectors also found two half-moon boards 150 yards apart, which they believe were designed to concentrate the gas in one section of tunnel, allowing the effluent to travel underneath. The downstream board was discovered lying on its side and probably allowed the concentrated gas to escape farther down the tunnel before it was ignited. Engineers think the board was dislodged by a weekly maintenance flush of that particular tunnel.

Inspectors have confirmed that twelve sewer tunnels in San Francisco and a total of nine in Washington have completely collapsed, blocking their ability to function. They are convinced it is a deliberate act of sabotage, probably the work of The 24th Revolution. One section of collapsed tunnel is reported to be a quarter of a mile in length.

Propane gas when mixed with air is highly explosive, but the reason the damage is so severe is probably due to the high levels of methane present in all sewerage systems. It is likely The 24th Revolution knew this, setting the timer to activate the spark plug after measuring the size of each tunnel and working out the distance and time required to ensure a volatile mixture of these three gases.

When ignited, a series of reactions would occur: the initial explosion creates a powerful shock wave, enough to crack and weaken the structure of the tunnel. Once the explosion has burnt all of the available oxygen it reverses: sucking in air to keep itself burning, causing an instant vacuum or implosion. Implosions are known to create powerful shock waves which are far more violent than explosions. This is probably why the destruction of the tunnels is so extensive.

The inspectors are saying The 24th Revolution targeted the main sewers in each city, at points where the sewage flow is greatest, to deliberately cause the most harm. Effectively, they have shut down the entire effluent system of Washington and a substantial portion of the San Francisco metropolis. There appears to be no quick or easy way to redirect the sewage which is why some sections of both cities, up to five miles from the nearest explosions, are also reporting over-flowing toilets, showers and sinks. Lakes of raw sewage are already pooling in the lower-lying regions of both cities and there is a likelihood of disease outbreaks in the coming weeks. As this is the hottest part of the year, doctors expect cholera and typhoid outbreaks to materialise in less than two weeks from now.

The Mayors of Washington and San Francisco have jointly appealed for calm. They have issued an order banning everyone from flushing toilets or conducting any type of washing for the next 72 hours, with a 10,000 dollar fine and a year's imprisonment for any person caught doing it. This becomes effective from 18:00 local times. Those fortunate enough to have alternative accommodation outside the cities are being asked to relocate until a solution can be found. Many residents are expressing dismay and alarm at being forced to leave their homes and vacate the area for the foreseeable future.

No one knows how long it will take to rectify the damage, but Craig Riner, a senior engineer in San Francisco, said it will take months to rebuild the affected tunnels. The reason he gave is that the blown-up sections have been churned into loose earth and stone debris which is impossible to bore through, so completely new tunnels will have to be excavated. This means stretches of busy roads will be closed for up to two months at a time. Additionally, due to the size of the tunnels and the need to build them in the shortest possible time, a substantial number of houses will need to be compulsory purchased. Details of their locations will be announced at the end of next week.

There is a lot of anger against The 24th Revolution, who most people assume are responsible for this pernicious act.

Police switchboards have been inundated with calls from as far away as New Orleans, Charleston and Phoenix, asking the authorities not to arrest the culprits, or to maintain secrecy over their arrest if they are apprehended. It is noteworthy that to date, none of these cities have been attacked by The 24th Revolution.

COUNTER GAMBIT

With the exception of the President and the Operations Director it had taken longer to prepare than anyone had anticipated, but the monumental task had finally come together. All the pieces were now in place for the operation they had codenamed "Orange Clockwork".

William Mann insisted from the outset on supervising the strategic planning and overall implementation, delaying the launch date twice after exposing several major flaws and a handful of fragile aspects. He made sure these were fully resolved before finally agreeing they were ready to launch.

'The stakes are extremely high and we only get one good shot at this. Let's make sure we get it right – and right from the get-go,' he constantly reminded the Operations Director.

When JJ and Leah had first arrived in Washington, a limousine drove them straight to the White House where they had been rigorously interviewed by the President – personally and in private. Expressing his delight at the end of their ordeal he added, 'I apologise for the severity of my questioning but there is a lot at stake here. I need to be certain you can help co-ordinate this effectively.'

For the first week they had worked on defining the plan, which was simple in theory but proved unwieldy in practice, mainly due to the large number of personnel who had to be brought in. From control of the carefully scripted press releases, right through to the security service and law enforcement response, was a logistical nightmare of mammoth proportion. The command and control centre alone held over 250 personnel and had to be set up from scratch, in secrecy.

They located the nerve centre in a disused building in a quiet corner of the CIA headquarters complex in Langley, Virginia. It had previously been used to monitor North Korean nuclear weapons manufacture and its advantages were considerable. The 12,000 sq foot building had all the necessary comms and sat-links in place, yet was far enough away from the other CIA buildings to ensure security could be guaranteed.

'This will blow up in our faces if some CIA middle manager with his own private agenda spills the beans,' JJ pointed out to William Mann; insisting on a separate security gate inside the Langley perimeter itself, which made the Director of the CIA fly into a rage.

The location did have one tricky aspect. Orange Clockwork did not draw on any CIA resources other than the building and the equipment it housed. William Mann told JJ about his heated discussion with the CIA Director, or as he put it, "his concerned interest in what is going on in his own back yard without his knowledge or approval". But the President had gone with JJ's instincts, warning the Director off by asking him where a leaked memo of a recent operation with Pakistan had originated.

'We will have to inform him eventually, Mr President,' JJ suggested. 'But let's do it when we start the Op, not while we are planning and preparing for it.' William had simply nodded his agreement.

Secrecy was the main bear they wrestled with throughout the painstaking process, but all the parts were now in place. They had spent the last week testing every contingency they could come up with, both real and imaginary, ironing out every last wrinkle. Satisfied the operation would perform as precisely as a sub-atomic clock, they awaited the 'Go' from the President and the launch date.

After two more days the call came through. 'I don't need to know the exact start date, but sometime next week will work well with my office and schedule,' he told the Operations Director.

'Next week it is, Mr President. We will shut down all information to the press for two weeks before releasing the dummy reports of the attacks.'

'Good. Because if this doesn't work out I will have to sign the order allowing our citizens to carry arms in public.'

This Bill had created a storm of protest on both sides of Congress. The Republicans were arguing that a war was being conducted on US soil and it was downright unconstitutional not to let people arm themselves. While the more sober thinkers in the House felt it would lead to shoot-outs between vigilante groups – each thinking the other was the enemy.

The President had gone on the record saying, 'I don't want to sign this Bill. It sends America down a dangerous path. One that will prove hard to reverse.'

'What do you want me to do with Leah and JJ?' asked the Operations Director. 'They've effectively worked themselves out of a job.'

'That sounds positive,' William replied. 'If you're sure you no longer need them, send them here for lunch on Monday. I'd like to thank them personally.'

'As a surprise, Sir?'

'No no, better warn them or Leah will turn up in jeans,' he joked.

The lunch didn't turn out to be quite the relaxed affair JJ and Leah were expecting. William Mann used the opportunity to go over the minutiae of the plan from start to finish, with JJ and Leah hardly touching their plates of Châteaubriand steak and double chocolate cake that had been lovingly presented by the White House chef. They explained how the real attacks would be supplemented in the media with fake reports, after a ten-day period of complete news blackout.

JJ reiterated that if were any longer the bloggers reporting the real attacks would start to gain credence, inadvertently tipping off The 24th Revolution that something else was in play. 'It will cause the exact opposite of what those concerned citizens are trying to achieve with their amateur reporting.'

'The 24th Revolution may realise what we're doing, the moment the fake arrests hit the media,' William posed.

'They might,' Leah replied. 'But they still have to come out when it's their turn, or the whole plan collapses like a house of cards. And I don't think your average religious fanatic enjoys burying his head in the sand. No, it's hide and wait, or fight. James MacCack thinks Khalifa recruited tribal groups and families – breaking them up to chain their loyalty to the cause. If he has done that, they will come out fighting.'

'And we are more than ready for them when they do, Mr President,' added JJ.

'It's the most extraordinary set of events I think any President has ever had to face. I must briefly become the terrorist of my own citizens to make our country safe once more. I hope my people forgive me.'

'If all goes to plan they will, Mr President,' Leah said supportively.

'If the plan works out they will, but things rarely go to plan. However, there is one great and good thing to come out of this. The Constitution Bill is about to be ratified by Congress. If it wasn't for these attacks, that Bill would never have seen the light of day. It will also ensure that any future president has a lot of campaigning to do before initiating another war on foreign soil. If the Bill had been in place when Bush Junior was President, I doubt we would have invaded Iraq and set the two greatest religions on a collision course. I have a feeling we are now paying for that with our own blood.'

'I saw Mr Bush being interviewed, saying he believed in the "End of Times",' Leah said in exasperation, referring to the belief that the Book of Revelations would come true and with it, an end to time on earth for anyone who wasn't devoutly Christian. 'So he had nothing to lose by starting a 100-year war between Christians and Muslims. Either his God wins or it's Armageddon. And for an extremist Christian, either one is a step forward.'

'Ha! That's funny,' the President laughed. 'But it's an unfortunate truth that he simply didn't realise the wider implications of what he did. He didn't have the world experience or the smarts. No, our people made a huge mistake electing a fool for their President.'

'I was told that his first election victory was partially due to vote-rigging in places like Miami,' Leah said. 'By someone who witnessed the voters getting channelled away from their polling booths.'

'Believe me that's been looked into thoroughly and it cannot happen again. As a direct result of that fiasco, I have managed to implement the Constitution Bill to include more frequent voting by our people, on a wide range of issues,' William explained, getting up from the table. Leaving JJ stunned by his admission.

'He should be held to account for that. Tried in court at the very least,' JJ burst out, forgetting in his anger to use the formal title of 'Mr President'.

'Really, JJ? And how would that promote people's belief in democracy?' William asked, gripping the back of his chair. 'Make no mistake about it: without that belief, without that trust and hope, democracy would disappear like smoke from a chimney, with nothing left to mark its passing. It's battered and bruised but democracy still lives. And post-mortems are for the dead, not the living.'

Seeing JJ had flushed to a deep red with outrage, Leah put a restraining hand on his arm. William noticed it. 'I understand how you feel, JJ, but true knowledge stems from experience and experience comes from making mistakes. So don't think we haven't learned from it and corrected it...It's curious that quite a few Presidents have used the medium of war to further their own agendas, while I'm using this more horrific attack to reinforce democracy throughout our great nation. Without this crisis, I would never in my wildest dreams have thought the Constitution Bill would get passed. Not in my lifetime anyway. But just before you arrived, I was informed that it will be voted into law tomorrow. "Never let a crisis go to waste" is an excellent dictum for all leaders,' his eyes shone. 'Rest assured, when all this is over I will fight to make it permanent – even at the price of my position as President – and it may come to that. There are some things and some beliefs that are worth sacrificing oneself for. The Constitution Bill is a step in the right direction for "Government by the People". I trust it will remain in place until a new, better way to structure society is found.'

Sitting back down he leaned towards them and said in the hushed tone of a co-conspirator. 'Now, where are you both going to take a well-earned break? I've got a Gulfstream on stand-by, awaiting only your itinerary.'

Leah and JJ looked across the table at each other. 'Barcelona,' they chorused.

COUNTER CHECK

REUTERS NEWS FEED

An investigation into the two freak waves which swept up and down the Colorado River yesterday morning causing widespread damage, has uncovered the likelihood of it being an act of sabotage.

Investigators believe the enormous piece of rock that fell into the river was deliberately engineered to break away from the cliff. Signs of a large fire have been discovered on the new cliff wall and the charring is too extensive to have been caused by any natural event. The report says the remains of burnt car tyres can be seen in the cracks of the newly exposed rock face and there is a strong smell of diesel fuel in the vicinity.

This is almost certainly the work of The 24th Revolution. They may have exploited one of the natural fissures in the sides of the canyon, filling it with car tyres and pouring in a tanker of diesel fuel which they set alight. The remote and uninhabited area has a small dirt road running parallel to the canyon and there are truck tyre marks leaving the road which end at the new cliff face.

The chief engineer, Dr Pellun, has said the fire would have created extremely high temperatures — heating the rock, then the well predicted rainstorm in the early hours of yesterday morning was torrential enough for water to collect in the fissure — cooling it rapidly. This heating and sudden cooling of the rock made it disintegrate, causing the massive section to peel away from the cliff. When it fell into the Colorado river some 300 feet below, it displaced more than an cubic acre of water. This displacement caused two gigantic waves to form, each over 100 feet high: one going up-river, the other sweeping downstream to impact the Hoover Dam.

The dam is currently being manned by a skeleton crew. Civilian air traffic has been denied airspace for a radius of fifty miles to prevent any interference with the rescue mission that will take place if the dam wall starts to fail.

Engineers inside the dam are lowering the water level. They are calling it 'a race against time'. Laser measurements of the larger cracks show they are moving apart at two hundredths of an inch per hour. This is fast enough to cause a catastrophic failure of the entire structure.

Photographs of the canyon walls show a clearly defined line, marking the height of each wave at 103 feet above mean water level. Up to this height the sides of the canyon have been scoured smooth. The wave which hit the Hoover Dam would have been loaded with stones and rock, making it behave more like liquid concrete on impact. This is why the dam has cracked so extensively.

At the time of the Hoover dam's construction in 1936, it was not known that rock displacing water will cause such gigantic waves to form, so the original design of the dam did not allow for waves more than forty feet high.

The sides of the canyon are high and straight in that area. They hemmed in the wave, channelling it straight towards the Hoover Dam. If the wall does fail, it will release some thirty million acre-feet of water, causing devastation for fifty miles downstream until it washes into Lake Mohave. Everyone has been evacuated from the area immediately below the dam and people are being told to clear the surrounding district, up to ten miles either side of the Colorado River.

THE BLACK KNIGHT'S MOVE

Fifteen days after the start of the news blackout, a computer program at the NSA monitoring facility in Fresno California, flagged up a purchase on the credit card Abdul had used to buy his laptop and flight to Cairo. It had been used to purchase a single cup of mint tea in Islamabad, Pakistan. The resulting bill for the spy satellite covering that area was 1,470,000 US dollars, paid for by the newly revamped Homeland Security.

It took eighteen minutes to realign the satellite, but Abdul had already left. Shielding himself from the searing eye of the sun with an umbrella. As many ladies are wont to do in Islamabad, when the heat is in the noonday.

COUNTER GAMBIT

Leah and JJ had their most heated row over what to do next. On Leah's side it was driven by her secret knowledge of the pact she had made with Abdul – the deal they had struck in the coffee shop in Cairo. She had first hand experience of how ingenious Abdul was and his abilities terrified her. He had nearly got her killed over her data download and because it was his credit card being used in Islamabad, she was sure it was being used intentionally. A thief would have made further purchases with the card after any initial success, and it had only been used once. She didn't think it was accidental or an oversight on Abdul's part and if it was deliberate, then he was summoning her to a meeting. Perhaps he was going to call off his attacks this time. Maybe he would hand himself in. Maybe. She couldn't think of another sensible explanation and if JJ discovered her and Abdul in conference, he would shoot first and regret it second. Ultimately though, meeting Abdul did involve risk; substantial risk on her part; probably life threatening. While she was prepared to risk her life trying to stop the attacks – and those were the stakes – getting killed by JJ as she attempted it seemed inherently unfair. It was a double dilemma, with the odds swinging in her favour if she went alone.

On the plus side, if she could meet Abdul she could try to persuade him to call off the attacks. And it would be a lot safer if she met him on her own. She was in no doubt as to how JJ would react if he caught them together. Now they were lovers, JJ would become instantly incensed by her concealment, then kill her. The cocktail of her personal betrayal combining with his patriotic duty would be more than enough to do it, and his loyalty to his country overshadowed his personal feelings. She knew JJ's sense of duty was strong. Strong enough for him to willingly sacrifice his own life and, if he was confronted by a traitor plotting and scheming with his sworn enemy…

But JJ wouldn't hear of her going to Islamabad alone. His initial response had been a dogged 'No, you can't go,' but she fought back and the next morning he tried a more conciliatory approach.

'You can't go solo, Leah.'

'JJ, you will stick out like a black choir at a Ku Klux Klan meeting and get us both hanged.'

'You don't know how to operate on your own. If anything goes wrong I have to explain it to James MacCack, remember? And honey, that ain't happening.'

'Look, it's Islamabad Pakistan. You don't speak any Urdu or Pashtu. You look Western, you're a spy, and now the Taliban are in effective control of the city you will get us both lynched.'

'I'll wear a beard.'

'Your eyes are blue.'

'No problem – I'll wear coloured contacts.'

'What about your skin colour?'

'Bottled tan.'

'You'll never pull it off.'

'I'm sorry, Leah, but you're not going without me. That's final.'

She stared at him, anxiously searching for a way out of her predicament. But the expression in his eyes was telling her that if she went, he was coming.

'I am a little worried about going there by myself,' she said carefully.

'A little worried? Grief Leah. No wonder you're a diplomat.'

'If you come along and blow it, we'll both get strung up.'

'Then let's do this: we'll fly to Morocco first, I'll get suited up in one of those fetching gowns Muslim men wear and if you're still worried I'll stay behind.'

'They're very comfortable and very sensible in the heat.'

'Yeah? Then why do they wear black under a hot sun? I'm going for the whitest white I can find. I don't feel a burning need to mourn their Prophet.'

'You think that's just religious? I thought you knew better.'

'It's to show mourning for the death of the Prophet, non?'

'Partly, but the black gets hot...'

'No kidding.'

'…and creates convection. So you get a cooling breeze wafting right up your hot spot.'

'You mean it's cooler than white?' he asked, incredulous.

'Much.'

'Really?'

'Really.'

'Wow, that's pretty cool.'

In the end, they dressed him as a pregnant woman in full veil, with Leah as the 'sister' accompanying him to a hospital in Islamabad. His attempt at disguise hadn't worked. His white even teeth shining out of a cigarette tan, turned his false beard into an object of suspicion. Like many pious Muslim women, he decided to wear black.

They put down at a Red Crescent base just after midnight as part of a shipment of 'humanitarian supplies'. A waiting car ferried them the last thirty miles to Islamabad, dropping them at a small hotel much favoured by the hard-working class of the small towns and villages which surround the city.

Everything they needed was in walking distance. Hundreds of small shops and stalls were selling everything from fruit to AK47s – three sold both. There two mosques only five minutes walk away.

Islamabad had a very different feel from Beirut or Cairo. The men shouldered rifles and sported curved daggers tied at their fronts, as they stalked through the streets pebble-eyed. They are the Taliban, their complex loyalties weaving back into the foothills and mountains from which they came. JJ saw them as shining examples of pure hate. Leah told him that their extreme form of Islam had outlawed almost everything, including dancing and teddy bears. She warned him repeatedly of their disgust at all things Western, especially the people: labelling them all as terrorists and modern-day Crusaders.

Their repression of women reflects a deep insecurity in themselves. Boil them down to their pure essence and they don't like anyone at all; happily mistrusting their own Taliban brotherhood when it comes to the more pleasurable pastime of blood feuding. Fighting is a ceaseless way of life to them, sparked by ancient rivalries and vendettas, some of which stretch back over hundreds of years. Many of the feuds continue to this day where the original reason for enmity has been given up to the mists of time.

'Abdul wouldn't have any problem recruiting his force from here,' JJ whispered under his gloved hand, noticing the scathing look one man gave them as he stalked past.

'They're not allowed ammo in the rifles,' Leah whispered back. 'The police hold it while they visit the city. This is all machismo.'

'Makes you wonder where they hide the bullets during the frisking. I doubt the body-search is quite as thorough as I would like, if I were a politician here.'

They left the hotel and went straight to the coffee shop where the credit card had been used and sat down. Leah ordered two mint teas, in the faltering Pashtu she had memorised on the flight over. 'No talking now or you'll get us both killed,' she whispered to JJ.

They sat in silence trying to blend, looking for anything which might hint at Abdul's presence there. After the second prolonged pot of tea they got up and went back to the hotel, frustrated.

'You know, it's ironic that you're here,' Leah said, watching him tear off the veil to gulp down fresher air.

'Why?' gasped JJ.

'Because I don't think I'd have been able to sit at that table alone.'

'Yeah, those Taliban look pretty fierce. We don't want to get on the wrong side of those boys.'

'We already are, JJ. We already are.'

'Yup, I can imagine Khalifa is feeling pretty comfortable right now. Look Leah, the sorry truth is that we can't operate here.'

'What do we do?'

'We wait quietly or leave now.'

'Let's wait.'

'Okay.' JJ suddenly held a finger to his lips, then went over to the small bamboo desk and wrote frantically on the notepad "Have u bug swept?"

'No,' she mouthed.

'Shit,' he wrote, picking up his BlackBerry to run the sweep. The flashing red arrow led him straight to a wall socket. JJ wriggled it out with an ease that surprised her. On the back of the metal box he pointed to a small magnetic disk no bigger than a penny. Holding his finger to his lips again, he carefully replaced the box before continuing his scan of the room. He found two more but instead of disabling them he replaced them and started putting his veil back on, waving at her to do the same.

Leading them into the park behind a mosque, JJ walked until he was sure they were out of earshot before turning to her, 'It's gotta be Abdul bugging us – but how?'

'How what?'

'How did he know our room number?'

'What about when we had our tea?'

'Even so, how did he get onto us so fast?'

'Maybe it's just coincidence. Perhaps a lot of the hotel rooms in Islamabad are bugged,' she offered.

'Those are British bugs.'

'What?'

'You can't buy them, Leah.'

'Either Abdul knew in advance, or we're being watched by our own side.'

'It can't be your outfit. They would be putting us in danger for no reason. But the good news is I can track the receiver,' JJ smiled.

'What's the bad?'

'Whoever is listening is close. Within 200 feet of our room.'

The realisation that Abdul could well be in the same hotel, hit Leah hard. She now had proof that he had summoned her to a meeting. No other explanation fit all the facts. There was no choice now, she had to get rid of JJ or leave Islamabad this instant. A paralysing fear grabbed her. If she bumped into Abdul it would be impossible to hide her reaction from JJ, and worse, Abdul might assume JJ had been told of their pact then introduce himself – thinking JJ was on-side. Her fear turned to near panic as she went through the possibilities of that encounter. 'What JJ? Merciful heaven, Abdul could be in the next room,' she gasped out.

'He would still need a bit of notice to set up our room without suspicion.'

'I don't understand. We only knew two days ago that we were coming here but we didn't know which hotel until we arrived,' Leah said, underscoring JJ's supposition.

'We didn't need to know. But it was booked by your outfit, wasn't it?'

'Yes. Why?'

'So MI6 has a record of the.... Oh my God.'

'What? What is it?'

'You remember that download you did?'

'I'll never forget it,' Leah replied.

'Twenty-three minutes! We never did get to the bottom of that.'

'If you're going to bring that up right now...'

'No, no. I believe it did take you that long– but not to download the data.'

'What then?'

'Perhaps he used your connection to the GCHQ server to piggyback in. Think about it, he's a computer expert and an authority on security systems for banks and it looks like he knew our hotel and room number before we did.'

'If Abdul had access to our computer systems, he would find out where we were staying the moment it was entered on the database. All he would have to do is monitor our file.'

'And he knows your name.'

Her chest-squeezing fear wrapped itself tighter. *What had she got herself into?* The game she was playing had been an exciting and risky up till now, but the knowledge that Abdul was playing with all the cards face up stopped her breathing. She could see the dire vulnerability of their situation, and she couldn't warn JJ.

'If ever I needed confirmation of whose side you're on – I've got it now,' he said, watching her face turn ashen.

'I shouldn't be here, JJ. I don't know what I'm doing. I'm a diplomat not a spy. I'm completely out of my depth.'

'We all are, Leah. That's the struggle.'

'What are we going to do?' she moaned.

'Turn the tables. For the very first time we are one step ahead of him.'

'You can't be serious? I say we cut and run without going back to that room,' she said, her lower lip trembling.

'We know he's bugging us. We know he's probably got access to Britain's security services database, but he doesn't know we know. We can track the bugs. We can mislead him with bogus intel. We may even be able to backtrack his connection to GCHQ's server. We have a really good shot at pinning him. It sure as hell takes the luck element out of the equation.'

'We're fish in a glass tank and you think it's good?'

'That's because I'm an agent, honey. Come on, we're wasting time. We've got a few things to get in place.'

'Every single damn duck in a row, JJ. Or you tell me. Deal?'

'It's not as straightforward as that. But I'll make sure you're always safe, okay?'

'What about you? Can you guarantee your safety?'

'As I said, it's never as straightforward as that. Let's go back to the hotel – I feel like a long cold shower.'

'*You what?* You can't want to get it on with him listening in, surely?'

'Well, he likes women and you're pretty easy on the eye. It might annoy him and throw him off his guard.'

'I see. Is this all part of your master plan to catch him?'

'No, not really,' he shook his head, grinning wolfishly.

'Okay, but on condition we bolt if anything goes wrong. Promise me, JJ.'

'Nothing will go wrong. Relax Leah, we're in control now.'

'Then let's run back to the hotel,' she replied, slanting her eyes back at him.

'Let's make him feel really safe to be listening, okay?'

'Abdul's going to feel safer than the Devil in Hell by the time I've finished with you,' she replied.

'That was fun,' JJ winked at her, lying back on the pillows with his hands behind his head.

Leah began fondling his flaccid penis. 'Ooh JJ, it's still so big, honey. And so soon after.'

JJ beseeched her with his eyes, whispering, 'It's okay, we've done enough.'

'Mmmm, Soooo big' she continued, ignoring his plea. 'Was your daddy a Cherokee or something?' she smiled, stirring his lifeless appendage like the hand of a clock.

He cupped a hand over her ear, 'I can fake it baby – can you?'

'All ma sweet life, honey chile,' Leah said, full voiced and throaty. 'All ma sweet life, I've just never known one that can do the things it does.'

'You ain't seen nothin', darlin'. Now bend over this pillow and let a man get to work,' he replied in the same southern drawl.

'I hope massa's not gonna wop me good. Just coz I've been a bad girl.'

JJ rolled his eyes at her, then slapped his own buttock. It stung.

'That the best you can do, honey?'

'So help me I'll make you scream,' he answered, wagging his finger in warning.

'Why don't you just let it all out darlin', while I do all the screaming,' she teased. JJ rolled his eyes, spanking himself loudly as Leah shrieked in the background.

They carried on with their charade until they both grabbed a pillow, hugging it to their mouths to smother their cries of laughter.

After hearing nothing for a further twenty minutes, Abdul stubbed out his Davidoff cigar angrily and wondered what the hell he was going to do now.

He had gone to a lot of trouble to get those particular bugs and they should have swept the room as soon as they were in it. But listening to them cavorting in the bedroom it was obvious they didn't realise they were being overheard.

'Fuck-it.'

It would cost him a day. At a crucial time. And time was the one luxury he couldn't afford.

He had sensed the endgame was in play when he noticed the American news coverage go quiet. Just when he knew his attacks were ramping up – not down. 'So the authorities are suppressing the media,' he realised. Once he read about the Hoover Dam being cracked by a monstrous wave, he knew exactly what was going on. The idiot who wrote it had conveniently overlooked the deep lake in front of the dam which would have dissipated and neutered the wave. The moron had even pointed to his own stupidity by detailing the huge volume of water in the lake in his 'report'. It had taken Abdul over ten minutes to stop laughing and cost him a bottle of 1960 Premier Cru Bollinger.

'I can't believe it took the Americans so long to get it together,' he had thought to himself as he poured out the first glass of champagne. But the result of the Americans' tardiness was that his timing was now critical. He had no leeway for error and these two were screwing it up royally and by the sound of their antics – literally. He could hardly phone her and tell her to look for the damn bugs as it was vitally important they found them on their own initiative. He knew he would lose the GCHQ connection with their discovery, but all good things come to an end and anyway, he already had a full copy SCOPE's data.

It was a tricky situation. He hadn't expected this. 'What the hells-fuck do I do now?' he swore.

With a white hot fury boiling up inside him, fed by the frustration that there was nothing he could do about their complete lack of professionalism, he stared up at the ceiling wracking his mind for a way to tip them off about the bugs, without also alerting them they were supposed to find the blasted things! If he didn't do something fast, his carefully planned endgame would vaporise like a moth attracted to a blast furnace.

Incandescent with anger, he got up from his desk and marched into the bathroom to fetch a bottle of lube from his wash bag, then threw open the door and strode purposefully into the sleeping girls' bedroom.

Early the next day, as the call to prayer echoed out across the city from the mosques nearby, Abdul pressed enter on his keyboard. He had friends of friends connected with the ISI – Pakistan's secret intelligence service. 'And in time of need, what are friends for?' he asked himself, as he scribbled down the phone number of a street vendor who sold intelligence to supplement the meagre earnings from his bakery. The baker's intel was normally accurate and as a result, he had the direct number of the Brigadier responsible for counterespionage – really, counter-terrorism. Fierce and completely ruthless, the Brigadier would make quick work of Leah and JJ's slapdash incompetence.

Picking up a street phone, Abdul dialled the vendor's number.

'Two western agents are staying at the Rashid Hotel, room 245.' He spoke quickly and hung up immediately. It wouldn't take the ISI long to get there and should be nearly as pleasurable as listening to them last night. 'No, far more enjoyable,' he thought as he walked back to his apartment. He sat down at his desk and switched on the wireless link to his computer, which hooked into the laptop he had set up in a room at the Rashid Hotel three days earlier.

The only thing to announce their arrival was a light tap on the door an hour later.

'Room service.'

'We didn't order room service.' JJ rolled out of bed, stepping next to the door. A second later Leah joined him.

'Leave it outside the door,' she said in faltering Pashtu.

'I cannot, people will steal the food and I get bad trouble.' Shockingly, it was spoken in broken English.

They exchanged a glance, then JJ motioned her into the bathroom. He turned the key in the door and pulled down the handle, which was as far as he got before the door crashed open throwing him backwards onto the bed. Five of ISI's finest stormed in shouting and levelling their automatics at him. JJ shouted for Leah to come out of the bathroom with her hands up as they pushed his face into the carpet.

Leah stepped out, trying to make sense of the scene confronting her. 'Okay, okay, whatever you want,' she said, lying down on the floor, head to head with JJ.

Plastic cuffs were forced roughly over her hands and pulled painfully tight. Another man frisked her and rolled her onto her back to continue his search. Satisfied, he called out over his shoulder. A tall man, in hand-tailored fatigues, wheeled into the room with his hands clasped behind his back. He looked like a thinner, fitter version of Saddam Hussein. Tall and moustachioed with the cold eyes of a leopard.

He looked down at them for a moment then waved at his men to sit them on the bed. Two guards lifted them bodily onto it then stood over them, guns pointing menacingly. The other three men began ransacking the room.

'You are under arrest for espionage,' the Brigadier said calmly.

'We are not spies. My name is Leah Mandrille. I am a senior diplomat for the United Kingdom and this is my boyfriend.'

'I see. This I can check. What are you both doing in Pakistan? Catching some rays? A little early for Christmas shopping is it not?'

JJ took a different line. 'We're tracking the man behind The 24th Revolution's attacks on the USA. I work for the NSA and this is a high-priority covert OP, which you have just wrecked.'

'Let me remind you that you are in Pakistan. You have no jurisdiction here Mr...?' He held out his hand and one of the men slapped their passports onto it. '...Mr Barberry.'

'No, but when I report your help and assistance to *my President*, I expect he will want to know from *your President* whose side the ISI is really on.'

'Good, that is also something I can check.' Turning to his men he ordered in Pashtu, 'Take them back to Headquarters.' Then switching into English, 'Make sure they have a safe and pleasant journey. We wouldn't want a British diplomat and a friend of the United States President to have any unforeseen accidents,' he smiled, stabbing them with his unblinking yellow eyes.

As they were frogmarched out, two men with large Samsonite suitcases hurried past them into the room. Their technicians had been trained by the American and British security forces.

'Shit,' thought JJ. 'There go the bugs and our connection to Abdul.' He shook the hand off his shoulder in frustration.

When they arrived at the ISI headquarters, the guards escorted them down three flights of stairs. As they went down deeper, the slime on the walls grew thicker. So did the stench of unwashed humanity. They threw JJ into a cell, then pulled Leah down two more flights and stopped outside a rusting iron door which squealed as they opened it. The air in the empty stone chamber was fetid with damp and the ammonium tang of stale urine; making Leah clasp a hand over her mouth as she was shoved inside. The door clanged shut then they switched off the light, leaving her marooned in the dark.

After three of the slowest hours of her life she heard running footsteps outside, then the solid clunk of a key turning in the lock and a man stepped inside. He held the door open. Smiling obsequiously, he motioned her out as if she were a guest at the Waldorf Manhattan rather than a prisoner in the dungeons of the ISI.

'Pliz, this way, pliz,' he said, grinning broken teeth at her.

They wound their way through the building and stopped outside an immaculate teak door. The guard tapped on it respectfully and stood to one side. The Brigadier opened it with a warm greeting painted on his face. JJ was sitting in front of the desk with an ankle crossed on his knee. He was puffing contentedly on a cigar.

In a show of overt courtesy, the Brigadier pulled out a chair and offered her a cigarette. 'I don't,' she said, shaking her head.

'Everything in moderation...including moderation,' JJ said to her. A signal they were safe.

The Brigadier sat down behind his desk and fixed bayonet eyes on them. 'We are most terribly sorry for any, ahh...inconvenience we caused. But in the cat and mouse game of counter-terrorism we are extremely tough. I hope you will remember that when you think of the ISI in future. It took us only a short time to check your credentials. An efficiency I trust you will admire in us. I am happy to inform you that you are both free to leave. Here are your passports and here is my number if I can be of any further assistance,' he finished.

Without moving from his chair, JJ blew a long plume of cigar smoke over the Brigadier's head. 'Actually, there is something you can help us with.'

'What is this...thing?' he asked, his hands tightening on the desk.

'The bugs,' JJ said flatly.

'Ah yes. The room was bugged. We found three. They are British,' he added, trying to steer JJ off course.

'Where did you find the receiver?'

'Receiver? We only found bugs in your room.'

'When this man says he's lying – he's lying. And stupid – he's stealing when he ought to be buying. God it's worth a try,' JJ thought,' saying, 'Two of your men had D5s on them. They can pinpoint a fart in a hurricane in ten seconds,' bluffing an informed guess, because he hadn't seen inside the suitcases.

'Ah yes, the D5s. I forgot them for a moment. We did locate a receiver. We found a laptop computer in the room directly above yours. It was connected to the internet via a wireless card. There were headphones and all the usual items but the window was open. Whoever was bugging your room must have escaped over the roof, as my men had the bottom of the building surrounded. Unfortunately, no one saw him leave, which I intend to investigate as soon as you are both safely on your way,' the Brigadier smirked, offering his open palm at the door.

JJ blew a thick blue smoke ring directly at the Brigadier's nose, 'I believe that man was Abdul-Azim Saqr Khalifa. Your interference tipped him off and your incompetence let him escape.'

'We are making enquiries. When we arrest him we will inform you immediately. Now I have several things to attend to, so if you wouldn't mind?' He flicked an expansive hand at the door again, this time in more forceful invitation.

JJ ignored it. 'We were going to track those bugs as soon as it was dark. We'd have caught him if you hadn't come crashing in. I think that's how my report to President Mann will read.'

'I understand your frustration, Mr Barberry, but there is nothing more I can do.'

'Certainly there is. You can give us the laptop. That way, I can see how your honest mistake and, as you point out, highly efficient operation might be seen in a more positive light.'

'I see,' he replied, narrowing still eyes at JJ dangerously. 'Well as soon as we've made sure it is not booby-trapped, I will have, it forwarded to your hotel.'

'That's not quite the spirit of co-operation I had in mind.'

'Oh? And what did you *imagine?*'

'Enough of this horseshit!' JJ shouted angrily, banging his fist on the desk. 'Get that laptop in here in one minute or I'll have you extradited to the US for acting in collaboration.'

'Pakistan no longer has an extradition treaty with the United States,' he responded coolly, smiling evenly at JJ's outburst.

'Legal extradition takes too long.'

'You don't frighten me with your threats, Mr Barberry,' he flared back. Then, getting hold of himself with a shrug, 'Perhaps however, in the spirit of co-operation between our two great nations, it would be better if you took it now,' and he reached over for the phone on his desk.

'And all copies of the data,' JJ added, as the Brigadier give the unintelligible order in Pashtu.

An ISI car dropped them outside the American Embassy. Leah hugged JJ's arm in relief as he flashed his pass at the sentry and they walked in through the gate.

'You know, darling, it's a funny thing about spies and diplomats,' Leah said.

'Uh huh. And what's that, gorgeous?'

'Well, we both get paid for collecting information, we both have our country's interests at heart and we both try and further those interests, but...'

'But what?'

'Listening to you in there...'

'Shocking, wasn't I?'

'It couldn't be more opposite from my approach.'

'That's why we're a great team,' he said, squeezing her waist. 'The only thing that ever impresses those military boys is angry authority.'

'So it's a boy thing is it?'

'No, more of a dick thing. But don't tell anyone my secret or I'll have to retire.'

'What secret?' Leah asked, suppressing her laughter.

'That I'm really a lamb in wolf's clothing.'

Leah nodded at the laptop. 'I can't wait to see what's on that. What do you reckon?' she said as the feeling of being a pawn in Abdul's game sharpened her nerves.

'Maybe nothing. Maybe everything. It damn well better yield something, or...'

'Or what?'

'I'm going to start biting people again.'

Once inside the magnificent colonial building, JJ showed his ID and they were escorted to an ornate room with a large window at one end. He went over to the desk in front of it and without sitting down, flipped open the laptop and turned it on.

Leah peered over his shoulder as he selected Windows Explorer. There was only one large file and they both started to read.

Leah reacted with cold shock. Staring at her from the screen was the undeniable proof that Abdul had held to his side of their agreement. Luckily, she was standing behind JJ and he didn't see her expression change. 'Perhaps this is a good time to tell him the truth,' she thought, then instantly dismissed the notion. As far as JJ was concerned they were at war with Abdul. He would never understand their deal. 'Besides,' she reasoned quickly, 'it will upend his world, making him doubt everything. It might even make him think the data is another false lead.'

And she knew it wasn't. Abdul was ending it. 'So that's why those bugs were British. We were guaranteed to find them. Abdul expected us to trace the connection to the laptop,' she realised.

'Jesus!' JJ exclaimed as he studied the information. 'We've got to get this to President Mann now.'

'The quickest, surest way is phone,' Leah suggested.

'You're right. Think he'll take my call immediately?'

'I think he will.'

It was 2:am in Washington when William Mann's voice came through on the other end. 'This had better be good news, JJ.'

'Good morning, Sir. The news is good. Shocking, but good. I'm looking at new intel detailing twenty terrorists in total – not 900. I repeat: there are only twenty-one if you include Ali. I've got full dossiers on each of them. Credit cards, fake IDs, the whole shebang. More than enough to round them up in a few days, Mr President.'

'Are you certain? How do you know it's complete?'

'I'm sure, because the intel's on Khalifa's laptop.'

'Remarkable. But are you sure it's complete?'

'Yes Sir, I think it is. We nearly caught Khalifa with it on him. He only just managed to slip away. It's also the right type of intel and it's way safer to keep it all in one place than hide it in fifty different locations. Less chance of accidental discovery that way, and Khalifa's smart. More importantly, it lists the times, places and addresses of the sixty-three suicide bombers who have attacked us over the last six months, including the man who blew up the San Fran Courthouse. It looks as though they were all set up without their knowledge, Sir. I'm looking at high definition pictures of the keys to their homes, offices and cars. It looks like all the suicide bombers were set up, Sir. Stooges, Mr President.'

'That is shocking. Thank you, JJ. Can you send over a more detailed report in six hours? It's 2:am here. But before you do, call your boss and tell him I said he must get that intel to Craig Mortimer at Homeland Security right this second. No delays. Tell him I said "Magenta" and he will know it's my order. Magenta, okay?'

'Yes Sir, Magenta. Consider it done, Mr President.'

'Okay. I look forward to reading your report. Anything else?'

'No. Goodnight Mr President.'

'What was that all about?' Julie asked with concern, when she saw the deep frown on Will's face as he slowly put the receiver down.

'Probably the best and worst news I've ever been given. I need to sleep now, darling. Ask me again in the morning,' he said, turning away from her onto his side.

But he didn't sleep again that night.

DOUBLE CHECK

President Mann had cleared his desk. All appointments were cancelled and his scheduled meeting with the Prime Minster of Greece had been postponed indefinitely. Alert, brooding and impatient, he waited in the Oval Office for the confirmation call to come through. At precisely 11:am the phone buzzed. He snatched up the receiver before it could ring twice.

'I have the Homeland Security chief on the line, Sir.'

'Put him straight through.'

'Mr President?'

'Yes Craig. Just give me the answer. Is it really possible?'

'It looks as though it is, Mr President.'

'You're telling me that all of those suicide bombers were set up? Are you absolutely sure?'

'How were we to know? They all had Middle Eastern origins and they were all carrying the bombs on them.'

'All sixty-three of them?'

'There wasn't much evidence left, Sir. They used C4 and they picked out people whose businesses had gone bust or had a history of disaffection.'

'I see. Are you one hundred percent certain that twenty people could logistically carry out all of those attacks and set up sixty-three suicide bombers? Because this is a career-minded choice you're making – probably for both of us.'

'I understand that, Sir. But we've re-analysed the timing and location of each suicide bomber. I've double-checked the analysis myself. If you use eight or nine teams of two men, operating in cells, I'm afraid it's not only possible, it's downright easy.'

'You assumed that all of those suicide bombers were part of this plot just because they had Arabic backgrounds or were Muslim? That's the blindest piece of bigotry I've ever heard.'

'What other choice did we have, Sir? Once the number of suicide bombers went past ten it was too dangerous to assume anything else. There wasn't another safe call we could make, Mr President.'

'My God. Where are you at on this now?'

'Twelve of them are still on the loose. We're onto them. I hope to have them in the next twenty-four to thirty-six hours, Sir. Mainly because the intel from Khalifa's laptop looks real and it's extremely well detailed. We've got more than enough here. It wouldn't surprise me if we have them fully contained within the next twelve hours.'

'I'm calling a meeting here at six. Can you make it over here by then?'

'I can if I leave now, Mr President.'

'Will your attendance affect the hunt for these criminals?'

'No, Mr President. It's fully delegated.'

'Then get your ass over here and don't be late. And I'm warning you, I'm not in the best of tempers,' Will finished, slamming the phone down.

A few minutes before six, the Homeland Security chief Craig Mortimer, Bruce Cougar, the Secretary for Defence and William's press spokesman Mike Hooper, assembled in the Oval Office and sat down on the chairs in front of the desk.

William thanked them for coming and asked if they had been briefed, to a chorus of 'yes sirs', before coming straight to his dilemma.

'I've been telling the American people there were 900 out there, when there were only twenty goddamit! Which means I've been terrorising my own people for the past six months. Not only that, but we are guilty of the most heinous racism I've ever come across. I'm fucking furious. I want a clear strategy to steer us out of this mess.'

'We can't tell the nation the truth for one simple reason, Mr President,' Craig Mortimer said.

'Why can't we?'

'It will open the floodgates against us. Any small group of dissidents could repeat this, knowing they will cause utter mayhem.'

'He's right, Mr President. If we announce there were only twenty people will think we didn't know what we were doing. With public sentiment running as high as it is at the moment, it will cause an immediate crisis of confidence in your Administration,' Mike Hooper said ominously.

'What's your view, Bruce?'

'For the sake of the future security of our nation you must bury this, Mr President. If the world finds out that twenty people can cause such horrific problems for us, it will snowball, with others trying it on.'

'There is one other aspect to consider as well, Sir,' added Craig.

'What?' William asked sharply.

'If we tell the world that twenty men put us on one knee, we can be sure as hell it will prompt another attack at some point. But what if the next one has a lot more people involved and they bluff us into thinking there's only a few of them?'

'That's a terrifying prospect.'

Bruce Cougar took a deep breath. 'It's the copycat syndrome, Sir. Any neo-Nazi or right-wing religious group could mount a similar attack, encouraged by the success of these few.'

'Is that what you all think? That we bury this? It doesn't sit well with me at all,' William said fiercely. 'You're the one who has to sell our decision to the People, Mike. Can you straight lie to the nation? Convincingly enough?'

'But if they find out the truth, Mr President...' his press spokesman answered warily.

'Who? The World?'

'Yes and no. If the American public ever discovers we were miles out on the number, then it's game-over for your Administration. The state of anxiety and anger out there can't be overemphasised. If we come clean, all the public will hear is that we screwed up. They will respond without tolerance, Sir.'

'I'm fully aware of that. How contained are we so far?' William shot out at Bruce Cougar.

'Fully contained, Mr President. Outside of this room only the two agents in Islamabad know the whole truth and I've already told them to keep this under wraps. One of them is British, as you know, but she's a long-time agent for MI6 and she's signed their Official Secrets Act. The Brits are pretty tough on enforcing it and I'm sure she's well aware of the consequences. Besides, the feedback from my agent is that she understands the need for silence,' Bruce finished.

'I still don't think I should lie about this,' William said bitterly.

'You must, Mr President. It's over now. Finished!' Craig burst out. 'I'll round up the rest of them within a few hours. None of them will know they were only twenty originally. It would be too risky if we caught one of them and broke him. The two we already interrogated believe they were part of a much bigger group. So our secret is safe and anyway, why trust the laptop intel beyond these twenty? What if it's designed to wrong-foot us? We go and announce there were only twenty when there are actually a lot more.'

'That is definitely the worst of both worlds,' William said with disgust.

'It's not a lie if we say nothing, Mr President. We just choose to keep it secret under the auspices of National Security,' Mike urged.

'Et tu Brutus?' William asked Cougar.

'I'm sorry, Mr President. But you can't advertise the fact that twenty people can do this much damage, spread this much fear and discord, without inspiring another group to have a go. I'm monitoring 117 extremist groups at the moment, and that's without stepping outside the country. Everyone thinks it was big. Involving a large number of people with a shed-load of money and organisation. Let them carry on believing it's hard to put together. A one-off attack that's very difficult to implement.'

'Unfortunately he's right, Mr President. And it's over now. Let's let it go without buying into any future crime waves like this again. I mean, any small gun club could get pissed at something and kick off. Look what happened after we took down Waco. Tim McVeigh blew up an FBI building and that was only a five man cell,' Craig said with exasperation.

Mike Hooper leaned forward and put both his hands on the desk. 'I'll support your decision, Mr President, whichever one you decide to go with. But now is not a good time to fall on our political swords – both for the sake of the nation today and certainly for our national security in future. Why add bringing down the American Government to their list of successes? It's under control now and successfully concluded. Or it will be shortly.'

William looked at his press spokesman in shock. 'Successfully concluded? The man behind all this is still out there, probably sipping tea with Al-Qaeda as I speak. The 24th Revolution indeed.

When I first interviewed Ali I thought the numbers against us were small. I was surprised when the number of suicide bombings went past ten then twenty, and I had to act accordingly. I had no other choice at the time. The people will understand that.'

'It will only sow a greater fear Mr President, when everyone realises how easy it is to do. God, it could spread a wave of similar attacks from our own extremist citizens. They are all armed to the teeth and dying to have a go. Let them think they need a large number to have this effect on us – it's the only brake we've got,' Bruce beseeched.

'How do we make up another 600-odd arrests for Christ's sake?' William challenged.

'Well Sir, we've got Orange Clockwork all set up. We simply broadcast the remaining 600 fake arrests in one go – then it's over. Even the people working there will think it's part of what they are supposed to be doing. They were going to issue those false statements anyway,' Bruce pointed out.

'That's right, Mr President. All we need do is bring Orange Clockwork forward a week or two,' Craig agreed.

William leaned back in his chair. 'I need to sleep on this overnight. But for the private record, let me say that my instincts are to come out with the truth – then deal with it. I thank you, gentlemen. You've each given excellent public service over the last six months and I appreciate it. Really I do. I've had to make some terrible decisions during this attack by The 24th Revolution. Some of our own citizens have died as a direct result, as I know you are aware. The first of those decisions was extremely distasteful. Holding off from arresting those first two snipers will be on my conscience for the rest of my life, however much I tell myself it was the right thing to do at the time. I suspect there is no known cure for that type of guilt.' He sighed. 'But this decision is mine alone to make. And as you are no doubt privately reflecting amongst yourselves at this very moment:

I too, wish someone else had to make it... ...'

END OF BOOK 2

BOOK 3

REVEALED CHECK

Opening the door of his large walk-in wardrobe with a key he kept on a light gold chain around his neck, Abdul wondered which outfit he should wear for this special occasion. Safely back in Cairo he felt much more at home, but it still paid to play it safe. Perhaps more so here than anywhere, he felt, because he was acutely aware of the size of the manhunt searching for him in every corner of the globe. Cairo was where it had all started and therefore, he hoped, the last place they would look for him.

'What to wear, what to wear,' he hummed to himself as he dug around for a few minutes before his eye fell on the padding.

'Oh, how appropriate,' he murmured, stripping down to his boxers then clipping it on. Deciding on a black silk thobe, he carefully stuck on the bushy beard, put his brown contact lenses in and inserted the black-toothed denture plate. He stared into the full-length mirror critically, gauging the overall effect. It bounced back the reflection of a small boy dressed in his father's robe, with a fake beard to complete the innocent game. But that was about to change. Gathering up the excess folds of fabric around his feet, he went over to the cupboard in the corner and tapped in his digital code, pleased to hear the click and hiss of it opening instantly.

His guns, ammunition, fifty-five communication devices, four million dollars in cash, twenty gold bars and twelve different identities were safely locked inside. The passports and driving licences had become his most treasured possessions.

He picked up his eighteen-inch platform boots and the pink prosthetic arms and sat down on the chair to put them on. The plastic limbs were cumbersome but necessary, in order for his arms to appear proportional to the extra height his platform boots gave him. It was the second forearm and hand that were such a nuisance, but he had long since mastered the art of tightening the last two straps with his teeth. Turning back to the mirror, he gave himself a quick but rigorous examination to ensure his disguise was perfect, then clumped out of the wardrobe, locking it behind him.

He called out to the girls as he went over to his writing bureau.

'Fatima, pick up this briefcase and follow me. We are going out.'

Dutifully, she did as he instructed in silence. She wasn't surprised to see him dressed in this way. He had worn it several times during the past eight months she had known him. Besides, it wasn't a good Muslim woman's place to question her future husband. A status Fatima hoped to achieve soon – her husband-to-be was a very wealthy man. Perhaps if things continued as they had done for a little while longer, she and Hana would both be able to marry the man who had taken them out of the slavery of Karida's and into a much better life. She hoped so. It was all she needed to complete her happiness.

Stepping into the sizzling heat of the mid afternoon they headed towards the souk a mile away. When he was certain they were not being followed, he hailed a cab and climbed into it.

'Main Post Office,' he instructed the driver.

Ten minutes later they got out and made their way up the steps to the entrance of the stone building. It had once been the German Embassy before Egypt's significance had waned and it glowered down at them gothically.

Stopping at the entrance, he waved his hand at the briefcase. Inside were forty-seven white vellum envelopes already sealed and stamped. Fatima took them out and went to post them in the slot in front of her, but he redirected her hand to the International Post box. 'Put them in this one,' he told her, and she fed them in several at a time.

With their errand complete, Abdul started back the way they had come. It was a nice day and he was in an ebullient mood.

'Perhaps I will walk,' he thought to himself, knowing it was more of a waddle.

His mood was heightened by the knowledge of what he had just despatched. Stepping from side to side down the steps he debated whether to celebrate his victory tonight, or wait the few days for the letters to arrive at their destinations, before going wild.

'We must leave here tomorrow, Fatima. But as soon as we get back to the apartment we will collect Hana, then I'm taking you both out shopping and you can buy whatever you wish. After that, we are going out for a night on the town…and you two can decide where we go,' he added unusually.

'Thank you,' she replied, noticing his good mood and the exceptional offer he had just made. It was the first time he had ever let them choose anything for themselves. 'Perhaps he is going to propose tonight,' she hoped, and in a rush of excitement she forgot her station for a moment. 'Hakim?' she asked sweetly.

'Yes, my dear,' Abdul replied.

PAWN ATTACK

Normally, George Hauler's first task after his morning latte was to open all of his mail. He liked to hone his deductive reasoning by arranging his correspondence in the correct order of importance before opening a single letter. It was good detective practice and he could tell a lot by the style of writing and other clues he had picked up during the twenty-two years he had been an investigative reporter for The USA Times.

One of the letters that morning had an unusual stamp. A stamp he had never seen before. It was on an expensive watermarked envelope posted Cairo, four days previously. He felt the hairs on the back of his neck rise and discarding the others, examined it more critically. For a disconcerting start, his name and address had been typed by typewriter – highly unusual in this modern age of PCs and printers.

He shook it a little and felt the envelope. It paid to be cautious as the anthrax letters had all been typewritten. The Unabomber was famous for using this more anonymous method to communicate his concerns to his victims.

He could feel a strangely shaped key and a document inside. He wondered whether to take it back to the post room for another x-raying and half got up from his desk, when his curiosity overcame him. He sat back down and picked up his silver paper knife, opening the envelope with extreme care. Turning his head away, he clamped his left hand over his nose and mouth then gently tipped out the contents at arm's length.

A brass key and a folded A4 sheet fell out. Using the point of the paper knife he opened the document to find a typed address of a Russian bank in Times Square and the number 24816. 'That's a safety deposit box key,' George realised, and jumping up from his desk, threw them in his leather satchel, grabbed the jacket off the back of his chair and hurried out through the open-plan office to the lifts.

His eagerness changed to avarice when he saw the reaction of the bank teller as he slid the key under the safety glass without saying a word. The man went from feigned politeness to fawning assistance the moment he saw the key. 'If you would kindly wait one moment, sir, I will call the assistant manager. He likes to handle these accounts personally. Please take a seat over there,' he indicated.

'Thank you, I will,' George replied, becoming increasingly more excited. Perhaps it was a bequest from a rich admirer for all the cracking work he had done over the years. 'Better late than never,' he thought with a grin.

'Hello, my name is Capuchin,' said a tall man walking over with a professional smile. 'I'm the assistant manager of this branch. If you would follow me this way, sir. Here at Bonobossa Bank we understand the need to treat these particular accounts with the importance and respect they deserve,' Capuchin added, rocketing Haular's hopes more than he would ever know.

After passing through several locked security grilles they arrived in front of a huge safe door, already open. To one side was an ornate wooden table with a blue book on it. Opening the book, Capuchin asked if he would care to sign.

'What is it?' George asked.

'It's the logbook, sir. If you prefer to remain anonymous, I can fill it in without your name. Here at Bonobossa Bank we understand the need for complete discretion.'

'Is there a name on this account?'

'Is the safety deposit box not your own, sir?'

'No.'

'Providing you can match the key to the correct box number and you know which branch of our bank holds it, there won't be problem. At Bonobossa Bank we consider that to be an intrinsic part of our fail-safe security.'

'Fail-safe security? Ermm, that sounds excellent. The box number is 24816. What's the name on the account?'

'Let me see, sir. Ahh, this box was rented anonymously on a two-year lease. Paid in advance.'

'How intriguing,' George replied. 'Do you remember who rented it? You did say you look after these accounts personally.'

'I'm afraid not, sir, and even if I did, I probably wouldn't recollect. Here at Bonobossa Bank we understand the need for absolute confidentiality.'

As George stood in the empty viewing room, looking down at the metal box on the table, he half-wondered whether he should open it or call the police. Nothing remotely like this had ever happened to him before. A second later, he put his key in the lock and lifted the lid a fraction to peer inside. His initial reaction was personal disappointment followed by a rising fever of professional curiosity when he saw that it contained neatly-typed documents. As he speed-read though the contents, his mouth fell open and he pulled out a chair to sit down without taking his eyes off what he was reading.

It was incredible – literally incredible. But giving the lie to that, was the level of detail the documents contained. Names, addresses. Everything. Full details of the attacks by The 24th Revolution: starting with Ali Mohammed and finishing with Duraq Baba. What sucked the breath out of him was the number of terrorists. There were only twenty-one.

Two months earlier, his Government had announced an end to the crisis as they rounded up the remaining 600 members of The 24th Revolution. Yet here he was, holding in his hands the precise detail of how twenty-one men could orchestrate all the chaos – attack by attack and blow by blow for the first 3 months. That part was all in exactly the right sequence.

'Only twenty-one?' he blurted out. 'It can't be true.'

Then his professional need for independent verification kicked in strongly. Perhaps he was being set up, because it wouldn't be the first time someone had tried that on. 'I must be careful how I report this. It'll cause the downfall of William Mann's Government in the same way Watergate destroyed Nixon's,' he thought. Because if what he was reading was true, it meant the authorities had not only lied about the number of terrorists, they had also invented atrocities which had never occurred. He was holding cast iron proof that his Government had barefaced lied to its people and the world. Trust in William Mann's administration would collapse like popped balloon.

Desperate now, George wracked his mind for any way to confirm the documents' authenticity; when the answer hit him like a lightning bolt and he rushed out of the room to the waiting manager.

'Hey, that log of yours – do you fill it out every time someone opens their deposit box?'

'Absolutely, sir. Here at Bonobossa Bank we understand the need to keep meticulous records of all transactions. Or in this case – all comings and goings.'

'How efficient. Then you must know when this box was last opened.'

'Let me see, sir. Ah yes, it was last Christmas. A year ago.'

'A year ago? Are you sure?'

'Yes, I'm certain, sir.'

'You couldn't have made a mistake?'

'Certainly not! Here at Bonobossa Bank we pride ourselves on not making mistakes – ever.'

'Is there any sign of tampering with the log?'

'See for yourself, sir.' Capuchin swivelled the book around and pointed with his index finger. 'The last entry for box 24816 is in my own handwriting.'

'So there's no way anyone can make a deposit or withdrawal without an entry into the log?'

'Definitely not. Is there something wrong, sir? Something missing?' Capuchin asked with concern.

'No, no – it's all here. Christ, it's all here,' George repeated excitedly, as he realised he was holding in his hands the news story he had been waiting to break all of his professional life. And it had to be true. Only the planner would have known anything about this a year ago – which was the last time the document could have been deposited in the box.

'Fuck me! Errrm sorry,' he waved the dossier at Capuchin. 'Bit of a shock, that's all. Look, I have to leave right now. Straight away. This instant. Can you show me out? As fast as you can?'

'Certainly sir. Here at Bonobossa Bank, we fully appreciate what a run is.'

THE WHITE QUEEN'S MOVE

10 months later

'So what do I call a lady Ambassador?' JJ asked Leah as they celebrated her new appointment. In three weeks time she would be the British Ambassador to Iran.

'You call me Mister Ambassador.'

'Really? Mr?'

'That's MISTER, mister.'

'The President was right. The world is upside down.'

'Yes, to us they are terrorists, but to half the world they are freedom fighters. Heroes, awarded the highest honour their religion can bestow – martyrdom.'

'We're not really the bad guys are we?'

'That depends on who you ask, JJ.'

'Meaning?'

'Meaning the winning side are always the freedom fighters and the losing side are always the terrorists. As it's always been and always will be. Even the first two Prime Ministers of Israel were charged with terrorism and sentenced to death in absentia by the British.'

'We are on the right side though, aren't we?'

'We're on our side JJ. And we will do the best we can.'

'I wonder what a terrorist's terrorist is called?'

'They are called Mr and Mrs Joe Public.'

'Aha. I suppose you're right.'

'I hope that in the long run we really are on the right side,' Leah said, half to herself.

348

'Yeah, it's a bitch that.'

'In the end, semantics always is,' she joked to lighten his mood.

'Semantics? I don' get it.'

'That either makes you a fool, which you are not, or me as mad as a box of frogs,' Leah smiled.

'Now that's mad,' JJ agreed, raising his glass of Pol Roger to hers.

'Salute,' they toasted, clinking glasses.

Leah's BlackBerry buzzed in her handbag on the kitchen table and she walked over to it. There was a new email message.

My warmest congratulations on your new appointment. We made an arrangement in a coffee shop not long ago. As you know, I kept to my side and cut it short. Perhaps not as short as you wanted but these things take time. In return, it seems only fair to swap Russian caviar for Iranian.

Let's do coffee again, once you've got your feet under the table. I'm buying several nice apartments in Tehran, only a stone's throw from the main Government building. I'll be in touch.

Yours sincerely,

One of the Chosen Few.

PS. Dad begs your forgiveness over his little publicity stunt and feels certain you went against his will. One all. He asks if you would be kind enough to bring him over something to read. By that, I think he means the whole library.

Without blinking, Leah smiled and hit delete. She put her BlackBerry on the table, looking calmly over at JJ while her mind caught on fire.

All the pieces fell into place. All of them. They positioned themselves so perfectly and so precisely that she knew it had to be true. Abdul had held to his side of their deal by deliberately leading her and JJ to his list of real terrorists. After misleading them with his first laptop, he probably felt it was necessary to let them almost catch him in order to convince JJ the intel was real.

And Victor was alive! He must have faked his own death to publicise his ideology, beautifully landing the British Government with the blame for his disappearance. Most people were convinced he had been quietly removed by the authorities. Even she, had been sure they had killed him. Recalling the time she first met Jimmy MacCack, she remembered how Victor had burst out laughing after saying he wouldn't be able to accomplish anything before he died. It was an unusual thing for anyone to laugh about. It was out of place, which is why she remembered it so clearly. That must have been the moment Victor saw the advantages to it. Or perhaps Jimmy's dire warning that he was in peril, had made Victor think he had to disappear or give up his fight for a new democracy.

'That's definitely part of it,' Leah thought. 'Victor faked his death to ensure nothing terrible happened to him.'

Self-preservation combining with enormous publicity for his ideals, leaving the finger of blame pointing squarely at the old Government's modus operandi – bolstering Victor's argument for change. All in one silent move. It was as ingenious as it was irresistible. No small wonder he had burst out laughing.

'What's up, Leah? You look like you've seen a ghost.'

'Oh… I'm just thinking about my new appointment, that's all. Would you refill my glass, please JJ?'

'Sure.'

Leah went back to her hypothesis. So Victor had teamed up with his son. The Professor must have deliberately set her up to keep his library – the one thing he treasured above all else. He must have been convinced that when the time came, she would never be able to burn his books. Victor would also know that her actions would fall under the close scrutiny of Jimmy MacCack – then go right past him. She had lost 90,000 pounds by keeping those books. Taken together, Jimmy would think she was acting on her own, not acting as the safe-keeper of Victor's intellectual treasure trove. Her complete innocence was delightfully described when she had gone against Victor's final wish. But how on earth had Victor known she would do that? Was she really that easy to read? 'God, I must be,' she murmured.

No wonder Jimmy suspected Victor was still alive. As head of MI6 he would have been party to Victor's removal and Jimmy knew he had given no such order. Victor had beaten him to it. For all she knew, the Professor could have set the entire plan in motion. From start to finish. He had the motive, ability and certainly the intellect; together with a disaffected son who had limitless resources. 'No, that can't be right,' Leah thought, 'Victor would never have condoned an attack on the US. He loves and admires the people there. He had a genuine concern that Abdul might attack America. That is why he told me about the Sword of Damocles in the first place,' she corrected herself.

'Who was that?' JJ nodded at the PDA on the table as he poured out her champagne.

'Oh, no one you know. Just an old work colleague wanting to have coffee in Tehran and wishing me luck,' Leah replied warily, as her dilemma over whether to tell JJ the whole truth about her secret deal with Abdul shot to the top of her mind.

She was in love with JJ. To continue her concealment was tantamount to betrayal – of both him and their love. It went against her most fundamental belief of what was honest, right and true. But how could she tell him about her pact with Abdul? At the same time how could she not? If she maintained her secrecy, the cancer of guilt would inevitably destroy their relationship. But if she did tell JJ, then he would leave her. Or more likely: kill her, then leave.

She knew JJ's feelings were reciprocal, as deep and sincere as her own, but he would only see it as a flagrant breach of trust – nothing less. His delineated mindset of right and wrong would unite with his patriotic duty to produce the most unholy rage. JJ would go berserk then kill her in anger. He might regret it afterwards but it would be too late for her, for both of them – she would be dead.

Fraught with anxiety, Leah turned away so JJ wouldn't see her trauma. She wandered over to the cupboard, ostensibly to get some olives out but really buying herself time to think. 'How can I tell JJ I was in partnership with Abdul...and I still am.' How could she tell him they had struck a deal which she had hidden throughout their ordeal. 'Find a solution, girl' she kicked herself mentally, only to be met by a blank wall, sterile of ideas.

Stepping close to JJ, Leah reached down and gave him a playful squeeze, 'Tell me something, darling, and I will transport you across the universe once again.'

'What's that, honey?'

'JJ is such a cool name and you're long overdue to tell me what it means.'

'It's a very cool name isn't it? What's wrong, Leah? You look worried.'

'What does JJ stand for?'

'I can't tell you.'

'Tell me,' she said in a throaty voice, caressing him more firmly.

'Okay. But promise you won't laugh?'

'I promise,' she replied silkily, gripping him tighter.

'It stands for...J J.'

'What?'

'When I was very young, learning to talk, someone must have pointed out a blue jay because afterward whenever I saw a flying bird I shouted Jay Jay.'

'I'm going to have to break that promise,' Leah said, unable to contain her mirth which erupted out of her like a geyser; forced up by the tremendous pressure of her dilemma. After gulping down air she roared again then doubled over, flapping her free hand up and down. 'That's... that's...' was all she could get out between shrieks of laughter.

'Dammit – I knew I should have kept that secret,' said Jay Jay.

And she suddenly stopped laughing and looked up at him in earnest; wondering if she would be able to sustain the burden of her own weighty secret, for a lifetime. 'It's impossible,' she told herself.

'Come on, Leah. I know you better than that.' JJ urged, with a questioning look. 'Something's not right. What is it?'

Instantly transfixed, Leah stared at him, her lower lip trembling slightly. A look of abject terror swept across her face as JJ threw her hand off him in a fit of pique. Taking three steps back, his eyes snapped into hard black bullets. Deadly serious, he spoke very slowly.

'Lovers rule number one, Leah – No secrets.'

'No JJ. Lovers rule number one is nurture your partner,' Leah replied, her fear turning to anger.

JJ glanced at her Blackberry, then walked quickly over to the table and picked it up with his left hand. When he turned around, his gun was in his right – levelled straight at her chest. 'That was Abdul, wasn't it? You've been in on this together. Right from the start. Well it's time to end your little two-step.'

Leah erupted with fury, her anger replacing calm rationale with a heady bravado. She had nothing to lose now and somewhere deep inside, knew that what she had agreed with Abdul was morally right. And she wasn't going to get killed without a fight. 'Right, JJ. You want the truth. I'll give you the truth. Afterwards you can shoot me or apologise, but if you don't shoot me your apology better be heartfelt or we're through.'

Raising her voice to a shout of accusation, 'Because I've had enough! I'm over with this crap. I'm done pussyfooting around the three blind mice of your patriotism, your programming and your perfect imprecision.'

'So. It really was Abdul,' JJ said coldly, clicking the safety catch off.

'You never asked why I chose Iran, did you? I chose Iran because I know I can effect real change there. Abdul turned me on to the idea in that coffee shop in Cairo. And you'd better get a grip here JJ, because guess what? I think he's right. I can change things fundamentally and Iran is a great place to start. Their regime is the most threatening confluence of political and religious extremism in the world and they are determined to get the bomb. They will use it to blackmail the world into doing whatever suits them. So yes, JJ, that was Abdul. And he emailed me from Tehran!'

'Dammit Leah, what have you done? Have you lost your mind? Abdul is a terrorist. You've betrayed me. You've betrayed the whole of the civilised world. Well I'm here to protect it. Goodbye,' and he lifted the Colt, moving his head a fraction to sight on her forehead.

'You shoot me and *you're* betraying *your* country, JJ. The country you so love and admire. The only country that has ever conducted a nuclear strike on civilians. Your country controls the world's money supply, issuing it with debt attached. That's modern day slavery. You're a slaver JJ! The World Bank and the IMF are controlled by the Federal Reserve which gives them their funding. The men who control the Fed are in effective control of your Government, JJ. Don't believe me? Think that's far-fetched? Then ask yourself: who provides the world with debt, JJ? I'm telling you – you won't like the answer. Your beloved country's social structure has the highest percentage of prisoners in the world. One percent of your fellow Americans are locked up. That's fifty percent higher than China. Hardly the Land of the Free, is it? If you piece those three jagged edges together you'll discover a perfect fit, JJ.'

'Shooting traitors is not betraying my country. I've had enough of this shit.'

'Abdul and I are going to take down the Iranian regime. If Abdul hadn't given us that laptop he would have taken down the US, JJ. He only gave us the laptop because I struck a deal with him. I agreed to join forces if he stopped attacking the US. If you shoot me, you also put a stop to Iran's regime being replaced by something up to date and non threatening.' Leah stabbed her finger at him. 'Here's shocker number two, JJ: I chose Iran – not Abdul. Providing our plan is practical and original it will work. Think for once! You can't deny how effective Abdul can be and you know what I'm capable of. The mullahs won't see us coming until it's over. You shoot me and your country's biggest enemy will grow into a demon, JJ. A demon with nuclear capability. When you pull that trigger you are also killing the inhabitants of twenty-odd US cities, alongside any capital city in the world. So go ahead. Do the right thing, JJ. Shut reason out of your mind and fire.'

'Why should I believe you? How *can* I believe you? You'd say anything to save your skin right now.' JJ's hand tightened on the pistol, knuckle-white. 'I can't take the chance. You've admitted your guilt, Leah.'

'Then don't believe me, believe Abdul. Read the email he just sent me. I deleted it. Look in deleted and read it for yourself. The password is LIBERTY101. All uppercase.'

'Get down on the floor. Sit on your hands on the floor. Don't move a muscle, Leah, or it's over.' JJ backed around to the other side of the table, holding the gun on her. He picked up her PDA and typed in her password.

'Before you read it, JJ, there is one more thing. I only discovered it when I saw the email just now.'

'What's that?'

'Victor is alive. He faked his death and he's teamed up with Abdul. I don't know when but I do know that he's alive and well.'

'Yeah, Abdul and Victor both used cars to hide their disappearance,' JJ said wryly. 'I had my suspicions about Victor when Abdul, as Guenaan, did a similar thing. I gave you the benefit of the doubt because you painted Victor as a saint. He disappeared right next to a river, didn't he?'

'Yes, the Severn.'

'Is it big enough to take an ocean going yacht?'

'It certainly is.'

'Must have been a delightful little cruise. We wouldn't have had to use radar to find him. Sound carries on water. We just listen for his shrieks of laughter.'

'Victor 'disappeared himself' because Jimmy MacCack told him he was in danger if he didn't reverse his stance on We the People.

When The 24th Revolution attacks were announced, Victor must have realised Abdul was behind it. He was genuinely concerned about his son wielding the Sword. They must have hooked up after the Mann announcement. Victor would not have approved of his son targeting the USA. He probably went in the same way I did – to try and stop Abdul. I now know they're lining up on the Iranian regime. And I'm going to help them, JJ, in whatever way I can. We'll make a devastating team. Now read that email and see for yourself.'

'Try stopping me.' JJ clicked on it, his face collapsing as he scanned the screen, 'Only a stone's throw from the main Gov...' his voice trailed off. 'One of the Chosen Few? That's the inscription on your ring,' he faltered. 'So Abdul's ring has the same...Whoa, I didn't realise they were completely identical.'

'Identical means identical,' Leah said firmly. 'And that's probably how they connected. Victor places ads in a few personal columns after he supposedly dies, signs it "One of the Chosen Few" and Abdul would know that he was really still alive – that they had overlap on some level. Because you don't fake your own death unless there's a damn good reason, JJ. And Abdul told me he knew all about "We the People". He would realise that his father's motive was probably survival. A ten-year-old could join those three dots and it's not much fun fighting the world on your own. That's why Abdul tried to recruit me, JJ. And that's probably why he got in touch with Victor.'

JJ's eyes filled with uncertainty. His gun hand trembled then fell to his side, 'I've never felt so out of my depth. You pulled Abdul off us, Leah? *And now he's going for Iran? Who the hell is this guy?* I'm sorry. I'm truly sorry. Oh God, I nearly shot you thirty seconds ago,' he cried out, dropping the gun, which clattered as it landed on the terracotta tiles. JJ kicked it into the far corner angrily, then pulled a chair out and collapsed into it. He looked shattered. Cupping his head in his hands he gave out a deep groan. Leah got up and went over to him, placing her arms gently around his shoulders.

'From now on, JJ. Lovers rule number one, is we trust each other first, everyone else third. Deal?'

'Deal,' he replied, looking up into her eyes.

And she leaned in to kiss him: passionately.

EPILOGUE

UNMASKING THE MONKEY

They sipped at their mint juleps in a contented silence, as the sun's rainbowic destruction filtered across an azure blue sea: rolling and dimpling before dissolving into horizon-less infinity. They were tired after fishing that afternoon. He had caught three Corbina and she had caught one, but hers was bigger: large enough to restock their fridge. When a brisk evening breeze had put a ripple on the waves they decided to decamp for cocktails and enjoy their books for the last hour of daylight.

Sitting next to her, high on the sand cliff, he glanced over and saw she was still engrossed in the book he had given her that morning: 'The 12th Planet' by Zacharia Sitchin. It was an in-depth analysis of the ancient Sumerian stones. It had a good translation of the legend of the Gods that came to earth to mine gold for their planet. He was glad to see she was enjoying it and he put down the book he had just finished reading, 'A New Earth' by Eckhart Tolle, the famed spiritual philosopher. It drew him to question his own existence; was there really a point to it all? A purpose?

The sun turned a deep red in a last act of angry defiance against the black night that was riding it down. The evening air cooled and a warm Santa Ana breeze began caressing his skin with fingers too soft and too sensual to let him notice his thoughts for a while. Seducing his being and suffusing his senses with their warm, dreamy beauty.

Slowly his thoughts meandered back, making him question why Man chose to fight his fellow man, when their universal foe was really that same Black Knight, lording over all. In the moment of stillness which precedes the dark, he spoke in wonder. 'It's strange to know that the all the technology we use for war: atomic reactions, missiles, computers and satellites, are exactly the same tools we need to conquer space, isn't it? Because we will have to focus on that one day – use them exclusively for that purpose. We are six billion inhabitants of the good ship Earth at present and at thirteen billion it becomes impossible to provide ourselves with enough water, and therefore food, to support ourselves.'

'Perhaps the Gods designed it that way. Gave us all the tools we need to rejoin them in the heavens, but only on the condition that we sort our own house first,' she offered.

'Ha! Maybe. Our DNA is 98% chimpanzee. The only ape which actively hunts, kills and eats its fellow monkeys. We've even allocated words for that behaviour – murder and cannibalism.'

'I don't think a higher intelligence would welcome the descendants of a murderous monkey roaming the universe: armed with atomic weapons and a lack of understanding. Holding virtually no compassion for any species which is different. 98%? Are you sure of that?'

'Actually it's 98.4.'

'Then what's the other 1.6?' she smiled.

'That's such a lovely question. I asked a priest and he said it was God. I asked a Darwinian who said it was evolution. If you ask a scientist they say it's mutating DNA, and when you ask an astronomer it's panspermia. Personally, I think the most likely explanation is all of them, but in combination. Three of them have a fundamental truth and the other is a widely held belief, or at the very least, a hope. The strange piece to our jigsaw is that we have not yet found a true missing link and we should have by now, it's noticeably overdue.' He sighed. 'Y'know, when you boil humankind down we are not so very different from each other. We like to think we are. We say we are unique but there is a selfish streak in Man which engineers an inevitability to our fate that transcends all. When people make mistakes, they do so en masse. We think we do things for different reasons but the truth is: we mainly act out of self-interest, then steam ahead and do them anyway. Our trial and error approach often ends with a body count in the millions and there is now a considerable risk involved.'

Shifting his weight in his chair, he added, 'Not only are we similar in nature, but only a small number of us realise that uniting to live together is the only way our grandchildren will survive and have a peaceful world to live in. It's that close to us now. It's "make our minds up time", because our nonsense will take several generations to resolve. That's why I believe people voting together, taking collective responsibility for their decisions and destiny is a giant leap forward for mankind. Not only will it make us more responsible, but it holds the incalculable by-product that we will unite in common causes which have long-term commonsense and goodness attached.'

'You are absolutely right, darling. It's a bit of an oxymoron to think we can have self-responsibility without self-governance,' she replied.

He glance at her with a widening smile, 'One of our American Presidents once said, "People get the Governments they deserve". There is way more truth than humour in that statement. Now that people are voting directly and getting to grips with controlling their own destinies, we have become entirely responsible for our own actions. It's the most delicious wake-up call because we can no longer blame carpetbagger politicians or anyone else but ourselves for a poisonous decision. Our preferences have become a transparent reflection of us all, making us responsible as a species for the very first time. What we choose to vote on directly impacts our own lives. It's not only the end of crooked politics, it's the dawning of a new era for Man.'

'Voting by the people has also reduced the amount of warring and killing,' she agreed. 'It's difficult to imagine what could induce the majority of people to vote for a war when they are not attacked first. I just hope it catches on around the rest of the globe,' she replied wistfully.

'I don't doubt it will. When people realise it's only the more feudal societies who initiate the wars, and only then as a result of their leaders' decision – not theirs. Don't worry, people are quite capable of working that one out for themselves. It won't take them long. Just another a war or two and it's done,' he winked.

'If you mean the people's commonsense leading them through a forest of good and bad decisions, then it should,' she returned the wink.

'The beautiful twist to the Constitution Bill, is that people are more good than bad. Certainly the majority are, and that's what counts in a democracy. Most of us have a conscience. That's always been a given; or as some might say, a God-given. But what I like the most about that Bill, is it not only unites people but is also the only way to bring voting up to date for our younger generation – the internet generation. Excluding them could well result in a high risk of despotism in the medium term. By voting together, people have discovered they had more in common than they previously thought. Borders will become administration zones for tax and population issues only. Patriotism and Nationalism: concepts responsible for the most heinous control of nations, will be seen as the separating Sin of Man. There will be one last great struggle between two of the largest religions on earth, that will present a choice between global unification or chaos and destruction. When faced with that consequence, people will realise that fighting over the name of God is the ultimate and most subtle ruse the Devil ever engineered for man. And if there is a God, He might well think our foolishness should end. One way or the other, and I can't blame Him for that. If I were God, and Man destroyed himself by warring, or gross planet mismanagement, I would invite the Devil over to supper, to thank him for pointing out how destructive and dangerous Man really is.'

She looked at him lovingly. 'That makes a funny kind of sense when you consider that we all have free will. Then there can be no doubting our intentions. No misunderstanding about what we are truly like, or how we are going to behave in future. And there's no backlash of guilt for God if we annihilate ourselves with our own hand. So free will is a double-edged sword for everyone but God.'

'That's funny. And in an awful way – makes perfect sense.'

'And if it is genuinely funny then it must have a grain of truth attached,' she grinned.

He gazed back at her with a feeling of equal joy; fascinated that they both saw the world in a similar way. It never ceased to amaze him how in tune they were – each to the other. Complementary without being duplicatory. It was a rare jewel and he leaned over to kiss her, settling back comfortably in his chair before leading their mutual love of discovery a little further up the lane.

'One of the most common beliefs among all religions is that God made us in his own image. Perhaps He did. Even we have the ability to do it now, through DNA. So far, all of the evidence points to us having materialised one day, then walked out of an African rainforest.'

'Perhaps we ran out of monkeys to kill and were forced to move on,' she laughed. 'We don't have a very good track record when it comes to peaceful co-existence, do we?'

'Not yet but one day, I hope. It may no longer be true to say: without

Man God is nothing. Our destiny is up to us. No one else. We will have to come together as a species and unite one day. The alternative to that harmony is our self-destruction through war, or usurping the resources of this wondrous planet to feed and water our exploding population. The report I read said we have 110 years at best before we reach thirteen billion.'

'At which point we have either found new territory out there in space, or we implode,' she agreed.

'Yup – disorganised people will always fight and kill for food and water, or energy. It became clear to me that the real, more imminent danger, was in not having the Constitution Bill. Our old system of Government was combining with our selfish streak to form us into large hierarchical societies, where the group with the biggest army eats and drinks, while the rest die of us of thirst.

'Perhaps I'm right,' she said emphatically.

'About what?'

'Perhaps the Gods really did devise it in this way – deliberately. We get one good chance to get our attitude together or we're just another failed experiment. Maybe that's why we have free will. So there can be no doubting our ability to co-exist with other species of the universe.'

'God's bigger picture, eh? If I were an advanced being or God, gifting my DNA, I wouldn't want the descendants of a killer ape with a capacity for intellect crashing about the heavens; switched to destroy anything different from themselves. Not until my own peaceful gene was dominant to a point where it countermanded our destructive aspect,' he spoke sadly. 'One scientific theory suggests that we are all descended from only two mothers. It makes me wonder who they were; what made them different; how they came to be here in the first place. At the very least it means we are all related to one another and if we can't live with our own direct relatives without fighting and killing them, then we wouldn't be too tolerant of any other species. I can see why it may not be in the interests of the Universe for us to focus on that bigger picture. Perhaps the Gods did design it that way.'

'Yes. All the tools necessary. The capacity for reason and a ticking clock to remind us we should unite against the challenge of space rather than fight each other over the name of God; or kill for water and food without care and consideration for our neighbour.'

A harvest moon lifted its shoulder over the horizon. The night sky deepened into black, unveiling the evening stars which sparkled diamantine brilliance across the water.

'You mustn't feel too badly about what happened, darling. What you did was the right thing to do. You must always remember that. Which ever way you went you were in trouble and that wasn't your fault. At least you found a way to end it and by hiding 'Orange Clockwork' for a while, you gave the new President time to prepare,' Julie soothed.

'I think Khalifa used us as his publicity machine to demonstrate the phenomenal power of The Sword of Damocles. It showed how effectively a few men, armed with a clear idea, can destabilise an advanced society with ease and speed,' William replied.

'Yes, twenty-one men creating that much havoc in six months is pretty conclusive,' Julie nodded.

'Khalifa has put a gun against the head of Man. Point-blank against the temple of incompetent or despised government. With a hair-trigger pull waiting for any dictator.'

'Is that what you really think, Will? The more extreme Governments of Russia and China will be the next targets of The Sword of Damocles?'

'Think of it this way: how do you stop the cut of The Sword, if you implement the plan without the flaw we uncovered?'

'By flaw, you mean publicising the fake arrests?'

'I do. If you instruct your operatives to wait and hide instead of fighting to the death, the defending Government will be highlighted for publishing fake arrests. If the militants resume their attacks after supposedly being rounded up, the Government will be seen as incompetent at best, or the terror of their own people at worst. That's a swift political drop with a short rope attached.'

'Yes – our fellow Americans were very upset by that, weren't they?'

'If a strict regime tries to hold onto power, by putting an end to those attacks in the way we did, then in reply, all the terrorists need do is hold off for a while and the Government will be torn to shreds by its own populace. Because when you publish fake arrests, you must also publicise fake attacks and people don't enjoy being misled and terrorized by their own Government. They won't tolerate it for long. Especially when it doesn't stop the chaos – but adds to it. I found that out the hard way.'

'So you don't fancy being the President of Russia or China, I take it?'

Julie joked.

'Not now The Sword of Damocles is hanging over the political table unsheathed. If I were the President there, I would be feeling distinctly uncomfortable right now. If they do get attacked by that Sword, they have only one choice, one way out, or they face the significant risk of their own people rising up against them – as they did with me.'

'Huh. I can't see any way out.'

'The only chance any despot has to survive that kind of attack, is to implement direct voting by the people: sidestepping the responsibility and the lethal back-cut of The Sword. A sword wielded by the hand of their own people. God, it nearly took my own head off so what chance does the leader of a feared or vilified regime have? No dictator has any chance of surviving that backslash. Look what they did to Ceausescu. Arrested, tried and shot in 24 hours! His wife too. Of course, the autocrats will resist until the last possible moment because they enjoy the power they hold. But if someone draws The Sword on them, they will be forced to take their foot off the throats of their people pretty fast – or face angry retribution. People won't tolerate terror by their own government. They don't enjoy being lied to and wilfully misled in a severe crisis. Thankfully those days are over.'

'So you think it will happen to a Superpower next?' Julie asked.

'I can't say that I do. But it might after it has happened to one or two dictators in smaller countries first. I think it's more likely to occur in Africa or South America next, or maybe Iran. Then once it's worked its magic there, it's only a matter of time before it happens to a dictatorial superpower.'

'Then perhaps we should be grateful The Sword attacked us first. Your Bill has given us immunity from its assault. America is finally leading mankind from the front; by peaceful example,' Julie said.

'There is that silver lining to it,' Will replied. 'Y'know, Khalifa must have thought this through carefully. He must have known what we would be forced into doing. Once we did, he ended it. I can only assume that his intention was to show the world he could remove a powerful government with ease, and demonstrate to stricter regimes just how vulnerable they really are. In fact, the stricter the regime the quicker they will arouse the anger and intolerance of their own people. I wouldn't trade all the assets of the world for a senior government post in a brutal regime right now. I might have considered it before, to try and change it from within; but not now. They will be twitching very nervously about the threat dangling over their throne of power, awaiting only the hand of a dissatisfied group to release The Sword of Damocles on their authority.'

'It's a bit of an odd coincidence that you came up with the Constitution Bill and you now think it's the only antidote to The Sword of Damocles.'

'Never repeat this to anyone, Julie – but it wasn't coincidence,' he looked at her steadily.

'Really?'

'No. When I found out that Victor Simmius had devised the Sword, I pulled every shred of information on him I could. In his last series of lectures, just before he died, he proposed the idea of controlling government through direct voting. Then you Julie, the fairest person I have ever known, suggested a similar concept. That's when I knew the timing was right.' He took a deep breath. 'You know I saw Professor Simmius once, a few years back. I was in a meeting with Alex Spyder and I had to go to the restroom. When I returned, Victor was in the middle of a blazing row with him. Apparently, he'd stormed into Alex's office unannounced, shouting that Alex had used his connections and skill to help elect George W; that he'd better set it straight. I could hear him at it as I waited outside. It was shockingly powerful and it didn't seem right to intrude. Then the door opened and Professor Simmius walked straight past me – angry as a bear. Alex asked me if I had overheard anything but I pretended ignorance. Old Spyder was pretty shaken and we had to reconvene.'

'I would love to have met the Professor. He must have been a remarkable man,' Julie said. 'But how did you know the Constitution Bill would be a good shield for The Sword?'

'You must never repeat this Julie, but I think I was tipped off...by Khalifa himself.'

'Really? How?'

'After I interviewed Ali, do you remember me saying that I thought there were only a few of them pitted against us? Do you remember me struggling with that?' Will asked.

'I certainly do. I remember your surprise when the number of suicide bombers went past ten, then twenty. Your first instinct was absolutely right, darling. What tipped you off?'

'It was their name – The 24th Revolution. It's an English name, not a Muslim one, and they weren't representing any particular entity or group. Ali said they were fighting for everyone.'

'Their name?' Julie questioned.

'Well, it's either The 24th Revolution or Two For Revolution. Khalifa on one side; me as the President on the other.'

'Ahaa. I see what you mean. You both wanted similar changes and you both got them. Goodness, did you know that from the start?'

'It went through my mind. I even asked Ali if he had any direct message for me and he said no, but when I quizzed him over the name he had three different explanations for it. Kinda underlined its multi-meaning in a way. I suddenly realised that perhaps the name itself was a message – and perhaps it was. I realised that if I couldn't stop the Sword directly, I could at least ensure society held together during the chaos: unified by a direct voting system; controlled by the people themselves. Once that idea occurred to me, I saw how important a backstop it was, and how good a shield it would be against the Sword of Khalifa's. Perhaps if they ever catch him, I will find out.'

'You clever old thing.'

'Without Khalifa's attack I would never have got the Constitution Bill through. Being forced to resign after the media were tipped off that we had lied about the number of terrorists, made everyone look at all my changes and decide whether to keep them on, or throw them in the garbage with me. And they kept that Bill. I'm delighted, because it makes my fall worthwhile. It's a great and good thing to know that even I was put in a position where I went against my true nature and lied to my people. With our new system of voting I don't think that can happen again in future. It shows how rotten our old system of government was.'

'Yes, our fellow Americans are now voting regularly and conscientiously on matters they had no say in before your Bill. I think what you accomplished is amazing, darling. The work of several lifetimes.'

'What amazes me is how the Founding Fathers were right all along. I can't see how they put it all together, in such a way that it would last for so long. That is truly amazing.'

'Well you've played your part as honourably as any man could. Now it's the citizens' turn to stand up, behave honourably and effect positive change for our world,' Julie volunteered.

'Looking back, I was lucky to escape with my own skin. If I hadn't implemented the Constitution Bill I would have been far less fortunate. That Bill clearly demonstrated my altruism to the people and they decided to let me go. It was quite an ordeal watching them vote on whether to go ahead and charge me.'

'Yes – the only thing that saved you was the very mechanism that could have imprisoned you, or worse.'

'When The Sword scythes down more autocratic forms of society, it will make me smile rather than cry. I can't wait to see the Ayatollah's face when his people demand more frequent voting,' Will leaned back contentedly, clasping his hands behind his head.

'So, what will you do now?'

'Well I used to write before I got mesmerised by maths.'

'That's a great idea – I didn't know you enjoyed writing.'

'When you think about it, most speeches are written.'

'Ha – I suppose they are,' she laughed.

'Perhaps at some point I will write the true account of what really happened. I've been giving it some thought. Maybe I should end with a personal letter to all the dictators and despots of the world. After all, I was once the President of the greatest power on earth. They might listen to me.'

'You should write it now, while it's fresh in your mind. If you include the whole truth about the Constitution Bill and your reasoning behind it, you might even win the Nobel Peace Prize.'

'Perhaps I should. For me, writing is the most revealing mirror of life I've ever looked into,' Will said curiously. 'Y'know, I like a book that can be read more than once. Maybe, if I make the human events metaphors for our behaviour, it will provide a different perspective the second time around.'

'It will also add depth to the first reading. But don't tell the whole truth. Make it a little fantastique, or it will scare.'

'You're right. I'll bend the tlimeline and show people the truth about themselves. None of them will believe that.'

'I would love to read your book, darling....but let's show it to the children when they are a little older.'

Getting up from his chair in one fluid motion, Will stepped in front of her. In a theatrical impersonation of Sir Walter Raleigh greeting his queen with the utmost courtesy, he plucked the fishing hat from his head and swept it across the grass at his feet, bowing deeply and speaking in the ringing tones of a thespian, 'I thank you. I thank you. I am indebted for your time, humbled by your effort and grateful for your understanding. But most of all, I would like to thank you personally for reading my book. Thank you.'

CHECKMATE
From the Persian "The King is Dead"

THE LAST AND FINAL WARNING TO ALL
DICTATORS ON EARTH

If you are the dictator of a country or superpower and in control of a strict regime, the combination of these two ideas is the most dangerous thing that will ever land on your desk. You will realise you are no longer safe, and neither are those who vie for your position of absolute authority. If you do not take your heel off your people, you face the same on/off mortality you reserve for all those who challenge your rule.

Why? Because many people are aware of these ideas now, and some will unsheathe The Sword of Damocles on you and your regime, should you not relinquish power as fast as your frightened mind will permit.

Consider this to be your very last warning. Before you wrongly dismiss this as mere revolutionary rhetoric, ask yourself Mr Dictator: when someone swings the Sword at you, how will you prevent it decapitating your domination?

I – a former President of the United States – can think of only one alternative. You must murder every one of your fellow citizens, quickly. Make sure you get them all, because they now know how to bring about your downfall efficiently, and they can snatch the crown from your head in less than a year. Replacing you with a freer and fairer system of government.

They no longer have to wait for someone to show them the way, to lead them, so there is no one to look for and destroy. Your people have a practical solution the moment they finish reading this. A solution: they themselves already control.

That's twelve months, Mr Tyrant. And the clock started ticking when this book sold its first copy – not from the point you first read it or heard about it.

If I were you, I'd have someone look into that timing. Ordering them to report back on when it was released by tomorrow morning – on pain of death. Never forget, Mr Oppressor, there are only six degrees of separation between the whole of mankind.

For the truly addicted – the paranoiacally insecure among you – for those of you who prefer to die with power than live without it, I promise you this: if you do not step back soon, your people will carry out their labour of love, with none of them wishing you remain on this earth a second longer than the moment they lay hands on you.

To all free men and women of this earth – I wish you continued happiness and tranquillity. And for all those trapped by the yoke of oppression: I wish you very good hunting in your next and final struggle. When it is over, you will find a permanent peace at the end of your fight. You will never have cause to take up arms again. Not if you all have the vote.

Please allow me the great privilege of being the first to welcome you.

Welcome to freedom.

William Jefferson Mann

The Implementer of the Constitution Bill and a former President of the United States of America.

Each and every descendant of the killer ape, which includes our politicians, must see and clearly recognize that one man's terrorist will always be another man's freedom fighter before we can unshackle ourselves from the forged manacles of war. But that, and the two ideas revealed in this book are all it should take – because as of right now, you are not the only person who knows of them, or understands what they capable of undoing.

No government can exist without our consent. The consent of Us – The people. That is their secret. The secret our Overlords and High Priests do not want you to know. It is Their fear. A secret fear which makes them murder dissent.

Their secret / Our destiny.

For those who cowardly resist change, ruminate on the dark message in this book. Your castle is paper thin. Capitalism cannot support 6 $\frac{1}{2}$ billion people.

Our Masters know this. The recent breakdowns and moral hazards created by our current financial system, even the oil spills and worldwide pollution, are symptoms of this underlying fault. Worse is coming. Ruinous destruction: lies, waiting in ambush on the road of Man, if we continue to blindly worship Mammon. Before you discard this, consider Capitalism in the context of China holding nearly 2 trillion dollars of debt: 70 % in dollars, the remainder almost entirely in Euros. To steal a march, they only have to dump these funds on the open market to reduce the Dollar and Euro to ten cents each. They do not have to fire a single shot.

Money is not the root cause of war; debt is the fuel of war and starvation.

Against all this, Our technology now works for Us. Even the Goddess of nature bows to our skill. Money does not give Us that power; and worse, it is now holding back Our advancement. Technology – our ability to use tools – solves our problems, lengthens our lives, delivers us from disease, feeds us, houses us, allows us to communicate and travel vast distances. Profit motive is starting to outweigh what we as a species can achieve. It is getting in the way of Our destiny. There is no longer any need for war or starvation. These are symptoms of a tiered society - a feudal society - that Equanimous Man has outgrown. We have the resources and ability to ride across the heavens if we wish – but not at a profit.

Debt is the first demon of capitalism we should exorcise. Debt is a man-made concept designed to maintain control over Us, so that a few may live in ease and authority. When you discover how it is engineered you will be extremely shocked and surprised. It is one thing for a retail bank to be rewarded with interest for its risk, quite another to have Central Banks manufacturing (printing) money – releasing it into society with interest/debt already attached to it. This mechanism, initially deflationary; in itself, is inflationary – the reason why They make the interest cumulative. They understand this.

Now you do.

I believe that one day, people will whisper: 'The time is come.' I go down on my knees to pray: Let it be us who make that shout.

To all those, right across the World, who value freedom; can embrace positive progress – change, hand-in-glove with Human values and therefore, our value as a species:

Let us grip Our destiny.

And, we hold the majority.

Now it's Our Turn.

This is not THE END